PARADISO

DOVER THRIFT EDITIONS

Dante Alighieri

Translated and with Notes by
Henry Wadsworth Longfellow

DOVER PUBLICATIONS, INC.
MINEOLA, NEW YORK

DOVER THRIFT EDITIONS

GENERAL EDITOR: SUSAN L. RATTINER
EDITOR OF THIS VOLUME: JIM MILLER

Bibliographical Note

This Dover edition, first published in 2017, is an unabridged republication of *Paradiso*, translated and with notes by Henry Wadsworth Longfellow, originally published in 1867 by George Routledge & Sons, London, as the third part of *The Divine Comedy of Dante Alighieri*.

International Standard Book Number

ISBN-13: 978-0-486-81534-3
ISBN-10: 0-486-81534-X

Manufactured in the United States by LSC Communications
81534X01   2017
www.doverpublications.com

Note

DANTE ALIGHIERI (1265–1321), born in Florence, would have a life-long affinity with his beloved city, even after being exiled in his later years. At the time of his birth, Italy was divided between those who supported the papacy, and those who were loyal to the German rulers of the Holy Roman Empire. Shortly after his birth, the Guelfs, with the help of French and papal troops, were successful in driving the pro-imperial Ghibellines from the city of Florence. This victory ushered in a period of Florentine prosperity, as well as its heightened stature among other Italian cities, and attracted a host of intellectuals there with whom Dante came to associate.

As a disciple of master rhetorician Brunetto Latini, Dante was influenced by his mentor's approach to philosophy and politics, and was also schooled in the burgeoning poetical movement in Italy. Dante became instrumental in the advancement of Stilnuovo ("New Style") poetry, by which he and friends Guido Cavalcanti and Cino de Pistoia used verse to analyze the psychology of love. Inspired by Latini's desire to employ the vernacular in literary works, Dante also pioneered the practice of using the laymen's Italian in literature, rather than the more technical Latin. At that time, there was no single Italian language; rather, people spoke local dialects that were all derived from Latin. Predictably, Dante chose to write many of his works in his native Florentine dialect.

Dante soon entered into local politics, joining a medical guild by way of his reputation as a philosopher. In 1300, he was elected *priore,* an office that granted him the power and burden of political involvement in turbulent Florence. At this time, the Florentine Guelfs were experiencing division within its party, and split into two factions—the Blacks and the Whites. Dante was a member of the Whites, who objected to the imperialistic ambitions of Pope Boniface VIII, and eventually lost control of the city. Detained at the Vatican, where he had gone as an emissary to speak to the pope, Dante was tried in absentia for crimes fabricated by the Blacks. Sentenced to death by burning should he ever return, Dante never again set foot in Florence. Instead, he roamed from city to city in Italy, where he was welcomed by scholars and nobles alike. He continued in his interest in politics, recording observations and writing a number of discourses on the volatile events of his time. He died in the city of Ravenna in 1321.

Dante began work on *The Divine Comedy* around 1308, and completed it shortly before his death. Originally titled *Commedia* (Comedy), the work adopted its lofty epithet after Dante was named "Divine Poet" by scholar Giovanni Boccaccio a few decades after his death. An epic poem that was his masterpiece, *The Divine Comedy* traces Dante's imagined journey through the three levels of the Roman Catholic afterlife—Hell, Purgatory, and Heaven. The first canto of *The Inferno* serves as an introduction to the entire poem, followed by the standard thirty-three cantos that serve as the structure for the two other canticles. At once an allegory of man's spiritual pilgrimage through life, as well as a thinly veiled political commentary on the circumstances of Dante's own exile, *The Divine Comedy* is a brilliant, multi-layered work that transcends time and culture in its ability to captivate readers and scholars alike.

It was in Italy, during a mandatory tour of Europe to qualify as a professor of modern languages, that Henry Wadsworth Longfellow (1807–1882) first encountered Dante's writings. Spending his evenings poring over the "gloomy pages," Longfellow later converted his many notes into lectures on Dante at Bowdoin College and Harvard University. Thus began Longfellow's lifelong interest in the poet, and, in 1843, he committed himself to the translation of *The Divine Comedy*—an endeavor that would span several decades, due to long respites from the project. Of the three canticles, he completed *The Inferno* last, marking the occasion in a diary entry on April 16, 1863. After several more years spent revising and annotating the translation, Longfellow finally published his work in 1867.

Contents

PARADISO

I lift mine eyes, and all the windows blaze
   With forms of Saints and holy men who died,
   Here martyred and hereafter glorified;
   And the great Rose upon its leaves displays
Christ's Triumph, and the angelic roundelays,
   With splendour upon splendour multiplied;
   And Beatrice again at Dante's side
   No more rebukes, but smiles her words of praise.
And then the organ sounds, and unseen choirs
   Sing the old Latin hymns of peace and love
   And benedictions of the Holy Ghost;
And the melodious bells among the spires
   O'er all the house-tops and through heaven above
   Proclaim the elevation of the Host!

PARADISO

Canto I

The glory of Him who moveth everything
   Doth penetrate the universe, and shine
   In one part more and in another less.
Within that heaven which most his light receives
   Was I, and things beheld which to repeat
   Nor knows, nor can, who from above descends;
Because in drawing near to its desire
   Our intellect ingulphs itself so far,
   That after it the memory cannot go.
Truly whatever of the holy realm   10
   I had the power to treasure in my mind
   Shall now become the subject of my song.
O good Apollo, for this last emprise
   Make of me such a vessel of thy power
   As giving the beloved laurel asks!
One summit of Parnassus hitherto
   Has been enough for me, but now with both
   I needs must enter the arena left.
Enter into my bosom, thou, and breathe
   As at the time when Marsyas thou didst draw   20
   Out of the scabbard of those limbs of his.
O power divine, lend'st thou thyself to me
   So that the shadow of the blessed realm
   Stamped in my brain I can make manifest,
Thou'lt see me come unto thy darling tree,
   And crown myself thereafter with those leaves
   Of which the theme and thou shall make me worthy.
So seldom, Father, do we gather them
   For triumph or of Cæsar or of Poet,
   The fault and shame of human inclinations,   30

1

That the Peneian foliage should bring forth
   Joy to the joyous Delphic deity,
   When any one it makes to thirst for it.
A little spark is followed by great flame;
   Perchance with better voices after me
   Shall prayer be made that Cyrrha may respond!
To mortal men by passages diverse
   Uprises the world's lamp; but by that one
   Which circles four uniteth with three crosses,
With better course and with a better star   40
   Conjoined it issues, and the mundane wax
   Tempers and stamps more after its own fashion.
Almost that passage had made morning there
   And evening here, and there was wholly white
   That hemisphere, and black the other part,
When Beatrice towards the left-hand side
   I saw turned round, and gazing at the sun;
   Never did eagle fasten so upon it!
And even as a second ray is wont
   To issue from the first and reascend,   50
   Like to a pilgrim who would fain return,
Thus of her action, through the eyes infused
   In my imagination, mine I made,
   And sunward fixed mine eyes beyond our wont.
There much is lawful which is here unlawful
   Unto our powers, by virtue of the place
   Made for the human species as its own.
Not long I bore it, nor so little while
   But I beheld it sparkle round about
   Like iron that comes molten from the fire;   60
And suddenly it seemed that day to day
   Was added, as if He who has the power
   Had with another sun the heaven adorned.
With eyes upon the everlasting wheels
   Stood Beatrice all intent, and I, on her
   Fixing my vision from above removed,
Such at her aspect inwardly became
   As Glaucus, tasting of the herb that made him
   Peer of the other gods beneath the sea.
To represent transhumanise in words   70
   Impossible were; the example, then, suffice

Him for whom Grace the experience reserves.
If I was merely what of me thou newly
   Createdst, Love who governest the heaven,
   Thou knowest, who didst lift me with thy light!
When now the wheel, which thou dost make eternal
   Desiring thee, made me attentive to it
   By harmony thou dost modulate and measure,
Then seemed to me so much of heaven enkindled
   By the sun's flame, that neither rain nor river   80
   E'er made a lake so widely spread abroad.
The newness of the sound and the great light
   Kindled in me a longing for their cause,
   Never before with such acuteness felt;
Whence she, who saw me as I saw myself,
   To quiet in me my perturbed mind,
   Opened her mouth, ere I did mine to ask,
And she began: "Thou makest thyself so dull
   With false imagining, that thou seest not
   What thou wouldst see if thou hadst shaken it off.   90
Thou art not upon earth, as thou believest;
   But lightning, fleeing its appropriate site,
   Ne'er ran as thou, who thitherward returnest."
If of my former doubt I was divested
   By these brief little words more smiled than spoken,
   I in a new one was the more ensnared;
And said: "Already did I rest content
   From great amazement; but am now amazed
   In what way I transcend these bodies light."
Whereupon she, after a pitying sigh,   100
   Her eyes directed tow'rds me with that look
   A mother casts on a delirious child;
And she began: "All things whate'er they be
   Have order among themselves, and this is form,
   That makes the universe resemble God.
Here do the higher creatures see the footprints
   Of the Eternal Power, which is the end
   Whereto is made the law already mentioned.
In the order that I speak of are inclined
   All natures, by their destinies diverse,   110
   More or less near unto their origin;
Hence they move onward unto ports diverse

O'er the great sea of being; and each one
  With instinct given it which bears it on.
This bears away the fire towards the moon;
  This is in mortal hearts the motive power;
  This binds together and unites the earth.
Nor only the created things that are
  Without intelligence this bow shoots forth,
  But those that have both intellect and love.   120
The Providence that regulates all this
  Makes with its light the heaven forever quiet,
  Wherein that turns which has the greatest haste.
And thither now, as to a site decreed,
  Bears us away the virtue of that cord
  Which aims its arrows at a joyous mark.
True is it, that as oftentimes the form
  Accords not with the intention of the art,
  Because in answering is matter deaf,
So likewise from this course doth deviate   130
  Sometimes the creature, who the power possesses,
  Though thus impelled, to swerve some other way,
(In the same wise as one may see the fire
  Fall from a cloud,) if the first impetus
  Earthward is wrested by some false delight.
Thou shouldst not wonder more, if well I judge,
  At thine ascent, than at a rivulet
  From some high mount descending to the lowland.
Marvel it would be in thee, if deprived
  Of hindrance, thou wert seated down below,   140
  As if on earth the living fire were quiet."
Thereat she heavenward turned again her face.

Canto II

O ye, who in some pretty little boat,
  Eager to listen, have been following
  Behind my ship, that singing sails along,
Turn back to look again upon your shores;
  Do not put out to sea, lest peradventure,
  In losing me, you might yourselves be lost.
The sea I sail has never yet been passed;

Minerva breathes, and pilots me Apollo,
And Muses nine point out to me the Bears.
Ye other few who have the neck uplifted   10
   Betimes to th' bread of Angels upon which
   One liveth here and grows not sated by it,
Well may you launch upon the deep salt-sea
   Your vessel, keeping still my wake before you
   Upon the water that grows smooth again.
Those glorious ones who unto Colchos passed
   Were not so wonder-struck as you shall be,
   When Jason they beheld a ploughman made!
The con-created and perpetual thirst
   For the realm deiform did bear us on,   20
   As swift almost as ye the heavens behold.
Upward gazed Beatrice, and I at her;
   And in such space perchance as strikes a bolt
   And flies, and from the notch unlocks itself,
Arrived I saw me where a wondrous thing
   Drew to itself my sight; and therefore she
   From whom no care of mine could be concealed,
Towards me turning, blithe as beautiful,
   Said unto me: "Fix gratefully thy mind
   On God, who unto the first star has brought us."   30
It seemed to me a cloud encompassed us,
   Luminous, dense, consolidate and bright
   As adamant on which the sun is striking.
Into itself did the eternal pearl
   Receive us, even as water doth receive
   A ray of light, remaining still unbroken.
If I was body, (and we here conceive not
   How one dimension tolerates another,
   Which needs must be if body enter body,)
More the desire should be enkindled in us   40
   That essence to behold, wherein is seen
   How God and our own nature were united.
There will be seen what we receive by faith,
   Not demonstrated, but self-evident
   In guise of the first truth that man believes.
I made reply: "Madonna, as devoutly
   As most I can do I give thanks to Him
   Who has removed me from the mortal world.

But tell me what the dusky spots may be
    Upon this body, which below on earth   50
    Make people tell that fabulous tale of Cain?"
Somewhat she smiled; and then, "If the opinion
    Of mortals be erroneous," she said,
    "Where'er the key of sense doth not unlock,
Certes, the shafts of wonder should not pierce thee
    Now, forasmuch as, following the senses,
    Thou seest that the reason has short wings.
But tell me what thou think'st of it thyself."
    And I: "What seems to us up here diverse,
    Is caused, I think, by bodies rare and dense."   60
And she: "Right truly shalt thou see immersed
    In error thy belief, if well thou hearest
    The argument that I shall make against it.
Lights many the eighth sphere displays to you
    Which in their quality and quantity
    May noted be of aspects different.
If this were caused by rare and dense alone,
    One only virtue would there be in all
    Or more or less diffused, or equally.
Virtues diverse must be perforce the fruits   70
    Of formal principles; and these, save one,
    Of course would by thy reasoning be destroyed.
Besides, if rarity were of this dimness
    The cause thou askest, either through and through
    This planet thus attenuate were of matter,
Or else, as in a body is apportioned
    The fat and lean, so in like manner this
    Would in its volume interchange the leaves.
Were it the former, in the sun's eclipse
    It would be manifest by the shining through   80
    Of light, as through aught tenuous interfused.
This is not so; hence we must scan the other,
    And if it chance the other I demolish,
    Then falsified will thy opinion be.
But if this rarity go not through and through,
    There needs must be a limit, beyond which
    Its contrary prevents the further passing,
And thence the foreign radiance is reflected,
    Even as a colour cometh back from glass,

The which behind itself concealeth lead.   90
Now thou wilt say the sunbeam shows itself
   More dimly there than in the other parts,
   By being there reflected farther back.
From this reply experiment will free thee
   If e'er thou try it, which is wont to be
   The fountain to the rivers of your arts.
Three mirrors shalt thou take, and two remove
   Alike from thee, the other more remote
   Between the former two shall meet thine eyes.
Turned towards these, cause that behind thy back   100
   Be placed a light, illuming the three mirrors
   And coming back to thee by all reflected.
Though in its quantity be not so ample
   The image most remote, there shalt thou see
   How it perforce is equally resplendent.
Now, as beneath the touches of warm rays
   Naked the subject of the snow remains
   Both of its former colour and its cold,
Thee, thus remaining in thy intellect,
   Will I inform with such a living light,   110
   That it shall tremble in its aspect to thee.
Within the heaven of the divine repose
   Revolves a body, in whose virtue lies
   The being of whatever it contains.
The following heaven, that has so many eyes,
   Divides this being by essences diverse,
   Distinguished from it, and by it contained.
The other spheres, by various differences,
   All the distinctions which they have within them
   Dispose unto their ends and their effects.   120
Thus do these organs of the world proceed,
   As thou perceivest now, from grade to grade;
   Since from above they take, and act beneath.
Observe me well, how through this place I come
   Unto the truth thou wishest, that hereafter
   Thou mayst alone know how to keep the ford.
The power and motion of the holy spheres,
   As from the artisan the hammer's craft,
   Forth from the blessed motors must proceed.
The heaven, which lights so manifold make fair,   130

From the Intelligence profound, which turns it,
    The image takes, and makes of it a seal.
And even as the soul within your dust
    Through members different and accommodated
    To faculties diverse expands itself,
So likewise this Intelligence diffuses
    Its virtue multiplied among the stars.
    Itself revolving on its unity.
Virtue diverse doth a diverse alloyage
    Make with the precious body that it quickens,   140
    In which, as life in you, it is combined.
From the glad nature whence it is derived,
    The mingled virtue through the body shines,
    Even as gladness through the living pupil.
From this proceeds whate'er from light to light
    Appeareth different, not from dense and rare:
    This is the formal principle that produces,
According to its goodness, dark and bright."

Canto III

That Sun, which erst with love my bosom warmed,
    Of beauteous truth had unto me discovered,
    By proving and reproving, the sweet aspect.
And, that I might confess myself convinced
    And confident, so far as was befitting,
    I lifted more erect my head to speak.
But there appeared a vision, which withdrew me
    So close to it, in order to be seen,
    That my confession I remembered not.
Such as through polished and transparent glass,   10
    Or waters crystalline and undisturbed,
    But not so deep as that their bed be lost,
Come back again the outlines of our faces
    So feeble, that a pearl on forehead white
    Comes not less speedily unto our eyes;
Such saw I many faces prompt to speak,
    So that I ran in error opposite
    To that which kindled love 'twixt man and fountain.
As soon as I became aware of them,

Esteeming them as mirrored semblances,   20
   To see of whom they were, mine eyes I turned,
And nothing saw, and once more turned them forward
   Direct into the light of my sweet Guide,
   Who smiling kindled in her holy eyes.
"Marvel thou not," she said to me, "because
   I smile at this thy puerile conceit,
   Since on the truth it trusts not yet its foot,
But turns thee, as 'tis wont, on emptiness.
   True substances are these which thou beholdest,
   Here relegate for breaking of some vow.   30
Therefore speak with them, listen and believe;
   For the true light, which giveth peace to them,
   Permits them not to turn from it their feet."
And I unto the shade that seemed most wishful
   To speak directed me, and I began,
   As one whom too great eagerness bewilders:
"O well-created spirit, who in the rays
   Of life eternal dost the sweetness taste
   Which being untasted ne'er is comprehended,
Grateful 'twill be to me, if thou content me   40
   Both with thy name and with your destiny."
   Whereat she promptly and with laughing eyes:
"Our charity doth never shut the doors
   Against a just desire, except as one
   Who wills that all her court be like herself.
I was a virgin sister in the world;
   And if thy mind doth contemplate me well,
   The being more fair will not conceal me from thee,
But thou shalt recognise I am Piccarda,
   Who, stationed here among these other blessed,   50
   Myself am blessed in the lowest sphere.
All our affections, that alone inflamed
   Are in the pleasure of the Holy Ghost,
   Rejoice at being of his order formed;
And this allotment, which appears so low,
   Therefore is given us, because our vows
   Have been neglected and in some part void."
Whence I to her: "In your miraculous aspects
   There shines I know not what of the divine,
   Which doth transform you from our first conceptions.   60

Therefore I was not swift in my remembrance;
  But what thou tellest me now aids me so,
  That the refiguring is easier to me.
But tell me, ye who in this place are happy,
  Are you desirous of a higher place,
  To see more or to make yourselves more friends?"
First with those other shades she smiled a little;
  Thereafter answered me so full of gladness,
  She seemed to burn in the first fire of love:
"Brother, our will is quieted by virtue   70
  Of charity, that makes us wish alone
  For what we have, nor gives us thirst for more.
If to be more exalted we aspired,
  Discordant would our aspirations be
  Unto the will of Him who here secludes us;
Which thou shalt see finds no place in these circles,
  If being in charity is needful here,
  And if thou lookest well into its nature;
Nay, 'tis essential to this blest existence
  To keep itself within the will divine,   80
  Whereby our very wishes are made one;
So that, as we are station above station
  Throughout this realm, to all the realm 'tis pleasing,
  As to the King, who makes his will our will.
And his will is our peace; this is the sea
  To which is moving onward whatsoever
  It doth create, and all that nature makes."
Then it was clear to me how everywhere
  In heaven is Paradise, although the grace
  Of good supreme there rain not in one measure.   90
But as it comes to pass, if one food sates,
  And for another still remains the longing,
  We ask for this, and that decline with thanks,
E'en thus did I, with gesture and with word,
  To learn from her what was the web wherein
  She did not ply the shuttle to the end.
"A perfect life and merit high in-heaven
  A lady o'er us," said she, "by whose rule
  Down in your world they vest and veil themselves,
That until death they may both watch and sleep   100
  Beside that Spouse who every vow accepts

Which charity conformeth to his pleasure.
To follow her, in girlhood from the world
    I fled, and in her habit shut myself,
    And pledged me to the pathway of her sect.
Then men accustomed unto evil more
    Than unto good, from the sweet cloister tore me;
    God knows what afterward my life became.
This other splendour, which to thee reveals
    Itself on my right side, and is enkindled   110
    With all the illumination of our sphere,
What of myself I say applies to her;
    A nun was she, and likewise from her head
    Was ta'en the shadow of the sacred wimple.
But when she too was to the world returned
    Against her wishes and against good usage,
    Of the heart's veil she never was divested.
Of great Costanza this is the effulgence,
    Who from the second wind of Suabia
    Brought forth the third and latest puissance."   120
Thus unto me she spake, and then began
    "Ave Maria" singing, and in singing
    Vanished, as through deep water something heavy.
My sight, that followed her as long a time
    As it was possible, when it had lost her
    Turned round unto the mark of more desire,
And wholly unto Beatrice reverted;
    But she such lightnings flashed into mine eyes,
    That at the first my sight endured it not;
And this in questioning more backward made me.   130

Canto IV

Between two viands, equally removed
    And tempting, a free man would die of hunger
    Ere either he could bring unto his teeth.
So would a lamb between the ravenings
    Of two fierce wolves stand fearing both alike;
    And so would stand a dog between two does.
Hence, if I held my peace, myself I blame not,
    Impelled in equal measure by my doubts,

Since it must be so, nor do I commend.
I held my peace; but my desire was painted   10
   Upon my face, and questioning with that
   More fervent far than by articulate speech.
Beatrice did as Daniel had done
   Relieving Nebuchadnezzar from the wrath
   Which rendered him unjustly merciless,
And said: "Well see I how attracteth thee
   One and the other wish, so that thy care
   Binds itself so that forth it does not breathe.
Thou arguest, if good will be permanent,
   The violence of others, for what reason   20
   Doth it decrease the measure of my merit?
Again for doubting furnish thee occasion
   Souls seeming to return unto the stars,
   According to the sentiment of Plato.
These are the questions which upon thy wish
   Are thrusting equally; and therefore first
   Will I treat that which hath the most of gall.
He of the Seraphim most absorbed in God,
   Moses, and Samuel, and whichever John
   Thou mayst select, I say, and even Mary,   30
Have not in any other heaven their seats,
   Than have those spirits that just appeared to thee,
   Nor of existence more or fewer years;
But all make beautiful the primal circle,
   And have sweet life in different degrees,
   By feeling more or less the eternal breath.
They showed themselves here, not because allotted
   This sphere has been to them, but to give sign
   Of the celestial which is least exalted.
To speak thus is adapted to your mind,   40
   Since only through the sense it apprehendeth
   What then it worthy makes of intellect.
On this account the Scripture condescends
   Unto your faculties, and feet and hands
   To God attributes, and means something else;
And Holy Church under an aspect human
   Gabriel and Michael represent to you,
   And him who made Tobias whole again.
That which Timæus argues of the soul

Doth not resemble that which here is seen,   50
   Because it seems that as he speaks he thinks.
He says the soul unto its star returns,
   Believing it to have been severed thence
   Whenever nature gave it as a form
Perhaps his doctrine is of other guise
   Than the words sound, and possibly may be
   With meaning that is not to be derided.
If he doth mean that to these wheels return
   The honour of their influence and the blame,
   Perhaps his bow doth hit upon some truth.   60
This principle ill understood once warped
   The whole world nearly, till it went astray
   Invoking Jove and Mercury and Mars.
The other doubt which doth disquiet thee
   Less venom has, for its malevolence
   Could never lead thee otherwhere from me.
That as unjust our justice should appear
   In eyes of mortals, is an argument
   Of faith, and not of sin heretical.
But still, that your perception may be able   70
   To thoroughly penetrate this verity,
   As thou desirest, I will satisfy thee.
If it be violence when he who suffers
   Co-operates not with him who uses force,
   These souls were not on that account excused;
For will is never quenched unless it will,
   But operates as nature doth in fire,
   If violence a thousand times distort it.
Hence, if it yieldeth more or less, it seconds
   The force; and these have done so, having power   80
   Of turning back unto the holy place.
If their will had been perfect, like to that
   Which Lawrence fast upon his gridiron held,
   And Mutius made severe to his own hand,
It would have urged them back along the road
   Whence they were dragged, as soon as they were free;
   But such a solid will is all too rare.
And by these words, if thou hast gathered them
   As thou shouldst do, the argument is refuted
   That would have still annoyed thee many times.   90

But now another passage runs across
    Before thine eyes, and such that by thyself
    Thou couldst not thread it ere thou wouldst be weary.
I have for certain put into thy mind
    That soul beatified could never lie,
    For it is ever near the primal Truth,
And then thou from Piccarda might'st have heard
    Costanza kept affection for the veil,
    So that she seemeth here to contradict me.
Many times, brother, has it come to pass,   100
    That, to escape from peril, with reluctance
    That has been done it was not right to do,
E'en as Alcmæon (who, being by his father
    Thereto entreated, his own mother slew)
    Not to lose pity pitiless became.
At this point I desire thee to remember
    That force with will commingles, and they cause
    That the offences cannot be excused.
Will absolute consenteth not to evil;
    But in so far consenteth as it fears,   110
    If it refrain, to fall into more harm.
Hence when Piccarda uses this expression,
    She meaneth the will absolute, and I
    The other, so that both of us speak truth."
Such was the flowing of the holy river
    That issued from the fount whence springs all truth;
    This put to rest my wishes one and all.
"O love of the first lover, O divine,"
    Said I forthwith, "whose speech inundates me
    And warms me so, it more and more revives me,   120
My own affection is not so profound
    As to suffice in rendering grace for grace;
    Let Him, who sees and can, thereto respond.
Well I perceive that never sated is
    Our intellect unless the Truth illume it,
    Beyond which nothing true expands itself.
It rests therein, as wild beast in his lair,
    When it attains it; and it can attain it;
    If not, then each desire would frustrate be.
Therefore springs up, in fashion of a shoot,   130
    Doubt at the foot of truth; and this is nature,

Which to the top from height to height impels us.
This doth invite me, this assurance give me
    With reverence, Lady, to inquire of you
    Another truth, which is obscure to me.
I wish to know if man can satisfy you
    For broken vows with other good deeds, so
    That in your balance they will not be light."
Beatrice gazed upon me with her eyes
    Full of the sparks of love, and so divine,   140
    That, overcome my power, I turned my back
And almost lost myself with eyes downcast.

Canto V

"If in the heat of love I flame upon thee
    Beyond the measure that on earth is seen,
    So that the valour of thine eyes I vanquish,
Marvel thou not thereat; for this proceeds
    From perfect sight, which as it apprehends
    To the good apprehended moves its feet.
Well I perceive how is already shining
    Into thine intellect the eternal light,
    That only seen enkindles always love;
And if some other thing your love seduce,   10
    'Tis nothing but a vestige of the same,
    Ill understood, which there is shining through.
Thou fain wouldst know if with another service
    For broken vow can such return be made
    As to secure the soul from further claim."
This Canto thus did Beatrice begin;
    And, as a man who breaks not off his speech,
    Continued thus her holy argument:
"The greatest gift that in his largess God
    Creating made, and unto his own goodness   20
    Nearest conformed, and that which he doth prize
Most highly, is the freedom of the will,
    Wherewith the creatures of intelligence
    Both all and only were and are endowed.
Now wilt thou see, if thence thou reasonest,
    The high worth of a vow, if it be made

So that when thou consentest God consents;
For, closing between God and man the compact,
    A sacrifice is of this treasure made,
    Such as I say, and made by its own act.   30
What can be rendered then as compensation?
    Think'st thou to make good use of what thou'st offered,
    With gains ill gotten thou wouldst do good deed.
Now art thou certain of the greater point;
    But because Holy Church in this dispenses,
    Which seems against the truth which I have shown thee,
Behoves thee still to sit awhile at table,
    Because the solid food which thou hast taken
    Requireth further aid for thy digestion.
Open thy mind to that which I reveal,   40
    And fix it there within; for 'tis not knowledge,
    The having heard without retaining it.
In the essence of this sacrifice two things
    Convene together; and the one is that
    Of which 'tis made, the other is the agreement.
This last for evermore is cancelled not
    Unless complied with, and concerning this
    With such precision has above been spoken.
Therefore it was enjoined upon the Hebrews
    To offer still, though sometimes what was offered   50
    Might be commuted, as thou ought'st to know.
The other, which is known to thee as matter,
    May well indeed be such that one errs not
    If it for other matter be exchanged.
But let none shift the burden on his shoulder
    At his arbitrament, without the turning
    Both of the white and of the yellow key;
And every permutation deem as foolish,
    If in the substitute the thing relinquished,
    As the four is in six, be not contained.   60
Therefore whatever thing has so great weight
    In value that it drags down every balance,
    Cannot be satisfied with other spending.
Let mortals never take a vow in jest;
    Be faithful and not blind in doing that,
    As Jephthah was in his first offering,
Whom more beseemed to say, 'I have done wrong,

Than to do worse by keeping; and as foolish
   Thou the great leader of the Greeks wilt find,
Whence wept Iphigenia her fair face,   70
   And made for her both wise and simple weep,
   Who heard such kind of worship spoken of.'
Christians, be ye more serious in your movements;
   Be ye not like a feather at each wind,
   And think not every water washes you.
Ye have the Old and the New Testament,
   And the Pastor of the Church who guideth you
   Let this suffice you unto your salvation.
If evil appetite cry aught else to you,
   Be ye as men, and not as silly sheep,   80
   So that the Jew among you may not mock you.
Be ye not as the lamb that doth abandon
   Its mother's milk, and frolicsome and simple
   Combats at its own pleasure with itself."
Thus Beatrice to me even as I write it;
   Then all desireful turned herself again
   To that part where the world is most alive.
Her silence and her change of countenance
   Silence imposed upon my eager mind,
   That had already in advance new questions;   90
And as an arrow that upon the mark
   Strikes ere the bowstring quiet hath become,
   So did we speed into the second realm.
My Lady there so joyful I beheld,
   As into the brightness of that heaven she entered,
   More luminous thereat the planet grew;
And if the star itself was changed and smiled,
   What became I, who by my nature am
   Exceeding mutable in every guise!
As, in a fish-pond which is pure and tranquil,   100
   The fishes draw to that which from without
   Comes in such fashion that their food they deem it;
So I beheld more than a thousand splendours
   Drawing towards us, and in each was heard:
   "Lo, this is she who shall increase our love."
And as each one was coming unto us,
   Full of beatitude the shade was seen,
   By the effulgence clear that issued from it.

Think, Reader, if what here is just beginning
    No farther should proceed, how thou wouldst have   110
    An agonizing need of knowing more;
And of thyself thou'lt see how I from these
    Was in desire of hearing their conditions,
    As they unto mine eyes were manifest.
"O thou well-born, unto whom Grace concedes
    To see the thrones of the eternal triumph,
    Or ever yet the warfare be abandoned,
With light that through the whole of heaven is spread
    Kindled are we, and hence if thou desirest
    To know of us, at thine own pleasure sate thee."   120
Thus by some one among those holy spirits
    Was spoken, and by Beatrice: "Speak, speak
    Securely, and believe them even as Gods."
"Well I perceive how thou dost nest thyself
    In thine own light, and drawest it from thine eyes,
    Because they coruscate when thou dost smile,
But know not who thou art, nor why thou hast,
    Spirit august, thy station in the sphere
    That veils itself to men in alien rays."
This said I in direction of the light   130
    Which first had spoken to me; whence it became
    By far more lucent than it was before.
Even as the sun, that doth conceal himself
    By too much light, when heat has worn away
    The tempering influence of the vapours dense,
By greater rapture thus concealed itself
    In its own radiance the figure saintly,
    And thus close, close enfolded answered me
In fashion as the following Canto sings.

Canto VI

"After that Constantine the eagle turned
    Against the course of heaven, which it had followed
    Behind the ancient who Lavinia took,
Two hundred years and more the bird of God
    In the extreme of Europe held itself,
    Near to the mountains whence it issued first;

And under shadow of the sacred plumes
 It governed there the world from hand to hand,
 And, changing thus, upon mine own alighted.
Cæsar I was, and am Justinian,   10
 Who, by the will of primal Love I feel,
 Took from the laws the useless and redundant;
And ere unto the work I was attent,
 One nature to exist in Christ, not more,
 Believed, and with such faith was I contented.
But blessed Agapetus, he who was
 The supreme pastor, to the faith sincere
 Pointed me out the way by words of his.
Him I believed, and what was his assertion
 I now see clearly, even as thou seest   20
 Each contradiction to be false and true.
As soon as with the Church I moved my feet,
 God in his grace it pleased with this high task
 To inspire me, and I gave me wholly to it,
And to my Belisarius I commended
 The arms, to which was heaven's right hand so joined
 It was a signal that I should repose.
Now here to the first question terminates
 My answer; but the character thereof
 Constrains me to continue with a sequel, 30
In order that thou see with how great reason
 Men move against the standard sacrosanct,
 Both who appropriate and who oppose it.
Behold how great a power has made it worthy
 Of reverence, beginning from the hour
 When Pallas died to give it sovereignty.
Thou knowest it made in Alba its abode
 Three hundred years and upward, till at last
 The three to three fought for it yet again.
Thou knowest what it achieved from Sabine wrong 40
 Down to Lucretia's sorrow, in seven kings
 O'ercoming round about the neighbouring nations;
Thou knowest what it achieved, borne by the Romans
 Illustrious against Brennus, against Pyrrhus,
 Against the other princes and confederates.
Torquatus thence and Quinctius, who from locks
 Unkempt was named, Decii and Fabii,

Received the fame I willingly embalm;
It struck to earth the pride of the Arabians,
    Who, following Hannibal, had passed across   50
    The Alpine ridges, Po, from which thou glidest;
Beneath it triumphed while they yet were young
    Pompey and Scipio, and to the hill
    Beneath which thou wast born it bitter seemed;
Then, near unto the time when heaven had willed
    To bring the whole world to its mood serene,
    Did Cæsar by the will of Rome assume it.
What it achieved from Var unto the Rhine,
    Isère beheld and Saône, beheld the Seine,
    And every valley whence the Rhone is filled;   60
What it achieved when it had left Ravenna,
    And leaped the Rubicon, was such a flight
    That neither tongue nor pen could follow it.
Round towards Spain it wheeled its legions; then
    Towards Durazzo, and Pharsalia smote
    That to the calid Nile was felt the pain.
Antandros and the Simois, whence it started,
    It saw again, and there where Hector lies,
    And ill for Ptolemy then roused itself.
From thence it came like lightning upon Juba;   70
    Then wheeled itself again into your West,
    Where the Pompeian clarion it heard.
From what it wrought with the next standard-bearer
    Brutus and Cassius howl in Hell together,
    And Modena and Perugia dolent were;
Still doth the mournful Cleopatra weep
    Because thereof, who, fleeing from before it,
    Took from the adder sudden and black death.
With him it ran even to the Red Sea shore;
    With him it placed the world in so great peace,   80
    That unto Janus was his temple closed.
But what the standard that has made me speak
    Achieved before, and after should achieve
    Throughout the mortal realm that lies beneath it,
Becometh in appearance mean and dim,
    If in the hand of the third Cæsar seen
    With eye unclouded and affection pure,
Because the living Justice that inspires me

Granted it, in the hand of him I speak of,
  The glory of doing vengeance for its wrath.   90
Now here attend to what I answer thee;
  Later it ran with Titus to do vengeance
  Upon the vengeance of the ancient sin.
And when the tooth of Lombardy had bitten
  The Holy Church, then underneath its wings
  Did Charlemagne victorious succour her.
Now hast thou power to judge of such as those
  Whom I accused above, and of their crimes,
  Which are the cause of all your miseries.
To the public standard one the yellow lilies   100
  Opposes, the other claims it for a party,
  So that 'tis hard to see which sins the most.
Let, let the Ghibellines ply their handicraft
  Beneath some other standard; for this ever
  Ill follows he who it and justice parts.
And let not this new Charles e'er strike it down,
  He and his Guelfs, but let him fear the talons
  That from a nobler lion stripped the fell.
Already oftentimes the sons have wept
  The father's crime; and let him not believe   110
  That God will change His scutcheon for the lilies.
This little planet doth adorn itself
  With the good spirits that have active been,
  That fame and honour might come after them;
And whensoever the desires mount thither,
  Thus deviating, must perforce the rays
  Of the true love less vividly mount upward.
But in commensuration of our wages
  With our desert is portion of our joy,
  Because we see them neither less nor greater.   120
Herein doth living Justice sweeten so
  Affection in us, that for evermore
  It cannot warp to any iniquity.
Voices diverse make up sweet melodies;
  So in this life of ours the seats diverse
  Render sweet harmony among these spheres;
And in the compass of this present pearl
  Shineth the sheen of Romeo, of whom
  The grand and beauteous work was ill rewarded.

But the Provençals who against him wrought,　　　　　130
    They have not laughed, and therefore ill goes he
    Who makes his hurt of the good deeds of others.
Four daughters, and each one of them a queen,
    Had Raymond Berenger, and this for him
    Did Romeo, a poor man and a pilgrim;
And then malicious words incited him
    To summon to a reckoning this just man,
    Who rendered to him seven and five for ten.
Then he departed poor and stricken in years,
    And if the world could know the heart he had,　　　　140
    In begging bit by bit his livelihood,
Though much it laud him, it would laud him more."

Canto VII

"*Osanna sanctus Deus Sabaoth,*
    Superillustrans claritate tua
    Felices ignes horum malahoth!"
In this wise, to his melody returning,
    This substance, upon which a double light
    Doubles itself, was seen by me to sing,
And to their dance this and the others moved,
    And in the manner of swift-hurrying sparks
    Veiled themselves from me with a sudden distance.
Doubting was I, and saying, "Tell her, tell her,"　　　　10
    Within me, "tell her," saying, "tell my Lady,"
    Who slakes my thirst with her sweet effluences;
And yet that reverence which doth lord it over
    The whole of me only by Beatrice,
    Bowed me again like unto one who drowses.
Short while did Beatrice endure me thus;
    And she began, lighting me with a smile
    Such as would make one happy in the fire:
"According to infallible advisement,
    After what manner a just vengeance justly　　　　20
    Could be avenged has put thee upon thinking,
But I will speedily thy mind unloose;
    And do thou listen, for these words of mine
    Of a great doctrine will a present make thee.
By not enduring on the power that wills

Curb for his good, that man who ne'er was born,
    Damning himself damned all his progeny;
Whereby the human species down below
    Lay sick for many centuries in great error,
    Till to descend it pleased the Word of God   30
To where the nature, which from its own Maker
    Estranged itself, he joined to him in person
    By the sole act of his eternal love.
Now unto what is said direct thy sight;
    This nature when united to its Maker,
    Such as created, was sincere and good;
But by itself alone was banished forth
    From Paradise, because it turned aside
    Out of the way of truth and of its life.
Therefore the penalty the cross held out,   40
    If measured by the nature thus assumed,
    None ever yet with so great justice stung,
And none was ever of so great injustice,
    Considering who the Person was that suffered,
    Within whom such a nature was contracted.
From one act therefore issued things diverse;
    To God and to the Jews one death was pleasing;
    Earth trembled at it and the Heaven was opened.
It should no longer now seem difficult
    To thee, when it is said that a just vengeance   50
    By a just court was afterward avenged.
But now do I behold thy mind entangled
    From thought to thought within a knot, from which
    With great desire it waits to free itself.
Thou sayest, 'Well discern I what I hear;
    But it is hidden from me why God willed
    For our redemption only this one mode.'
Buried remaineth, brother, this decree
    Unto the eyes of every one whose nature
    Is in the flame of love not yet adult.   60
Verily, inasmuch as at this mark
    One gazes long and little is discerned,
    Wherefore this mode was worthiest will I say.
Goodness Divine, which from itself doth spurn
    All envy, burning in itself so sparkles
    That the eternal beauties it unfolds.
Whate'er from this immediately distils

Has afterwards no end, for ne'er removed
    Is its impression when it sets its seal.
Whate'er from this immediately rains down   70
    Is wholly free, because it is not subject
    Unto the influences of novel things.
The more conformed thereto, the more it pleases;
    For the blest ardour that irradiates all things
    In that most like itself is most vivacious.
With all of these things has advantaged been
    The human creature; and if one be wanting,
    From his nobility he needs must fall.
'Tis sin alone which doth disfranchise him,
    And render him unlike the Good Supreme,   80
    So that he little with its light is blanched,
And to his dignity no more returns,
    Unless he fill up where transgression empties
    With righteous pains for criminal delights.
Your nature when it sinned so utterly
    In its own seed, out of these dignities
    Even as out of Paradise was driven,
Nor could itself recover, if thou notest
    With nicest subtlety, by any way,
    Except by passing one of these two fords: 90
Either that God through clemency alone
    Had pardon granted, or that man himself
    Had satisfaction for his folly made.
Fix now thine eye deep into the abyss
    Of the eternal counsel, to my speech
    As far as may be fastened steadfastly!
Man in his limitations had not power
    To satisfy, not having power to sink
    In his humility obeying then,
Far as he disobeying thought to rise;   100
    And for this reason man has been from power
    Of satisfying by himself excluded.
Therefore it God behoved in his own ways
    Man to restore unto his perfect life,
    I say in one, or else in both of them.
But since the action of the doer is
    So much more grateful, as it more presents
    The goodness of the heart from which it issues,

Goodness Divine, that doth imprint the world,
  Has been contented to proceed by each   110
  And all its ways to lift you up again;
Nor 'twixt the first day and the final night
  Such high and such magnificent proceeding
  By one or by the other was or shall be;
For God more bounteous was himself to give
  To make man able to uplift himself,
  Than if he only of himself had pardoned;
And all the other modes were insufficient
  For justice, were it not the Son of God
  Himself had humbled to become incarnate.   120
Now, to fill fully each desire of thine,
  Return I to elucidate one place,
  In order that thou there mayst see as I do.
Thou sayst: 'I see the air, I see the fire,
  The water, and the earth, and all their mixtures
  Come to corruption, and short while endure;
And these things notwithstanding were created;'
  Therefore if that which I have said were true,
  They should have been secure against corruption.
The Angels, brother, and the land sincere   130
  In which thou art, created may be called
  Just as they are in their entire existence;
But all the elements which thou hast named,
  And all those things which out of them are made,
  By a created virtue are informed.
Created was the matter which they have;
  Created was the informing influence
  Within these stars that round about them go.
The soul of every brute and of the plants
  By its potential temperament attracts   140
  The ray and motion of the holy lights;
But your own life immediately inspires
  Supreme Beneficence, and enamours it
  So with herself, it evermore desires her.
And thou from this mayst argue furthermore
  Your resurrection, if thou think again
  How human flesh was fashioned at that time
When the first parents both of them were made."

Canto VIII

The world used in its peril to believe
　　That the fair Cypria delirious love
　　Rayed out, in the third epicycle turning;
Wherefore not only unto her paid honour
　　Of sacrifices and of votive cry
　　The ancient nations in the ancient error,
But both Dione honoured they and Cupid,
　　That as her mother, this one as her son,
　　And said that he had sat in Dido's lap;
And they from her, whence I beginning take,　　　　10
　　Took the denomination of the star
　　That wooes the sun, now following, now in front.
I was not ware of our ascending to it;
　　But of our being in it gave full faith
　　My Lady whom I saw more beauteous grow.
And as within a flame a spark is seen,
　　And as within a voice a voice discerned,
　　When one is steadfast, and one comes and goes,
Within that light beheld I other lamps
　　Move in a circle, speeding more and less,　　　　20
　　Methinks in measure of their inward vision.
From a cold cloud descended never winds,
　　Or visible or not, so rapidly
　　They would not laggard and impeded seem
To any one who had those lights divine
　　Seen come towards us, leaving the gyration
　　Begun at first in the high Seraphim.
And behind those that most in front appeared
　　Sounded "*Osanna!*" so that never since
　　To hear again was I without desire.　　　　30
Then unto us more nearly one approached,
　　And it alone began: "We all are ready
　　Unto thy pleasure, that thou joy in us.
We turn around with the celestial Princes,
　　One gyre and one gyration and one thirst,
　　To whom thou in the world of old didst say,
'*Ye who, intelligent, the third heaven are moving;*'
　　And are so full of love, to pleasure thee
　　A little quiet will not be less sweet."

After these eyes of mine themselves had offered 40
  Unto my Lady reverently, and she
  Content and certain of herself had made them,
Back to the light they turned, which so great promise
  Made of itself, and "Say, who art thou?" was
  My voice, imprinted with a great affection.
O how and how much I beheld it grow
  With the new joy that superadded was
  Unto its joys, as soon as I had spoken!
Thus changed, it said to me: "The world possessed me
  Short time below; and, if it had been more, 50
  Much evil will be which would not have been.
My gladness keepeth me concealed from thee,
  Which rayeth round about me, and doth hide me
  Like as a creature swathed in its own silk.
Much didst thou love me, and thou hadst good reason;
  For had I been below, I should have shown thee
  Somewhat beyond the foliage of my love.
That left-hand margin, which doth bathe itself
  In Rhone, when it is mingled with the Sorgue,
  Me for its lord awaited in due time, 60
And that horn of Ausonia, which is towned
  With Bari, with Gaeta and Catona,
  Whence Tronto and Verde in the sea disgorge.
Already flashed upon my brow the crown
  Of that dominion which the Danube waters
  After the German borders it abandons;
And beautiful Trinacria, that is murky
  'Twixt Pachino and Peloro, (on the gulf
  Which greatest scath from Eurus doth receive,)
Not through Typhœus, but through nascent sulphur, 70
  Would have awaited her own monarchs still,
  Through me from Charles descended and from Rudolph,
If evil lordship, that exasperates ever
  The subject populations, had not moved
  Palermo to the outcry of 'Death! death!'
And if my brother could but this foresee,
  The greedy poverty of Catalonia
  Straight would he flee, that it might not molest him;
For verily 'tis needful to provide,
  Through him or other, so that on his bark 80

Already freighted no more freight be placed.
His nature, which from liberal covetous
 Descended, such a soldiery would need
 As should not care for hoarding in a chest."
"Because I do believe the lofty joy
 Thy speech infuses into me, my Lord,
 Where every good thing doth begin and end
Thou seest as I see it, the more grateful
 Is it to me; and this too hold I dear,
 That gazing upon God thou dost discern it.   90
Glad hast thou made me; so make clear to me,
 Since speaking thou hast stirred me up to doubt,
 How from sweet seed can bitter issue forth."
This I to him; and he to me: "If I
 Can show to thee a truth, to what thou askest
 Thy face thou'lt hold as thou dost hold thy back.
The Good which all the realm thou art ascending
 Turns and contents, maketh its providence
 To be a power within these bodies vast;
And not alone the natures are foreseen   100
 Within the mind that in itself is perfect,
 But they together with their preservation.
For whatsoever thing this bow shoots forth
 Falls foreordained unto an end foreseen,
 Even as a shaft directed to its mark.
If that were not, the heaven which thou dost walk
 Would in such manner its effects produce,
 That they no longer would be arts, but ruins.
This cannot be, if the Intelligences
 That keep these stars in motion are not maimed,   110
 And maimed the First that has not made them perfect.
Wilt thou this truth have clearer made to thee?"
 And I: "Not so; for 'tis impossible
 That nature tire, I see, in what is needful."
Whence he again: "Now say, would it be worse
 For men on earth were they not citizens?"
 "Yes," I replied; "and here I ask no reason."
"And can they be so, if below they live not
 Diversely unto offices diverse?
 No, if your master writeth well for you."   120
So came he with deductions to this point;

Then he concluded: "Therefore it behoves
    The roots of your effects to be diverse.
Hence one is Solon born, another Xerxes,
    Another Melchisedec, and another he
    Who, flying through the air, his son did lose.
Revolving Nature, which a signet is
    To mortal wax, doth practise well her art,
    But not one inn distinguish from another;
Thence happens it that Esau differeth   130
    In seed from Jacob; and Quirinus comes
    From sire so vile that he is given to Mars.
A generated nature its own way
    Would always make like its progenitors,
    If Providence divine were not triumphant.
Now that which was behind thee is before thee;
    But that thou know that I with thee am pleased,
    With a corollary will I mantle thee.
Evermore nature, if it fortune find
    Discordant to it, like each other seed   140
    Out of its region, maketh evil thrift;
And if the world below would fix its mind
    On the foundation which is laid by nature,
    Pursuing that, 'twould have the people good.
But you unto religion wrench aside
    Him who was born to gird him with the sword,
    And make a king of him who is for sermons;
Therefore your footsteps wander from the road."

Canto IX

Beautiful Clemence, after that thy Charles
    Had me enlightened, he narrated to me
    The treacheries his seed should undergo;
But said: "Be still and let the years roll round;"
    So I can only say, that lamentation
    Legitimate shall follow on your wrongs.
And of that holy light the life already
    Had to the Sun which fills it turned again,
    As to that good which for each thing sufficeth.
Ah, souls deceived, and creatures impious,   10

Who from such good do turn away your hearts,
Directing upon vanity your foreheads!
And now, behold, another of those splendours
Approached me, and its will to pleasure me
It signified by brightening outwardly.
The eyes of Beatrice, that fastened were
Upon me, as before, of dear assent
To my desire assurance gave to me.
"Ah, bring swift compensation to my wish,
Thou blessed spirit," I said, "and give me proof   20
That what I think in thee I can reflect!"
Whereat the light, that still was new to me,
Out of its depths, whence it before was singing,
As one delighted to do good, continued:
"Within that region of the land depraved
Of Italy, that lies between Rialto
And fountain-heads of Brenta and of Piava,
Rises a hill, and mounts not very high,
Wherefrom descended formerly a torch
That made upon that region great assault.   30
Out of one root were born both I and it;
Cunizza was I called, and here I shine
Because the splendour of this star o'ercame me.
But gladly to myself the cause I pardon
Of my allotment, and it does not grieve me;
Which would perhaps seem strong unto your vulgar.
Of this so luculent and precious jewel,
Which of our heaven is nearest unto me,
Great fame remained; and ere it die away
This hundredth year shall yet quintupled be.   40
See if man ought to make him excellent,
So that another life the first may leave!
And thus thinks not the present multitude
Shut in by Adige and Tagliamento,
Nor yet for being scourged is penitent.
But soon 'twill be that Padua in the marsh
Will change the water that Vicenza bathes,
Because the folk are stubborn against duty;
And where the Sile and Cagnano join
One lordeth it, and goes with lofty head,   50
For catching whom e'en now the net is making.

Feltro moreover of her impious pastor
    Shall weep the crime, which shall so monstrous be
    That for the like none ever entered Malta.
Ample exceedingly would be the vat
    That of the Ferrarese could hold the blood,
    And weary who should weigh it ounce by ounce,
Of which this courteous priest shall make a gift
    To show himself a partisan; and such gifts
    Will to the living of the land conform.   60
Above us there are mirrors, Thrones you call them,
    From which shines out on us God Judicant,
    So that this utterance seems good to us."
Here it was silent, and it had the semblance
    Of being turned elsewhither, by the wheel
    On which it entered as it was before.
The other joy, already known to me,
    Became a thing transplendent in my sight,
    As a fine ruby smitten by the sun.
Through joy effulgence is acquired above,   70
    As here a smile; but down below, the shade
    Outwardly darkens, as the mind is sad.
"God seeth all things, and in Him, blest spirit,
    Thy sight is," said I, "so that never will
    Of his can possibly from thee be hidden;
Thy voice, then, that for ever makes the heavens
    Glad, with the singing of those holy fires
    Which of their six wings make themselves a cowl,
Wherefore does it not satisfy my longings?
    Indeed, I would not wait thy questioning   80
    If I in thee were as thou art in me."
"The greatest of the valleys where the water
    Expands itself," forthwith its words began,
    "That sea excepted which the earth engarlands,
Between discordant shores against the sun
    Extends so far, that it meridian makes
    Where it was wont before to make the horizon.
I was a dweller on that valley's shore
    'Twixt Ebro and Magra that with journey short
    Doth from the Tuscan part the Genoese.   90
With the same sunset and same sunrise nearly
    Sit Buggia and the city whence I was,

That with its blood once made the harbour hot.
Folco that people called me unto whom
    My name was known; and now with me this heaven
    Imprints itself, as I did once with it;
For more the daughter of Belus never burned,
    Offending both Sichæus and Creusa,
    Than I, so long as it became my locks,
Nor yet that Rodophean, who deluded   100
    Was by Demophoön, nor yet Alcides,
    When Iole he in his heart had locked.
Yet here is no repenting, but we smile,
    Not at the fault, which comes not back to mind,
    But at the power which ordered and foresaw.
Here we behold the art that doth adorn
    With such affection, and the good discover
    Whereby the world above turns that below.
But that thou wholly satisfied mayst bear
    Thy wishes hence which in this sphere are born,   110
    Still farther to proceed behoveth me.
Thou fain wouldst know who is within this light
    That here beside me thus is scintillating,
    Even as a sunbeam in the limpid water.
Then know thou, that within there is at rest
    Rahab, and being to our order joined,
    With her in its supremest grade 'tis sealed.
Into this heaven, where ends the shadowy cone
    Cast by your world, before all other souls
    First of Christ's triumph was she taken up.   120
Full meet it was to leave her in some heaven,
    Even as a palm of the high victory
    Which he acquired with one palm and the other,
Because she favoured the first glorious deed
    Of Joshua upon the Holy Land,
    That little stirs the memory of the Pope.
Thy city, which an offshoot is of him
    Who first upon his Maker turned his back,
    And whose ambition is so sorely wept,
Brings forth and scatters the accursed flower   130
    Which both the sheep and lambs hath led astray,
    Since it has turned the shepherd to a wolf.
For this the Evangel and the mighty Doctors

Are derelict, and only the Decretals
   So studied that it shows upon their margins.
On this are Pope and Cardinals intent;
   Their meditations reach not Nazareth,
   There where his pinions Gabriel unfolded;
But Vatican and the other parts elect
   Of Rome, which have a cemetery been   140
   Unto the soldiery that followed Peter,
Shall soon be free from this adultery."

Canto X

Looking into his Son with all the Love
   Which each of them eternally breathes forth,
   The Primal and unutterable Power
Whate'er before the mind or eye revolves
   With so much order made, there can be none
   Who this beholds without enjoying Him.
Lift up then, Reader, to the lofty wheels
   With me thy vision straight unto that part
   Where the one motion on the other strikes,
And there begin to contemplate with joy   10
   That Master's art, who in himself so loves it
   That never doth his eye depart therefrom.
Behold how from that point goes branching off
   The oblique circle, which conveys the planets,
   To satisfy the world that calls upon them;
And if their pathway were not thus inflected,
   Much virtue in the heavens would be in vain,
   And almost every power below here dead.
If from the straight line distant more or less
   Were the departure, much would wanting be   20
   Above and underneath of mundane order.
Remain now, Reader, still upon thy bench,
   In thought pursuing that which is foretasted,
   If thou wouldst jocund be instead of weary.
I've set before thee; henceforth feed thyself,
   For to itself diverteth all my care
   That theme whereof I have been made the scribe.
The greatest of the ministers of nature,

Who with the power of heaven the world imprints
  And measures with his light the time for us,   30
With that part which above is called to mind
  Conjoined, along the spirals was revolving,
  Where each time earlier he presents himself;
And I was with him; but of the ascending
  I was not conscious, saving as a man
  Of a first thought is conscious ere it come;
And Beatrice, she who is seen to pass
  From good to better, and so suddenly
  That not by time her action is expressed,
How lucent in herself must she have been!   40
  And what was in the sun, wherein I entered,
  Apparent not by colour but by light,
I, though I call on genius, art, and practice,
  Cannot so tell that it could be imagined;
  Believe one can, and let him long to see it.
And if our fantasies too lowly are
  For altitude so great, it is no marvel,
  Since o'er the sun was never eye could go.
Such in this place was the fourth family
  Of the high Father, who forever sates it,   50
  Showing how he breathes forth and how begets.
And Beatrice began: "Give thanks, give thanks
  Unto the Sun of Angels, who to this
  Sensible one has raised thee by his grace!"
Never was heart of mortal so disposed
  To worship, nor to give itself to God
  With all its gratitude was it so ready,
As at those words did I myself become;
  And all my love was so absorbed in Him,
  That in oblivion Beatrice was eclipsed.   60
Nor this displeased her; but she smiled at it
  So that the splendour of her laughing eyes
  My single mind on many things divided.
Lights many saw I, vivid and triumphant,
  Make us a centre and themselves a circle,
  More sweet in voice than luminous in aspect.
Thus girt about the daughter of Latona
  We sometimes see, when pregnant is the air,

So that it holds the thread which makes her zone.
Within the court of Heaven, whence I return,   70
   Are many jewels found, so fair and precious
   They cannot be transported from the realm;
And of them was the singing of those lights.
   Who takes not wings that he may fly up thither,
   The tidings thence may from the dumb await!
As soon as singing thus those burning suns
   Had round about us whirled themselves three times,
   Like unto stars neighbouring the steadfast poles,
Ladies they seemed, not from the dance released,
   But who stop short, in silence listening   80
   Till they have gathered the new melody.
And within one I heard beginning: "When
   The radiance of grace, by which is kindled
   True love, and which thereafter grows by loving,
Within thee multiplied is so resplendent
   That it conducts thee upward by that stair,
   Where without reascending none descends,
Who should deny the wine out of his vial
   Unto thy thirst, in liberty were not
   Except as water which descends not seaward.   90
Fain wouldst thou know with what plants is enflowered
   This garland that encircles with delight
   The Lady fair who makes thee strong for heaven.
Of the lambs was I of the holy flock
   Which Dominic conducteth by a road
   Where well one fattens if he strayeth not.
He who is nearest to me on the right
   My brother and master was; and he Albertus
   Is of Cologne, I Thomas of Aquinum.
If thou of all the others wouldst be certain,   100
   Follow behind my speaking with thy sight
   Upward along the blessed garland turning.
That next effulgence issues from the smile
   Of Gratian, who assisted both the courts
   In such wise that it pleased in Paradise.
The other which near by adorns our choir
   That Peter was who, e'en as the poor widow,
   Offered his treasure unto Holy Church.

The fifth light, that among us is the fairest,
    Breathes forth from such a love, that all the world   110
    Below is greedy to learn tidings of it.
Within it is the lofty mind, where knowledge
    So deep was put, that, if the true be true,
    To see so much there never rose a second.
Thou seest next the lustre of that taper,
    Which in the flesh below looked most within
    The angelic nature and its ministry.
Within that other little light is smiling
    The advocate of the Christian centuries,
    Out of whose rhetoric Augustine was furnished.   120
Now if thou trainest thy mind's eye along
    From light to light pursuant of my praise,
    With thirst already of the eighth thou waitest.
By seeing every good therein exults
    The sainted soul, which the fallacious world
    Makes manifest to him who listeneth well;
The body whence 'twas hunted forth is lying
    Down in Cieldauro, and from martyrdom
    And banishment it came unto this peace.
See farther onward flame the burning breath   130
    Of Isidore, of Beda, and of Richard
    Who was in contemplation more than man.
This, whence to me returneth thy regard,
    The light is of a spirit unto whom
    In his grave meditations death seemed slow.
It is the light eternal of Sigier,
    Who, reading lectures in the Street of Straw,
    Did syllogize invidious verities."
Then, as a horologe that calleth us
    What time the Bride of God is rising up   140
    With matins to her Spouse that he may love her,
Wherein one part the other draws and urges,
    Ting! ting! resounding with so sweet a note,
    That swells with love the spirit well disposed,
Thus I beheld the glorious wheel move round,
    And render voice to voice, in modulation
    And sweetness that can not be comprehended,
Excepting there where joy is made eternal.

Canto XI

O Thou insensate care of mortal men,
　　How inconclusive are the syllogisms
　　That make thee beat thy wings in downward flight!
One after laws and one to aphorisms
　　Was going, and one following the priesthood,
　　And one to reign by force or sophistry,
And one in theft, and one in state affairs,
　　One in the pleasures of the flesh involved
　　Wearied himself, one gave himself to ease;
When I, from all these things emancipate,   10
　　With Beatrice above there in the Heavens
　　With such exceeding glory was received!
When each one had returned unto that point
　　Within the circle where it was before,
　　It stood as in a candlestick a candle;
And from within the effulgence which at first
　　Had spoken unto me, I heard begin
　　Smiling while it more luminous became:
"Even as I am kindled in its ray,
　　So, looking into the Eternal Light,   20
　　The occasion of thy thoughts I apprehend.
Thou doubtest, and wouldst have me to resift
　　In language so extended and so open
　　My speech, that to thy sense it may be plain,
Where just before I said, 'where well one fattens,'
　　And where I said, 'there never rose a second';
　　And here 'tis needful we distinguish well.
The Providence, which governeth the world
　　With counsel, wherein all created vision
　　Is vanquished ere it reach unto the bottom,   30
(So that towards her own Beloved might go
　　The bride of Him who, uttering a loud cry,
　　Espoused her with his consecrated blood,
Self-confident and unto Him more faithful,)
　　Two Princes did ordain in her behoof,
　　Which on this side and that might be her guide.
The one was all seraphical in ardour;
　　The other by his wisdom upon earth
　　A splendour was of light cherubical.

One will I speak of, for of both is spoken   40
    In praising one, whichever may be taken,
    Because unto one end their labours were.
Between Tupino and the stream that falls
    Down from the hill elect of blessed Ubald,
    A fertile slope of lofty mountain hangs,
From which Perugia feels the cold and heat
    Through Porta Sole, and behind it weep
    Gualdo and Nocera their grievous yoke.
From out that slope, there where it breaketh most
    Its steepness, rose upon the world a sun   50
    As this one does sometimes from out the Ganges;
Therefore let him who speaketh of that place,
    Say not Ascesi, for he would say little,
    But Orient, if he properly would speak.
He was not yet far distant from his rising
    Before he had begun to make the earth
    Some comfort from his mighty virtue feel.
For he in youth his father's wrath incurred
    For certain Dame, to whom, as unto death,
    The gate of pleasure no one doth unlock;   60
And was before his spiritual court
    Et coram patre unto her united;
    Then day by day more fervently he loved her.
She, reft of her first husband, scorned, obscure,
    One thousand and one hundred years and more,
    Waited without a suitor till he came.
Naught it availed to hear, that with Amyclas
    Found her unmoved at sounding of his voice
    He who struck terror into all the world;
Naught it availed being constant and undaunted,   70
    So that, when Mary still remained below,
    She mounted up with Christ upon the cross!
But that too darkly I may not proceed,
    Francis and Poverty for these two lovers
    Take thou henceforward in my speech diffuse.
Their concord and their joyous semblances,
    The love, the wonder, and the sweet regard,
    They made to be the cause of holy thoughts;
So much so that the venerable Bernard
    First bared his feet, and after so great peace   80

Ran, and, in running, thought himself too slow.
O wealth unknown! O veritable good!
   Giles bares his feet, and bares his feet Sylvester
   Behind the bridegroom, so doth please the bride!
Then goes his way that father and that master,
   He and his Lady and that family
   Which now was girding on the humble cord;
Nor cowardice of heart weighed down his brow
   At being son of Peter Bernardone,
   Nor for appearing marvellously scorned;   90
But regally his hard determination
   To Innocent he opened, and from him
   Received the primal seal upon his Order.
After the people mendicant increased
   Behind this man, whose admirable life
   Better in glory of the heavens were sung,
Incoronated with a second crown
   Was through Honorius by the Eternal Spirit
   The holy purpose of this Archimandrite.
And when he had, through thirst of martyrdom,   100
   In the proud presence of the Sultan preached
   Christ and the others who came after him,
And, finding for conversion too unripe
   The folk, and not to tarry there in vain,
   Returned to fruit of the Italic grass,
On the rude rock 'twixt Tiber and the Arno
   From Christ did he receive the final seal,
   Which during two whole years his members bore.
When He, who chose him unto so much good,
   Was pleased to draw him up to the reward   110
   That he had merited by being lowly,
Unto his friars, as to the rightful heirs,
   His most dear Lady did he recommend,
   And bade that they should love her faithfully;
And from her bosom the illustrious soul
   Wished to depart, returning to its realm,
   And for its body wished no other bier.
Think now what man was he, who was a fit
   Companion over the high seas to keep
   The bark of Peter to its proper bearings.   120
And this man was our Patriarch; hence whoever

Doth follow him as he commands can see
   That he is laden with good merchandise.
But for new pasturage his flock has grown
   So greedy, that it is impossible
   They be not scattered over fields diverse;
And in proportion as his sheep remote
   And vagabond go farther off from him,
   More void of milk return they to the fold.
Verily some there are that fear a hurt,   130
   And keep close to the shepherd; but so few,
   That little cloth doth furnish forth their hoods.
Now if my utterance be not indistinct,
   If thine own hearing hath attentive been,
   If thou recall to mind what I have said,
In part contented shall thy wishes be;
   For thou shalt see the plant that's chipped away,
   And the rebuke that lieth in the words,
'Where well one fattens, if he strayeth not.'"

Canto XII

Soon as the blessed flame had taken up
   The final word to give it utterance,
   Began the holy millstone to revolve,
And in its gyre had not turned wholly round,
   Before another in a ring enclosed it,
   And motion joined to motion, song to song;
Song that as greatly doth transcend our Muses,
   Our Sirens, in those dulcet clarions,
   As primal splendour that which is reflected.
And as are spanned athwart a tender cloud   10
   Two rainbows parallel and like in colour,
   When Juno to her handmaid gives command,
(The one without born of the one within,
   Like to the speaking of that vagrant one
   Whom love consumed as doth the sun the vapours,)
And make the people here, through covenant
   God set with Noah, presageful of the world
   That shall no more be covered with a flood,
In such wise of those sempiternal roses

The garlands twain encompassed us about,   20
  And thus the outer to the inner answered.
After the dance, and other grand rejoicings,
  Both of the singing, and the flaming forth
  Effulgence with effulgence blithe and tender,
Together, at once, with one accord had stopped,
  (Even as the eyes, that, as volition moves them,
  Must needs together shut and lift themselves,)
Out of the heart of one of the new lights
  There came a voice, that needle to the star
  Made me appear in turning thitherward.   30
And it began: "The love that makes me fair
  Draws me to speak about the other leader,
  By whom so well is spoken here of mine.
'Tis right, where one is, to bring in the other,
  That, as they were united in their warfare,
  Together likewise may their glory shine.
The soldiery of Christ, which it had cost
  So dear to arm again, behind the standard
  Moved slow and doubtful and in numbers few,
When the Emperor who reigneth evermore   40
  Provided for the host that was in peril,
  Through grace alone and not that it was worthy;
And, as was said, he to his Bride brought succour
  With champions twain, at whose deed, at whose word
  The straggling people were together drawn.
Within that region where the sweet west wind
  Rises to open the new leaves, wherewith
  Europe is seen to clothe herself afresh,
Not far off from the beating of the waves,
  Behind which in his long career the sun   50
  Sometimes conceals himself from every man,
Is situate the fortunate Calahorra,
  Under protection of the mighty shield
  In which the Lion subject is and sovereign.
Therein was born the amorous paramour
  Of Christian Faith, the athlete consecrate,
  Kind to his own and cruel to his foes;
And when it was created was his mind
  Replete with such a living energy,
  That in his mother her it made prophetic.   60

As soon as the espousals were complete
   Between him and the Faith at holy font,
   Where they with mutual safety dowered each other,
The woman, who for him had given assent,
   Saw in a dream the admirable fruit
   That issue would from him and from his heirs;
And that he might be construed as he was,
   A spirit from this place went forth to name him
   With His possessive whose he wholly was.
Dominic was he called; and him I speak of   70
   Even as of the husbandman whom Christ
   Elected to his garden to assist him.
Envoy and servant sooth he seemed of Christ,
   For the first love made manifest in him
   Was the first counsel that was given by Christ.
Silent and wakeful many a time was he
   Discovered by his nurse upon the ground,
   As if he would have said, 'For this I came.'
O thou his father, Felix verily!
   O thou his mother, verily Joanna,   80
   If this, interpreted, means as is said!
Not for the world which people toil for now
   In following Ostiense and Taddeo,
   But through his longing after the true manna,
He in short time became so great a teacher,
   That he began to go about the vineyard,
   Which fadeth soon, if faithless be the dresser;
And of the See, (that once was more benignant
   Unto the righteous poor, not through itself,
   But him who sits there and degenerates,)   90
Not to dispense or two or three for six,
   Not any fortune of first vacancy,
   Non decimas quæ sunt pauperum Dei,
He asked for, but against the errant world
   Permission to do battle for the seed,
   Of which these four and twenty plants surround thee
Then with the doctrine and the will together,
   With office apostolical he moved,
   Like torrent which some lofty vein out-presses;
And in among the shoots heretical   100
   His impetus with greater fury smote,

Wherever the resistance was the greatest.
Of him were made thereafter divers runnels,
   Whereby the garden catholic is watered,
   So that more living its plantations stand.
If such the one wheel of the Biga was,
   In which the Holy Church itself defended
   And in the field its civic battle won,
Truly full manifest should be to thee
   The excellence of the other, unto whom   110
   Thomas so courteous was before my coming.
But still the orbit, which the highest part
   Of its circumference made, is derelict,
   So that the mould is where was once the crust.
His family, that had straight forward moved
   With feet upon his footprints, are turned round
   So that they set the point upon the heel.
And soon aware they will be of the harvest
   Of this bad husbandry, when shall the tares
   Complain the granary is taken from them.   120
Yet say I, he who searcheth leaf by leaf
   Our volume through, would still some page discover
   Where he could read, 'I am as I am wont.'
'Twill not be from Casal nor Acquasparta,
   From whence come such unto the written word
   That one avoids it, and the other narrows.
Bonaventura of Bagnoregio's life
   Am I, who always in great offices
   Postponed considerations sinister.
Here are Illuminato and Agostino,   130
   Who of the first barefooted beggars were
   That with the cord the friends of God became.
Hugh of Saint Victor is among them here,
   And Peter Mangiador, and Peter of Spain,
   Who down below in volumes twelve is shining;
Nathan the seer, and metropolitan
   Chrysostom, and Anselmus, and Donatus
   Who deigned to lay his hand to the first art;
Here is Rabanus, and beside me here
   Shines the Calabrian Abbot Joachim,   140
   He with the spirit of prophecy endowed.
To celebrate so great a paladin

Have moved me the impassioned courtesy
    And the discreet discourses of Friar Thomas,
And with me they have moved this company."

Canto XIII

Let him imagine, who would well conceive
    What now I saw, and let him while I speak
    Retain the image as a steadfast rock,
The fifteen stars, that in their divers regions
    The sky enliven with a light so great
    That it transcends all clusters of the air;
Let him the Wain imagine unto which
    Our vault of heaven sufficeth night and day,
    So that in turning of its pole it fails not;
Let him the mouth imagine of the horn   10
    That in the point beginneth of the axis
    Round about which the primal wheel revolves,—
To have fashioned of themselves two signs in heaven,
    Like unto that which Minos' daughter made,
    The moment when she felt the frost of death;
And one to have its rays within the other,
    And both to whirl themselves in such a manner
    That one should forward go, the other backward;
And he will have some shadowing forth of that
    True constellation and the double dance   20
    That circled round the point at which I was;
Because it is as much beyond our wont,
    As swifter than the motion of the Chiana
    Moveth the heaven that all the rest outspeeds.
There sang they neither Bacchus, nor Apollo,
    But in the divine nature Persons three,
    And in one person the divine and human.
The singing and the dance fulfilled their measure,
    And unto us those holy lights gave need,
    Growing in happiness from care to care.   30
Then broke the silence of those saints concordant
    The light in which the admirable life
    Of God's own mendicant was told to me,
And said: "Now that one straw is trodden out

Now that its seed is garnered up already,
Sweet love invites me to thresh out the other.
Into that bosom, thou believest, whence
    Was drawn the rib to form the beauteous cheek
    Whose taste to all the world is costing dear,
And into that which, by the lance transfixed,   40
    Before and since, such satisfaction made
    That it weighs down the balance of all sin,
Whate'er of light it has to human nature
    Been lawful to possess was all infused
    By the same power that both of them created;
And hence at what I said above dost wonder,
    When I narrated that no second had
    The good which in the fifth light is enclosed.
Now ope thine eyes to what I answer thee,
    And thou shalt see thy creed and my discourse   50
    Fit in the truth as centre in a circle.
That which can die, and that which dieth not,
    Are nothing but the splendour of the idea
    Which by his love our Lord brings into being;
Because that living Light, which from its fount
    Effulgent flows, so that it disunites not
    From Him nor from the Love in them intrined,
Through its own goodness reunites its rays
    In nine subsistences, as in a mirror,
    Itself eternally remaining One.   60
Thence it descends to the last potencies,
    Downward from act to act becoming such
    That only brief contingencies it makes;
And these contingencies I hold to be
    Things generated, which the heaven produces
    By its own motion, with seed and without.
Neither their wax, nor that which tempers it,
    Remains immutable, and hence beneath
    The ideal signet more and less shines through;
Therefore it happens, that the selfsame tree   70
    After its kind bears worse and better fruit,
    And ye are born with characters diverse.
If in perfection tempered were the wax,
    And were the heaven in its supremest virtue,
    The brilliance of the seal would all appear;

But nature gives it evermore deficient,
    In the like manner working as the artist,
    Who has the skill of art and hand that trembles.
If then the fervent Love, the Vision clear,
    Of primal Virtue do dispose and seal,   80
    Perfection absolute is there acquired.
Thus was of old the earth created worthy
    Of all and every animal perfection;
    And thus the Virgin was impregnate made;
So that thine own opinion I commend,
    That human nature never yet has been,
    Nor will be, what it was in those two persons.
Now if no farther forth I should proceed,
    'Then in what way was he without a peer?'
    Would be the first beginning of thy words.   90
But, that may well appear what now appears not,
    Think who he was, and what occasion moved him
    To make request, when it was told him, 'Ask.'
I've not so spoken that thou canst not see
    Clearly he was a king who asked for wisdom,
    That he might be sufficiently a king;
'Twas not to know the number in which are
    The motors here above, or if *necesse*
    With a contingent e'er *necesse* make,
Non si est dare primum motum esse,   100
    Or if in semicircle can be made
    Triangle so that it have no right angle.
Whence, if thou notest this and what I said,
    A regal prudence is that peerless seeing
    In which the shaft of my intention strikes
And if on 'rose' thou turnest thy clear eyes,
    Thou'lt see that it has reference alone
    To kings who're many, and the good are rare.
With this distinction take thou what I said,
    And thus it can consist with thy belief   110
    Of the first father and of our Delight.
And lead shall this be always to thy feet,
    To make thee, like a weary man, move slowly
    Both to the Yes and No thou seest not;
For very low among the fools is he
    Who affirms without distinction, or denies,

As well in one as in the other case;
Because it happens that full often bends
    Current opinion in the false direction,
    And then the feelings bind the intellect.   120
Far more than uselessly he leaves the shore,
    (Since he returneth not the same he went,)
    Who fishes for the truth, and has no skill;
And in the world proofs manifest thereof
    Parmenides, Melissus, Brissus are,
    And many who went on and knew not whither;
Thus did Sabellius, Arius, and those fools
    Who have been even as swords unto the Scriptures
    In rendering distorted their straight faces.
Nor yet shall people be too confident   130
    In judging, even as he is who doth count
    The corn in field or ever it be ripe.
For I have seen all winter long the thorn
    First show itself intractable and fierce,
    And after bear the rose upon its top;
And I have seen a ship direct and swift
    Run o'er the sea throughout its course entire,
    To perish at the harbour's mouth at last.
Let not Dame Bertha nor Ser Martin think,
    Seeing one steal, another offering make,   140
    To see them in the arbitrament divine;
For one may rise, and fall the other may."

Canto XIV

From centre unto rim, from rim to centre,
    In a round vase the water moves itself,
    As from without 'tis struck or from within.
Into my mind upon a sudden dropped
    What I am saying, at the moment when
    Silent became the glorious life of Thomas,
Because of the resemblance that was born
    Of his discourse and that of Beatrice,
    Whom, after him, it pleased thus to begin:
"This man has need (and does not tell you so,   10
    Nor with the voice, nor even in his thought)

Of going to the root of one truth more.
Declare unto him if the light wherewith
    Blossoms your substance shall remain with you
    Eternally the same that it is now;
And if it do remain, say in what manner,
    After ye are again made visible,
    It can be that it injure not your sight."
As by a greater gladness urged and drawn
    They who are dancing in a ring sometimes   20
    Uplift their voices and their motions quicken;
So, at that orison devout and prompt,
    The holy circles a new joy displayed
    In their revolving and their wondrous song.
Whoso lamenteth him that here we die
    That we may live above, has never there
    Seen the refreshment of the eternal rain.
The One and Two and Three who ever liveth,
    And reigneth ever in Three and Two and One,
    Not circumscribed and all things circumscribing,   30
Three several times was chanted by each one
    Among those spirits, with such melody
    That for all merit it were just reward;
And, in the lustre most divine of all
    The lesser ring, I heard a modest voice,
    Such as perhaps the Angel's was to Mary,
Answer: "As long as the festivity
    Of Paradise shall be, so long our love
    Shall radiate round about us such a vesture.
Its brightness is proportioned to the ardour,   40
    The ardour to the vision; and the vision
    Equals what grace it has above its worth.
When, glorious and sanctified, our flesh
    Is reassumed, then shall our persons be
    More pleasing by their being all complete;
For will increase whate'er bestows on us
    Of light gratuitous the Good Supreme,
    Light which enables us to look on Him;
Therefore the vision must perforce increase,
    Increase the ardour which from that is kindled,   50
    Increase the radiance which from this proceeds.
But even as a coal that sends forth flame,

And by its vivid whiteness overpowers it
 So that its own appearance it maintains,
Thus the effulgence that surrounds us now
 Shall be o'erpowered in aspect by the flesh,
 Which still to-day the earth doth cover up;
Nor can so great a splendour weary us,
 For strong will be the organs of the body
 To everything which hath the power to please us." 60
So sudden and alert appeared to me
 Both one and the other choir to say Amen,
 That well they showed desire for their dead bodies;
Nor sole for them perhaps, but for the mothers,
 The fathers, and the rest who had been dear
 Or ever they became eternal flames
And lo! all round about of equal brightness
 Arose a lustre over what was there,
 Like an horizon that is clearing up.
And as at rise of early eve begin   70
 Along the welkin new appearances,
 So that the sight seems real and unreal,
It seemed to me that new subsistences
 Began there to be seen, and make a circle
 Outside the other two circumferences.
O very sparkling of the Holy Spirit,
 How sudden and incandescent it became
 Unto mine eyes, that vanquished bore it not!
But Beatrice so beautiful and smiling
 Appeared to me, that with the other sights 80
 That followed not my memory I must leave her.
Then to uplift themselves mine eyes resumed
 The power, and I beheld myself translated
 To higher salvation with my Lady only.
Well was I ware that I was more uplifted
 By the enkindled smiling of the star,
 That seemed to me more ruddy than its wont.
With all my heart, and in that dialect
 Which is the same in all, such holocaust
 To God I made as the new grace beseemed; 90
And not yet from my bosom was exhausted
 The ardour of sacrifice, before I knew
 This offering was accepted and auspicious;

For with so great a lustre and so red
    Splendours appeared to me in twofold rays,
    I said: "O Helios who dost so adorn them!"
Even as distinct with less and greater lights
    Glimmers between the two poles of the world
    The Galaxy that maketh wise men doubt,
Thus constellated in the depths of Mars,   100
    Those rays described the venerable sign
    That quadrants joining in a circle make.
Here doth my memory overcome my genius;
    For on that cross as levin gleamed forth Christ,
    So that I cannot find ensample worthy;
But he who takes his cross and follows Christ
    Again will pardon me what I omit,
    Seeing in that aurora lighten Christ.
From horn to horn, and 'twixt the top and base,
    Lights were in motion, brightly scintillating   110
    As they together met and passed each other;
Thus level and aslant and swift and slow
    We here behold, renewing still the sight,
    The particles of bodies long and short,
Across the sunbeam move, wherewith is listed
    Sometimes the shade, which for their own defence
    People with cunning and with art contrive.
And as a lute and harp, accordant strung
    With many strings, a dulcet tinkling make
    To him by whom the notes are not distinguished,   120
So from the lights that there to me appeared
    Upgathered through the cross a melody,
    Which rapt me, not distinguishing the hymn.
Well was I ware it was of lofty laud,
    Because there came to me, "Arise and conquer!"
    As unto him who hears and comprehends not.
So much enamoured I became therewith,
    That until then there was not anything
    That e'er had fettered me with such sweet bonds.
Perhaps my word appears somewhat too bold,   130
    Postponing the delight of those fair eyes,
    Into which gazing my desire has rest;
But who bethinks him that the living seals

Of every beauty grow in power ascending,
  And that I there had not turned round to those,
Can me excuse, if I myself accuse
  To excuse myself, and see that I speak truly:
  For here the holy joy is not disclosed,
Because ascending it becomes more pure.

Canto XV

A will benign, in which reveals itself
  Ever the love that righteously inspires,
  As in the iniquitous, cupidity,
Silence imposed upon that dulcet lyre,
  And quieted the consecrated chords,
  That Heaven's right hand doth tighten and relax.
How unto just entreaties shall be deaf
  Those substances, which, to give me desire
  Of praying them, with one accord grew silent?
'Tis well that without end he should lament,   10
  Who for the love of thing that doth not last
  Eternally despoils him of that love!
As through the pure and tranquil evening air
  There shoots from time to time a sudden fire,
  Moving the eyes that steadfast were before,
And seems to be a star that changeth place,
  Except that in the part where it is kindled
  Nothing is missed, and this endureth little;
So from the horn that to the right extends
  Unto that cross's foot there ran a star   20
  Out of the constellation shining there;
Nor was the gem dissevered from its ribbon,
  But down the radiant fillet ran along,
  So that fire seemed it behind alabaster.
Thus piteous did Anchises' shade reach forward,
  If any faith our greatest Muse deserve,
  When in Elysium he his son perceived.
"*O sanguis meus, O super infusa*
  Gratia Dei, sicut tibi, cui
  Bis unquam Cæli janua reclusa?"   30

Thus that effulgence; whence I gave it heed;
    Then round unto my Lady turned my sight,
    And on this side and that was stupefied;
For in her eyes was burning such a smile
    That with mine own methought I touched the bottom
    Both of my grace and of my Paradise!
Then, pleasant to the hearing and the sight,
    The spirit joined to its beginning things
    I understood not, so profound it spake;
Nor did it hide itself from me by choice,   40
    But by necessity; for its conception
    Above the mark of mortals set itself.
And when the bow of burning sympathy
    Was so far slackened, that its speech descended
    Towards the mark of our intelligence,
The first thing that was understood by me
    Was "Benedight be Thou, O Trine and One,
    Who hast unto my seed so courteous been!"
And it continued: "Hunger long and grateful,
    Drawn from the reading of the mighty volume   50
    Wherein is never changed the white nor dark,
Thou hast appeased, my son, within this light
    In which I speak to thee, by grace of her
    Who to this lofty flight with plumage clothed thee.
Thou thinkest that to me thy thought doth pass
    From Him who is the first, as from the unit,
    If that be known, ray out the five and six;
And therefore who I am thou askest not,
    And why I seem more joyous unto thee
    Than any other of this gladsome crowd.   60
Thou think'st the truth; because the small and great
    Of this existence look into the mirror
    Wherein, before thou think'st, thy thought thou showest.
But that the sacred love, in which I watch
    With sight perpetual, and which makes me thirst
    With sweet desire, may better be fulfilled,
Now let thy voice secure and frank and glad
    Proclaim the wishes, the desire proclaim,
    To which my answer is decreed already."
To Beatrice I turned me, and she heard   70

Before I spake, and smiled to me a sign,
That made the wings of my desire increase;
Then in this wise began I: "Love and knowledge,
    When on you dawned the first Equality,
    Of the same weight for each of you became;
For in the Sun, which lighted you and burned
    With heat and radiance, they so equal are,
    That all similitudes are insufficient.
But among mortals will and argument,
    For reason that to you is manifest,   80
    Diversely feathered in their pinions are.
Whence I, who mortal am, feel in myself
    This inequality; so give not thanks,
    Save in my heart, for this paternal welcome.
Truly do I entreat thee, living topaz!
    Set in this precious jewel as a gem,
    That thou wilt satisfy me with thy name."
"O leaf of mine, in whom I pleasure took
    E'en while awaiting, I was thine own root!"
    Such a beginning he in answer made me.   90
Then said to me: "That one from whom is named
    Thy race, and who a hundred years and more
    Has circled round the mount on the first cornice,
A son of mine and thy great-grandsire was;
    Well it behoves thee that the long fatigue
    Thou shouldst for him make shorter with thy works.
Florence, within the ancient boundary
    From which she taketh still her tierce and nones,
    Abode in quiet, temperate and chaste.
No golden chain she had, nor coronal,   100
    Nor ladies shod with sandal shoon, nor girdle
    That caught the eye more than the person did.
Not yet the daughter at her birth struck fear
    Into the father, for the time and dower
    Did not o'errun this side or that the measure.
No houses had she void of families,
    Not yet had thither come Sardanapalus
    To show what in a chamber can be done;
Not yet surpassed had Montemalo been
    By your Uccellatojo, which surpassed   110

Shall in its downfall be as in its rise.
Bellincion Berti saw I go begirt
    With leather and with bone, and from the mirror
    His dame depart without a painted face;
And him of Nerli saw, and him of Vecchio,
    Contented with their simple suits of buff,
    And with the spindle and the flax their dames.
O fortunate women! and each one was certain
    Of her own burial-place, and none as yet
    For sake of France was in her bed deserted.   120
One o'er the cradle kept her studious watch,
    And in her lullaby the language used
    That first delights the fathers and the mothers;
Another, drawing tresses from her distaff,
    Told o'er among her family the tales
    Of Trojans and of Fesole and Rome.
As great a marvel then would have been held
    A Lapo Salterello, a Cianghella,
    As Cincinnatus or Cornelia now.
To such a quiet, such a beautiful   130
    Life of the citizen, to such a safe
    Community, and to so sweet an inn,
Did Mary give me, with loud cries invoked,
    And in your ancient Baptistery at once
    Christian and Cacciaguida I became.
Moronto was my brother, and Eliseo;
    From Val di Pado came to me my wife,
    And from that place thy surname was derived.
I followed afterward the Emperor Conrad,
    And he begirt me of his chivalry,   140
    So much I pleased him with my noble deeds.
I followed in his train against that law's
    Iniquity, whose people doth usurp
    Your just possession, through your Pastor's fault.
There by that execrable race was I
    Released from bonds of the fallacious world,
    The love of which defileth many souls,
And came from martyrdom unto this peace."

Canto XVI

O thou our poor nobility of blood,
   If thou dost make the people glory in thee
   Down here where our affection languishes,
A marvellous thing it ne'er will be to me;
   For there where appetite is not perverted,
   I say in Heaven, of thee I made a boast!
Truly thou art a cloak that quickly shortens,
   So that unless we piece thee day by day
   Time goeth round about thee with his shears!
With *You,* which Rome was first to tolerate,   10
   (Wherein her family less perseveres,)
   Yet once again my words beginning made;
Whence Beatrice, who stood somewhat apart,
   Smiling, appeared like unto her who coughed
   At the first failing writ of Guenever.
And I began: "You are my ancestor,
   You give to me all hardihood to speak,
   You lift me so that I am more than I.
So many rivulets with gladness fill
   My mind, that of itself it makes a joy   20
   Because it can endure this and not burst.
Then tell me, my beloved root ancestral,
   Who were your ancestors, and what the years
   That in your boyhood chronicled themselves?
Tell me about the sheepfold of Saint John,
   How large it was, and who the people were
   Within it worthy of the highest seats."
As at the blowing of the winds a coal
   Quickens to flame, so I beheld that light
   Become resplendent at my blandishments.   30
And as unto mine eyes it grew more fair,
   With voice more sweet and tender, but not in
   This modern dialect, it said to me:
"From uttering of the *Ave,* till the birth
   In which my mother, who is now a saint,
   Of me was lightened who had been her burden,
Unto its Lion had this fire returned
   Five hundred fifty times and thirty more,
   To reinflame itself beneath his paw.

My ancestors and I our birthplace had　　　　　　　40
　　Where first is found the last ward of the city
　　By him who runneth in your annual game.
Suffice it of my elders to hear this;
　　But who they were, and whence they thither came,
　　Silence is more considerate than speech.
All those who at that time were there between
　　Mars and the Baptist, fit for bearing arms,
　　Were a fifth part of those who now are living;
But the community, that now is mixed
　　With Campi and Certaldo and Figghine,　　　　　50
　　Pure in the lowest artisan was seen.
O how much better 'twere to have as neighbours
　　The folk of whom I speak, and at Galluzzo
　　And at Trespiano have your boundary,
Than have them in the town, and bear the stench
　　Of Aguglione's churl, and him of Signa
　　Who has sharp eyes for trickery already.
Had not the folk, which most of all the world
　　Degenerates, been a step-dame unto Cæsar,
　　But as a mother to her son benignant,　　　　　60
Some who turn Florentines, and trade and discount,
　　Would have gone back again to Simifonte
　　There where their grandsires went about as beggars.
At Montemurlo still would be the Counts,
　　The Cerchi in the parish of Acone,
　　Perhaps in Valdigrieve the Buondelmonti.
Ever the intermingling of the people
　　Has been the source of malady in cities,
　　As in the body food it surfeits on;
And a blind bull more headlong plunges down　　70
　　Than a blind lamb; and very often cuts
　　Better and more a single sword than five.
If Luni thou regard, and Urbisaglia,
　　How they have passed away, and how are passing
　　Chiusi and Sinigaglia after them,
To hear how races waste themselves away,
　　Will seem to thee no novel thing nor hard,
　　Seeing that even cities have an end.
All things of yours have their mortality,
　　Even as yourselves; but it is hidden in some　　80

That a long while endure, and lives are short;
And as the turning of the lunar heaven
   Covers and bares the shores without a pause,
   In the like manner fortune does with Florence.
Therefore should not appear a marvellous thing
   What I shall say of the great Florentines
   Of whom the fame is hidden in the Past.
I saw the Ughi, saw the Catellini,
   Filippi, Greci, Ormanni, and Alberichi,
   Even in their fall illustrious citizens;   90
And saw, as mighty as they ancient were,
   With him of La Sannella him of Arca,
   And Soldanier, Ardinghi, and Bostichi.
Near to the gate that is at present laden
   With a new felony of so much weight
   That soon it shall be jetsam from the bark,
The Ravignani were, from whom descended
   The County Guido, and whoe'er the name
   Of the great Bellincione since hath taken.
He of La Pressa knew the art of ruling   100
   Already, and already Galigajo
   Had hilt and pommel gilded in his house.
Mighty already was the Column Vair,
   Sacchetti, Giuochi, Fifant, and Barucci,
   And Galli, and they who for the bushel blush.
The stock from which were the Calfucci born
   Was great already, and already chosen
   To curule chairs the Sizii and Arrigucci.
O how beheld I those who are undone
   By their own pride! and how the Balls of Gold   110
   Florence enflowered in all their mighty deeds!
So likewise did the ancestors of those
   Who evermore, when vacant is your church,
   Fatten by staying in consistory.
The insolent race, that like a dragon follows
   Whoever flees, and unto him that shows
   His teeth or purse is gentle as a lamb,
Already rising was, but from low people;
   So that it pleased not Ubertin Donato
   That his wife's father should make him their kin.   120
Already had Caponsacco to the Market

From Fesole descended, and already
    Giuda and Infangato were good burghers.
I'll tell a thing incredible, but true;
    One entered the small circuit by a gate
    Which from the Della Pera took its name!
Each one that bears the beautiful escutcheon
    Of the great baron whose renown and name
    The festival of Thomas keepeth fresh,
Knighthood and privilege from him received;   130
    Though with the populace unites himself
    To-day the man who binds it with a border.
Already were Gualterotti and Importuni;
    And still more quiet would the Borgo be
    If with new neighbours it remained unfed.
The house from which is born your lamentation,
    Through just disdain that death among you brought
    And put an end unto your joyous life,
Was honoured in itself and its companions.
    O Buondelmonte, how in evil hour   140
    Thou fled'st the bridal at another's promptings!
Many would be rejoicing who are sad,
    If God had thee surrendered to the Ema
    The first time that thou camest to the city.
But it behoved the mutilated stone
    Which guards the bridge, that Florence should provide
    A victim in her latest hour of peace.
With all these families, and others with them,
    Florence beheld I in so great repose,
    That no occasion had she whence to weep;   150
With all these families beheld so just
    And glorious her people, that the lily
    Never upon the spear was placed reversed,
Nor by division was vermilion made."

Canto XVII

As came to Clymene, to be made certain
    Of that which he had heard against himself,
    He who makes fathers chary still to children,
Even such was I, and such was I perceived
    By Beatrice and by the holy light

That first on my account had changed its place.
    Therefore my Lady said to me: "Send forth
    The flame of thy desire, so that it issue
    Imprinted well with the internal stamp;
Not that our knowledge may be greater made
    By speech of thine, but to accustom thee
    To tell thy thirst, that we may give thee drink."
"O my beloved tree, (that so dost lift thee,
    That even as minds terrestrial perceive
    No triangle containeth two obtuse,
So thou beholdest the contingent things
    Ere in themselves they are, fixing thine eyes
    Upon the point in which all times are present,)
While I was with Virgilius conjoined
    Upon the mountain that the souls doth heal,
    And when descending into the dead world,
Were spoken to me of my future life
    Some grievous words; although I feel myself
    In sooth foursquare against the blows of chance.
On this account my wish would be content
    To hear what fortune is approaching me,
    Because foreseen an arrow comes more slowly."
Thus did I say unto that selfsame light
    That unto me had spoken before; and even
    As Beatrice willed was my own will confessed.
Not in vague phrase, in which the foolish folk
    Ensnared themselves of old, ere yet was slain
    The Lamb of God who taketh sins away,
But with clear words and unambiguous
    Language responded that paternal love,
    Hid and revealed by its own proper smile:
"Contingency, that outside of the volume
    Of your materiality extends not,
    Is all depicted in the eternal aspect.
Necessity however thence it takes not,
    Except as from the eye, in which 'tis mirrored,
    A ship that with the current down descends.
From thence, e'en as there cometh to the ear
    Sweet harmony from an organ, comes in sight
    To me the time that is preparing for thee.
As forth from Athens went Hippolytus,
    By reason of his step–dame false and cruel,

So thou from Florence must perforce depart.
Already this is willed, and this is sought for;
 And soon it shall be done by him who thinks it,   50
 Where every day the Christ is bought and sold.
The blame shall follow the offended party
 In outcry as is usual; but the vengeance
 Shall witness to the truth that doth dispense it.
Thou shalt abandon everything beloved
 Most tenderly, and this the arrow is
 Which first the bow of banishment shoots forth.
Thou shalt have proof how savoureth of salt
 The bread of others, and how hard a road
 The going down and up another's stairs.   60
And that which most shall weigh upon thy shoulders
 Will be the bad and foolish company
 With which into this valley thou shalt fall;
For all ingrate, all mad and impious
 Will they become against thee; but soon after
 They, and not thou, shall have the forehead scarlet
Of their bestiality their own proceedings
 Shall furnish proof; so 'twill be well for thee
 A party to have made thee by thyself.
Thine earliest refuge and thine earliest inn   70
 Shall be the mighty Lombard's courtesy,
 Who on the Ladder bears the holy bird,
Who such benign regard shall have for thee
 That 'twixt you twain, in doing and in asking,
 That shall be first which is with others last.
With him shalt thou see one who at his birth
 Has by this star of strength been so impressed,
 That notable shall his achievements be.
Not yet the people are aware of him
 Through his young age, since only nine years yet   80
 Around about him have these wheels revolved.
But ere the Gascon cheat the noble Henry,
 Some sparkles of his virtue shall appear
 In caring not for silver nor for toil.
So recognized shall his magnificence
 Become hereafter, that his enemies
 Will not have power to keep mute tongues about it.
On him rely, and on his benefits;

By him shall many people be transformed,
  Changing condition rich and mendicant;   90
And written in thy mind thou hence shalt bear
  Of him, but shalt not say it"—and things said he
  Incredible to those who shall be present.
Then added: "Son, these are the commentaries
  On what was said to thee; behold the snares
  That are concealed behind few revolutions;
Yet would I not thy neighbours thou shouldst envy,
  Because thy life into the future reaches
  Beyond the punishment of their perfidies."
When by its silence showed that sainted soul   100
  That it had finished putting in the woof
  Into that web which I had given it warped,
Began I, even as he who yearneth after,
  Being in doubt, some counsel from a person
  Who seeth, and uprightly wills, and loves:
"Well see I, father mine, how spurreth on
  The time towards me such a blow to deal me
  As heaviest is to him who most gives way.
Therefore with foresight it is well I arm me,
  That, if the dearest place be taken from me,   110
  I may not lose the others by my songs.
Down through the world of infinite bitterness,
  And o'er the mountain, from whose beauteous summit
  The eyes of my own Lady lifted me,
And afterward through heaven from light to light,
  I have learned that which, if I tell again,
  Will be a savour of strong herbs to many.
And if I am a timid friend to truth,
  I fear lest I may lose my life with those
  Who will hereafter call this time the olden."   120
The light in which was smiling my own treasure
  Which there I had discovered, flashed at first
  As in the sunshine doth a golden mirror;
Then made reply: "A conscience overcast
  Or with its own or with another's shame,
  Will taste forsooth the tartness of thy word;
But ne'ertheless, all falsehood laid aside,
  Make manifest thy vision utterly,
  And let them scratch wherever is the itch;

For if thine utterance shall offensive be   130
    At the first taste, a vital nutriment
    'Twill leave thereafter, when it is digested.
This cry of thine shall do as doth the wind,
    Which smiteth most the most exalted summits,
    And that is no slight argument of honour.
Therefore are shown to thee within these wheels,
    Upon the mount and in the dolorous valley,
    Only the souls that unto fame are known;
Because the spirit of the hearer rests not,
    Nor doth confirm its faith by an example   140
    Which has the root of it unknown and hidden,
Or other reason that is not apparent."

Canto XVIII

Now was alone rejoicing in its word
    That soul beatified, and I was tasting
    My own, the bitter tempering with the sweet,
And the Lady who to God was leading me
    Said: "Change thy thought; consider that I am
    Near unto Him who every wrong disburdens."
Unto the loving accents of my comfort
    I turned me round, and then what love I saw
    Within those holy eyes I here relinquish;
Not only that my language I distrust,   10
    But that my mind cannot return so far
    Above itself, unless another guide it.
Thus much upon that point can I repeat,
    That, her again beholding, my affection
    From every other longing was released.
While the eternal pleasure, which direct
    Rayed upon Beatrice, from her fair face
    Contented me with its reflected aspect,
Conquering me with the radiance of a smile,
    She said to me, "Turn thee about and listen;   20
    Not in mine eyes alone is Paradise."
Even as sometimes here do we behold
    The affection in the look, if it be such
    That all the soul is wrapt away by it,

So, by the flaming of the effulgence holy
    To which I turned, I recognized therein
    The wish of speaking to me somewhat farther.
And it began: "In this fifth resting-place
    Upon the tree that liveth by its summit,
    And aye bears fruit, and never loses leaf,   30
Are blessed spirits that below, ere yet
    They came to Heaven, were of such great renown
    That every Muse therewith would affluent be.
Therefore look thou upon the cross's horns;
    He whom I now shall name will there enact
    What doth within a cloud its own swift fire."
I saw athwart the Cross a splendour drawn
    By naming Joshua, (even as he did it,)
    Nor noted I the word before the deed;
And at the name of the great Maccabee   40
    I saw another move itself revolving,
    And gladness was the whip unto that top.
Likewise for Charlemagne and for Orlando,
    Two of them my regard attentive followed
    As followeth the eye its falcon flying.
William thereafterward, and Renouard,
    And the Duke Godfrey, did attract my sight
    Along upon that Cross, and Robert Guiscard.
Then, moved and mingled with the other lights,
    The soul that had addressed me showed how great   50
    An artist 'twas among the heavenly singers.
To my right side I turned myself around,
    My duty to behold in Beatrice
    Either by words or gesture signified;
And so translucent I beheld her eyes,
    So full of pleasure, that her countenance
    Surpassed its other and its latest wont.
And as, by feeling greater delectation,
    A man in doing good from day to day
    Becomes aware his virtue is increasing,   60
So I became aware that my gyration
    With heaven together had increased its arc,
    That miracle beholding more adorned.
And such as is the change, in little lapse
    Of time, in a pale woman, when her face

Is from the load of bashfulness unladen,
Such was it in mine eyes, when I had turned,
    Caused by the whiteness of the temperate star,
    The sixth, which to itself had gathered me.
Within that Jovial torch did I behold   70
    The sparkling of the love which was therein
    Delineate our language to mine eyes.
And even as birds uprisen from the shore,
    As in congratulation o'er their food,
    Make squadrons of themselves, now round, now long,
So from within those lights the holy creatures
    Sang flying to and fro, and in their figures
    Made of themselves now D, now I, now L.
First singing they to their own music moved;
    Then one becoming of these characters,   80
    A little while they rested and were silent.
O divine Pegasea, thou who genius
    Dost glorious make, and render it long-lived,
    And this through thee the cities and the kingdoms,
Illume me with thyself, that I may bring
    Their figures out as I have them conceived!
    Apparent be thy power in these brief verses!
Themselves then they displayed in five times seven
    Vowels and consonants; and I observed
    The parts as they seemed spoken unto me.   90
Diligite justitiam, these were
    First verb and noun of all that was depicted;
    Qui judicatis terram were the last.
Thereafter in the M of the fifth word
    Remained they so arranged, that Jupiter
    Seemed to be silver there with gold inlaid.
And other lights I saw descend where was
    The summit of the M, and pause there singing
    The good, I think, that draws them to itself.
Then, as in striking upon burning logs   100
    Upward there fly innumerable sparks,
    Whence fools are wont to look for auguries,
More than a thousand lights seemed thence to rise,
    And to ascend, some more, and others less,
    Even as the Sun that lights them had allotted;
And, each one being quiet in its place,

The head and neck beheld I of an eagle
   Delineated by that inlaid fire.
He who there paints has none to be his guide;
   But Himself guides; and is from Him remembered   110
   That virtue which is form unto the nest.
The other beatitude, that contented seemed
   At first to bloom a lily on the M,
   By a slight motion followed out the imprint.
O gentle star! what and how many gems
   Did demonstrate to me, that all our justice
   Effect is of that heaven which thou ingemmest!
Wherefore I pray the Mind, in which begin
   Thy motion and thy virtue, to regard
   Whence comes the smoke that vitiates thy rays;   120
So that a second time it now be wroth
   With buying and with selling in the temple
   Whose walls were built with signs and martyrdoms!
O soldiery of heaven, whom I contemplate,
   Implore for those who are upon the earth
   All gone astray after the bad example!
Once 'twas the custom to make war with swords;
   But now 'tis made by taking here and there
   The bread the pitying Father shuts from none.
Yet thou, who writest but to cancel, think   130
   That Peter and that Paul, who for this vineyard
   Which thou art spoiling died, are still alive!
Well canst thou say: "So steadfast my desire
   Is unto him who willed to live alone,
   And for a dance was led to martyrdom,
That I know not the Fisherman nor Paul."

Canto XIX

Appeared before me with its wings outspread
   The beautiful image that in sweet fruition
   Made jubilant the interwoven souls;
Appeared a little ruby each, wherein
   Ray of the sun was burning so enkindled
   That each into mine eyes refracted it.
And what it now behoves me to retrace

Nor voice has e'er reported, nor ink written,
Nor was by fantasy e'er comprehended;
For speak I saw, and likewise heard, the beak,   10
    And utter with its voice both *I* and *My,*
    When in conception it was *We* and *Our.*
And it began: "Being just and merciful
    Am I exalted here unto that glory
    Which cannot be exceeded by desire;
And upon earth I left my memory
    Such, that the evil-minded people there
    Commend it, but continue not the story."
So doth a single heat from many embers
    Make itself felt, even as from many loves   20
    Issued a single sound from out that image.
Whence I thereafter: "O perpetual flowers
    Of the eternal joy, that only one
    Make me perceive your odours manifold,
Exhaling, break within me the great fast
    Which a long season has in hunger held me,
    Not finding for it any food on earth.
Well do I know, that if in heaven its mirror
    Justice Divine another realm doth make,
    Yours apprehends it not through any veil.   30
You know how I attentively address me
    To listen; and you know what is the doubt
    That is in me so very old a fast."
Even as a falcon, issuing from his hood,
    Doth move his head, and with his wings applaud him,
    Showing desire, and making himself fine,
Saw I become that standard, which of lauds
    Was interwoven of the grace divine,
    With such songs as he knows who there rejoices.
Then it began: "He who a compass turned   40
    On the world's outer verge, and who within it
    Devised so much occult and manifest,
Could not the impress of his power so make
    On all the universe, as that his Word
    Should not remain in infinite excess.
And this makes certain that the first proud being,
    Who was the paragon of every creature,
    By not awaiting light fell immature.

And hence appears it, that each minor nature
   Is scant receptacle unto that good   50
   Which has no end, and by itself is measured.
In consequence our vision, which perforce
   Must be some ray of that intelligence
   With which all things whatever are replete,
Cannot in its own nature be so potent,
   That it shall not its origin discern
   Far beyond that which is apparent to it.
Therefore into the justice sempiternal
   The power of vision that your world receives,
   As eye into the ocean, penetrates;   60
Which, though it see the bottom near the shore,
   Upon the deep perceives it not, and yet
   'Tis there, but it is hidden by the depth.
There is no light but comes from the serene
   That never is o'ercast, nay, it is darkness
   Or shadow of the flesh, or else its poison.
Amply to thee is opened now the cavern
   Which has concealed from thee the living justice
   Of which thou mad'st such frequent questioning.
For saidst thou: 'Born a man is on the shore   70
   Of Indus, and is none who there can speak
   Of Christ, nor who can read, nor who can write;
And all his inclinations and his actions
   Are good, so far as human reason sees,
   Without a sin in life or in discourse:
He dieth unbaptised and without faith;
   Where is this justice that condemneth him?
   Where is his fault, if he do not believe?'
Now who art thou, that on the bench wouldst sit
   In judgment at a thousand miles away,   80
   With the short vision of a single span?
Truly to him who with me subtilizes,
   If so the Scripture were not over you,
   For doubting there were marvellous occasion.
O animals terrene, O stolid minds,
   The primal will, that in itself is good,
   Ne'er from itself, the Good Supreme, has moved.
So much is just as is accordant with it;
   No good created draws it to itself,

But it, by raying forth, occasions that." 90
Even as above her nest goes circling round
    The stork when she has fed her little ones,
    And he who has been fed looks up at her,
So lifted I my brows, and even such
    Became the blessed image, which its wings
    Was moving, by so many counsels urged.
Circling around it sang, and said: "As are
    My notes to thee, who dost not comprehend them,
    Such is the eternal judgment to you mortals."
Those lucent splendours of the Holy Spirit 100
    Grew quiet then, but still within the standard
    That made the Romans reverend to the world.
It recommenced: "Unto this kingdom never
    Ascended one who had not faith in Christ,
    Before or since he to the tree was nailed.
But look thou, many crying are, 'Christ, Christ!'
    Who at the judgment shall be far less near
    To him than some shall be who knew not Christ.
Such Christians shall the Ethiop condemn,
    When the two companies shall be divided, 110
    The one for ever rich, the other poor.
What to your kings may not the Persians say,
    When they that volume opened shall behold
    In which are written down all their dispraises?
There shall be seen, among the deeds of Albert,
    That which ere long shall set the pen in motion,
    For which the realm of Prague shall be deserted.
There shall be seen the woe that on the Seine
    He brings by falsifying of the coin,
    Who by the blow of a wild boar shall die. 120
There shall be seen the pride that causes thirst,
    Which makes the Scot and Englishman so mad
    That they within their boundaries cannot rest;
Be seen the luxury and effeminate life
    Of him of Spain, and the Bohemian,
    Who valour never knew and never wished;
Be seen the Cripple of Jerusalem,
    His goodness represented by an I,
    While the reverse an M shall represent;
Be seen the avarice and poltroonery 130

Of him who guards the Island of the Fire,
  Wherein Anchises finished his long life;
And to declare how pitiful he is
  Shall be his record in contracted letters
  Which shall make note of much in little space.
And shall appear to each one the foul deeds
  Of uncle and of brother who a nation
  So famous have dishonoured, and two crowns.
And he of Portugal and he of Norway
  Shall there be known, and he of Rascia too,   140
  Who saw in evil hour the coin of Venice.
O happy Hungary, if she let herself
  Be wronged no farther! and Navarre the happy,
  If with the hills that gird her she be armed!
And each one may believe that now, as hansel
  Thereof, do Nicosìa and Famagosta
  Lament and rage because of their own beast,
Who from the others' flank departeth not."

Canto XX

When he who all the world illuminates
  Out of our hemisphere so far descends
  That on all sides the daylight is consumed,
The heaven, that erst by him alone was kindled,
  Doth suddenly reveal itself again
  By many lights, wherein is one resplendent.
And came into my mind this act of heaven,
  When the ensign of the world and of its leaders
  Had silent in the blessed beak become;
Because those living luminaries all,   10
  By far more luminous, did songs begin
  Lapsing and falling from my memory.
O gentle Love, that with a smile dost cloak thee,
  How ardent in those sparks didst thou appear,
  That had the breath alone of holy thoughts!
After the precious and pellucid crystals,
  With which begemmed the sixth light I beheld,
  Silence imposed on the angelic bells,
I seemed to hear the murmuring of a river

That clear descendeth down from rock to rock,   20
    Showing the affluence of its mountain-top.
And as the sound upon the cithern's neck
    Taketh its form, and as upon the vent
    Of rustic pipe the wind that enters it,
Even thus, relieved from the delay of waiting,
    That murmuring of the eagle mounted up
    Along its neck, as if it had been hollow.
There it became a voice, and issued thence
    From out its beak, in such a form of words
    As the heart waited for wherein I wrote them.   30
"The part in me which sees and bears the sun
    In mortal eagles," it began to me,
    "Now fixedly must needs be looked upon;
For of the fires of which I make my figure,
    Those whence the eye doth sparkle in my head
    Of all their orders the supremest are.
He who is shining in the midst as pupil
    Was once the singer of the Holy Spirit,
    Who bore the ark from city unto city;
Now knoweth he the merit of his song,   40
    In so far as effect of his own counsel,
    By the reward which is commensurate.
Of five, that make a circle for my brow,
    He that approacheth nearest to my beak
    Did the poor widow for her son console;
Now knoweth he how dearly it doth cost
    Not following Christ, by the experience
    Of this sweet life and of its opposite.
He who comes next in the circumference
    Of which I speak, upon its highest arc,   50
    Did death postpone by penitence sincere;
Now knoweth he that the eternal judgment
    Suffers no change, albeit worthy prayer
    Maketh below to-morrow of to-day.
The next who follows, with the laws and me,
    Under the good intent that bore bad fruit
    Became a Greek by ceding to the pastor;
Now knoweth he how all the ill deduced
    From his good action is not harmful to him,
    Although the world thereby may be destroyed.   60

And he, whom in the downward arc thou seest,
    Guglielmo was, whom the same land deplores
    That weepeth Charles and Frederick yet alive;
Now knoweth he how heaven enamoured is
    With a just king; and in the outward show
    Of his effulgence he reveals it still.
Who would believe, down in the errant world,
    That e'er the Trojan Ripheus in this round
    Could be the fifth one of the holy lights?
Now knoweth he enough of what the world   70
    Has not the power to see of grace divine,
    Although his sight may not discern the bottom."
Like as a lark that in the air expatiates,
    First singing and then silent with content
    Of the last sweetness that doth satisfy her,
Such seemed to me the image of the imprint
    Of the eternal pleasure, by whose will
    Doth everything become the thing it is.
And notwithstanding to my doubt I was
    As glass is to the colour that invests it,   80
    To wait the time in silence it endured not,
But forth from out my mouth, "What things are these?"
    Extorted with the force of its own weight;
    Whereat I saw great joy of coruscation.
Thereafterward with eye still more enkindled
    The blessed standard made to me reply,
    To keep me not in wonderment suspended:
"I see that thou believest in these things
    Because I say them, but thou seest not how;
    So that, although believed in, they are hidden.   90
Thou doest as he doth who a thing by name
    Well apprehendeth, but its quiddity
    Cannot perceive, unless another show it.
Regnum cælorum suffereth violence
    From fervent love, and from that living hope
    That overcometh the Divine volition;
Not in the guise that man o'ercometh man,
    But conquers it because it will be conquered,
    And conquered conquers by benignity.
The first life of the eyebrow and the fifth   100
    Cause thee astonishment, because with them

Thou seest the region of the angels painted.
They passed not from their bodies, as thou thinkest,
　　Gentiles, but Christians in the steadfast faith
　　Of feet that were to suffer and had suffered.
For one from Hell, where no one e'er turns back
　　Unto good will, returned unto his bones,
　　And that of living hope was the reward,—
Of living hope, that placed its efficacy
　　In prayers to God made to resuscitate him,　　　　110
　　So that 'twere possible to move his will.
The glorious soul concerning which I speak,
　　Returning to the flesh, where brief its stay,
　　Believed in Him who had the power to aid it;
And, in believing, kindled to such fire
　　Of genuine love, that at the second death
　　Worthy it was to come unto this joy.
The other one, through grace, that from so deep
　　A fountain wells that never hath the eye
　　Of any creature reached its primal wave,　　　　120
Set all his love below on righteousness;
　　Wherefore from grace to grace did God unclose
　　His eye to our redemption yet to be,
Whence he believed therein, and suffered not
　　From that day forth the stench of paganism,
　　And he reproved therefor the folk perverse.
Those Maidens three, whom at the right-hand wheel
　　Thou didst behold, were unto him for baptism
　　More than a thousand years before baptizing.
O thou predestination, how remote　　　　130
　　Thy root is from the aspect of all those
　　Who the First Cause do not behold entire!
And you, O mortals! hold yourselves restrained
　　In judging; for ourselves, who look on God,
　　We do not know as yet all the elect;
And sweet to us is such a deprivation,
　　Because our good in this good is made perfect,
　　That whatsoe'er God wills, we also will."
After this manner by that shape divine,
　　To make clear in me my short-sightedness,　　　　140
　　Was given to me a pleasant medicine;
And as good singer a good lutanist

Accompanies with vibrations of the chords,
    Whereby more pleasantness the song acquires,
So, while it spake, do I remember me
    That I beheld both of those blessed lights,
    Even as the winking of the eyes concords,
Moving unto the words their little flames.

Canto XXI

Already on my Lady's face mine eyes
    Again were fastened, and with these my mind,
    And from all other purpose was withdrawn;
And she smiled not; but "If I were to smile,"
    She unto me began, "thou wouldst become
    Like Semele, when she was turned to ashes.
Because my beauty, that along the stairs
    Of the eternal palace more enkindles,
    As thou hast seen, the farther we ascend,
If it were tempered not, is so resplendent   10
    That all thy mortal power in its effulgence
    Would seem a leaflet that the thunder crushes.
We are uplifted to the seventh splendour,
    That underneath the burning Lion's breast
    Now radiates downward mingled with his power.
Fix in direction of thine eyes the mind,
    And make of them a mirror for the figure
    That in this mirror shall appear to thee."
He who could know what was the pasturage
    My sight had in that blessed countenance,   20
    When I transferred me to another care,
Would recognize how grateful was to me
    Obedience unto my celestial escort,
    By counterpoising one side with the other.
Within the crystal which, around the world
    Revolving, bears the name of its dear leader,
    Under whom every wickedness lay dead,
Coloured like gold, on which the sunshine gleams,
    A stairway I beheld to such a height
    Uplifted, that mine eye pursued it not.   30
Likewise beheld I down the steps descending

So many splendours, that I thought each light
　That in the heaven appears was there diffused.
And as accordant with their natural custom
　The rooks together at the break of day
　Bestir themselves to warm their feathers cold;
Then some of them fly off without return,
　Others come back to where they started from,
　And others, wheeling round, still keep at home;
Such fashion it appeared to me was there　　　　　　40
　Within the sparkling that together came,
　As soon as on a certain step it struck,
And that which nearest unto us remained
　Became so clear, that in my thought I said,
　"Well I perceive the love thou showest me;
But she, from whom I wait the how and when
　Of speech and silence, standeth still; whence I
　Against desire do well if I ask not."
She thereupon, who saw my silentness
　In the sight of Him who seeth everything,　　　　　50
　Said unto me, "Let loose thy warm desire."
And I began: "No merit of my own
　Renders me worthy of response from thee;
　But for her sake who granteth me the asking,
Thou blessed life that dost remain concealed
　In thy beatitude, make known to me
　The cause which draweth thee so near my side;
And tell me why is silent in this wheel
　The dulcet symphony of Paradise,
　That through the rest below sounds so devoutly."　　60
"Thou hast thy hearing mortal as thy sight,"
　It answer made to me; "they sing not here,
　For the same cause that Beatrice has not smiled.
Thus far adown the holy stairway's steps
　Have I descended but to give thee welcome
　With words, and with the light that mantles me;
Nor did more love cause me to be more ready,
　For love as much and more up there is burning,
　As doth the flaming manifest to thee.
But the high charity, that makes us servants　　　　70
　Prompt to the counsel which controls the world,
　Allotteth here, even as thou dost observe."

"I see full well," said I, "O sacred lamp!
   How love unfettered in this court sufficeth
   To follow the eternal Providence;
But this is what seems hard for me to see,
   Wherefore predestinate wast thou alone
   Unto this office from among thy consorts."
No sooner had I come to the last word,
   Than of its middle made the light a centre,   80
   Whirling itself about like a swift millstone.
Then answer made the love that was therein:
   "On me directed is a light divine,
   Piercing through this in which I am embosomed,
Of which the virtue with my sight conjoined
   Lifts me above myself so far, I see
   The supreme essence from which this is drawn.
Hence comes the joyfulness with which I flame,
   For to my sight, as far as it is clear,
   The clearness of the flame I equal make.   90
But that soul in the heaven which is most pure,
   That seraph which his eye on God most fixes,
   Could this demand of thine not satisfy;
Because so deeply sinks in the abyss
   Of the eternal statute what thou askest,
   From all created sight it is cut off.
And to the mortal world, when thou returnest,
   This carry back, that it may not presume
   Longer tow'rd such a goal to move its feet.
The mind, that shineth here, on earth doth smoke;   100
   From this observe how can it do below
   That which it cannot though the heaven assume it?"
Such limit did its words prescribe to me,
   The question I relinquished, and restricted
   Myself to ask it humbly who it was.
"Between two shores of Italy rise cliffs,
   And not far distant from thy native place,
   So high, the thunders far below them sound,
And form a ridge that Catria is called,
   'Neath which is consecrate a hermitage   110
   Wont to be dedicate to worship only."
Thus unto me the third speech recommenced,
   And then, continuing, it said: "Therein

Unto God's service I became so steadfast,
    That feeding only on the juice of olives
      Lightly I passed away the heats and frosts,
      Contented in my thoughts contemplative.
That cloister used to render to these heavens
    Abundantly, and now is empty grown,
      So that perforce it soon must be revealed.   120
I in that place was Peter Damiano;
    And Peter the Sinner was I in the house
      Of Our Lady on the Adriatic shore.
Little of mortal life remained to me,
    When I was called and dragged forth to the hat
      Which shifteth evermore from bad to worse.
Came Cephas, and the mighty Vessel came
    Of the Holy Spirit, meagre and barefooted,
      Taking the food of any hostelry.
Now some one to support them on each side   130
    The modern shepherds need, and some to lead them,
      So heavy are they, and to hold their trains.
They cover up their palfreys with their cloaks,
    So that two beasts go underneath one skin;
      O Patience, that dost tolerate so much!"
At this voice saw I many little flames
    From step to step descending and revolving,
      And every revolution made them fairer.
Round about this one came they and stood still,
    And a cry uttered of so loud a sound,   140
      It here could find no parallel, nor I
Distinguished it, the thunder so o'ercame me.

Canto XXII

Oppressed with stupor, I unto my guide
    Turned like a little child who always runs
      For refuge there where he confideth most;
And she, even as a mother who straightway
    Gives comfort to her pale and breathless boy
      With voice whose wont it is to reassure him,
Said to me: "Knowest thou not thou art in heaven,
    And knowest thou not that heaven is holy all,

And what is done here cometh from good zeal?
After what wise the singing would have changed thee   10
  And I by smiling, thou canst now imagine,
  Since that the cry has startled thee so much,
In which if thou hadst understood its prayers
  Already would be known to thee the vengeance
  Which thou shalt look upon before thou diest.
The sword above here smiteth not in haste
  Nor tardily, howe'er it seem to him
  Who fearing or desiring waits for it.
But turn thee round towards the others now,
  For very illustrious spirits shalt thou see,   20
  If thou thy sight directest as I say."
As it seemed good to her mine eyes I turned,
  And saw a hundred spherules that together
  With mutual rays each other more embellished.
I stood as one who in himself represses
  The point of his desire, and ventures not
  To question, he so feareth the too much.
And now the largest and most luculent
  Among those pearls came forward, that it might
  Make my desire concerning it content.   30
Within it then I heard: "If thou couldst see
  Even as myself the charity that burns
  Among us, thy conceits would be expressed;
But, that by waiting thou mayst not come late
  To the high end, I will make answer even
  Unto the thought of which thou art so chary.
That mountain on whose slope Cassino stands
  Was frequented of old upon its summit
  By a deluded folk and ill-disposed;
And I am he who first up thither bore   40
  The name of Him who brought upon the earth
  The truth that so much sublimateth us.
And such abundant grace upon me shone
  That all the neighbouring towns I drew away
  From the impious worship that seduced the world.
These other fires, each one of them, were men
  Contemplative, enkindled by that heat
  Which maketh holy flowers and fruits spring up.
Here is Macarius, here is Romualdus,

Here are my brethren, who within the cloisters 50
    Their footsteps stayed and kept a steadfast heart."
And I to him: "The affection which thou showest
    Speaking with me, and the good countenance
    Which I behold and note in all your ardours,
In me have so my confidence dilated
    As the sun doth the rose, when it becomes
    As far unfolded as it hath the power.
Therefore I pray, and thou assure me, father,
    If I may so much grace receive, that I
    May thee behold with countenance unveiled." 60
He thereupon: "Brother, thy high desire
    In the remotest sphere shall be fulfilled,
    Where are fulfilled all others and my own.
There perfect is, and ripened, and complete,
    Every desire; within that one alone
    Is every part where it has always been;
For it is not in space, nor turns on poles,
    And unto it our stairway reaches up,
    Whence thus from out thy sight it steals away.
Up to that height the Patriarch Jacob saw it 70
    Extending its supernal part, what time
    So thronged with angels it appeared to him.
But to ascend it now no one uplifts
    His feet from off the earth, and now my Rule
    Below remaineth for mere waste of paper.
The walls that used of old to be an Abbey
    Are changed to dens of robbers, and the cowls
    Are sacks filled full of miserable flour.
But heavy usury is not taken up
    So much against God's pleasure as that fruit 80
    Which maketh so insane the heart of monks;
For whatsoever hath the Church in keeping
    Is for the folk that ask it in God's name,
    Not for one's kindred or for something worse.
The flesh of mortals is so very soft,
    That good beginnings down below suffice not
    From springing of the oak to bearing acorns.
Peter began with neither gold nor silver,
    And I with orison and abstinence,
    And Francis with humility his convent. 90

And if thou lookest at each one's beginning,
   And then regardest whither he has run,
   Thou shalt behold the white changed into brown.
In verity the Jordan backward turned,
   And the sea's fleeing, when God willed, were more
   A wonder to behold, than succour here."
Thus unto me he said; and then withdrew
   To his own band, and the band closed together;
   Then like a whirlwind all was upward rapt.
The gentle Lady urged me on behind them   100
   Up o'er that stairway by a single sign,
   So did her virtue overcome my nature;
Nor here below, where one goes up and down
   By natural law, was motion e'er so swift
   That it could be compared unto my wing.
Reader, as I may unto that devout
   Triumph return, on whose account I often
   For my transgressions weep and beat my breast,—
Thou hadst not thrust thy finger in the fire
   And drawn it out again, before I saw   110
   The sign that follows Taurus, and was in it.
O glorious stars, O light impregnated
   With mighty virtue, from which I acknowledge
   All of my genius, whatsoe'er it be,
With you was born, and hid himself with you,
   He who is father of all mortal life,
   When first I tasted of the Tuscan air;
And then when grace was freely given to me
   To enter the high wheel which turns you round,
   Your region was allotted unto me.   120
To you devoutly at this hour my soul
   Is sighing, that it virtue may acquire
   For the stern pass that draws it to itself.
"Thou art so near unto the last salvation,"
   Thus Beatrice began, "thou oughtest now
   To have thine eyes unclouded and acute;
And therefore, ere thou enter farther in,
   Look down once more, and see how vast a world
   Thou hast already put beneath thy feet;
So that thy heart, as jocund as it may,   130
   Present itself to the triumphant throng

That comes rejoicing through this rounded ether."
I with my sight returned through one and all
    The sevenfold spheres, and I beheld this globe
    Such that I smiled at its ignoble semblance;
And that opinion I approve as best
    Which doth account it least; and he who thinks
    Of something else may truly be called just.
I saw the daughter of Latona shining
    Without that shadow, which to me was cause   140
    That once I had believed her rare and dense.
The aspect of thy son, Hyperion,
    Here I sustained, and saw how move themselves
    Around and near him Maia and Dione.
Thence there appeared the temperateness of Jove
    'Twixt son and father, and to me was clear
    The change that of their whereabout they make;
And all the seven made manifest to me
    How great they are, and eke how swift they are,
    And how they are in distant habitations.   150
The threshing-floor that maketh us so proud,
    To me revolving with the eternal Twins,
    Was all apparent made from hill to harbour!
Then to the beauteous eyes mine eyes I turned.

Canto XXIII

Even as a bird, 'mid the beloved leaves,
    Quiet upon the nest of her sweet brood
    Throughout the night, that hideth all things from us,
Who, that she may behold their longed-for looks
    And find the food wherewith to nourish them,
    In which, to her, grave labours grateful are,
Anticipates the time on open spray
    And with an ardent longing waits the sun,
    Gazing intent as soon as breaks the dawn:
Even thus my Lady standing was, erect   10
    And vigilant, turned round towards the zone
    Underneath which the sun displays less haste;
So that beholding her distraught and wistful,
    Such I became as he is who desiring

For something yearns, and hoping is appeased.
But brief the space from one When to the other;
  Of my awaiting, say I, and the seeing
  The welkin grow resplendent more and more.
And Beatrice exclaimed: "Behold the hosts
  Of Christ's triumphal march, and all the fruit   20
  Harvested by the rolling of these spheres!"
It seemed to me her face was all aflame;
  And eyes she had so full of ecstasy
  That I must needs pass on without describing.
As when in nights serene of the full moon
  Smiles Trivia among the nymphs eternal
  Who paint the firmament through all its gulfs,
Saw I, above the myriads of lamps,
  A Sun that one and all of them enkindled,
  E'en as our own doth the supernal sights,   30
And through the living light transparent shone
  The lucent substance so intensely clear
  Into my sight, that I sustained it not.
O Beatrice, thou gentle guide and dear!
  To me she said: "What overmasters thee
  A virtue is from which naught shields itself.
There are the wisdom and the omnipotence
  That oped the thoroughfares 'twixt heaven and earth,
  For which there erst had been so long a yearning."
As fire from out a cloud unlocks itself,   40
  Dilating so it finds not room therein,
  And down, against its nature, falls to earth,
So did my mind, among those aliments
  Becoming larger, issue from itself,
  And that which it became cannot remember.
"Open thine eyes, and look at what I am:
  Thou hast beheld such things, that strong enough
  Hast thou become to tolerate my smile."
I was as one who still retains the feeling
  Of a forgotten vision, and endeavours   50
  In vain to bring it back into his mind,
When I this invitation heard, deserving
  Of so much gratitude, it never fades
  Out of the book that chronicles the past.
If at this moment sounded all the tongues

That Polyhymnia and her sisters made
  Most lubrical with their delicious milk,
To aid me, to a thousandth of the truth
  It would not reach, singing the holy smile
  And how the holy aspect it illumed.   60
And therefore, representing Paradise,
  The sacred poem must perforce leap over,
  Even as a man who finds his way cut off;
But whoso thinketh of the ponderous theme,
  And of the mortal shoulder laden with it,
  Should blame it not, if under this it tremble.
It is no passage for a little boat
  This which goes cleaving the audacious prow,
  Nor for a pilot who would spare himself.
"Why doth my face so much enamour thee,   70
  That to the garden fair thou turnest not,
  Which under the rays of Christ is blossoming?
There is the Rose in which the Word Divine
  Became incarnate; there the lilies are
  By whose perfume the good way was discovered."
Thus Beatrice; and I, who to her counsels
  Was wholly ready, once again betook me
  Unto the battle of the feeble brows.
As in the sunshine, that unsullied streams
  Through fractured cloud, ere now a meadow of flowers 80
  Mine eyes with shadow covered o'er have seen,
So troops of splendours manifold I saw
  Illumined from above with burning rays,
  Beholding not the source of the effulgence.
O power benignant that dost so imprint them!
  Thou didst exalt thyself to give more scope
  There to mine eyes, that were not strong enough.
The name of that fair flower I e'er invoke
  Morning and evening utterly enthralled
  My soul to gaze upon the greater fire.   90
And when in both mine eyes depicted were
  The glory and greatness of the living star
  Which there excelleth, as it here excelled,
Athwart the heavens a little torch descended
  Formed in a circle like a coronal,
  And cinctured it, and whirled itself about it.

Whatever melody most sweetly soundeth
   On earth, and to itself most draws the soul,
   Would seem a cloud that, rent asunder, thunders,
Compared unto the sounding of that lyre   100
   Wherewith was crowned the sapphire beautiful,
   Which gives the clearest heaven its sapphire hue.
"I am Angelic Love, that circle round
   The joy sublime which breathes from out the womb
   That was the hostelry of our Desire;
And I shall circle, Lady of Heaven, while
   Thou followest thy Son, and mak'st diviner
   The sphere supreme, because thou enterest there."
Thus did the circulated melody
   Seal itself up; and all the other lights   110
   Were making to resound the name of Mary.
The regal mantle of the volumes all
   Of that world, which most fervid is and living
   With breath of God and with his works and ways,
Extended over us its inner border,
   So very distant, that the semblance of it
   There where I was not yet appeared to me.
Therefore mine eyes did not possess the power
   Of following the incoronated flame,
   Which mounted upward near to its own seed.   120
And as a little child, that towards its mother
   Stretches its arms, when it the milk has taken,
   Through impulse kindled into outward flame,
Each of those gleams of whiteness upward reached
   So with its summit, that the deep affection
   They had for Mary was revealed to me.
Thereafter they remained there in my sight,
   Regina cæli singing with such sweetness,
   That ne'er from me has the delight departed.
O, what exuberance is garnered up   130
   Within those richest coffers, which had been
   Good husbandmen for sowing here below!
There they enjoy and live upon the treasure
   Which was acquired while weeping in the exile
   Of Babylon, wherein the gold was left.
There triumpheth, beneath the exalted Son
   Of God and Mary, in his victory,

Both with the ancient council and the new,
He who doth keep the keys of such a glory.

Canto XXIV

"O company elect to the great supper
  Of the Lamb benedight, who feedeth you
  So that for ever full is your desire,
If by the grace of God this man foretaste
  Something of that which falleth from your table,
  Or ever death prescribe to him the time,
Direct your mind to his immense desire,
  And him somewhat bedew; ye drinking are
  For ever at the fount whence comes his thought."
Thus Beatrice; and those souls beatified   10
  Transformed themselves to spheres on steadfast poles,
  Flaming intensely in the guise of comets.
And as the wheels in works of horologes
  Revolve so that the first to the beholder
  Motionless seems, and the last one to fly,
So in like manner did those carols, dancing
  In different measure, of their affluence
  Give me the gauge, as they were swift or slow.
From that one which I noted of most beauty
  Beheld I issue forth a fire so happy   20
  That none it left there of a greater brightness;
And around Beatrice three several times
  It whirled itself with so divine a song,
  My fantasy repeats it not to me;
Therefore the pen skips, and I write it not,
  Since our imagination for such folds,
  Much more our speech, is of a tint too glaring.
"O holy sister mine, who us implorest
  With such devotion, by thine ardent love
  Thou dost unbind me from that beautiful sphere!"   30
Thereafter, having stopped, the blessed fire
  Unto my Lady did direct its breath,
  Which spake in fashion as I here have said.
And she: "O light eterne of the great man
  To whom our Lord delivered up the keys

He carried down of this miraculous joy,
This one examine on points light and grave,
As good beseemeth thee, about the Faith
By means of which thou on the sea didst walk.
If he love well, and hope well, and believe,   40
From thee 'tis hid not; for thou hast thy sight
There where depicted everything is seen.
But since this kingdom has made citizens
By means of the true Faith, to glorify it
'Tis well he have the chance to speak thereof."
As baccalaureate arms himself, and speaks not
Until the master doth propose the question,
To argue it, and not to terminate it,
So did I arm myself with every reason,
While she was speaking, that I might be ready   50
For such a questioner and such profession.
"Say, thou good Christian; manifest thyself;
What is the Faith?" Whereat I raised my brow
Unto that light wherefrom was this breathed forth.
Then turned I round to Beatrice, and she
Prompt signals made to me that I should pour
The water forth from my internal fountain.
"May grace, that surfers me to make confession,"
Began I, "to the great centurion,
Cause my conceptions all to be explicit!"   60
And I continued: "As the truthful pen,
Father, of thy dear brother wrote of it,
Who put with thee Rome into the good way,
Faith is the substance of the things we hope for,
And evidence of those that are not seen;
And this appears to me its quiddity."
Then heard I: "Very rightly thou perceivest,
If well thou understandest why he placed it
With substances and then with evidences."
And I thereafterward: "The things profound,   70
That here vouchsafe to me their apparition,
Unto all eyes below are so concealed,
That they exist there only in belief,
Upon the which is founded the high hope,
And hence it takes the nature of a substance.
And it behoveth us from this belief

To reason without having other sight,
And hence it has the nature of evidence."
Then heard I: "If whatever is acquired
Below by doctrine were thus understood,   80
No sophist's subtlety would there find place."
Thus was breathed forth from that enkindled love;
Then added: "Very well has been gone over
Already of this coin the alloy and weight;
But tell me if thou hast it in thy purse?"
And I: "Yes, both so shining and so round,
That in its stamp there is no peradventure."
Thereafter issued from the light profound
That there resplendent was: "This precious jewel,
Upon the which is every virtue founded,   90
Whence hadst thou it?"And I: "The large outpouring
Of Holy Spirit, which has been diffused
Upon the ancient parchments and the new,
A syllogism is, which proved it to me
With such acuteness, that, compared therewith,
All demonstration seems to me obtuse."
And then I heard: "The ancient and the new
Postulates, that to thee are so conclusive,
Why dost thou take them for the word divine?"
And I: "The proofs, which show the truth to me,   100
Are the works subsequent, whereunto Nature
Ne'er heated iron yet, nor anvil beat."
'Twas answered me: "Say, who assureth thee
That those works ever were? the thing itself
That must be proved, nought else to thee affirms it."
"Were the world to Christianity converted,"
I said, "withouten miracles, this one
Is such, the rest are not its hundredth part;
Because that poor and fasting thou didst enter
Into the field to sow there the good plant,   110
Which was a vine and has become a thorn!"
This being finished, the high, holy Court
Resounded through the spheres, "One God we praise!"
In melody that there above is chanted.
And then that Baron, who from branch to branch,
Examining, had thus conducted me,
Till the extremest leaves we were approaching,

Again began: "The Grace that dallying
   Plays with thine intellect thy mouth has opened,
    Up to this point, as it should opened be,   120
So that I do approve what forth emerged;
   But now thou must express what thou believest,
    And whence to thy belief it was presented."
"O holy father, spirit who beholdest
   What thou believedst so that thou o'ercamest,
    Towards the sepulchre, more youthful feet,"
Began I, "thou dost wish me in this place
   The form to manifest of my prompt belief,
    And likewise thou the cause thereof demandest.
And I respond: In one God I believe,   130
   Sole and eterne, who moveth all the heavens
    With love and with desire, himself unmoved;
And of such faith not only have I proofs
   Physical and metaphysical, but gives them
    Likewise the truth that from this place rains down
Through Moses, through the Prophets and the Psalms,
   Through the Evangel, and through you, who wrote
    After the fiery Spirit sanctified you;
In Persons three eterne believe, and these
   One essence I believe, so one and trine   140
    They bear conjunction both with *sunt* and *est*.
With the profound condition and divine
   Which now I touch upon, doth stamp my mind
    Ofttimes the doctrine evangelical.
This the beginning is, this is the spark
   Which afterwards dilates to vivid flame,
    And, like a star in heaven, is sparkling in me."
Even as a lord who hears what pleaseth him
   His servant straight embraces, gratulating
    For the good news as soon as he is silent;   150
So, giving me its benediction, singing,
   Three times encircled me, when I was silent,
    The apostolic light, at whose command
I spoken had, in speaking I so pleased him.

Canto XXV

If e'er it happen that the Poem Sacred,
   To which both heaven and earth have set their hand,
   So that it many a year hath made me lean,
O'ercome the cruelty that bars me out
   From the fair sheepfold, where a lamb I slumbered,
   An enemy to the wolves that war upon it,
With other voice forthwith, with other fleece
   Poet will I return, and at my font
   Baptismal will I take the laurel crown;
Because into the Faith that maketh known   10
   All souls to God there entered I, and then
   Peter for her sake thus my brow encircled.
Thereafterward towards us moved a light
   Out of that band whence issued the first-fruits
   Which of his vicars Christ behind him left,
And then my Lady, full of ecstasy,
   Said unto me: "Look, look! behold the Baron
   For whom below Galicia is frequented."
In the same way as, when a dove alights
   Near his companion, both of them pour forth,   20
   Circling about and murmuring, their affection,
So one beheld I by the other grand
   Prince glorified to be with welcome greeted,
   Lauding the food that there above is eaten.
But when their gratulations were complete,
   Silently *coram me* each one stood still,
   So incandescent it o'ercame my sight.
Smiling thereafterwards, said Beatrice:
   "Illustrious life, by whom the benefactions
   Of our Basilica have been described,   30
Make Hope resound within this altitude;
   Thou knowest as oft thou dost personify it
   As Jesus to the three gave greater clearness."—
"Lift up thy head, and make thyself assured;
   For what comes hither from the mortal world
   Must needs be ripened in our radiance."
This comfort came to me from the second fire;
   Wherefore mine eyes I lifted to the hills,
   Which bent them down before with too great weight.

"Since, through his grace, our Emperor wills that thou 40
   Shouldst find thee face to face, before thy death,
   In the most secret chamber, with his Counts,
So that, the truth beholden of this court,
   Hope, which below there rightfully enamours,
   Thereby thou strengthen in thyself and others,
Say what it is, and how is flowering with it
   Thy mind, and say from whence it came to thee."
   Thus did the second light again continue.
And the Compassionate, who piloted
   The plumage of my wings in such high flight, 50
   Did in reply anticipate me thus:
"No child whatever the Church Militant
   Of greater hope possesses, as is written
   In that Sun which irradiates all our band;
Therefore it is conceded him from Egypt
   To come into Jerusalem to see,
   Or ever yet his warfare be completed.
The two remaining points, that not for knowledge
   Have been demanded, but that he report
   How much this virtue unto thee is pleasing, 60
To him I leave; for hard he will not find them,
   Nor of self-praise; and let him answer them;
   And may the grace of God in this assist him!"
As a disciple, who his teacher follows,
   Ready and willing, where he is expert,
   That his proficiency may be displayed,
"Hope," said I, "is the certain expectation
   Of future glory, which is the effect
   Of grace divine and merit precedent.
From many stars this light comes unto me; 70
   But he instilled it first into my heart
   Who was chief singer unto the chief captain.
'*Sperent in te,*' in the high Theody
   He sayeth, 'those who know thy name;' and who
   Knoweth it not, if he my faith possess?
Thou didst instil me, then, with his instilling
   In the Epistle, so that I am full,
   And upon others rain again your rain."
While I was speaking, in the living bosom
   Of that combustion quivered an effulgence, 80

Sudden and frequent, in the guise of lightning;
Then breathed: "The love wherewith I am inflamed
   Towards the virtue still which followed me
   Unto the palm and issue of the field,
Wills that I breathe to thee that thou delight
   In her; and grateful to me is thy telling
   Whatever things Hope promises to thee."
And I: "The ancient Scriptures and the new
   The mark establish, and this shows it me,
   Of all the souls whom God hath made his friends.   90
Isaiah saith, that each one garmented
   In his own land shall be with twofold garments
   And his own land is this delightful life.
Thy brother, too, far more explicitly,
   There where he treateth of the robes of white,
   This revelation manifests to us."
And first, and near the ending of these words,
   "*Sperent in te*" from over us was heard,
   To which responsive answered all the carols.
Thereafterward a light among them brightened,   100
   So that, if Cancer one such crystal had,
   Winter would have a month of one sole day.
And as uprises, goes, and enters the dance
   A winsome maiden, only to do honour
   To the new bride, and not from any failing,
Even thus did I behold the brightened splendour
   Approach the two, who in a wheel revolved
   As was beseeming to their ardent love.
Into the song and music there it entered;
   And fixed on them my Lady kept her look,   110
   Even as a bride silent and motionless.
"This is the one who lay upon the breast
   Of him our Pelican; and this is he
   To the great office from the cross elected."
My Lady thus; but therefore none the more
   Did move her sight from its attentive gaze
   Before or afterward these words of hers.
Even as a man who gazes, and endeavours
   To see the eclipsing of the sun a little,
   And who, by seeing, sightless doth become,   120
So I became before that latest fire,

While it was said, "Why dost thou daze thyself
　　To see a thing which here hath no existence?
Earth in the earth my body is, and shall be
　　With all the others there, until our number
　　With the eternal proposition tallies.
With the two garments in the blessed cloister
　　Are the two lights alone that have ascended:
　　And this shalt thou take back into your world."
And at this utterance the flaming circle   130
　　Grew quiet, with the dulcet intermingling
　　Of sound that by the trinal breath was made,
As to escape from danger or fatigue
　　The oars that erst were in the water beaten
　　Are all suspended at a whistle's sound.
Ah, how much in my mind was I disturbed,
　　When I turned round to look on Beatrice,
　　That her I could not see, although I was
Close at her side and in the Happy World!

Canto XXVI

While I was doubting for my vision quenched,
　　Out of the flame refulgent that had quenched it
　　Issued a breathing, that attentive made me,
Saying: "While thou recoverest the sense
　　Of seeing which in me thou hast consumed,
　　'Tis well that speaking thou shouldst compensate it.
Begin then, and declare to what thy soul
　　Is aimed, and count it for a certainty,
　　Sight is in thee bewildered and not dead;
Because the Lady, who through this divine   10
　　Region conducteth thee, has in her look
　　The power the hand of Ananias had."
I said: "As pleaseth her, or soon or late
　　Let the cure come to eyes that portals were
　　When she with fire I ever burn with entered.
The Good, that gives contentment to this Court,
　　The Alpha and Omega is of all
　　The writing that love reads me low or loud."
The selfsame voice, that taken had from me

The terror of the sudden dazzlement,   20
   To speak still farther put it in my thought;
And said: "In verity with finer sieve
   Behoveth thee to sift; thee it behoveth
   To say who aimed thy bow at such a target."
And I: "By philosophic arguments,
   And by authority that hence descends,
   Such love must needs imprint itself in me;
For Good, so far as good, when comprehended
   Doth straight enkindle love, and so much greater
   As more of goodness in itself it holds;   30
Then to that Essence (whose is such advantage
   That every good which out of it is found
   Is nothing but a ray of its own light)
More than elsewhither must the mind be moved
   Of every one, in loving, who discerns
   The truth in which this evidence is founded.
Such truth he to my intellect reveals
   Who demonstrates to me the primal love
   Of all the sempiternal substances.
The voice reveals it of the truthful Author,   40
   Who says to Moses, speaking of Himself,
   'I will make all my goodness pass before thee.'
Thou too revealest it to me, beginning
   The loud Evangel, that proclaims the secret
   Of heaven to earth above all other edict."
And I heard say: "By human intellect
   And by authority concordant with it,
   Of all thy loves reserve for God the highest.
But say again if other cords thou feelest,
   Draw thee towards Him, that thou mayst proclaim   50
   With how many teeth this love is biting thee."
The holy purpose of the Eagle of Christ
   Not latent was, nay, rather I perceived
   Whither he fain would my profession lead.
Therefore I recommenced: "All of those bites
   Which have the power to turn the heart to God
   Unto my charity have been concurrent.
The being of the world, and my own being,
   The death which He endured that I may live,
   And that which all the faithful hope, as I do,   60

With the forementioned vivid consciousness
   Have drawn me from the sea of love perverse,
   And of the right have placed me on the shore.
The leaves, wherewith embowered is all the garden
   Of the Eternal Gardener, do I love
   As much as he has granted them of good."
As soon as I had ceased, a song most sweet
   Throughout the heaven resounded, and my Lady
   Said with the others, "Holy, holy, holy!"
And as at some keen light one wakes from sleep   70
   By reason of the visual spirit that runs
   Unto the splendour passed from coat to coat,
And he who wakes abhorreth what he sees,
   So all unconscious is his sudden waking,
   Until the judgment cometh to his aid,
So from before mine eyes did Beatrice
   Chase every mote with radiance of her own,
   That cast its light a thousand miles and more.
Whence better after than before I saw,
   And in a kind of wonderment I asked   80
   About a fourth light that I saw with us.
And said my Lady: "There within those rays
   Gazes upon its Maker the first soul
   That ever the first virtue did create."
Even as the bough that downward bends its top
   At transit of the wind, and then is lifted
   By its own virtue, which inclines it upward,
Likewise did I, the while that she was speaking,
   Being amazed, and then I was made bold
   By a desire to speak wherewith I burned.   90
And I began: "O apple, that mature
   Alone hast been produced, O ancient father,
   To whom each wife is daughter and daughter-in-law,
Devoutly as I can I supplicate thee
   That thou wouldst speak to me; thou seest my wish;
   And I, to hear thee quickly, speak it not."
Sometimes an animal, when covered, struggles
   So that his impulse needs must be apparent,
   By reason of the wrappage following it;
And in like manner the primeval soul   100
   Made clear to me athwart its covering

How jubilant it was to give me pleasure.
Then breathed: "Without thy uttering it to me,
    Thine inclination better I discern
    Than thou whatever thing is surest to thee;
For I behold it in the truthful mirror,
    That of Himself all things parhelion makes,
    And none makes Him parhelion of itself.
Thou fain wouldst hear how long ago God placed me
    Within the lofty garden, where this Lady   110
    Unto so long a stairway thee disposed.
And how long to mine eyes it was a pleasure,
    And of the great disdain the proper cause,
    And the language that I used and that I made.
Now, son of mine, the tasting of the tree
    Not in itself was cause of so great exile,
    But solely the o'erstepping of the bounds.
There, whence thy Lady moved Virgilius,
    Four thousand and three hundred and two circuits
    Made by the sun, this Council I desired;   120
And him I saw return to all the lights
    Of his highway nine hundred times and thirty,
    Whilst I upon the earth was tarrying.
The language that I spake was quite extinct
    Before that in the work interminable
    The people under Nimrod were employed;
For nevermore result of reasoning
    (Because of human pleasure that doth change,
    Obedient to the heavens) was durable.
A natural action is it that man speaks;   130
    But whether thus or thus, doth nature leave
    To your own art, as seemeth best to you.
Ere I descended to the infernal anguish,
    El was on earth the name of the Chief Good,
    From whom comes all the joy that wraps me round;
Eli he then was called, and that is proper,
    Because the use of men is like a leaf
    On bough, which goeth and another cometh.
Upon the mount that highest o'er the wave
    Rises was I, in life or pure or sinful,   140
    From the first hour to that which is the second,
As the sun changes quadrant, to the sixth."

Canto XXVII

"Glory be to the Father, to the Son,
  And Holy Ghost!" all Paradise began,
  So that the melody inebriate made me.
What I beheld seemed unto me a smile
  Of the universe; for my inebriation
  Found entrance through the hearing and the sight.
O joy! O gladness inexpressible!
  O perfect life of love and peacefulness!
  O riches without hankering secure!
Before mine eyes were standing the four torches   10
  Enkindled, and the one that first had come
  Began to make itself more luminous;
And even such in semblance it became
  As Jupiter would become, if he and Mars
  Were birds, and they should interchange their feathers.
That Providence, which here distributeth
  Season and service, in the blessed choir
  Had silence upon every side imposed.
When I heard say: "If I my colour change,
  Marvel not at it; for while I am speaking   20
  Thou shalt behold all these their colour change.
He who usurps upon the earth my place,
  My place, my place, which vacant has become
  Before the presence of the Son of God,
Has of my cemetery made a sewer
  Of blood and stench, whereby the Perverse One,
  Who fell from here, below there is appeased!"
With the same colour which, through sun adverse,
  Painteth the clouds at evening or at morn,
  Beheld I then the whole of heaven suffused.   30
And as a modest woman, who abides
  Sure of herself, and at another's failing,
  From listening only, timorous becomes,
Even thus did Beatrice change countenance;
  And I believe in heaven was such eclipse,
  When suffered the supreme Omnipotence;
Thereafterward proceeded forth his words
  With voice so much transmuted from itself,
  The very countenance was not more changed.

"The spouse of Christ has never nurtured been   40
     On blood of mine, of Linus and of Cletus,
     To be made use of in acquest of gold;
But in acquest of this delightful life
     Sixtus and Pius, Urban and Calixtus,
     After much lamentation, shed their blood.
Our purpose was not, that on the right hand
     Of our successors should in part be seated
     The Christian folk, in part upon the other;
Nor that the keys which were to me confided
     Should e'er become the escutcheon on a banner,   50
     That should wage war on those who are baptized;
Nor I be made the figure of a seal
     To privileges venal and mendacious,
     Whereat I often redden and flash with fire.
In garb of shepherds the rapacious wolves
     Are seen from here above o'er all the pastures!
     O wrath of God, why dost thou slumber still?
To drink our blood the Caorsines and Gascons
     Are making ready. O thou good beginning,
     Unto how vile an end must thou needs fall!   60
But the high Providence, that with Scipio
     At Rome the glory of the world defended,
     Will speedily bring aid, as I conceive;
And thou, my son, who by thy mortal weight
     Shalt down return again, open thy mouth;
     What I conceal not, do not thou conceal."
As with its frozen vapours downward falls
     In flakes our atmosphere, what time the horn
     Of the celestial Goat doth touch the sun,
Upward in such array saw I the ether   70
     Become, and flaked with the triumphant vapours,
     Which there together with us had remained.
My sight was following up their semblances,
     And followed till the medium, by excess,
     The passing farther onward took from it;
Whereat the Lady, who beheld me freed
     From gazing upward, said to me: "Cast down
     Thy sight, and see how far thou art turned round."
Since the first time that I had downward looked,
     I saw that I had moved through the whole arc   80

Which the first climate makes from midst to end;
So that I saw the mad track of Ulysses
    Past Gades, and this side, well nigh the shore
    Whereon became Europa a sweet burden.
And of this threshing-floor the site to me
    Were more unveiled, but the sun was proceeding
    Under my feet, a sign and more removed.
My mind enamoured, which is dallying
    At all times with my Lady, to bring back
    To her mine eyes was more than ever ardent.   90
And if or Art or Nature has made bait
    To catch the eyes and so possess the mind,
    In human flesh or in its portraiture,
All joined together would appear as nought
    To the divine delight which shone upon me
    When to her smiling face I turned me round.
The virtue that her look endowed me with
    From the fair nest of Leda tore me forth,
    And up into the swiftest heaven impelled me.
Its parts exceeding full of life and lofty   100
    Are all so uniform, I cannot say
    Which Beatrice selected for my place.
But she, who was aware of my desire,
    Began, the while she smiled so joyously
    That God seemed in her countenance to rejoice:
"The nature of that motion, which keeps quiet
    The centre, and all the rest about it moves,
    From hence begins as from its starting point.
And in this heaven there is no other Where
    Than in the Mind Divine, wherein is kindled   110
    The love that turns it, and the power it rains.
Within a circle light and love embrace it,
    Even as this doth the others, and that precinct
    He who encircles it alone controls.
Its motion is not by another meted,
    But all the others measured are by this,
    As ten is by the half and by the fifth.
And in what manner time in such a pot
    May have its roots, and in the rest its leaves,
    Now unto thee can manifest be made.   120
O Covetousness, that mortals dost ingulf

Beneath thee so, that no one hath the power
  Of drawing back his eyes from out thy waves!
Full fairly blossoms in mankind the will;
  But the uninterrupted rain converts
  Into abortive wildings the true plums.
Fidelity and innocence are found
  Only in children; afterwards they both
  Take flight or e'er the cheeks with down are covered.
One, while he prattles still, observes the fasts,   130
  Who, when his tongue is loosed, forthwith devours
  Whatever food under whatever moon;
Another, while he prattles, loves and listens
  Unto his mother, who when speech is perfect
  Forthwith desires to see her in her grave.
Even thus is swarthy made the skin so white
  In its first aspect of the daughter fair
  Of him who brings the morn, and leaves the night.
Thou, that it may not be a marvel to thee,
  Think that on earth there is no one who governs;   140
  Whence goes astray the human family.
Ere January be unwintered wholly
  By the centesimal on earth neglected,
  Shall these supernal circles roar so loud
The tempest that has been so long awaited
  Shall whirl the poops about where are the prows;
  So that the fleet shall run its course direct,
And the true fruit shall follow on the flower."

Canto XXVIII

After the truth against the present life
  Of miserable mortals was unfolded
  By her who doth imparadise my mind,
As in a looking-glass a taper's flame
  He sees who from behind is lighted by it,
  Before he has it in his sight or thought,
And turns him round to see if so the glass
  Tell him the truth, and sees that it accords
  Therewith as doth a music with its metre,
In similar wise my memory recollecteth   10

That I did, looking into those fair eyes,
    Of which Love made the springes to ensnare me.
And as I turned me round, and mine were touched
    By that which is apparent in that volume,
    Whenever on its gyre we gaze intent,
A point beheld I, that was raying out
    Light so acute, the sight which it enkindles
    Must close perforce before such great acuteness.
And whatsoever star seems smallest here
    Would seem to be a moon, if placed beside it   20
    As one star with another star is placed.
Perhaps at such a distance as appears
    A halo cincturing the light that paints it,
    When densest is the vapour that sustains it,
Thus distant round the point a circle of fire
    So swiftly whirled, that it would have surpassed
    Whatever motion soonest girds the world;
And this was by another circumcinct,
    That by a third, the third then by a fourth,
    By a fifth the fourth, and then by a sixth the fifth;   30
The seventh followed thereupon in width
    So ample now, that Juno's messenger
    Entire would be too narrow to contain it.
Even so the eighth and ninth; and every one
    More slowly moved, according as it was
    In number distant farther from the first.
And that one had its flame most crystalline
    From which less distant was the stainless spark,
    I think because more with its truth imbued.
My Lady, who in my anxiety   40
    Beheld me much perplexed, said: "From that point
    Dependent is the heaven and nature all.
Behold that circle most conjoined to it,
    And know thou, that its motion is so swift
    Through burning love whereby it is spurred on."
And I to her: "If the world were arranged
    In the order which I see in yonder wheels,
    What's set before me would have satisfied me;
But in the world of sense we can perceive
    That evermore the circles are diviner   50
    As they are from the centre more remote

Wherefore if my desire is to be ended
  In this miraculous and angelic temple,
  That has for confines only love and light,
To hear behoves me still how the example
  And the exemplar go not in one fashion,
  Since for myself in vain I contemplate it."
"If thine own fingers unto such a knot
  Be insufficient, it is no great wonder,
  So hard hath it become for want of trying."   60
My Lady thus; then said she: "Do thou take
  What I shall tell thee, if thou wouldst be sated,
  And exercise on that thy subtlety.
The circles corporal are wide and narrow
  According to the more or less of virtue
  Which is distributed through all their parts.
The greater goodness works the greater weal,
  The greater weal the greater body holds,
  If perfect equally are all its parts.
Therefore this one which sweeps along with it   70
  The universe sublime, doth correspond
  Unto the circle which most loves and knows.
On which account, if thou unto the virtue
  Apply thy measure, not to the appearance
  Of substances that unto thee seem round,
Thou wilt behold a marvellous agreement,
  Of more to greater, and of less to smaller,
  In every heaven, with its Intelligence."
Even as remaineth splendid and serene
  The hemisphere of air, when Boreas   80
  Is blowing from that cheek where he is mildest,
Because is purified and resolved the rack
  That erst disturbed it, till the welkin laughs
  With all the beauties of its pageantry;
Thus did I likewise, after that my Lady
  Had me provided with her clear response,
  And like a star in heaven the truth was seen.
And soon as to a stop her words had come,
  Not otherwise does iron scintillate
  When molten, than those circles scintillated.   90
Their coruscation all the sparks repeated,
  And they so many were, their number makes

More millions than the doubling of the chess.
I heard them sing hosanna choir by choir
    To the fixed point which holds them at the *Ubi*,
    And ever will, where they have ever been.
And she, who saw the dubious meditations
    Within my mind, "The primal circles," said,
    "Have shown thee Seraphim and Cherubim.
Thus rapidly they follow their own bonds,   100
    To be as like the point as most they can,
    And can as far as they are high in vision.
Those other Loves, that round about them go,
    Thrones of the countenance divine are called,
    Because they terminate the primal Triad.
And thou shouldst know that they all have delight
    As much as their own vision penetrates
    The Truth, in which all intellect finds rest.
From this it may be seen how blessedness
    Is founded in the faculty which sees,   110
    And not in that which loves, and follows next;
And of this seeing merit is the measure,
    Which is brought forth by grace, and by good will;
    Thus on from grade to grade doth it proceed.
The second Triad, which is germinating
    In such wise in this sempiternal spring,
    That no nocturnal Aries despoils,
Perpetually hosanna warbles forth
    With threefold melody, that sounds in three
    Orders of joy, with which it is intrined.   120
The three Divine are in this hierarchy,
    First the Dominions, and the Virtues next;
    And the third order is that of the Powers.
Then in the dances twain penultimate
    The Principalities and Archangels wheel;
    The last is wholly of angelic sports.
These orders upward all of them are gazing,
    And downward so prevail, that unto God
    They all attracted are and all attract.
And Dionysius with so great desire   130
    To contemplate these Orders set himself,
    He named them and distinguished them as I do.
But Gregory afterwards dissented from him;

Wherefore, as soon as he unclosed his eyes
    Within this heaven, he at himself did smile.
And if so much of secret truth a mortal
    Proffered on earth, I would not have thee marvel,
    For he who saw it here revealed it to him,
With much more of the truth about these circles."

Canto **XXIX**

At what time both the children of Latona,
    Surmounted by the Ram and by the Scales,
    Together make a zone of the horizon,
As long as from the time the zenith holds them
    In equipoise, till from that girdle both
    Changing their hemisphere disturb the balance,
So long, her face depicted with a smile,
    Did Beatrice keep silence while she gazed
    Fixedly at the point which had o'ercome me.
Then she began: "I say, and I ask not   10
    What thou dost wish to hear, for I have seen it
    Where centres every When and every *Ubi*.
Not to acquire some good unto himself,
    Which is impossible, but that his splendour
    In its resplendency may say, '*Subsisto*,'
In his eternity outside of time,
    Outside all other limits, as it pleased him,
    Into new Loves the Eternal Love unfolded.
Nor as if torpid did he lie before;
    For neither after nor before proceeded   20
    The going forth of God upon these waters.
Matter and Form unmingled and conjoined
    Came into being that had no defect,
    E'en as three arrows from a three-stringed bow.
And as in glass, in amber, or in crystal
    A sunbeam flashes so, that from its coming
    To its full being is no interval,
So from its Lord did the triform effect
    Ray forth into its being all together,
    Without discrimination of beginning.   30
Order was con-created and constructed

In substances, and summit of the world
   Were those wherein the pure act was produced.
Pure potentiality held the lowest part;
   Midway bound potentiality with act
   Such bond that it shall never be unbound.
Jerome has written unto you of angels
   Created a long lapse of centuries
   Or ever yet the other world was made;
But written is this truth in many places   40
   By writers of the Holy Ghost, and thou
   Shalt see it, if thou lookest well thereat.
And even reason seeth it somewhat,
   For it would not concede that for so long
   Could be the motors without their perfection.
Now dost thou know both where and when these Loves
   Created were, and how; so that extinct
   In thy desire already are three fires.
Nor could one reach, in counting, unto twenty
   So swiftly, as a portion of these angels   50
   Disturbed the subject of your elements.
The rest remained, and they began this art
   Which thou discernest, with so great delight
   That never from their circling do they cease.
The occasion of the fall was the accursed
   Presumption of that One, whom thou hast seen
   By all the burden of the world constrained.
Those whom thou here beholdest modest were
   To recognise themselves as of that goodness
   Which made them apt for so much understanding;   60
On which account their vision was exalted
   By the enlightening grace and their own merit,
   So that they have a full and steadfast will.
I would not have thee doubt, but certain be,
   'Tis meritorious to receive this grace,
   According as the affection opens to it.
Now round about in this consistory
   Much mayst thou contemplate, if these my words
   Be gathered up, without all further aid.
But since upon the earth, throughout your schools,   70
   They teach that such is the angelic nature
   That it doth hear, and recollect, and will,

More will I say, that thou mayst see unmixed
   The truth that is confounded there below,
   Equivocating in such like prelections.
These substances, since in God's countenance
   They jocund were, turned not away their sight
   From that wherefrom not anything is hidden;
Hence they have not their vision intercepted
   By object new, and hence they do not need   80
   To recollect, through interrupted thought.
So that below, not sleeping, people dream,
   Believing they speak truth, and not believing;
   And in the last is greater sin and shame.
Below you do not journey by one path
   Philosophising; so transporteth you
   Love of appearance and the thought thereof.
And even this above here is endured
   With less disdain, than when is set aside
   The Holy Writ, or when it is distorted.   90
They think not there how much of blood it costs
   To sow it in the world, and how he pleases
   Who in humility keeps close to it.
Each striveth for appearance, and doth make
   His own inventions; and these treated are
   By preachers, and the Evangel holds its peace.
One sayeth that the moon did backward turn,
   In the Passion of Christ, and interpose herself
   So that the sunlight reached not down below;
And lies; for of its own accord the light   100
   Hid itself; whence to Spaniards and to Indians,
   As to the Jews, did such eclipse respond.
Florence has not so many Lapi and Bindi
   As fables such as these, that every year
   Are shouted from the pulpit back and forth,
In such wise that the lambs, who do not know,
   Come back from pasture fed upon the wind,
   And not to see the harm doth not excuse them.
Christ did not to his first disciples say,
   'Go forth, and to the world preach idle tales,'   110
   But unto them a true foundation gave;
And this so loudly sounded from their lips,
   That, in the warfare to enkindle Faith,

They made of the Evangel shields and lances.
Now men go forth with jests and drolleries
   To preach, and if but well the people laugh,
   The hood puffs out, and nothing more is asked.
But in the cowl there nestles such a bird,
   That, if the common people were to see it,
   They would perceive what pardons they confide in,   120
For which so great on earth has grown the folly,
   That, without proof of any testimony,
   To each indulgence they would flock together.
By this Saint Anthony his pig doth fatten,
   And many others, who are worse than pigs,
   Paying in money without mark of coinage.
But since we have digressed abundantly,
   Turn back thine eyes forthwith to the right path,
   So that the way be shortened with the time.
This nature doth so multiply itself   130
   In numbers, that there never yet was speech
   Nor mortal fancy that can go so far.
And if thou notest that which is revealed
   By Daniel, thou wilt see that in his thousands
   Number determinate is kept concealed.
The primal light, that all irradiates it,
   By modes as many is received therein,
   As are the splendours wherewith it is mated.
Hence, inasmuch as on the act conceptive
   The affection followeth, of love the sweetness   140
   Therein diversely fervid is or tepid.
The height behold now and the amplitude
   Of the eternal power, since it hath made
   Itself so many mirrors, where 'tis broken,
One in itself remaining as before."

Canto XXX

Perchance six thousand miles remote from us
   Is glowing the sixth hour, and now this world
   Inclines its shadow almost to a level,
When the mid-heaven begins to make itself
   So deep to us, that here and there a star

Ceases to shine so far down as this depth,
And as advances bright exceedingly
   The handmaid of the sun, the heaven is closed
   Light after light to the most beautiful;
Not otherwise the Triumph, which for ever   10
   Plays round about the point that vanquished me,
   Seeming enclosed by what itself encloses,
Little by little from my vision faded;
   Whereat to turn mine eyes on Beatrice
   My seeing nothing and my love constrained me.
If what has hitherto been said of her
   Were all concluded in a single praise,
   Scant would it be to serve the present turn.
Not only does the beauty I beheld
   Transcend ourselves, but truly I believe   20
   Its Maker only may enjoy it all.
Vanquished do I confess me by this passage
   More than by problem of his theme was ever
   O'ercome the comic or the tragic poet;
For as the sun the sight that trembles most,
   Even so the memory of that sweet smile
   My mind depriveth of its very self.
From the first day that I beheld her face
   In this life, to the moment of this look,
   The sequence of my song has ne'er been severed;   30
But now perforce this sequence must desist
   From following her beauty with my verse,
   As every artist at his uttermost.
Such as I leave her to a greater fame
   Than any of my trumpet, which is bringing
   Its arduous matter to a final close,
With voice and gesture of a perfect leader
   She recommenced: "We from the greatest body
   Have issued to the heaven that is pure light;
Light intellectual replete with love,   40
   Love of true good replete with ecstasy,
   Ecstasy that transcendeth every sweetness.
Here shalt thou see the one host and the other
   Of Paradise, and one in the same aspects
   Which at the final judgment thou shalt see."
Even as a sudden lightning that disperses

The visual spirits, so that it deprives
The eye of impress from the strongest objects
Thus round about me flashed a living light,
    And left me swathed around with such a veil 50
    Of its effulgence, that I nothing saw.
"Ever the Love which quieteth this heaven
    Welcomes into itself with such salute,
    To make the candle ready for its flame."
No sooner had within me these brief words
    An entrance found, than I perceived myself
    To be uplifted over my own power,
And I with vision new rekindled me,
    Such that no light whatever is so pure
    But that mine eyes were fortified against it. 60
And light I saw in fashion of a river
    Fulvid with its effulgence, 'twixt two banks
    Depicted with an admirable Spring.
Out of this river issued living sparks,
    And on all sides sank down into the flowers,
    Like unto rubies that are set in gold;
And then, as if inebriate with the odours,
    They plunged again into the wondrous torrent,
    And as one entered issued forth another.
"The high desire, that now inflames and moves thee 70
    To have intelligence of what thou seest,
    Pleaseth me all the more, the more it swells.
But of this water it behoves thee drink
    Before so great a thirst in thee be slaked."
    Thus said to me the sunshine of mine eyes;
And added: "The river and the topazes
    Going in and out, and the laughing of the herbage,
    Are of their truth foreshadowing prefaces;
Not that these things are difficult in themselves,
    But the deficiency is on thy side, 80
    For yet thou hast not vision so exalted."
There is no babe that leaps so suddenly
    With face towards the milk, if he awake
    Much later than his usual custom is,
As I did, that I might make better mirrors
    Still of mine eyes, down stooping to the wave
    Which flows that we therein be better made.

And even as the penthouse of mine eyelids
   Drank of it, it forthwith appeared to me
   Out of its length to be transformed to round.   90
Then as a folk who have been under masks
   Seem other than before, if they divest
   The semblance not their own they disappeared in,
Thus into greater pomp were changed for me
   The flowerets and the sparks, so that I saw
   Both of the Courts of Heaven made manifest.
O splendour of God! by means of which I saw
   The lofty triumph of the realm veracious,
   Give me the power to say how it I saw!
There is a light above, which visible   100
   Makes the Creator unto every creature,
   Who only in beholding Him has peace,
And it expands itself in circular form
   To such extent, that its circumference
   Would be too large a girdle for the sun.
The semblance of it is all made of rays
   Reflected from the top of Primal Motion,
   Which takes therefrom vitality and power.
And as a hill in water at its base
   Mirrors itself, as if to see its beauty   110
   When affluent most in verdure and in flowers,
So, ranged aloft all round about the light,
   Mirrored I saw in more ranks than a thousand
   All who above there have from us returned
And if the lowest row collect within it
   So great a light, how vast the amplitude
   Is of this Rose in its extremest leaves!
My vision in the vastness and the height
   Lost not itself, but comprehended all
   The quantity and quality of that gladness.   120
There near and far nor add nor take away;
   For there where God immediately doth govern,
   The natural law in naught is relevant.
Into the yellow of the Rose Eternal
   That spreads, and multiplies, and breathes an odour
   Of praise unto the ever-vernal Sun,
As one who silent is and fain would speak,
   Me Beatrice drew on, and said: "Behold

Of the white stoles how vast the convent is!
Behold how vast the circuit of our city!   130
    Behold our seats so filled to overflowing,
    That here henceforward are few people wanting!
On that great throne whereon thine eyes are fixed
    For the crown's sake already placed upon it,
    Before thou suppest at this wedding feast
Shall sit the soul (that is to be Augustus
    On earth) of noble Henry, who shall come
    To redress Italy ere she be ready.
Blind covetousness, that casts its spell upon you,
    Has made you like unto the little child,   140
    Who dies of hunger and drives off the nurse.
And in the sacred forum then shall be
    A Prefect such, that openly or covert
    On the same road he will not walk with him.
But long of God he will not be endured
    In holy office: he shall be thrust down
    Where Simon Magus is for his deserts,
And make him of Alagna lower go!"

Canto XXXI

In fashion then as of a snow-white rose
    Displayed itself to me the saintly host,
    Whom Christ in his own blood had made his bride,
But the other host, that flying sees and sings
    The glory of Him who doth enamour it,
    And the goodness that created it so noble,
Even as a swarm of bees, that sinks in flowers
    One moment, and the next returns again
    To where its labour is to sweetness turned,
Sank into the great flower, that is adorned   10
    With leaves so many, and thence reascended
    To where its love abideth evermore.
Their faces had they all of living flame,
    And wings of gold, and all the rest so white
    No snow unto that limit doth attain.
From bench to bench, into the flower descending,
    They carried something of the peace and ardour

Which by the fanning of their flanks they won.
Nor did the interposing 'twixt the flower
  And what was o'er it of such plenitude   20
  Of flying shapes impede the sight and splendour;
Because the light divine so penetrates
  The universe, according to its merit,
  That naught can be an obstacle against it.
This realm secure and full of gladsomeness,
  Crowded with ancient people and with modern,
  Unto one mark had all its look and love.
O Trinal Light, that in a single star
  Sparkling upon their sight so satisfies them,
  Look down upon our tempest here below!   30
If the barbarians, coming from some region
  That every day by Helice is covered,
  Revolving with her son whom she delights in,
Beholding Rome and all her noble works,
  Were wonder-struck, what time the Lateran
  Above all mortal things was eminent,—
I who to the divine had from the human,
  From time unto eternity, had come,
  From Florence to a people just and sane,
With what amazement must I have been filled!   40
  Truly between this and the joy, it was
  My pleasure not to hear, and to be mute.
And as a pilgrim who delighteth him
  In gazing round the temple of his vow,
  And hopes some day to retell how it was,
So through the living light my way pursuing
  Directed I mine eyes o'er all the ranks,
  Now up, now down, and now all round about.
Faces I saw of charity persuasive,
  Embellished by His light and their own smile,   50
  And attitudes adorned with every grace.
The general form of Paradise already
  My glance had comprehended as a whole,
  In no part hitherto remaining fixed,
And round I turned me with rekindled wish
  My Lady to interrogate of things
  Concerning which my mind was in suspense.

One thing I meant, another answered me;
   I thought I should see Beatrice, and saw
   An Old Man habited like the glorious people.   60
O'erflowing was he in his eyes and cheeks
   With joy benign, in attitude of pity
   As to a tender father is becoming.
And "She, where is she?" instantly I said;
   Whence he: "To put an end to thy desire,
   Me Beatrice hath sent from mine own place.
And if thou lookest up to the third round
   Of the first rank, again shalt thou behold her
   Upon the throne her merits have assigned her."
Without reply I lifted up mine eyes,   70
   And saw her, as she made herself a crown
   Reflecting from herself the eternal rays.
Not from that region which the highest thunders
   Is any mortal eye so far removed,
   In whatsoever sea it deepest sinks,
As there from Beatrice my sight; but this
   Was nothing unto me; because her image
   Descended not to me by medium blurred.
"O Lady, thou in whom my hope is strong,
   And who for my salvation didst endure   80
   In Hell to leave the imprint of thy feet,
Of whatsoever things I have beheld,
   As coming from thy power and from thy goodness
   I recognise the virtue and the grace.
Thou from a slave hast brought me unto freedom,
   By all those ways, by all the expedients,
   Whereby thou hadst the power of doing it.
Preserve towards me thy magnificence,
   So that this soul of mine, which thou hast healed,
   Pleasing to thee be loosened from the body."   90
Thus I implored; and she, so far away,
   Smiled, as it seemed, and looked once more at me;
   Then unto the eternal fountain turned.
And said the Old Man holy: "That thou mayst
   Accomplish perfectly thy journeying,
   Whereunto prayer and holy love have sent me,
Fly with thine eyes all round about this garden;

For seeing it will discipline thy sight
   Farther to mount along the ray divine.
And she, the Queen of Heaven, for whom I burn   100
   Wholly with love, will grant us every grace,
   Because that I her faithful Bernard am."
As he who peradventure from Croatia
   Cometh to gaze at our Veronica,
   Who through its ancient fame is never sated,
But says in thought, the while it is displayed,
   "My Lord, Christ Jesus, God of very God,
   Now was your semblance made like unto this?"
Even such was I while gazing at the living
   Charity of the man, who in this world   110
   By contemplation tasted of that peace.
"Thou son of grace, this jocund life," began he,
   "Will not be known to thee by keeping ever
   Thine eyes below here on the lowest place;
But mark the circles to the most remote,
   Until thou shalt behold enthroned the Queen
   To whom this realm is subject and devoted."
I lifted up mine eyes, and as at morn
   The oriental part of the horizon
   Surpasses that wherein the sun goes down,   120
Thus, as if going with mine eyes from vale
   To mount, I saw a part in the remoteness
   Surpass in splendour all the other front.
And even as there, where we await the pole
   That Phaeton drove badly, blazes more
   The light, and is on either side diminished,
So likewise that pacific oriflamme
   Gleamed brightest in the centre, and each side
   In equal measure did the flame abate.
And at that centre, with their wings expanded,   130
   More than a thousand jubilant Angels saw I,
   Each differing in effulgence and in kind.
I saw there at their sports and at their songs
   A beauty smiling, which the gladness was
   Within the eyes of all the other saints;
And if I had in speaking as much wealth
   As in imagining, I should not dare
   To attempt the smallest part of its delight

Bernard, as soon as he beheld mine eyes
  Fixed and intent upon its fervid fervour,
  His own with such affection turned to her
That it made mine more ardent to behold. 140

Canto **XXXII**

Absorbed in his delight, that contemplator
  Assumed the willing office of a teacher,
  And gave beginning to these holy words:
"The wound that Mary closed up and anointed,
  She at her feet who is so beautiful,
  She is the one who opened it and pierced it.
Within that order which the third seats make
  Is seated Rachel, lower than the other,
  With Beatrice, in manner as thou seest.
Sarah, Rebecca, Judith, and her who was   10
  Ancestress of the Singer, who for dole
  Of the misdeed said, *'Miserere mei,'*
Canst thou behold from seat to seat descending
  Down in gradation, as with each one's name
  I through the Rose go down from leaf to leaf.
And downward from the seventh row, even as
  Above the same, succeed the Hebrew women,
  Dividing all the tresses of the flower;
Because, according to the view which Faith
  In Christ had taken, these are the partition   20
  By which the sacred stairways are divided.
Upon this side, where perfect is the flower
  With each one of its petals, seated are
  Those who believed in Christ who was to come.
Upon the other side, where intersected
  With vacant spaces are the semicircles,
  Are those who looked to Christ already come.
And as, upon this side, the glorious seat
  Of the Lady of Heaven, and the other seats
  Below it, such a great division make,   30
So opposite doth that of the great John,
  Who, ever holy, desert and martyrdom
  Endured, and afterwards two years in Hell.

And under him thus to divide were chosen
    Francis, and Benedict, and Augustine,
    And down to us the rest from round to round.
Behold now the high providence divine;
    For one and other aspect of the Faith
    In equal measure shall this garden fill.
And know that downward from that rank which cleaves   40
    Midway the sequence of the two divisions,
    Not by their proper merit are they seated;
But by another's under fixed conditions;
    For these are spirits one and all assoiled
    Before they any true election had.
Well canst thou recognise it in their faces,
    And also in their voices puerile,
    If thou regard them well and hearken to them.
Now doubtest thou, and doubting thou art silent;
    But I will loosen for thee the strong bond   50
    In which thy subtile fancies hold thee fast.
Within the amplitude of this domain
    No casual point can possibly find place,
    No more than sadness can, or thirst, or hunger;
For by eternal law has been established
    Whatever thou beholdest, so that closely
    The ring is fitted to the finger here.
And therefore are these people, festinate
    Unto true life, not *sine causa* here
    More and less excellent among themselves.   60
The King, by means of whom this realm reposes
    In so great love and in so great delight
    That no will ventureth to ask for more,
In his own joyous aspect every mind
    Creating, at his pleasure dowers with grace
    Diversely; and let here the effect suffice.
And this is clearly and expressly noted
    For you in Holy Scripture, in those twins
    Who in their mother had their anger roused.
According to the colour of the hair,   70
    Therefore, with such a grace the light supreme
    Consenteth that they worthily be crowned.
Without, then, any merit of their deeds,
    Stationed are they in different gradations,

Differing only in their first acuteness.
'Tis true that in the early centuries,
　　With innocence, to work out their salvation
　　Sufficient was the faith of parents only.
After the earlier ages were completed,
　　Behoved it that the males by circumcision   80
　　Unto their innocent wings should virtue add;
But after that the time of grace had come
　　Without the baptism absolute of Christ,
　　Such innocence below there was retained.
Look now into the face that unto Christ
　　Hath most resemblance; for its brightness only
　　Is able to prepare thee to see Christ."
On her did I behold so great a gladness
　　Rain down, borne onward in the holy minds
　　Created through that altitude to fly,   90
That whatsoever I had seen before
　　Did not suspend me in such admiration,
　　Nor show me such similitude of God.
And the same Love that first descended there,
　　"*Ave Maria, gratia plena,*" singing,
　　In front of her his wings expanded wide.
Unto the canticle divine responded
　　From every part the court beatified,
　　So that each sight became serener for it.
"O holy father, who for me endurest   100
　　To be below here, leaving the sweet place
　　In which thou sittest by eternal lot,
Who is the Angel that with so much joy
　　Into the eyes is looking of our Queen,
　　Enamoured so that he seems made of fire?"
Thus I again recourse had to the teaching
　　Of that one who delighted him in Mary
　　As doth the star of morning in the sun.
And he to me: "Such gallantry and grace
　　As there can be in Angel and in soul,   110
　　All is in him; and thus we fain would have it;
Because he is the one who bore the palm
　　Down unto Mary, when the Son of God
　　To take our burden on himself decreed.
But now come onward with thine eyes, as I

Speaking shall go, and note the great patricians
    Of this most just and merciful of empires.
Those two that sit above there most enraptured,
    As being very near unto Augusta,
    Are as it were the two roots of this Rose.   120
He who upon the left is near her placed
    The father is, by whose audacious taste
    The human species so much bitter tastes.
Upon the right thou seest that ancient father
    Of Holy Church, into whose keeping Christ
    The keys committed of this lovely flower.
And he who all the evil days beheld,
    Before his death, of her the beauteous bride
    Who with the spear and with the nails was won,
Beside him sits, and by the other rests   130
    That leader under whom on manna lived
    The people ingrate, fickle, and stiff-necked.
Opposite Peter seest thou Anna seated,
    So well content to look upon her daughter,
    Her eyes she moves not while she sings Hosanna.
And opposite the eldest household father
    Lucia sits, she who thy Lady moved
    When to rush downward thou didst bend thy brows.
But since the moments of thy vision fly,
    Here will we make full stop, as a good tailor   140
    Who makes the gown according to his cloth,
And unto the first Love will turn our eyes,
    That looking upon Him thou penetrate
    As far as possible through his effulgence.
Truly, lest peradventure thou recede,
    Moving thy wings believing to advance,
    By prayer behoves it that grace be obtained;
Grace from that one who has the power to aid thee;
    And thou shalt follow me with thy affection
    That from my words thy heart turn not aside."   150
And he began this holy orison.

Canto **XXXIII**

"Thou Virgin Mother, daughter of thy Son,
   Humble and high beyond all other creature,
   The limit fixed of the eternal counsel,
Thou art the one who such nobility
   To human nature gave, that its Creator
   Did not disdain to make himself its creature.
Within thy womb rekindled was the love,
   By heat of which in the eternal peace
   After such wise this flower has germinated.
Here unto us thou art a noonday torch   10
   Of charity, and below there among mortals
   Thou art the living fountain-head of hope.
Lady, thou art so great, and so prevailing,
   That he who wishes grace, nor runs to thee,
   His aspirations without wings would fly.
Not only thy benignity gives succour
   To him who asketh it, but oftentimes
   Forerunneth of its own accord the asking.
In thee compassion is, in thee is pity,
   In thee magnificence; in thee unites   20
   Whate'er of goodness is in any creature.
Now doth this man, who from the lowest depth
   Of the universe as far as here has seen
   One after one the spiritual lives,
Supplicate thee through grace for so much power
   That with his eyes he may uplift himself
   Higher towards the uttermost salvation.
And I, who never burned for my own seeing
   More than I do for his, all of my prayers
   Proffer to thee, and pray they come not short,   30
That thou wouldst scatter from him every cloud
   Of his mortality so with thy prayers,
   That the Chief Pleasure be to him displayed.
Still farther do I pray thee, Queen, who canst
   Whate'er thou wilt, that sound thou mayst preserve
   After so great a vision his affections.
Let thy protection conquer human movements;
   See Beatrice and all the blessed ones
   My prayers to second clasp their hands to thee!"

The eyes beloved and revered of God,   40
    Fastened upon the speaker, showed to us
    How grateful unto her are prayers devout;
Then unto the Eternal Light they turned,
    On which it is not credible could be
    By any creature bent an eye so clear.
And I, who to the end of all desires
    Was now approaching, even as I ought
    The ardour of desire within me ended.
Bernard was beckoning unto me, and smiling,
    That I should upward look; but I already   50
    Was of my own accord such as he wished;
Because my sight, becoming purified,
    Was entering more and more into the ray
    Of the High Light which of itself is true.
From that time forward what I saw was greater
    Than our discourse, that to such vision yields,
    And yields the memory unto such excess.
Even as he is who seeth in a dream,
    And after dreaming the imprinted passion
    Remains, and to his mind the rest returns not,   60
Even such am I, for almost utterly
    Ceases my vision, and distilleth yet
    Within my heart the sweetness born of it;
Even thus the snow is in the sun unsealed,
    Even thus upon the wind in the light leaves
    Were the soothsayings of the Sibyl lost.
O Light Supreme, that dost so far uplift thee
    From the conceits of mortals, to my mind
    Of what thou didst appear re-lend a little,
And make my tongue of so great puissance,   70
    That but a single sparkle of thy glory
    It may bequeath unto the future people;
For by returning to my memory somewhat,
    And by a little sounding in these verses,
    More of thy victory shall be conceived!
I think the keenness of the living ray
    Which I endured would have bewildered me,
    If but mine eyes had been averted from it;
And I remember that I was more bold
    On this account to bear, so that I joined   80

My aspect with the Glory Infinite.
O grace abundant, by which I presumed
    To fix my sight upon the Light Eternal,
    So that the seeing I consumed therein!
I saw that in its depth far down is lying
    Bound up with love together in one volume,
    What through the universe in leaves is scattered;
Substance, and accident, and their operations,
    All interfused together in such wise
    That what I speak of is one simple light.   90
The universal fashion of this knot
    Methinks I saw, since more abundantly
    In saying this I feel that I rejoice.
One moment is more lethargy to me,
    Than five and twenty centuries to the emprise
    That startled Neptune with the shade of Argo!
My mind in this wise wholly in suspense,
    Steadfast, immovable, attentive gazed,
    And evermore with gazing grew enkindled.
In presence of that light one such becomes,   100
    That to withdraw therefrom for other prospect
    It is impossible he e'er consent;
Because the good, which object is of will,
    Is gathered all in this, and out of it
    That is defective which is perfect there.
Shorter henceforward will my language fall
    Of what I yet remember, than an infant's
    Who still his tongue doth moisten at the breast.
Not because more than one unmingled semblance
    Was in the living light on which I looked,   110
    For it is always what it was before;
But through the sight, that fortified itself
    In me by looking, one appearance only
    To me was ever changing as I changed.
Within the deep and luminous subsistence
    Of the High Light appeared to me three circles,
    Of threefold colour and of one dimension,
And by the second seemed the first reflected
    As Iris is by Iris, and the third
    Seemed fire that equally from both is breathed.   120
O how all speech is feeble and falls short

Of my conceit, and this to what I saw
Is such, 'tis not enough to call it little!
O Light Eterne, sole in thyself that dwellest,
Sole knowest thyself, and, known unto thyself
And knowing, lovest and smilest on thyself!
That circulation, which being thus conceived
Appeared in thee as a reflected light,
When somewhat contemplated by mine eyes,
Within itself, of its own very colour   130
Seemed to me painted with our effigy,
Wherefore my sight was all absorbed therein.
As the geometrician, who endeavours
To square the circle, and discovers not,
By taking thought, the principle he wants,
Even such was I at that new apparition;
I wished to see how the image to the circle
Conformed itself, and how it there finds place;
But my own wings were not enough for this,
Had it not been that then my mind there smote   140
A flash of lightning, wherein came its wish.
Here vigour failed the lofty fantasy:
But now was turning my desire and will,
Even as a wheel that equally is moved,
The Love which moves the sun and the other stars.

NOTES TO PARADISO

NOTES TO PARADISO

Canto I

1. Dante's theory of the universe is the old one, which made the earth a stationary central point, around which all the heavenly bodies revolved; a theory, that, according to Milton, *Par. Lost,* VIII. 15, astonished even Adam in Paradise:—

> "When I behold this goodly frame, this world,
> Of heaven and earth consisting, and compute
> Their magnitudes; this earth, a spot, a grain,
> An atom, with the firmament compared
> And all her numbered stars, that seem to roll
> Spaces incomprehensible (for such
> Their distance argues, and their swift return
> Diurnal), merely to officiate light
> Round this opacous earth, this punctual spot,
> One day and night; in all their vast survey
> Useless besides; reasoning I oft admire,
> How Nature, wise and frugal, could commit
> Such disproportions, with superfluous hand
> So many nobler bodies to create,
> Greater so manifold, to this one use,
> For aught appears, and on their orbs impose
> Such restless revolution day by day
> Repeated; while the sedentary earth,
> That better might with far less compass move,
> Served by more noble than herself, attains
> Her end without least motion, and receives,
> As tribute, such a sumless journey brought
> Of incorporeal speed, her warmth and light,—
> Speed, to describe whose swiftness number fails."

The reply that Raphael makes to "our general ancestor," may be addressed to every reader of the Paradiso:—

> "Whether the sun, predominant in heaven,
> Rise on the earth, or earth rise on the sun;

123

> He from the east his flaming road begin,
> Or she from west her silent course advance,
> With inoffensive pace that spinning sleeps
> On her soft axle; while she paces even,
> And bears thee soft with the smooth air along;
> Solicit not thy thoughts with matters hid."

Thus, taking the earth as the central point, and speaking of the order of the Ten Heavens, Dante says, *Convito,* II. 4: "The first is that where the Moon is; the second is that where Mercury is; the third is that where Venus is; the fourth is that where the Sun is; the fifth is that where Mars is; the sixth is that where Jupiter is; the seventh is that where Saturn is; the eighth is that of the Stars; the ninth is not visible, save by the motion mentioned above, and is called by many the Crystalline: that is, diaphanous, or wholly transparent. Beyond all these, indeed, the Catholics place the Empyrean Heaven; that is to say, the Heaven of flame, or luminous; and this they suppose to be immovable, from having within itself, in every part, that which its matter demands. And this is the cause why the Primum Mobile has a very swift motion; from the fervent longing which each part of that ninth heaven has to be conjoined with that Divinest Heaven, the Heaven of Rest, which is next to it, it revolves therein with so great desire, that its velocity is almost incomprehensible; and quiet and peaceful is the place of that supreme Deity, who alone doth perfectly see himself."

Of the symbolism of these Heavens he says, *Convito,* II. 14: "As narrated above, the seven Heavens nearest to us are those of the Planets; and above these are two movable Heavens, and one motionless over all. To the first seven correspond the seven sciences of the Trivium and Quadrivium; that is, Grammar, Dialectics, Rhetoric, Arithmetic, Music, Geometry, and Astrology. To the eighth, that is, to the starry sphere, Natural Science, called Physics, corresponds, and the first science which is called Metaphysics; and to the ninth sphere corresponds Moral Science; and to the Heaven of Rest, the Divine Science, which is called Theology."

The details of these correspondences will be given later in their appropriate places.

These Ten Heavens are the heavens of the Paradiso; nine of them revolving about the earth as a central point, and the motionless Empyrean encircling and containing all.

In the first Heaven, or that of the Moon, are seen the spirits of those who, having taken monastic vows, were forced to violate them. In the second, or that of Mercury, the spirits of those whom desire of fame, incited to noble deeds. In the third, or that of Venus, the spirits of Lovers. In the fourth, or that of the Sun, the spirits of Theologians and Fathers of the Church. In the fifth, or that of Mars, the spirits of Crusaders and those who died for the true Faith. In the sixth, or that of Jupiter, the spirits of righteous Kings and Rulers.

In the seventh, or that of Saturn, the spirits of the Contemplative. In the eighth, or that of the Fixed Stars, the Triumph of Christ. In the ninth, or Primum Mobile, the Angelic Hierarchies. In the tenth, or the Empyrean, is the Visible Presence of God.

It must be observed, however, that the lower spheres, in which the spirits appear, are not assigned them as their places or dwellings. They show themselves in these different places only to indicate to Dante the different degrees of glory which they enjoy, and to show that while on earth they were under the influence of the planets in which they here appear. Dante expressly says, in Canto IV. 28:—

> "He of the Seraphim most absorbed in God,
>   Moses, and Samuel, and whichever John
>   Thou mayst select, I say, and even Mary,
> Have not in any other heaven their thrones
>   Than have those spirits that just appeared to thee,
>   Nor of existence more or fewer years;
> But all make beautiful the primal circle,
>   And have sweet life in different degrees,
>   By feeling more or less the eternal breath,
> They showed themselves here, not because allotted
>   This sphere has been to them, but to give sign
>   Of the celestial which is least exalted."

The threefold main division of the Paradiso, indicated by a longer prelude, or by a natural pause in the action of the poem, is:—1. From Canto I. to Canto X. 2. From Canto X. to Canto XXIII. 3. From Canto XXIII. to the end.

2. *Wisdom of Solomon*, i. 7: "For the spirit of the Lord filleth the world"; and *Ecclesiasticus*, xlii. 16: "The sun that giveth light looketh upon all things, and the work thereof is full of the glory of the Lord."

4. The Empyrean. Milton, *Par. Lost*, III. 57:—

> "From the pure Empyrean where he sits
> High throned above all highth."

5. 2 *Corinthians*, xii. 2: "I knew a man in Christ about fourteen years ago, (whether in the body, I cannot tell; or whether out of the body, I cannot tell: God knoweth;) such an one caught up to the third heaven. And I knew such a man, (whether in the body, or out of the body, I cannot tell; God knoweth:) how that he was caught up into paradise, and heard unspeakable words, which it is not lawful for a man to utter."

7. *Convito*, III. 2.: "Hence the human soul, which is the noblest form of those created under heaven, receiveth more of the divine nature than any

other. . . . . . And inasmuch as its being depends upon God, and is preserved
by him, it naturally desires and wishes to be united with God, in order to
strengthen its being."

And again, *Convito,* III. 6: "Each thing chiefly desireth its own perfection,
and in it quieteth every desire, and for it is each thing desired. And this is the
desire which always maketh each delight seem insufficient; for in this life is
no delight so great that it can satisfy the thirst of the soul, so that the desire
I speak of shall not remain in our thoughts."

13. Chaucer, *House of Fame,* III. 1:—

> "God of science and of light,
>   Apollo! thorough thy grete might
>   This litel last boke now thou gye.
>
>   . . . .
>
>   And if that divine virtue thou
>   Wilte helpen me to showen now
>   That in my hed ymarked is,
>
>   . . . .
>
>   Thou shalt yse me go as blive
>   Unto the next laurer I se,
>   And kysse it for it is thy tre.
>   Nowe entre in my brest anone."

19. Chaucer, *Ballade in Commendacion of Our Ladie,* 12:—

> "O winde of grace! now blowe unto my saile;
>   O auriate licour of Clio! to write
>   My penne enspire, of that I woll indite."

20. Ovid, *Met.,* VI., Croxall's Tr.:—

> "When straight another pictures to their view
>   The Satyr's fate, whom angry Phœbus slew;
>   Who, raised with high conceit, and puffed with pride,
>   At his own pipe the skilful God defied.
>   Why do you tear me from myself, he cries?
>   Ah, cruel! must my skin be made the prize?
>   This for a silly pipe? he roaring said,
>   Meanwhile the skin from off his limbs was flayed."

And Chaucer, *House of Fame,* 139, changing the sex of Marsyas:—

> "And Mercia that lost hire skinne,
>   Bothe in the face, bodie, and chinne,
>   For that she would envyen, lo!
>   To pipen bette than Apollo."

36. A town at the foot of Parnassus, dedicated to Apollo, and here used for Apollo.

Chaucer, *Quene Annelida and False Arcite,* 15:—

> "Be favorable eke thou, Polymnia!
> On Parnassus that, with thy susters glade
> By Helicon, and not ferre from Cirrha,
> Singed, with voice memoriall, in the shade
> Under the laurer, which that maie not fade."

39. That point of the horizon where the sun rises at the equinox; and where the Equator, the Zodiac, and the equinoctial Colure meet, and form each a cross with the Horizon.

41. The world is as wax, which the sun softens and stamps with his seal.

44. "This word *almost,*" says Buti, "gives us to understand that it was not the exact moment when the sun enters Aries."

60. Milton, *Par. Lost,* III. 593:—

> "Not all parts like, but all alike informed
> With radiant light, as glowing iron with fire."

61. Milton, *Par. Lost,* V. 310:—

> "Seems another morn
> Risen on mid-noon."

68. Glaucus, changed to a sea-god by eating of the salt-meadow grass. Ovid, *Met.,* XIII., Rowe's Tr.:—

> "Restless I grew, and every place forsook,
> And still upon the seas I bent my look.
> Farewell for ever! Farewell, land! I said;
> And plunged amidst the waves my sinking head.
> The gentle powers, who that low empire keep,
> Received me as a brother of the deep;
> To Tethys, and to Ocean old, they pray
> To purge my mortal earthy parts away."

"As Glaucus," says Buti, "was changed from a fisherman to a sea-god by tasting of the grass that had that power, so the human soul, tasting of things divine, becomes divine."

73. Whether I were spirit only. 2 *Corinthians,* xii. 3: "Whether in the body, or out of the body, I cannot tell; God knoweth."

One of the questions which exercised the minds of the Fathers and the Schoolmen was, whether the soul were created before the body or after it. Origen, following Plato, supposes all souls to have been created at once, and to await their bodies. Thomas Aquinas combats this opinion, *Sum. Theol.*, I. Quæst. cxviii. 3, and maintains, that "creation and infusion are simultaneous in regard to the soul." This seems also to be Dante's belief. See *Purg.* XXV. 70:—

> "The primal Motor turns to it well pleased
>   At so great art of nature, and inspires
>   A spirit new, with virtue all replete."

76. It is a doctrine of Plato that the heavens are always in motion, seeking the Soul of the World, which has no determinate place, but is everywhere diffused. See also Note 1.

78. The music of the spheres.

Shakespeare, *Merchant of Venice,* V. 1:—

> "Look, how the floor of heaven
> Is thick inlaid with patines of bright gold;
> There's not the smallest orb which thou behold'st,
> But in his motion like an angel sings,
> Still quiring to the young-eyed cherubins;
> Such harmony is in immortal souls;
> But, whilst this muddy vesture of decay
> Doth grossly close it in, we cannot hear it."

And Milton, *Hymn on Christ's Nativity:*—

> "Ring out, ye crystal spheres,
>   Once bless our human ears,
>   If ye have power to touch our senses so;
>   And let your silver chime
>   Move in melodious time;
>   And let the bass of Heaven's deep organ blow;
>   And, with your ninefold harmony,
>   Make up full consort to the angelic symphony."

Rixner, *Handbuch der Geschichte der Philosophie,* I. 100, speaking of the ten heavens, or the Lyre of Pythagoras, says: "These ten celestial spheres are arranged among themselves in an order so mathematical and musical, that is so harmonious, that the sphere of the fixed stars, which is above the sphere of Saturn, gives forth the deepest tone in the music of the universe (the World-Lyre strung with ten strings), and that of the Moon the highest."

Cicero, in his *Vision of Scipio,* inverts the tones. He says, Edmonds's Tr.:—

"Which as I was gazing at in amazement, I said, as I recovered myself, from whence proceed these sounds so strong, and yet so sweet, that fill my ears? 'The melody,' replies he, 'which you hear, and which, though composed in unequal time, is nevertheless divided into regular harmony, is effected by the impulse and motion of the spheres themselves, which, by a happy temper of sharp and grave notes, regularly produces various harmonic effects. Now it is impossible that such prodigious movements should pass in silence; and nature teaches that the sounds which the spheres at one extremity utter must be sharp, and those on the other extremity must be grave; on which account, that highest revolution of the star-studded heaven, whose motion is more rapid, is carried on with a sharp and quick sound; whereas this of the moon, which is situated the lowest, and at the other extremity, moves with the gravest sound. For the earth, the ninth sphere, remaining motionless, abides invariably in the innermost position, occupying the central spot in the universe.

" 'Now these eight directions, two of which have the same powers, effect seven sounds, differing in their modulations, which number is the connecting principle of almost all things. Some learned men, by imitating this harmony with strings and vocal melodies, have opened a way for their return to this place: as all others have done, who, endued with pre-eminent qualities, have cultivated in their mortal life the pursuits of heaven.

" 'The ears of mankind, filled with these sounds, have become deaf, for of all your senses it is the most blunted. Thus, the people who live near the place where the Nile rushes down from very high mountains to the parts which are called Catadupa, are destitute of the sense of hearing, by reason of the greatness of the noise. Now this sound, which is effected by the rapid rotation of the whole system of nature, is so powerful that human hearing cannot comprehend it, just as you cannot look directly upon the sun, because your sight and sense are overcome by his beams.' "

92. The region of fire. Brunetto Latini, *Tresor*, Ch. CVIII.: "After the zone of the air is placed the fourth element. This is an orb of fire without any moisture, which extends as far as the moon, and surrounds this atmosphere in which we are. And know that above the fire is first the moon, and the other stars, which are all of the nature of fire."

109. Milton, *Par. Lost.* V. 469:—

> "One Almighty is, from whom
> All things proceed, and up to him return,
> If not depraved from good; created all
> Such to perfection, one first matter all,
> Endued with various forms, various degrees
> Of substance, and, in things that live, of life;
> But more refined, more spiritous, and pure,
> As nearer to him placed, or nearer tending
> Each in their several active spheres assigned,
> Till body up to spirit work, in bounds

Proportioned to each kind. So from the root
Springs lighter the green stalk; from thence the leaves
More aery; last, the bright consummate flower
Spirits odorous breathes: flowers and their fruit,
Man's nourishment, by gradual scale sublimed,
To vital spirits aspire, to animal,
To intellectual; give both life and sense,
Fancy and understanding: whence the soul
Reason receives, and reason is her being,
Discursive or intuitive."

121. Filicaja's beautiful sonnet on Providence is thus translated by Leigh Hunt:—

"Just as a mother, with sweet, pious face,
     Yearns towards her little children from her seat,
     Gives one a kiss, another an embrace,
     Takes this upon her knees, that on her feet;
And while from actions, looks, complaints, pretences,
     She learns their feelings and their various will,
     To this a look, to that a word, dispenses,
     And, whether stern or smiling, loves them still;—
So Providence for us, high, infinite,
     Makes our necessities its watchful task,
     Hearkens to all our prayers, helps all our wants,
And even if it denies what seems our right,
     Either denies because 'twould have us ask,
     Or seems but to deny, or in denying grants."

122. The Empyrean, within which the Primum Mobile revolves "with so great desire that its velocity is almost incomprehensible."

141. *Convito,* III. 2: "The human soul, ennobled by the highest power, that is by reason, partakes of the divine nature in the manner of an eternal Intelligence; because the soul is so ennobled by that sovereign power, and denuded of matter, that the divine light shines in it as in an angel; and therefore man has been called by the philosophers a divine animal."

Canto II

1. The Heaven of the Moon, in which are seen the spirits of those who, having taken monastic vows, were forced to violate them.

In Dante's symbolism this heaven represents the first science of the Trivium. *Convito,* II. 14: "I say that the heaven of the Moon resembles Grammar; because it may be compared therewith; for if the Moon be well observed, two things are seen peculiar to it, which are not seen in the other stars. One is the shadow in it, which is nothing but the rarity of its body, in which the rays of the sun cannot terminate and be reflected as in the other parts. The other is the variation of its brightness, which now shines on one side, and now upon the other, according as the sun looks upon it. And Grammar has these two properties; since, on account of its infinity, the rays of reason do not terminate in it in any special part of its words; and it shines now on this side, and now on that, inasmuch as certain words, certain declinations, certain constructions, are in use which once were not, and many once were which will be again."

For the influences of the Moon, see Canto III. Note 30.

The introduction to this canto is at once a warning and an invitation. Balbi, *Life and Times of Dante,* II. Ch. 15, Mrs. Bunbury's Tr., says:—

"The last part of the Commedia, which Dante finished about this time (1320). . . . . is said to be the most difficult and obscure part of the whole poem. And it is so; and it would be in vain for us to attempt to awaken in the generality of readers that attention which Dante has not been able to obtain for himself. Readers in general will always be repulsed by the difficulties of its numerous allegories, by the series of heavens, arranged according to the now forgotten Ptolemaic system, and more than all by disquisitions on philosophy and theology which often degenerate into mere scholastic themes. With the exception of the three cantos relating to Cacciaguida, and a few other episodes which recall us to earth, as well as those verses in which frequently Dante's love for Beatrice shines forth, the Paradiso must not be considered as pleasant reading for the general reader, but as an especial recreation for those who find there, expressed in sublime verse, those contemplations that have been the subjects of their philosophical and theological studies. . . . . But few will always be the students of philosophy and theology, and much fewer those who look upon these sciences as almost one and the same thing, pursued by two different methods; these, if I am not mistaken, will find in Dante's Paradiso, a treasure of thought, and the loftiest and most soothing words of comfort, forerunners of the joys of Heaven itself. Above all, the Paradiso will delight those who find themselves, when they are reading it, in a somewhat similar disposition of mind to that of Dante when he was writing it; those in short who, after having in their youth lived in the world, and sought happiness in it, have now arrived at maturity, old age, or satiety, and seek by the means of philosophy and theology to know as far as possible of that other world on which their hopes now rest. Philosophy is the romance of the aged, and Religion the only future history for us all. Both these subjects of contemplation we find in Dante's Paradiso, and pursued with a rare modesty, not beyond the limits of our understanding, and with due submission to the Divine Law which placed these limits."

8. In the other parts of the poem "one summit of Parnassus" has sufficed; but in this Minerva, Apollo, and the nine Muses come to his aid, as wind, helmsman, and compass.

11. The bread of the Angels is Knowledge or Science, which Dante calls the "ultimate perfection." *Convito,* I. 1:—"Everything, impelled by the providence of its own nature, inclines towards its own perfection; whence, inasmuch as knowledge is the ultimate perfection of our soul, wherein consists our ultimate felicity, we are all naturally subject to its desire. . . . . O blessed those few who sit at the table where the bread of the Angels is eaten."

16. The Argonauts, when they saw their leader Jason ploughing with the wild bulls of Æetes, and sowing the land with serpents' teeth. Ovid, *Met.,* VII., Tate's Tr.:—

> "To unknown yokes their brawny necks they yield,
> And, like tame oxen, plough the wondering field.
> The Colchians stare; the Grecians shout, and raise
> Their champion's courage with inspiring praise.
> Emboldened now, on fresh attempts he goes,
> With serpents' teeth the fertile furrows sows;
> The glebe, fermenting with enchanted juice,
> Makes the snakes' teeth a human crop produce."

19. This is generally interpreted as referring to the natural aspiration of the soul for higher things; characterized in *Purg.* XXI. 1, as

> "The natural thirst that ne'er is satisfied,
> Excepting with the water for whose grace
> The woman of Samaria besought."

But Venturi says that it means the "being borne onward by the motion of the Primum Mobile, and swept round so as to find himself directly beneath the moon."

23. As if looking back upon his journey through the air, Dante thus rapidly describes it in an inverse order, the arrival, the ascent, the departure;—the striking of the shaft, the flight, the discharge from the bow-string. Here again we are reminded of the arrow of Pandarus, *Iliad,* IV. 120.

51. Cain with his bush of thorns. See *Inf.* XX. Note 126.

59. The spots in the Moon, which Dante thought were caused by rarity or density of the substance of the planet. *Convito,* II. 14: "The shadow in it, which is nothing but the rarity of its body, in which the rays of the sun cannot terminate and be reflected, as in the other parts."

Milton, *Par. Lost,* V. 419:—

> "Whence in her visage round those spots unpurged,
> Vapours not yet into her substance turned."

64. The Heaven of the Fixed Stars.

73. Either the diaphanous parts must run through the body of the Moon, or the rarity and density must be in layers one above the other.

90. As in a mirror, which Dante elsewhere, *Inf.* XXIII. 25, calls *impiombato vetro,* leaded glass.

107. The subject of the snow is what lies under it; "the mountain that remains naked," says Buti. Others give a scholastic interpretation to the word, defining it "the cause of accident," the cause of colour and cold.

111. Shall tremble like a star. "When a man looks at the stars," says Buti, "he sees their effulgence tremble, and this is because their splendour scintillates as fire does, and moves to and fro like the flame of the fire." The brighter they burn, the more they tremble.

112. The Primum Mobile, revolving in the Empyrean, and giving motion to all the heavens beneath it.

115. The Heaven of the Fixed Stars. *Greek Epigrams,* III. 62:—

"If I were heaven,
With all the eyes of heaven would I look down on thee."

Also Catullus, *Carm.,* V.:—

"How many stars, when night is silent,
Look on the furtive loves of men."

And Milton, *Par. Lost,* V. 44:—

"Heaven wakes with all his eyes
Whom to behold but thee, nature's desire?"

131. The Intelligences, ruling and guiding the several heavens (receiving power from above, and distributing it downward, taking their impression from God and stamping it like a seal upon the spheres below), according to Dionysius the Areopagite are as follows:—

The Seraphim,	Primum Mobile.
The Cherubim,	The Fixed Stars.
The Thrones,	Saturn.
The Dominions,	Jupiter.
The Virtues,	Mars.
The Powers,	The Sun.
The Principalities,	Venus.
The Archangels,	Mercury.
The Angels,	The Moon.

See Canto XXVIII. Note 99, and also the article *Cabala* at the end of the volume.

147. The principle which gives being to all created things.

Canto III

1. The Heaven of the Moon continued. Of the influence of this planet, Buti, quoting the astrologer Albumasar, says: "The Moon is cold, moist, and phlegmatic, sometimes warm, and gives lightness, aptitude in all things, desire of joy, of beauty, and of praise, beginning of all works, knowledge of the rich and noble, prosperity in life, acquisition of things desired, devotion in faith, superior sciences, multitude of thoughts, necromancy, acuteness of mind in things, geometry, knowledge of lands and waters and of their measure and number, weakness of the sentiments, noble women, marriages, pregnancies, nursings, embassies, falsehoods, accusations; the being lord among lords, servant among servants, and conformity with every man of like nature, oblivion thereof, timid, of simple heart, flattering, honourable towards men, useful to them, not betraying secrets, a multitude of infirmities and the care of healing bodies, cutting hair, liberality of food, chastity. These are the significations (influences) of the Moon upon the things it finds, the blame and honour of which, according to the astrologers, belong to the planet; but the wise man follows the good influences, and leaves the bad; though all are good and necessary to the life of the universe."

18. Narcissus mistook his shadow for a substance; Dante, falling into the opposite error, mistakes these substances for shadows.

41. Your destiny; that is, of yourself and the others with you.

49. Piccarda was a sister of Forese and Corso Donati, and of Gemma, Dante's wife. In *Purg.* XXIV. 13, Forese says of her:—

> "My sister, who, 'twixt beautiful and good,
>> I know not which was more, triumphs rejoicing
>> Already in her crown on high Olympus."

She was a nun of Santa Clara, and was dragged by violence from the cloister by her brother Corso Donati, who married her to Rosselin della Tosa. As she herself says:—

> "God knows what afterward my life became."

It was such that she did not live long. For this crime the "excellent Baron," according to the *Ottimo,* had to do penance in his shirt.

70. Milton, *Par. Lost,* XII. 583:—

> "Add Love,
>> By name to come called Charity, the soul
>> Of all the rest."

118. Constance, daughter of Roger of Sicily. She was a nun at Palermo, but was taken from the convent and married to the Emperor Henry V., son of Barbarossa and father of Frederic II. Of these "winds of Suabia," or Emperors

of the house of Suabia, Barbarossa was the first, Henry V. the second, and Frederic II. the third, and, as Dante calls him in the *Convito,* IV. 3, "the last of the Roman Emperors," meaning the last of the Suabian line.

Canto IV

1. The Heaven of the Moon continued.

2. Montaigne says: "If any one should place us between the bottle and the bacon (*entre la bouteille et le jambon*), with an equal appetite for food and drink, there would doubtless be no remedy but to die of thirst and hunger."

6. Ovid, *Met,* V., Maynwaring's Tr.:—

> "As when a hungry tiger near him hears
>   Two lowing herds, awhile he both forbears;
>   Nor can his hopes of this or that renounce,
>   So strong he lusts to prey on both at once."

9. "A similitude," says Venturi, "of great poetic beauty, but of little philosophic soundness."

13. When he recalled and interpreted the forgotten dream of Nebuchadnezzar, *Daniel,* ii. 10: "The Chaldeans answered before the king, and said, There is not a man upon the earth that can show the king's matter: therefore there is no king, lord, nor ruler, that asked such things at any magician, or astrologer, or Chaldean. And it is a rare thing that the king requireth: and there is none other that can show it before the king except the gods, whose dwelling is not with flesh."

24. Plato, *Timæus,* Davis's Tr., says: "And after having thus framed the universe, he allotted to it souls equal in number to the stars, inserting each in each. . . . . And he declared also, that after living well for the time appointed to him, each one should once more return to the habitation of his associate star, and spend a blessed and suitable existence."

26. The word "thrust," *pontano,* is here used in its architectural sense, as in *Inf.* XXXII. 3. There it is literal, here figurative.

28. *Che più s' india,* that most in-God's himself. As in Canto IX. 81, *S' io m' intuassi come tu t' immii,* "if I could in-thee myself as thou dost in-me thyself"; and other expressions of a similar kind.

42. The dogma of the Peripatetics, that nothing is in Intellect which was not first in Sense.

48. Raphael, "the affable archangel," of whom Milton says, *Par. Lost,* V. 220:—

> "Raphael, the sociable spirit, that deigned
>   To travel with Tobias, and secured
>   His marriage with the seven-times-wedded maid."

See *Tobit* xii. 14: "And now God hath sent me to heal thee and Sara thy daughter-in-law. I am Raphael, one of the seven holy angels which present the prayers of the saints, and which go in and out before the glory of the Holy One."

It must be remarked, however, that it was Tobit, and not Tobias, who was cured of his blindness.

49. Plato's Dialogue, entitled *Timæus,* the name of the philosopher of Locri.

51. Plato means it literally, and the Scriptures figuratively.

54. When it was infused into the body, or the body became informed with it.

Thomas Aquinas, *Sum. Theol.,* I., Quæst. LXXVI. I, says: "Form is that by which a thing is. . . . .This principle therefore, by which we first think, whether it be called intellect, or intellectual soul, is the form of the body."

And Spenser, *Hymne in Honour of Beautie,* says:—

> "For of the soule the bodie forme doth take,
>   For soule is forme and doth the bodie make."

63. Joachim di Flora, Dante's "Calabrian Abbot Joachim," the mystic of the twelfth century, says in his *Exposition of the Apocalypse:* "The deceived Gentiles believed that the planets to which they gave the names of Jupiter, Saturn, Venus, Mercury, Mars, the Moon, and the Sun, were gods."

64. Stated in line 20:—

> "The violence of others, for what reason
>   Doth it decrease the measure of my merit?"

83. St. Lawrence. In Mrs. Jameson's *Sacred and Legendary Art,* II. 156, his martyrdom is thus described:—

"The satellites of the tyrant, hearing that the treasures of the church had been confided to Lawrence, carried him before the tribunal, and he was questioned, but replied not one word; therefore he was put into a dungeon, under the charge of a man named Hippolytus, whom with his whole family he converted to the faith of Christ, and baptized; and when he was called again before the Prefect, and required to say where the treasures were concealed, he answered that in three days he would show them. The third day being come, St. Lawrence gathered together the sick and the poor, to whom he had dispensed alms, and, placing them before the Prefect, said, 'Behold, here are the treasures of Christ's Church.' Upon this the Prefect, thinking he was mocked, fell into a great rage, and ordered St. Lawrence to be tortured till he had made known where the treasures were concealed; but no suffering could subdue the patience and constancy of the holy martyr. Then the Prefect commanded that he should be carried by night to the baths of Olympias, near the villa of Sallust the historian, and that a new kind of torture should be prepared for him, more strange and cruel than had ever entered into the heart of a tyrant to conceive; for he ordered him to be stretched on a sort of bed, formed of iron bars in the manner of a gridiron, and a fire to be lighted beneath, which should gradually consume his body to ashes: and the executioners did as they were commanded, kindling the fire and adding coals from time to time, so that the victim was in a manner roasted alive; and those who were present looked on with horror, and wondered at the cruelty of the Prefect, who could condemn to such torments a youth of such fair person and courteous and gentle bearing, and all for the lust of gold."

84. Plutarch thus relates the story of Mutius Scævola, Dryden's Tr.:—

"The story of Mutius is variously given; we, like others, must follow the commonly received statement. He was a man endowed with every virtue, but most eminent in war, and resolving to kill Porsenna, attired himself in the Tuscan habit, and using the Tuscan language, came to the camp, and approaching the seat where the king sat amongst his nobles, but not certainly knowing the king, and fearful to inquire, drew out his sword, and stabbed one who he thought had most the appearance of king. Mutius was taken in the act, and whilst he was under examination, a pan of fire was brought to the king, who intended to sacrifice; Mutius thrust his right hand into the flame, and whilst it burnt stood looking at Porsenna with a steadfast and undaunted countenance; Porsenna at last in admiration dismissed him, and returned his sword, reaching it from his seat; Mutius received it in his left hand, which occasioned the name of Scævola, left-handed, and said, 'I have overcome the terrors of Porsenna, yet am vanquished by his generosity, and gratitude obliges me to disclose what no punishment could extort;' and assured him then, that three hundred Romans, all of the same resolution, lurked about his camp only waiting for an opportunity; he, by lot appointed to the enterprise, was not sorry that he had miscarried in it, because so brave and good a man deserved rather to be a friend to the Romans than an enemy."

103. Alcmæon, who slew his mother Eriphyle to avenge his father Amphiaraüs the soothsayer. See *Purg.* XII. Note 50.

Ovid, *Met.,* IX.:—

> "The son shall bathe his hands in parent's blood
> And in one act be both unjust and good."

118. Beatrice, beloved of God; "that blessed Beatrice, who lives in heaven with the angels and on earth with my soul."

131. Lessing, *Theol. Schrift.,* I. 108: "If God held all Truth shut up in his right hand, and in his left only the ever restless instinct for Truth, ... and

said to me, Choose! I should humbly fall down at his left, and say, Father, give! Pure Truth is for Thee alone!"

139. It must not be forgotten, that Beatrice is the symbol of Divine Wisdom. Dante says, *Convito,* III. 15: "In her countenance appear things which display some of the pleasures of Paradise;" and notes particularly "the eyes and smile." He then adds: "And here it should be known that the eyes of Wisdom are its demonstrations, by which the truth is most clearly seen; and its smile the persuasions, in which is displayed the interior light of Wisdom under a veil; and in these two things is felt the exceeding pleasure of beatitude, which is the chief good in Paradise. This pleasure cannot exist in anything here below, except in beholding these eyes and this smile."

Canto V

1. The Heaven of Mercury, where are seen the spirits of those who for the love of fame achieved great deeds. Of its symbolism Dante says, *Convito,* II. 14: "The Heaven of Mercury may be compared to Dialectics, on account of two properties; for Mercury is the smallest star of heaven, since the quantity of its diameter is not more than two thousand and thirty-two miles, according to the estimate of Alfergano, who declares it to be one twenty-eighth part of the diameter of the Earth, which is six thousand and fifty-two miles. The other property is, that it is more veiled by the rays of the Sun than any other star. And these two properties are in Dialectics; for Dialectics are less in body than any Science; since in them is perfectly compiled and bounded as much doctrine as is found in ancient and modern Art; and it is more veiled than any Science, inasmuch as it proceeds by more sophistic and probable arguments than any other."

For the influences of Mercury, see Canto VI. Note 114.

10. Burns, *The Vision:*—

> "I saw thy pulse's maddening play
>   Wild send thee pleasure's devious way,
>   Misled by fancy's meteor ray,
>   By passion driven;
>   And yet the light that led astray
>   Was light from heaven."

24. Milton, *Par. Lost,* V. 235:—

> "Happiness in his power left free to will,
>   Left to his own free will, his will though free,
>   Yet mutable."

33. In illustration of this line, Venturi quotes the following epigram:—

> "This hospital a pious person built,
> But first he made the poor wherewith to fill't."

And Biagioli this:—

> "C'est un homme d'honneur, de piété profonde,
> Et qui veut rendre à Dieu ce qu'il a pris au monde."

52. That which is sacrificed, or of which an offering is made.

57. Without the permission of Holy Church, symbolized by the two keys; the silver key of Knowledge, and the golden key of Authority. See *Purg.* IX. 118:—

> "One was of gold, and the other was of silver;
>
> . . . . .
>
> More precious one is, but the other needs
> More art and intellect ere it unlock,
> For it is that which doth the knot unloose."

60. The thing substituted must be greater than the thing relinquished.

66. *Judges* xi. 30: "And Jephthah vowed a vow unto the Lord, and said, If thou shalt without fail deliver the children of Ammon into my hands, then it shall be, that whatsoever cometh forth of the doors of my house to meet me, when I return in peace from the children of Ammon, shall surely be the Lord's, and I will offer it up for a burnt-offering. . . . And Jephthah came to Mizpeh unto his house, and, behold, his daughter came out to meet him with timbrels and with dances; and she was his only child: besides her he had neither son nor daughter."

69. Agamemnon.

70. Euripides, *Iphigenia in Tauris,* I. 1, Buckley's Tr.:—

"O thou who rulest over this Grecian expedition, Agamemnon, thou wilt not lead forth thy ships from the ports of this land, before Diana shall receive thy daughter Iphigenia as a victim; for thou didst vow to sacrifice to the light-bearing Goddess whatsoever the year should bring forth most beautiful. Now your wife Clytæmnestra has brought forth a daughter in your house, referring to me the title of the most beautiful, whom thou must needs sacrifice. And so, by the arts of Ulysses, they drew me from my mother under pretence of being wedded to Achilles. But I wretched coming to Aulis, being seized and raised aloft above the pyre, would have been slain by the sword; but Diana, giving to the Greeks a stag in my stead, stole me away, and, sending me through the clear ether, she settled me in this land of the Tauri, where barbarian Thoas rules the land."

80. Dante, *Convito,* I. 11: "These should be called sheep, and not men; for if one sheep should throw itself down a precipice of a thousand feet, all the others would follow, and if one sheep, in passing along the road, leaps

from any cause, all the others leap, though seeing no cause for it. And I once saw several leap into a well, on account of one that had leaped in, thinking perhaps it was leaping over a wall; notwithstanding that the shepherd, weeping and wailing, opposed them with arms and breast."

82. Lucretius, *Nature of Things,* II. 324, Good's Tr.:—

> "The fleecy flocks, o'er yonder hill that browse,
>   From glebe to glebe, where'er, impearled with dew,
>   The jocund clover call them, and the lambs
>   That round them gambol, saturate with milk,
>   Proving their frontlets in the mimic fray."

87. Towards the Sun, where the heaven is brightest.

95. The Heaven of Mercury.

97. Brunetto Latini, *Tresor,* I., Ch. 3, says, the planet Mercury "is easily moved according to the goodness or malice of the planets to which it is joined." Dante here represents himself as being of a peculiarly mercurial temperament.

108. The joy of spirits in Paradise is shown by greater brightness.

121. The spirit of Justinian.

129. Mercury is the planet nearest the Sun, and being thus "veiled with alien rays," is only visible to the naked eye at the time of its greatest elongation, and then but for a few minutes.

Dante, *Convito,* II. 14, says, that Mercury "is more veiled by the rays of the Sun than any other star." And yet it will be observed that in his planetary system he places Venus between Mercury and the Sun.

133. Milton, *Par. Lost,* III. 380:—

> "Dark with excessive bright thy skirts appear,
>   Yet dazzle heaven."

And again, V. 598:—

> "A flaming mount, whose top
> Brightness had made invisible."

Canto VI

1. The Heaven of Mercury continued.

In the year 330, Constantine, after his conversion and baptism by Sylvester (*Inf.* XXVII. Note 94), removed the seat of empire from Rome to Byzantium, which received from him its more modern name of Constantinople. He called it also New Rome; and, having promised to the Senators and their families that they should soon tread again on Roman soil, he had the streets of Constantinople strewn with earth which he had brought from Rome in ships.

The transfer of the empire from west to east was turning the imperial eagle against the course of heaven, which it had followed in coming from Troy to Italy with Æneas, who married Lavinia, daughter of King Latinus, and was the founder of the Roman Empire.

4. From 324, when the seat of empire was transferred to Constantinople by Constantine, to 527, when the reign of Justinian began.

5. The mountains of Asia, between Constantinople and the site of Troy.

10. Cæsar, or Kaiser, the general title of all the Roman Emperors.

The character of Justinian is thus sketched by Gibbon, *Decline and Fall,* Ch. XLIII.:—

"The Emperor was easy of access, patient of hearing, courteous and affable in discourse, and a master of the angry passions, which rage with such destructive violence in the breast of a despot. Procopius praises his temper to reproach him with calm and deliberate cruelty; but in the conspiracies which attacked his authority and person, a more candid judge will approve the justice or admire the clemency of Justinian. He excelled in the private virtues of chastity and temperance; but the impartial love of beauty would have been less mischievous than his conjugal tenderness for Theodora; and his abstemious diet was regulated, not by the prudence of a philosopher, but the superstition of a monk. His repasts were short and frugal; on solemn fasts he contented himself with water and vegetables; and such was his strength as well as fervour, that he frequently passed two days, and as many nights, without tasting any food. The measure of his sleep was not less rigorous; after the repose of a single hour the body was awakened by the soul, and, to the astonishment of his chamberlain, Justinian walked or studied till the morning light. Such restless application prolonged his time for the acquisition of knowledge and the despatch of business; and he might seriously deserve the reproach of confounding, by minute and preposterous diligence, the general order of his administration. The Emperor professed himself a musician and architect, a poet and philosopher, a lawyer and theologian; and if he failed in the enterprise of reconciling the Christian sects, the review of the Roman jurisprudence is a noble monument of his spirit and industry. In the government of the empire he was less wise or less successful: the age was unfortunate; the people was oppressed and discontented; Theodora abused her power; a succession of bad ministers disgraced his judgment; and Justinian was neither beloved in his life, nor regretted at his death. The love of fame was deeply implanted in his breast, but he condescended to the poor ambition of titles, honours, and contemporary praise; and while he laboured to fix the admiration, he forfeited the esteem and affection of the Romans."

12. Of the reform of the Roman Laws, by which they were reduced from two thousand volumes to fifty, Gibbon, *Decline and Fall,* Ch. XLIV., says: "The vain titles of the victories of Justinian are crumbled into dust; but the

name of the legislator is inscribed on a fair and everlasting monument. Under his reign, and by his care, the civil jurisprudence was digested in the immortal works of the CODE, the PANDECT, and the INSTITUTES; the public reason of the Romans has been silently or studiously transfused into the domestic institutions of Europe, and the laws of Justinian still command the respect or obedience of independent nations. Wise or fortunate is the prince who connects his own reputation with the honour and interest of a perpetual order of men."

This is what Dante alludes to, *Purg.* VI. 89:—

> "What boots it, that for thee Justinian
> The bridle mend, if empty be the saddle?"

14. The heresy of Eutyches, who maintained that only the Divine nature existed in Christ, not the human; and consequently that the Christ crucified was not the real Christ, but a phantom.

16. Agapetus was Pope, or Bishop of Rome, in the year 515, and was compelled by King Theodotus the Ostrogoth, to go upon an embassy to the Emperor Justinian at Constantinople, where he refused to hold any communication with Anthimus, Bishop of Trebizond, who, against the canon of the Church, had been transferred from his own see to that of Constantinople. Milman, *Hist. Latin Christ.,* I. 460, says: "Agapetus, in a conference, condescended to satisfy the Emperor as to his own unimpeachable orthodoxy. Justinian sternly commanded him to communicate with Anthimus. 'With the Bishop of Trebizond,' replied the unawed ecclesiastic, 'when he has returned to his diocese, and accepted the Council of Chalcedon and the letters of Leo.' The Emperor in a louder voice commanded him to acknowledge the Bishop of Constantinople on pain of immediate exile. 'I came hither in my old age to see, as I supposed, a religious and a Christian Emperor; I find a new Diocletian. But I fear not kings' menaces, I am ready to lay down my life for the truth.' The feeble mind of Justinian passed at once from the height of arrogance to admiration and respect; he listened to the charges advanced by Agapetus against the orthodoxy of Anthimus. In his turn the Bishop of Constantinople was summoned to render an account of his theology before the Emperor, convicted of Eutychianism, and degraded from the see."

25. Belisarius, the famous general, to whom Justinian gave the leadership of his armies in Africa and Italy. In his old age he was suspected of conspiring against the Emperor's life; but the accusation was not proved. Gibbon, *Decline and Fall,* Ch. XLI., speaks of him thus: "The Africanus of new Rome was born, and perhaps educated, among the Thracian peasants, without any of those advantages which had formed the virtues of the elder and the younger Scipio,—a noble origin, liberal studies, and the emulation of a free state. The silence of a loquacious secretary may be admitted, to prove that the youth of Belisarius could not afford any subject of praise: he served, most

assuredly with valour and reputation among the private guards of Justinian; and when his patron became Emperor, the domestic was promoted to military command."

And of his last years as follows, Ch. XLIII.: "Capricious pardon and arbitrary punishment embittered the irksomeness and discontent of a long reign; a conspiracy was formed in the palace, and, unless we are deceived by the names of Marcellus and Sergius, the most virtuous and the most profligate of the courtiers were associated in the same designs. They had fixed the time of the execution; their rank gave them access to the royal banquet, and their black slaves were stationed in the vestibule and porticoes to announce the death of the tyrant, and to excite a sedition in the capital. But the indiscretion of an accomplice saved the poor remnant of the days of Justinian. The conspirators were detected and seized, with daggers hidden under their garments; Marcellus died by his own hand, and Sergius was dragged from the sanctuary. Pressed by remorse, or tempted by the hopes of safety, he accused two officers of the household of Belisarius; and torture forced them to declare that they had acted according to the secret instructions of their patron. Posterity will not hastily believe that a hero who, in the vigour of life, had disdained the fairest offers of ambition and revenge, should stoop to the murder of his prince, whom he could not long expect to survive. His followers were impatient to fly; but flight must have been supported by rebellion, and he had lived enough for nature and for glory. Belisarius appeared before the council with less fear than indignation; after forty years' service, the Emperor had prejudged his guilt; and injustice was sanctified by the presence and authority of the patriarch. The life of Belisarius was graciously spared; but his fortunes were sequestered, and from December to July he was guarded as a prisoner in his own palace. At length his innocence was acknowledged; his freedom and honours were restored; and death, which might be hastened by resentment and grief, removed him from the world about eight months after his deliverance. The name of Belisarius can never die; but instead of the funeral, the monuments, the statues, so justly due to his memory, I only read that his treasures, the spoils of the Goths and Vandals, were immediately confiscated for the Emperor. Some decent portion was reserved, however, for the use of his widow; and as Antonina had much to repent, she devoted the last remains of her life and fortune to the foundation of a convent. Such is the simple and genuine narrative of the fall of Belisarius and the ingratitude of Justinian. That he was deprived of his eyes, and reduced by envy to beg his bread,—'Give a penny to Belisarius the general!'—is a fiction of later times, which has obtained credit, or rather favour, as a strange example of the vicissitudes of fortune."

36. The son of Evander, sent to assist Æneas, and slain by Turnus. Virgil, *Æneid*, X., Davidson's Tr.: "Turnus, long poising a javelin tipped with sharpened steel, darts it at Pallas, and thus speaks: See whether ours be not the more

penetrating dart. He said; and with a quivering stroke the point pierces through the mid-shield, through so many plates of iron, so many of brass, while the bull's hide so many times encompasses it, and through the corslet's cumbrous folds transfixes his breast with a hideous gash. He in vain wrenches out the reeking weapon from the wound; at one and the same passage the blood and soul issue forth. Down on his wound he falls: over him his armour gave a clang; and in death with bloody jaws he bites the hostile ground."

37. In Alba Longa, built by Ascanius, son of Æneas, on the borders of the Alban Lake. The period of three hundred years is traditionary, not historic.

39. The Horatii and Curatii.

40. From the rape of the Sabine women, in the days of Romulus, the first of the seven kings of Rome, down to the violence done to Lucretia by Tarquinius Superbus, the last of them.

44. Brennus was the king of the Gauls, who, entering Rome unopposed, found the city deserted, and the Senators seated in their ivory chairs in the Forum, so silent and motionless that his soldiers took them for the statues of gods. He burned the city and laid siege to the Capitol, whither the people had fled for safety, and which was preserved from surprise by the cackling of the sacred geese in the Temple of Juno. Finally Brennus and his army were routed by Camillus, and tradition says that not one escaped.

Pyrrhus was a king of Epirus, who boasted his descent from Achilles, and whom Hannibal called "the greatest of commanders." He was nevertheless driven out of Italy by Curius, his army of eighty thousand being routed by thirty thousand Romans; whereupon he said that, "if he had soldiers like the Romans, or if the Romans had him for a general, he would leave no corner of the earth unseen, and no nation unconquered."

46. Titus Manlius, surnamed Torquatus, from the collar (*torques*) which he took from a fallen foe; and Quinctius, surnamed Cincinnatus, or "the curly-haired."

47. Three of the Decii, father, son, and grandson, sacrificed their lives in battle at different times for their country. The Fabii also rendered signal services to the state, but are chiefly known in history through one of their number, Quinctius Maximus, surnamed Cunctator, or the Delayer, from whom we have "the Fabian policy."

53. The hill of Fiesole, overlooking Florence, where Dante was born. Fiesole was destroyed by the Romans for giving refuge to Catiline and his fellow conspirators.

55. The birth of Christ. Milton, *Hymn on the Morning of Christ's Nativity*, 3, 4:—

> "But he, her fears to cease,
>   Sent down the meek-eyed Peace:
>   She, crowned with olive-green, came softly sliding
>   Down through the turning sphere,
>   His ready harbinger,
>   With turtle wing the amorous clouds dividing;

And, waving wide her myrtle wand,
She strikes a universal peace through sea and land.

"No war or battle's sound
Was heard the world around:
    The idle spear and shield were high up hung;
The hooked chariot stood
Unstained with hostile blood;
    The trumpet spake not to the arméd throng;
And kings sat still with awful eye,
As if they surely knew their sovran Lord was by."

65. Durazzo in Macedonia, and Pharsalia in Thessaly.
66. Gower, *Conf. Amant.*, II.:—

"That one sleeth. and that other sterveth,
But aboven all his prise deserveth
This knightly Romain; where he rode
His dedly swerd no man abode,
Ayen the which was no defence:
Egipte fledde in his presence."

67. Antandros, a city, and Simois, a river, near Troy, whence came the Roman eagle with Æneas into Italy.
69. It was an evil hour for Ptolemy, when Cæsar took from him the kingdom of Egypt, and gave it to Cleopatra.
70. Juba, king of Numidia, who protected Pompey, Cato, and Scipio after the battle of Pharsalia. Being conquered by Cæsar, his realm became a Roman province, of which Sallust the historian was the first governor.
Milton, *Sams. Agon.*, 1695:—

"But as an eagle
His cloudless thunder bolted on their heads."

71. Towards Spain, where some remnants of Pompey's army still remained under his two sons. When these were subdued the civil war was at an end.
73. Octavius Augustus, nephew of Julius Cæsar. At the battle of Philippi he defeated Brutus and Cassius, and established the Empire.
75. On account of the great slaughter made by Augustus in his battles with Mark Antony and his brother Lucius, in the neighbourhood of these cities.
81. Augustus closed the gates of the temple of Janus as a sign of universal peace, in the year of Christ's birth.
86. Tiberius Cæsar.
90. The crucifixion of Christ, in which the Romans took part in the person of Pontius Pilate.

92. The destruction of Jerusalem under Titus, which avenged the cruci-
fixion.

94. When the Church was assailed by the Lombards, who were subdued
by Charlemagne.

98. Referring back to line 31:—

> "In order that thou see with how great reason
> Men move against the standard sacrosanct,
> Both who appropriate and who oppose it."

100. The Golden Lily, or Fleur-de-lis of France. The Guelfs, uniting with
the French, opposed the Ghibellines, who had appropriated the imperial
standard to their own party purposes.

106. Charles II. of Apulia, son of Charles of Anjou.

111. Change the imperial eagle for the lilies of France.

112. Mercury is the smallest of the planets, with the exception of the
Asteroids, being sixteen times smaller than the Earth.

114. Speaking of the planet Mercury, Buti says: "We are now to consider
the effects which Mercury produces upon us in the world below, for which
honour and blame are given to the planet; for as Albumasar says in the
introduction to his seventh treatise, ninth division, where he treats of the
nature of the planets and of their properties, Mercury signifies these twenty-
two things among others, namely, desire of knowledge and of seeing secret
things; interpretation of the Deity, of oracles and prophecies; foreknowledge
of things future; knowledge and profundity of knowledge in profound
books; study of wisdom; memory of stories and tales; eloquence with pol-
ish of language; subtilty of genius; desire of lordship; appetite of praise and
fame; colour and subtilty of speech; subtilty of genius in everything to
which man betakes himself; desire of perfection; cunning of hand in all arts;
practice of trade; selling, buying, giving, receiving, stealing, cheating; con-
cealing thoughts in the mind; change of habits; youthfulness, lust, abundance,
murmurs, lies, false testimony, and many other things as being therein
contained. And therefore our author feigns, that those who have been active
in the world, and have lived with political and moral virtues, show them-
selves in the sphere of Mercury, because Mercury exercises such influence,
according to the astrologers, as has been shown; but it is in man's free will
to follow the good influence and avoid the bad, and hence springs the merit
and demerit."

Milton, *Lycidas,* 70:—

> "Fame is the spur that the clear spirit doth raise,
> (That last infirmity of noble mind,)
> To scorn delights, and live laborious days;
> But the fair guerdon when we hope to find,
> And think to burst out into sudden blaze,
> Comes the blind Fury with the abhorred shears

And slits the thin-spun life. 'But not the praise,'
Phœbus replied, and touched my trembling ears:
'Fame is no plant that grows on mortal soil,
Nor in the glistering foil
Set off to the world, nor in broad rumour lies;
But lives and spreads aloft by those pure eyes,
And perfect witness of all-judging Jove:
As he pronounces lastly on each deed,
Of so much fame in heaven expect thy meed.'"

121. Piccarda, Canto III. 70, says:—

"Brother, our will is quieted by virtue
    Of charity, that makes us wish alone
    For what we have, nor gives us thirst for more."

128. Villani, VI. Ch. 90, relates the story of Romeo (in Italian Roméo)
as follows, though it will be observed that he uses the word *romeo* not as a
proper, but as a common noun, in its sense of pilgrim: "There arrived at his
court a pilgrim, who was returning from St. James; and hearing of the good-
ness of Count Raymond, he tarried in his court, and was so wise and worthy,
and found such favour with the Count, that he made him master and direc-
tor of all things. He was always clad in a decent and clerical habit, and in a
short time, by his dexterity and wisdom, increased the income of his lord
threefold, maintaining always a grand and honourable court. . . . . Four
daughters had the Count, and no son. By the wisdom and address of the good
pilgrim, he first married the eldest to the good King Louis of France by means
of money, saying to the Count, 'Let me manage this, and do not be troubled
at the cost; for if thou marry the first well, on account of this relationship
thou wilt marry all the others better, and at less cost.' And so it came to pass;
for straightway the King of England, in order to be brother-in-law of the
King of France, took the second for a small sum of money; then his brother,
being elected King of the Romans, took the third; and the fourth still remain-
ing to be married, the good pilgrim said, 'With this one I want thee to have
a brave son, who shall be thy heir;' and so he did. Finding Charles, Count
of Anjou, brother of King Louis of France, he said, 'Give her to this man,
for he will be the best man in the world;' prophesying concerning him, and
so it was done. Then it came to pass through envy, which spoils every good
thing, that the barons of Provence accused the good pilgrim of having badly
managed the treasury of the Count, and had him called to a reckoning. The
noble pilgrim said: 'Count, I have served thee a long time, and brought thee
from low to high estate, and for this, through false counsel of thy folk, thou
art little grateful. I came to thy court a poor pilgrim, and have lived modestly
on thy bounty. Have my mule and my staff and scrip given back to me as
when I came, and I ask no further wages.' The Count would not have him
go; but on no account would he remain; and he departed as he had come,

and never was it known whence he came, nor whither he went. Many thought that his was a sainted soul."

142. Lord Bacon says in his *Essay on Adversity:* "Prosperity is the blessing of the Old Testament; adversity is the blessing of the New, which carrieth the greater benediction and the clearer revelation of God's favour. Yet, even in the Old Testament, if you listen to David's harp, you shall hear as many hearse-like airs as carols; and the pencil of the Holy Ghost hath laboured more in describing the afflictions of Job than the felicities of Solomon."

Canto VII

1. "Hosanna, holy God of Sabaoth, illuminating with thy brightness the happy fires of these realms."

Dante is still in the planet Mercury, which receives from the sun six times more light and heat than the earth.

5. By Substance is here meant spirit, or angel; the word having the sense of Subsistence. See Canto XIII. Note 58.

7. The rapidity of the motion of the flying spirits is beautifully expressed in these lines.

10. Namely, the doubt in his mind.

14. Bice, or Beatrice.

17. *Convito,* III. 8: "And in these two places I say these pleasures appear, saying, *In her eyes and in her sweet smile;* which two places by a beautiful similitude may be called balconies of the Lady who inhabits the edifice of the body, that is, the Soul; since here, although as if veiled, she often shows herself. She shows herself in the eyes so manifestly, that he who looks carefully can recognize her present passion. Hence, inasmuch as six passions are peculiar to the human soul, of which the Philosopher makes mention in his Rhetoric, that is, grace, zeal, mercy, envy, love, and shame, with none of these can the Soul be impassioned, without its semblance coming to the window of the eyes, unless it be kept within by great effort. Hence one of old plucked out his eyes, so that his inward shame might not appear outwardly, as Statius the poet relates of Theban Œdipus, when he says, that in eternal night he hid his shame accursed. She shows herself in the mouth, as colour behind glass. And what is laughter but a coruscation of the delight of the soul, that is, a light appearing outwardly, as it exists within? And therefore it behoveth man to show his soul in moderate joy, to laugh moderately with dignified severity, and with slight motion of the arms; so that the Lady who then shows herself, as has been said, may appear modest, and not dissolute. Hence the Book of the Four Cardinal Virtues commands us, 'Let thy laughter be without cachinnation, that is to say, without cackling like a hen.' Ah, wonderful laughter of my Lady, that never was perceived but by the eye!"

20. Referring back to Canto VI. 92:—

> "To do vengeance
> Upon the vengeance of the ancient sin."

27. Milton, *Par. Lost,* I. 1, the story

> "Of man's first disobedience, and the fruit
> Of that forbidden tree, whose mortal taste
> Brought death into the world, and all our woe,
> With loss of Eden, till one greater Man
> Restore us, and regain the blissful seat."

36. Sincere in the sense of pure.

65. Plato, *Timæus,* Davis's Tr., X.: "Let us declare then on what account the framing Artificer settled the formation of this universe. He was good; and in the good envy is never engendered about anything whatever. Hence, being free from this, he desired that all things should as much as possible resemble himself."

Also Milton, *Par. Lost,* I. 259:—

> "The Almighty hath not built
> Here for his envy."

And again, VIII. 491:—

> "Thou hast fulfilled
> Thy words, Creator bounteous and benign,
> Giver of all things fair! but fairest this
> Of all thy gifts! nor enviest."

67. Dante here discriminates between the direct or immediate inspirations of God, and those influences that come indirectly through the stars. In the *Convito,* VII. 3, he says: "The goodness of God is received in one manner by disembodied substances, that is, by the Angels (who are without material grossness, and as it were diaphanous on account of the purity of their form), and in another manner by the human soul, which, though in one part it is free from matter, in another is impeded by it; (as a man who is wholly in the water, except his head, of whom it cannot be said he is wholly in the water nor wholly out of it;) and in another manner by the animals, whose soul is all absorbed in matter, but somewhat ennobled; and in another manner by the metals, and in another by the earth; because it is the most material, and therefore the most remote from and the most inappropriate for the first most simple and noble virtue, which is solely intellectual, that is, God."

And in Canto XXIX. 136:—

> "The primal light, that all irradiates,
>   By modes as many is received therein,
>   As are the splendours wherewith it is mated."

76. *Convito,* VII. 3: "Between the angelic nature, which is an intellectual thing, and the human soul there is no step, but they are both almost continuous in the order of gradation. . . . . Thus we are to suppose and firmly to believe, that a man may be so noble, and of such lofty condition, that he shall be almost an angel."

130. The Angels, and the Heavens, and the human soul, being immediately inspired by God, are immutable and indestructible. But the elements and the souls of brutes and plants are controlled by the stars, and are mutable and perishable.

142. See *Purg.* XVI. 85:—

> "Forth from the hand of Him, who fondles it
>   Before it is, like to a little girl
>   Weeping and laughing in her childish sport,
> Issues the simple soul, that nothing knows,
>   Save that, proceeding from a joyous Maker,
>   Gladly it turns to that which gives it pleasure."

And also *Purg.* XXV. 70:—

> "The primal Motor turns to it well pleased
>   At so great art of nature, and inspires
>   A spirit new with virtue all replete."

Canto VIII

1. The ascent to the Third Heaven, or that of Venus, where are seen the spirits of Lovers. Of this Heaven Dante says, *Convito,* II. 14:—

"The Heaven of Venus may be compared to Rhetoric for two properties; the first is the brightness of its aspect, which is most sweet to look upon, more than any other star; the second is its appearance, now in the morning, now in the evening. And these two properties are in Rhetoric, the sweetest of all the sciences, for that is principally its intention. It appears in the morning when the rhetorician speaks before the face of his audience; it appears in the evening, that is, retrograde, when the letter in part remote speaks for the rhetorician."

For the influences of Venus, see Canto IX. Note 33.

2. In the days of "the false and lying gods," when the world was in peril of damnation for misbelief. Cypria, or Cyprigna, was a title of Venus, from the place of her birth, Cyprus.

3. The third Epicycle, or that of Venus, the third planet, was its supposed motion from west to east, while the whole heavens were swept onward from east to west by the motion of the Primum Mobile.

In the *Convito*, II. 4, Dante says: "Upon the back of this circle (the Equatorial) in the Heaven of Venus, of which we are now treating, is a little sphere, which revolves of itself in this heaven, and whose orbit the astrologers call Epicycle." And again, II. 7: "All this heaven moves and revolves with its Epicycle from east to west, once every natural day; but whether this movement be by any Intelligence, or by the sweep of the Primum Mobile, God knoweth; in me it would be presumptuous to judge."

Milton, *Par. Lost,* VIII. 72:—

> "From man or angel the great Architect
> Did wisely to conceal, and not divulge
> His secrets to be scanned by them who ought
> Rather admire; or, if they list to try
> Conjecture, He his fabric of the heavens
> Hath left to their disputes; perhaps to move
> His laughter at their quaint opinions wide
> Hereafter, when they come to model heaven
> And calculate the stars; how they will wield
> The mighty frame; how build, unbuild, contrive,
> To save appearances; how gird the sphere
> With centric and eccentric scribbled o'er,
> Cycle and epicycle, orb in orb."

See also Nichol, *Solar System,* p. 7: "Nothing in later times ought to obscure the glory of Hipparchus, and, as some think, the still greater Ptolemy. Amid the bewilderment of these planetary motions, what could they say, except that the 'gods never act without design;' and thereon resolve to discern it? The motion of the Earth was concealed from them: nor was aught intelligible or explicable concerning the wanderings of the planets, except the grand revolution of the sky around the Earth. That Earth, small to us, they therefore, on the ground of phenomena, considered the centre of the Universe,—thinking, perhaps, not more confinedly than persons in repute in modern days. Around that centre all motion seemed to pass in order the most regular; and if a few bodies appeared to interrupt the regularity of that order, why not conceive the existence of some arrangement by which they might be reconciled with it? It was a strange, but most ingenious idea. They could not tell how, by any simple system of circular and uniform motion, the ascertained courses of the planets, as *directly observed,* were to be accounted for; but they made a most artificial scheme, that still saved the immobility of the Earth. Suppose a person passing around a room holding a lamp, and all the while turning on his heel. If he turned round uniformly, there would be no actual interruption of the uniform circular motion both of the carrier and the carried; but the light, *as seen by an observer in the interior,* would make strange gyrations. Unable to account otherwise for the irregularities of the planets, they mounted them in this manner, on small circles, whose *centres only* revolved regularly around the Earth, but which, during their revolutionary motion, also revolved around their own centres. Styling these cycles and epicycles, the ancient learned men framed that grand system of the Heavens concerning which Ptolemy composed his 'Syntax.'"

7. Shakespeare, *Love's Labour's Lost,* III. 1:—

> "This wimpled, whining, purblind, wayward boy;
> This senior-junior, giant-dwarf, Dan Cupid;
> Regent of love-rhymes, lord of folded arms,
> The anointed sovereign of sighs and groans,
> Liege of all loiterers and malcontents."

9. Cupid in the semblance of Ascanius. *Æneid,* I. 718, Davidson's Tr.: "She clings to him with her eyes, her whole soul, and sometimes fondles him in her lap, Dido not thinking what a powerful god is settling on her, hapless one. Meanwhile he, mindful of his Acidalian mother, begins insensibly to efface the memory of Sichæus, and with a living flame tries to prepossess her languid affections, and her heart, chilled by long disuse."

10. Venus, with whose name this canto begins.

12. Brunetto Latini, *Tresor,* I. Ch. 3, says that Venus "always follows the sun, and is beautiful and gentle, and is called the Goddess of Love."

Dante says, it plays with or caresses the sun, "now behind and now in front." When it follows, it is Hesperus, the Evening Star; when it precedes, it is Phosphor, the Morning Star.

21. The rapidity of the motion of the spirits, as well as their brightness, is in proportion to their vision of God. Compare Canto XIV. 40:—

> "Its brightness is proportioned to the ardour,
> The ardour to the vision; and the vision
> Equals what grace it has above its worth."

23. Made visible by mist and cloud-rack.

27. Their motion originates in the *Primum Mobile,* whose Regents, or Intelligences, are the Seraphim.

34. The Regents, or Intelligences, of Venus are the Principalities.

37. This is the first line of the first canzone in the *Convito,* and in his commentary upon it, II. 5, Dante says: "In the first place, then, be it known, that the movers of this heaven are substances separate from matter, that is, Intelligences, which the common people call Angels." And farther on, II. 6: "It is reasonable to believe that the motors of the Heaven of the Moon are of the order of the Angels; and those of Mercury are the Archangels; and those of Venus are the Thrones." It will be observed, however, that in line 34 he alludes to the Principalities as the Regents of

Venus; and in Canto IX. 61, speaks of the Thrones as reflecting the justice of God:—

> "Above us there are mirrors, Thrones you call them,
> From which shines out on us God Judicant;"

thus referring the Thrones to a higher heaven than that of Venus.

40. After he had by looks asked and gained assent from Beatrice.

46. The spirit shows its increase of joy by increase of brightness. As Picarda in Canto III. 67:—

> "First with those other shades she smiled a little;
> Thereafter answered me so joyously,
> She seemed to burn in the first fire of love."

And Justinian, in Canto V. 133:—

> "Even as the sun, that doth conceal himself
> By too much light, when heat has worn away
> The tempering influence of the vapours dense,
> By greater rapture thus concealed itself
> In its own radiance the figure saintly."

49. The spirit who speaks is Charles Martel of Hungary, the friend and benefactor of Dante. He was the eldest son of Charles the Lame (Charles II. of Naples) and of Mary of Hungary. He was born in 1272, and in 1291 married the "beautiful Clemence," daughter of Rudolph of Hapsburg, Emperor of Germany. He died in 1295, at the age of twenty-three, to which he alludes in the words,

> "The world possessed me
> Short time below."

58. That part of Provence, embracing Avignon, Aix, Arles, and Marseilles, of which his father was lord, and which he would have inherited had he lived. This is "the great dowry of Provence," which the daughter of Raymond Berenger brought to Charles of Anjou in marriage, and which is mentioned in *Purg.* XX. 61, as taking the sense of shame out of the blood of the Capets.

61. The kingdom of Apulia in Ausonia, or Lower Italy, embracing Bari on the Adriatic, Gaeta in the Terra di Lavoro on the Mediterranean, and Crotona in Calabria; a region bounded on the north by the Tronto emptying into the Adriatic, and the Verde (or Garigliano) emptying into the Mediterranean.

65. The kingdom of Hungary.

67. Sicily, called of old Trinacria, from its three promontories Peloro, Pachino, and Lilibeo.

68. Pachino is the south-eastern promontory of Sicily, and Peloro the north-eastern. Between them lies the Gulf of Catania, receiving with open arms the east wind. Horace speaks of Eurus as "riding the Sicilian seas."

70. Both Pindar and Ovid speak of the giant Typhœus, as struck by Jove's thunderbolt, and lying buried under Ætna. Virgil says it is Enceladus, a brother of Typhœus. Charles Martel here gives the philosophical, not the poetical, cause of the murky atmosphere of the bay.

72. Through him from his grandfather Charles of Anjou, and his father-in-law the Emperor Rudolph.

75. The Sicilian Vespers and revolt of Palermo, in 1282. Milman, *Hist. Latin Christ.*, VI. 155: "It was at a festival on Easter Tuesday that a multitude of the inhabitants of Palermo and the neighbourhood had thronged to a church, about half a mile out of the town, dedicated to the Holy Ghost. The religious service was over, the merriment begun; tables were spread, the amusements of all sorts, games, dances under the trees, were going gaily on; when the harmony was suddenly interrupted and the joyousness chilled by the appearance of a body of French soldiery, under the pretext of keeping the peace. The French mingled familiarly with the people, paid court, not in the most respectful manner, to the women; the young men made sullen remonstrances, and told them to go their way. The Frenchmen began to draw together. 'These rebellious Paterins must have arms, or they would not venture on such insolence.' They began to search some of them for arms. The two parties were already glaring at each other in angry hostility. At that moment the beautiful daughter of Roger Mastrangelo, a maiden of exquisite loveliness and modesty, with her bridegroom, approached the church. A Frenchman, named Drouet, either in wantonness or insult, came up to her, and, under the pretence of searching for arms, thrust his hand into her bosom. The girl fainted in her bridegroom's arms. He uttered in his agony the fatal cry, 'Death to the French!' A youth rushed forward, stabbed Drouet to the heart with his own sword, was himself struck down. The cry, the shriek, ran through the crowd, 'Death to the French!' Many Sicilians fell, but, of two hundred on the spot, not one Frenchman escaped. The cry spread to the city: Mastrangelo took the lead; every house was stormed, every hole and corner searched; their dress, their speech, their persons, their manners, denounced the French. The palace was forced; the Justiciary, being luckily wounded in the face, and rolled in the dust, and so undetected, mounted a horse, and fled with two followers. Two thousand French were slain. They denied them decent burial, heaped them together in a great pit. The horrors of the scene were indescribable; the insurgents broke into the convents, the churches. The friars, especial objects of hatred, were massacred; they slew the French monks, the French priests. Neither old age, nor sex, nor infancy was spared."

76. Robert, Duke of Calabria, third son of Charles II. and younger brother of Charles Martel. He was King of Sicily from 1309 to 1343. He brought with him from Catalonia a band of needy adventurers, whom he put into

high offices of state, "and like so many leeches," says Biagioli, "they filled themselves with the blood of that poor people, not dropping off so long as there remained a drop to suck."

80. Sicily already heavily laden with taxes of all kinds.

82. Born of generous ancestors, he was himself avaricious.

84. Namely, ministers and officials who were not greedy of gain.

87. In God, where all things are reflected as in a mirror. *Rev.* xxi. 6: "I am Alpha and Omega; the beginning and the end." Buti interprets thus: "Because I believe that thou seest my joy in God, even as I see it, I am pleased; and this also is dear to me, that thou seest in God, that I believe it."

97. *Convito,* III. 14: "The first agent, that is, God, sends his influence into some things by means of direct rays, and into others by means of reflected splendour. Hence into the Intelligences the divine light rays out immediately; in others it is reflected from these Intelligences first illuminated. But as mention is here made of light and splendour, in order to a perfect understanding, I will show the difference of these words, according to Avicenna. I say, the custom of the philosophers is to call the Heaven *light,* in reference to its existence in its fountain head; to call it *ray,* in reference to its passing from the fountainhead to the first body, in which it is arrested; to call it *splendour,* in reference to its reflection upon some other part illuminated."

116. If men lived isolated from each other, and not in communities.

120. Aristotle, whom Dante in the *Convito,* III. 5, calls "that glorious philosopher to whom Nature most laid open her secrets;" and in *Inf.* IV. 131, "the master of those who know."

124. The Jurist, the Warrior, the Priest and the Artisan are here typified in Solon, Xerxes, Melchisedec, and Dædalus.

129. Nature, like death, makes no distinction between palace and hovel. Her gentlemen are born alike in each, and so her churls.

130. Esau and Jacob, though twin brothers, differed in character, Esau being warlike and Jacob peaceable. *Genesis* xxv. 27: "And the boys grew: and Esau was a cunning hunter, a man of the field; and Jacob was a plain man, dwelling in tents."

131. Romulus, called Quirinus, because he always carried a spear *(quiris),* was of such obscure birth, that the Romans, to dignify their origin, pretended he was born of Mars.

141. *Convito,* III. 3: "Animate plants have a very manifest affection for certain places, according to their character; and therefore we see certain plants rooting themselves by the waterside, and others upon mountainous places, and others on the slopes and at the foot of the mountains, which, if they are transplanted, either wholly perish, or live a kind of melancholy life, as things separated from what is friendly to them."

145. Another allusion to King Robert of Sicily. Villani, XII. 9, says of him: "This king Robert was the wisest king that had been known among Christians for five hundred years, both in natural ability and in knowledge,

being a very great master in theology, and a consummate philosopher." And
the Postillatore of the Monte Cassino Codex: "This King Robert delighted
in preaching and studying, and would have made a better monk than king."

Canto IX

1. The Heaven of Venus is continued in this canto. The beautiful Clemence
here addressed is the daughter of the Emperor Rudolph, and wife of Charles
Martel. Some commentators say it is his daughter, but for what reason is not
apparent, as the form of address would rather indicate the wife than the
daughter; and moreover, at the date of the poem, 1300, the daughter was
only six or seven years old. So great was the affection of this "beautiful
Clemence" for her husband, that she is said to have fallen dead on hearing
the news of his death.

3. Charles the Lame, dying in 1309, gave the kingdom of Naples and Sicily
to his third son, Robert, Duke of Calabria, thus dispossessing Carlo Roberto
(or Caroberto) son of Charles Martel and Clemence, and rightful heir to the
throne.

22. Unknown to me by name.

25. The region here described is the Marca Trivigiana, lying between
Venice (here indicated by one of its principal wards, the Rialto) and the Alps,
dividing Italy from Germany.

28. The hill on which stands the Castello di Romano, the birthplace of
the tyrant Ezzelino, or Azzolino, whom, for his cruelties, Dante punished in
the river of boiling blood. *Inf.* XII. 110. Before his birth his mother is said
to have dreamed of a lighted torch, as Hecuba did before the birth of Paris,
Althæa before the birth of Meleager, and the mother of St. Dominic before
the birth of

> "The amorous paramour
> Of Christian Faith, the athlete consecrate,
> Kind to his own and cruel to his foes."

32. Cunizza was the sister of Azzolino di Romano. Her story is told by
Rolandino, *Liber Chronicorum,* in Muratori, *Rer. Ital. Script.,* VIII. 173. He
says that she was first married to Richard of St. Boniface; and soon after had
an intrigue with Sordello, as already mentioned, *Purg.* VI. Note 74. Afterwards
she wandered about the world with a soldier of Treviso, named Bonius,
"taking much solace," says the old chronicler, "and spending much money,"—
multa habendo solatia, et maximas faciendo expensas. After the death of Bonius,
she was married to a nobleman of Braganzo; and finally and for a third time
to a gentleman of Verona.

The *Ottimo* alone among the commentators takes up the defence of Cunizza,
and says: "This lady lived lovingly in dress, song, and sport; but consented

not to any impropriety or unlawful act; and she passed her life in enjoyment, as Solomon says in Ecclesiastes,"—alluding probably to the first verse of the second chapter, "I said in my heart, Go to now, I will prove thee with mirth; therefore enjoy pleasure; and, behold, this is also vanity."

33. Of the influences of the planet Venus, quoting Albumasar, as before, Buti says: "Venus is cold and moist, and of phlegmatic temperament, and signifies beauty, liberality, patience, sweetness, dignity of manners, love of dress and ornaments of gold and silver, humility towards friends, pride and adjunction, delectation and delight in singing and use of ornaments, joy and gladness, dancing, song with pipe and lute, bridals, ornaments and precious ointments, cunning in the composition of songs, skill in the game of chess, indolence, drunkenness, lust, adultery, gesticulations, and lasciviousness of courtesans, abundance of perjuries, of lies and all kinds of wantonness, love of children, delight in men, strength of body, weakness of mind, abundance of food and corporal delights, observance of faith and justice, traffic in odoriferous merchandise; and as was said of the Moon, all are not found in one man, but a part in one, and a part in another, according to Divine Providence; and the wise man adheres to the good, and overcomes the others."

34. Since God has pardoned me, I am no longer troubled for my past errors, on account of which I attain no higher glory in Paradise. She had tasted of the waters of Lethe, and all the ills and errors of the past were forgotten. *Purg.* XXXIII. 94:—

> " 'And if thou art not able to remember,'
> Smiling she answered, 'recollect thee now
> How thou this very day hast drunk of Lethe.' "

Hugo of St. Victor, in a passage quoted by Philalethes in the notes to his translation of the *Divina Commedia,* says: "In that city . . . . there will be Free Will, emancipated from all evil, and filled with all good, enjoying without interruption the delight of eternal joys, oblivious of sins, oblivious of punishments; yet not so oblivious of its liberation as to be ungrateful to its liberator. So far, therefore, as regards intellectual knowledge, it will be mindful of its past evils; but wholly unmindful, as regards any feeling of what it has passed through."

37. The spirit of Folco, or Folchetto, of Marseilles, as mentioned later in this canto; the famous Troubadour whose renown was not to perish for five centuries, but is small enough now, save in the literary histories of Millot and the Benedictines of St. Maur.

44. The Marca Trivigiana is again alluded to, lying between the Adige, that empties into the Adriatic south of Venice, and the Tagliamento to the north-east, towards Trieste. This region embraces the cities of Padua and Vicenza in the south, Treviso in the centre, and Feltro in the north.

46. The rout of the Paduans near Vicenza, in those endless quarrels that run through Italian history like the roll of a drum. Three times the Paduan Guelphs were defeated by the Ghibellines,—in 1311, in 1314, and in 1318,

when Can Grande della Scala was chief of the Ghibelline league. The river stained with blood is the Bacchiglione, on which Vicenza stands.

49. In Treviso, where the Sile and Cagnano unite.

50. Riccardo da Camino, who was assassinated while playing at chess. He was a son of the "good Gherardo," and brother of the beautiful Gaja, mentioned *Purg*. XVI. 40. He succeeded his father as lord of Treviso; but carried on his love adventures so openly and with so high a hand, that he was finally assassinated by an outraged husband. The story of his assassination is told in the *Hist. Cartusiorum* in Muratori, XII. 784.

53. A certain bishop of the town of Feltro in the Marca Trivigiana, whose name is doubtful, but who was both lord spiritual and temporal of the town, broke faith with certain gentlemen of Ferrara, guilty of political crimes, who sought refuge and protection in his diocese. They were delivered up, and executed in Ferrara. Afterward the Bishop himself came to a violent end, being beaten to death with bags of sand.

54. Malta was a prison on the shores of Lake Bolsena, where priests were incarcerated for their crimes. There Pope Boniface VIII. imprisoned the Abbot of Monte Cassino for letting the fugitive Celestine V. escape from his convent.

58. This "courteous priest" was a Guelph, and showed his zeal for his party in the persecution of the Ghibellines.

60. The treachery and cruelty of this man will be in conformity to the customs of the country.

61. Above in the Crystalline Heaven, or *Primum Mobile,* is the Order of Angels called Thrones. These are mirrors reflecting the justice and judgments of God.

69. The *Balascio* (in French *rubi balais)* is supposed to take its name from the place in the East where it was found.

Chaucer, *Court of Love,* 78:—

> "No saphire of Inde, no rube riche of price,
> There lacked then, nor emeraude so grene,
> Balais Turkis, ne thing to my devise
> That may the castel maken for to shene."

The mystic virtues of this stone are thus enumerated by Mr. King, *Antique Gems,* p. 419: "The *Balais Ruby* represses vain and lascivious thoughts, appeases quarrels between friends, and gives health of body. Its powder taken in water cures diseases of the eyes, and pains in the liver. If you touch with this gem the four corners of a house, orchard, or vineyard, they will be safe from lightning, storms, and blight."

70. Joy is shown in heaven by greater light, as here on earth by smiles, and as in the infernal regions the grief of souls in torment is by greater darkness.

73. In Him thy sight is; in the original, *tuo veder s' inluia,* thy sight *in-Hims-itself.*

76. There is a similar passage in one of the Troubadours, who, in an Elegy, commends his departed friend to the Virgin as a good singer. "He sang so well, that the nightingales grew silent with admiration, and listened to him. Therefore God took him for his own service. . . . . If the Virgin Mary is fond of genteel young men, I advise her to take him."

77. The Seraphim, clothed with six wings, as seen in the vision of the Prophet Isaiah vi. 2: "Above it stood the seraphims: each one had six wings; with twain he covered his face, and with twain he covered his feet, and with twain he did fly."

81. In the original, *S' io m' intuassi come tu t'immii;* if I in-theed myself as thou in-meest thyself. Dantesque words, like *inluia,* Note 73.

82. The Mediterranean, the greatest of seas, except the ocean, surrounding the earth.

Bryant, *Thanatopsis:*—

> "And poured round all
> Old Ocean's gray and melancholy waste."

85. Extending eastward between Europe and Africa. Dante gives the length of the Mediterranean as ninety degrees. Modern geographers make it less than fifty.

89. Marseilles, about equidistant from the Ebro, in Spain, and the Magra, which divides the Genoese and Tuscan territories. Being a small river, it has but a short journey to make.

92. Buggia is a city in Africa, on nearly the same parallel of longitude as Marseilles.

93. The allusion here is to the siege of Marseilles by a portion of Cæsar's army under Tribonius, and the fleet under Brutus. *Purg.* XVIII. 101:—

> "And Cæsar, that he might subdue Ilerda,
>   Thrust at Marseilles, and then ran into Spain."

Lucan, who describes the siege and sea-fight in the third book of his *Pharsalia,* says:—

> "Meanwhile, impatient of the lingering war,
>   The chieftain to Iberia bends afar,
>   And gives the leaguer to Tribonius' care."

94. Folco, or Folchetto, of Marseilles (Folquet de Marseilles) was a noted Troubadour, who flourished at the end of the twelfth century. He was the son of a rich merchant of Marseilles, and after his father's death, giving up business for pleasure and poetry, became a frequenter of courts and favourite of lords and princes. Among his patrons are mentioned King Richard of England, King Alfonso of Aragon, Count Raymond of Toulouse, and the Sire Barral of Marseilles. The old Provençal chronicler in Raynouard, V.

150, says: "He was a good Troubadour, and very attractive in person. He paid court to the wife of his lord, Sire Barral, and besought her love, and made songs about her. But neither for prayers nor songs could he find favour with her so as to procure any mark of love, of which he was always complaining in his songs."

Nevertheless this Lady Alazais listened with pleasure to his songs and praises; and was finally moved to jealousy, if not to love. The Troubadour was at the same time paying his homage to the two sisters of the Sire Barral, Lady Laura and Lady Mabel, both beautiful and *de gran valor,* and being accused thereof, fell into disfavour and banishment, the Lady Alazais wishing to hear no more his prayers nor his songs. In his despair he took refuge at the court of William, Lord of Montpellier, whose wife, daughter of the Emperor Manuel, "comforted him a little, and besought him not to be downcast and despairing, but for love of her to sing and make songs."

And now a great change came over him. The old chronicler goes on to say: "And it came to pass that the Lady Alazais died; and the Sire Barral, her husband and his lord, died; and died the good King Richard, and the good Count Raymond of Toulouse, and King Alfonso of Aragon: whereat, in grief for his lady and for the princes who were dead, he abandoned the world, and retired to a Cistercian convent, with his wife and two sons. And he became Abbot of a rich abbey in Provence, called Torondet, and afterwards Bishop of Toulouse, and there he died."

It was in 1200 that he became a Cistercian, and he died in 1233. It would be pleasant to know that he atoned for his youthful follies by an old age of virtues. But unfortunately for his fame, the old nightingale became a bird of prey. He was deeply implicated in the persecutions of the Albigenses, and the blood of those "slaughtered saints" makes a ghastly rubric in his breviary.

97. Dido, queen of Carthage. The *Ottimo* says: "He seems to mean, that Folco loved indifferently married women, virgins, and widows, gentle and simple."

100. Phillis of Thrace, called Rodopeia from Mount Rodope near which she lived, was deserted by her Athenian lover Demophoön, of whom Chaucer, *Legende of Good Women,* 2442, gives this portrait:—

> "Men knewe him well and didden hym honour,
> For at Athenis duke and lorde was he,
> As Theseus his father hath ibe,
> That in his tyme was of grete renown,
> No man so grete in all his regioun,
> And like his father of face and of stature;
> And false of love, it came hym of nature;
> As doeth the foxe, Renarde the foxes sonne,
> Of kinde, he coulde his olde father wonne,

> Withouten lore; as can a drake swimme,
> When it is caught and caried to the brimme."

101. Hercules was so subdued by love for Iole, that he sat among her maidens spinning with a distaff.

103. See Note 34 of this canto.

106. The ways of Providence,

> "From seeming evil still educing good."

116. Rahab, who concealed the spies of Joshua among the flax-stalks on the roof of her house. *Joshua,* ii. 6.

118. Milton, *Par. Lost,* IV. 776:—

> "Now had night measured with her shadowy cone
> Half-way up hill this vast sublunar vault."

120. The first soul redeemed when Christ descended into Limbo. "The first shall be last, and the last first."

123. The Crucifixion. If any one is disposed to criticise the play upon words in this beautiful passage, let him remember the *Tu es Petrus et super hanc petram edificabo ecclesiam meam.*

124. *Hebrews* xi. 31: "By faith the harlot Rahab perished not with them that believed not, when she had received the spies with peace."

125. Forgetful that it was in the hands of the Saracens.

127. The heathen Gods were looked upon by the Christians as demons. Hence Florence was the city of Satan to Dante in his dark hours, when he thought of Mars; but in his better moments, when he remembered John the Baptist, it was "the fairest and most renowned daughter of Rome."

130. The Lily on the golden florin of Florence.

133. To gain the golden florin the study of the Gospels and the Fathers was abandoned, and the Decretals, or books of Ecclesiastical Law, so diligently conned, that their margins were worn and soiled with thumb-marks. The first five books of the Decretals were compiled by Gregory IX., and the sixth by Boniface VIII.

138. A prophecy of the death of Boniface VIII. in 1303, and the removal of the Holy See to Avignon in 1305.

Canto X

1. The Heaven of the Sun, "a good planet and imperial," says Brunetto Latini. Dante makes it the symbol of Arithmetic. *Convito,* II. 14: "The Heaven of the Sun may be compared to Arithmetic on account of two properties; the first is, that with its light all the other stars are informed; the second is, that the eye cannot behold it. And these two properties are in Arithmetic, for with its light all the sciences are illuminated, since their subjects are all considered under some number, and in the consideration thereof we always proceed with numbers; as in natural science the subject is the movable body, which movable body has in it ratio of continuity, and this has in it ratio of infinite number. And the chief consideration of natural science is to consider the principles of natural things, which are three, namely, matter, species, and form; in which this number is visible, not only in all together, but, if we consider well, in each one separately. Therefore Pythagoras, according to Aristotle in the first book of his Physics, gives the odd and even as the principles of natural things, considering all things to be number. The other property of the Sun is also seen in number, to which Arithmetic belongs, for the eye of the intellect cannot behold it, for number considered in itself is infinite; and this we cannot comprehend."

In this Heaven of the Sun are seen the spirits of theologians and Fathers of the Church; and its influences, according to Albumasar, cited by Buti, are as follows: "The Sun signifies the vital soul, light and splendour, reason and intellect, science and the measure of life; it signifies kings, princes and leaders, nobles and magnates and congregations of men, strength and victory, voluptuousness, beauty and grandeur, subtleness of mind, pride and praise, good desire of kingdom and of subjects, and great love of gold, and affluence of speech, and delight in neatness and beauty. It signifies faith and the worship of God, judges and wise men, fathers and brothers and mediators; it joins itself to men and mingles among them, it gives what is asked for, and is strong in vengeance, that is to say, it punishes rebels and malefactors."

2. Adam of St. Victor, *Hymn to the Holy Ghost:*—

> "Veni, Creator Spiritus,
> Spiritus recreator,
> Tu dans, tu datus cœlitus,
> Tu donum, tu donator;
> Tu lex, tu digitus,
> Alens et alitus,
> Spirans et spiritus,
> Spiratus et spirator."

9. Where the Zodiac crosses the Equator, and the motion of the planets, which is parallel to the former, comes into apparent collision with that of the fixed stars, which is parallel to the latter.

14. The Zodiac, which cuts the Equator obliquely.

16. Milton, *Par. Lost,* X. 668:—

> "Some say, he bid his angels turn askance
>   The poles of earth, twice ten degrees and more,
>   From the sun's axle; they with labour pushed
>   Oblique the centric globe: some say, the sun
>   Was bid turn reins from the equinoctial road
>   Like-distant breadth to Taurus with the seven
>   Atlantic Sisters, and the Spartan twins,
>   Up to the tropic Crab: thence down amain
>   By Leo, and the Virgin, and the Scales,
>   As deep as Capricorn; to bring in change
>   Of seasons to each clime: else had the spring
>   Perpetual smiled on earth with vernant flowers,
>   Equal in days and nights, except to those
>   Beyond the polar circles; to them day
>   Had unbenighted shone; while the low sun,
>   To recompense his distance, in their sight
>   Had rounded still the horizon, and not known
>   Or east or west; which had forbid the snow
>   From cold Estotiland, and south as far
>   Beneath Magellan."

28. The Sun.

31. The Sun in Aries, as indicated in line 9; that being the sign in which the Sun is at the vernal equinox.

32. Such is the apparent motion of the Sun round the earth, as he rises earlier and earlier in Spring.

48. No eye has ever seen any light greater than that of the Sun, nor can we conceive of any greater.

51. How the Son is begotten of the Father, and how from these two is breathed forth the Holy Ghost. The Heaven of the Sun being the Fourth Heaven, the spirits seen in it are called the fourth family of the Father; and to these theologians is revealed the mystery of the Trinity.

67. The moon with a halo about her.

82. The spirit of Thomas Aquinas.

87. The stairway of Jacob's dream, with its angels ascending and descending.

89. Whoever should refuse to gratify thy desire for knowledge, would no more follow his natural inclination than water which did not flow downward.

98. Albertus Magnus, at whose twenty-one ponderous folios one gazes with awe and amazement, was born of a noble Swabian family at the beginning of the thirteenth century. In his youth he studied at Paris and at Padua; became a Dominican monk, and, retiring to a convent in Cologne, taught

in the schools of that city. He became Provincial of his Order in Germany; and was afterward made Grand-Master of the Palace at Rome, and then Bishop of Ratisbon. Resigning his bishopric in 1262, he returned to his convent in Cologne, where he died in 1280, leaving behind him great fame for his learning and his labour.

Milman, *Hist. Latin Christ.*, VIII. 259, says of him: "Albert the Great at once awed by his immense erudition and appalled his age. His name, the Universal Doctor, was the homage to his all-embracing knowledge. He quotes, as equally familiar, Latin, Greek, Arabic, Jewish philosophers. He was the first Schoolman who lectured on Aristotle himself, on Aristotle from Græco-Latin or Arabo-Latin copies. The whole range of the Stagirite's physical and metaphysical philosophy was within the scope of Albert's teaching. In later days he was called the Ape of Aristotle; he had dared to introduce Aristotle into the Sanctuary itself. One of his Treatises is a refutation of the Arabian Averrhoes. Nor is it Aristotle and Averrhoes alone that come within the pale of Albert's erudition; the commentators and glossators of Aristotle, the whole circle of the Arabians, are quoted; their opinions, their reasonings, even their words, with the utmost familiarity. But with Albert, Theology was still the master-science. The Bishop of Ratisbon was of unimpeached orthodoxy; the vulgar only, in his wonderful knowledge of the secrets of Nature, in his studies of Natural History, could not but see something of the magician. Albert had the ambition of reconciling Plato and Aristotle, and of reconciling this harmonized Aristotelian and Platonic philosophy with Christian Divinity. He thus, in some degree, misrepresented or misconceived both the Greeks; he hardened Plato into Aristotelism, expanded Aristotelism into Platonism; and his Christianity, though Albert was a devout man, while it constantly subordinates, in strong and fervent language, knowledge to faith and love, became less a religion than a philosophy."

99. Thomas Aquinas, the Angelic Doctor of the Schools. Milman, *Hist. Latin Christ.*, VIII. 265, gives the following sketch of him:—

"Of all the schoolmen Thomas Aquinas has left the greatest name. He was a son of the Count of Aquino, a rich fief in the kingdom of Naples. His mother, Theodora, was of the line of the old Norman kings; his brothers, Reginald and Landolph, held high rank in the Imperial armies. His family was connected by marriage with the Hohenstaufens; they had Swabian blood in their veins, and so the great schoolman was of the race of Frederick II. Monasticism seized on Thomas in his early youth; he became an inmate of Monte Casino; at sixteen years of age he caught the more fiery and vigorous enthusiasm of the Dominicans. By them he was sent—no unwilling proselyte and pupil—to France. He was seized by his worldly brothers, and sent back to Naples; he was imprisoned in one of the family castles, but resisted even the fond entreaties of his mother and his sisters. He persisted in his pious disobedience, his holy hardness of heart; he was released after two years' imprisonment—it might seem strange—at the command of the Emperor Frederick II. The godless Emperor, as he was called, gave Thomas to the

Church. Aquinas took the irrevocable vow of a Friar Preacher. He became a scholar of Albert the Great at Cologne and at Paris. He was dark, silent, unapproachable even by his brethren, perpetually wrapt in profound meditation. He was called, in mockery, the great dumb ox of Sicily. Albert questioned the mute disciple on the most deep and knotty points of theology; he found, as he confessed, his equal, his superior. 'That dumb ox will make the world resound with his doctrines.' With Albert the faithful disciple returned to Cologne. Again he went back to Paris, received his academic degrees, and taught with universal wonder. Under Alexander IV. he stood up in Rome in defence of his Order against the eloquent William de St. Amour; he repudiated for his Order, and condemned by his authority, the prophesies of the Abbot Joachim. He taught at Cologne with Albert the Great; also at Paris, at Rome, at Orvieto, at Viterbo, at Perugia. Where he taught, the world listened in respectful silence. He was acknowledged by two Popes, Urban IV. and Clement IV., as the first theologian of the age. He refused the Archbishopric of Naples. He was expected at the Council of Lyons, as the authority before whom all Christendom might be expected to bow down. He died ere he had passed the borders of Naples, at the Abbey of Rossa Nuova, near Terracina, at the age of forty-eight. Dark tales were told of his death; only the wickedness of man could deprive the world so early of such a wonder. The University of Paris claimed, but in vain, the treasure of his mortal remains. He was canonized by John XXII.

"Thomas Aquinas is throughout, above all, the Theologian. God and the soul of man are the only objects truly worthy of his philosophic investigation. This is the function of the Angelic Doctor, the mission of the Angel of the Schools. In his works, or rather in his one great work, is the final result of all which has been decided by Pope or Council, taught by the Fathers, accepted by tradition, argued in the schools, inculcated in the confessional. The Sum of Theology is the authentic, authoritative, acknowledged code of Latin Christianity. We cannot but contrast this vast work with the original Gospel: to this bulk has grown the New Testament, or rather the doctrinal and moral part of the New Testament. But Aquinas is an intellectual theologian: he approaches more nearly than most philosophers, certainly than most divines, to pure embodied intellect. He is perfectly passionless; he has no polemic indignation, nothing of the Churchman's jealousy and suspicion; he has no fear of the result of any investigation; he hates nothing, hardly heresy; loves nothing, unless perhaps naked, abstract truth. In his serene confidence that all must end in good, he moves the most startling and even perilous questions, as if they were the most indifferent, the very Being of God. God must be revealed by syllogistic process. Himself inwardly conscious of the absolute harmony of his own intellectual and moral being, he places sin not so much in the will as in the understanding. The perfection of man is the perfection of his intelligence. He examines with the same perfect self-command, it might almost be said apathy, the converse as well as the proof of the most vital religious truths. He is nearly as consummate a sceptic, almost atheist, as he is a divine and theologian. Secure, as it should seem, in impenetrable armour, he has not only no apprehension, but seems not to suppose the possibility of danger; he has nothing of the boastfulness of self-confidence, but, in calm assurance of victory, gives every advantage to his adversary. On both sides of every question he casts the argument into one of his clear, distinct syllogisms, and calmly places himself as Arbiter, and passes judgment in one or a series of still more unanswerable syllogisms. He has assigned its unassailable province to Church authority, to tradition or the Fathers, faith and works; but beyond, within the proper sphere of philosophy, he asserts full freedom. There is no Father, even St. Augustine, who may not be examined by the fearless intellect."

104. Gratian was a Franciscan friar, and teacher in the school of the convent of St. Felix in Bologna. He wrote the *Decretum Gratiani,* or "Concord of the Discordant Canons," in which he brought into agreement the laws of the courts secular and ecclesiastical.

107. Peter Lombard, the "Master of Sentences," so called from his *Libri Sententiarum*. In the dedication of this work to the Church he says that he wishes "to contribute, like the poor widow, his mite to the treasury of the Lord." The following account of him and his doctrines is from Milman, *Hist. Latin Christ.,* VIII. 238: "Peter the Lombard was born near Novara, the native place of Lanfranc and of Anselm. He was Bishop of Paris in 1159. His famous Book of the Sentences was intended to be, and became to a great extent, the Manual of the Schools. Peter knew not, or disdainfully threw aside, the philosophical cultivation of his day. He adhered rigidly to all which passed for Scripture, and was the authorized interpretation of the Scripture, to all which had become the creed in the traditions, and law in the decretals, of the Church. He seems to have no apprehension of doubt in his stern dogmatism; he will not recognize any of the difficulties suggested by philosophy; he cannot, or will not, perceive the weak points of his own system. He has the great merit that, opposed as he was to the prevailing Platonism, throughout the Sentences the ethical principle predominates; his excellence is perspicuity, simplicity, definiteness of moral purpose. His distinctions are endless, subtile, idle; but he wrote from conflicting authorities to reconcile writers at war with each other, at war with themselves. Their quarrels had been wrought to intentional or unintentional antagonism in the 'Sic et Non' of Abelard. That philosopher, whether Pyrrhonist or more than Pyrrhonist, had left them all in the confusion of strife; he had set Fathers against Fathers, each Father against himself, the Church against the Church, tradition against tradition, law against law. The Lombard announced himself and was accepted as the mediator, the final arbiter in this endless litigation; he would sternly fix the positive, proscribe the negative or sceptical view in all these questions. The litigation might still go on, but within the limits which he had rigidly established; he had determined those ultimate results against which there was no appeal. The mode of proof might be interminably contested in the schools; the conclusion was already irrefragably fixed. On the sacramental system Peter

the Lombard is loftily, severely hierarchical. Yet he is moderate on the power of the keys; he holds only a declaratory power of binding and loosing,—of showing how the souls of men were to be bound and loosed."

Peter Lombard was born at the beginning of the twelfth century, when the Novarese territory, his birthplace, was a part of Lombardy, and hence his name. He studied at the University of Paris, under Abelard; was afterwards made Professor of Theology in the University, and then Bishop of Paris. He died in 1164.

109. Solomon, whose Song of Songs breathes such impassioned love.

111. To know if he were saved or not, a grave question having been raised upon that point by theologians.

115. Dionysius the Areopagite, who was converted by St. Paul. *Acts* xvii. 34: "Howbeit, certain men clave unto him, and believed; among the which was Dionysius the Areopagite." A book attributed to him, on the "Celestial Hierarchy," was translated into Latin by Johannes Erigena, and became in the Middle Ages the text-book of angelic lore. "The author of those extraordinary treatises," says Milman, *Hist. Latin Christ.*, VIII. 189, "which, from their obscure and doubtful parentage, now perhaps hardly maintain their fame for imaginative richness, for the occasional beauty of their language, and their deep piety,—those treatises which, widely popular in the West, almost created the angel-worship of the popular creed, and were also the parents of Mystic Theology and of the higher Scholasticism,—this Poet-Theologian was a Greek. The writings which bear the venerable name of Dionysius the Areopagite, the proselyte of St. Paul, first appear under a suspicious and suspected form, as authorities cited by the heterodox Severians in a conference at Constantinople. The orthodox stood aghast: how was it that writings of the holy convert of St. Paul had never been heard of before? that Cyril of Alexandria, that Athanasius himself, were ignorant of their existence? But these writings were in themselves of too great power, too captivating, too congenial to the monastic mind, not to find bold defenders. Bearing this venerable name in their front, and leaving behind them, in the East, if at first a doubtful, a growing faith in their authenticity, they appeared in the West as a precious gift from the Byzantine Emperor to the Emperor Louis the Pious. France in that age was not likely to throw cold and jealous doubts on writings which bore the hallowed name of that great Saint, whom she had already boasted to have left his primal Bishopric of Athens to convert her forefathers, whom Paris already held to be her tutelar patron, the rich and powerful Abbey of St. Denys to be her founder. There was living in the West, by happy coincidence, the one man who at that period, by his knowledge of Greek, by the congenial speculativeness of his mind, by the vigour and richness of his imagination, was qualified to translate into Latin the mysterious doctrines of the Areopagite, both as to the angelic world and the subtile theology. John Erigena hastened to make known in the West the 'Celestial Hierarchy,' the treatise 'On the Name of God,' and the brief chapters on the 'Mystic Philosophy.'"

119. Paul Orosius. He was a Spanish presbyter, born at Tarragona near the close of the fourth century. In his youth he visited St. Augustine in Africa, who in one of his books describes him thus: "There came to me a young monk, in the catholic peace our brother, in age our son, in honour our fellow-presbyter, Orosius, alert in intellect, ready of speech, eager in study, desiring to be a useful vessel in the house of the Lord for the refutation of false and pernicious doctrines, which have slain the souls of the Spaniards much more unhappily than the sword of the barbarians their bodies."

On leaving St. Augustine, he went to Palestine to complete his studies under St. Jerome at Bethlehem, and while there arraigned Palagius for heresy before the Bishop of Jerusalem. The work by which he is chiefly known is his "Seven Books of Histories;" a world-chronicle from the creation to his own time. Of this work St. Augustine availed himself in writing his "City of God;" and it had also the honour of being translated into Anglo-Saxon by King Alfred. Dante calls Orosius "the advocate of the Christian centuries," because this work was written to refute the misbelievers who asserted that Christianity had done more harm to the world than good.

125. Severinus Boethius, the Roman Senator and philosopher in the days of Theodoric the Goth, born in 475, and put to death in 524. His portrait is thus drawn by Gibbon, *Decline and Fall,* Ch. XXXIX.: "The Senator Boethius is the last of the Romans whom Cato or Tully could have acknowl-edged for their countryman. As a wealthy orphan, he inherited the patrimony and honours of the Anician family, a name ambitiously assumed by the kings and emperors of the age; and the appellation of Manlius asserted his genuine or fabulous descent from a race of consuls and dictators, who had repulsed the Gauls from the Capitol, and sacrificed their sons to the discipline of the Republic. In the youth of Boethius, the studies of Rome were not totally abandoned; a Virgil is now extant, corrected by the hand of a consul; and the professors of grammar, rhetoric, and jurisprudence were maintained in their privileges and pensions by the liberality of the Goths. But the erudition of the Latin language was insufficient to satiate his ardent curiosity; and Boethius is said to have employed eighteen laborious years in the schools of Athens, which were supported by the zeal, the learning, and the diligence of Proclus and his disciples. The reason and piety of their Roman pupil were fortunately saved from the contagion of mystery and magic, which polluted the groves of the Academy; but he imbibed the spirit, and imitated the method of his dead and living masters, who attempted to reconcile the strong and subtle sense of Aristotle with the devout contemplation and sublime fancy of Plato. After his return to Rome, and his marriage with the daugh-ter of his friend, the patrician Symmachus, Boethius still continued in a palace of ivory and marble to prosecute the same studies. The Church was edified by his profound defence of the orthodox creed against the Arian, the Eutychian, and the Nestorian heresies; and the Catholic unity was explained or exposed in a formal treatise by the *indifference* of three distinct, though con-substantial persons. For the benefit of his Latin readers, his genius

submitted to teach the first elements of the arts and sciences of Greece. The geometry of Euclid, the music of Pythagoras, the arithmetic of Nicomachus, the mechanics of Archimedes, the astronomy of Ptolemy, the theology of Plato, and the logic of Aristotle, with the commentary of Porphyry, were translated and illustrated by the indefatigable pen of the Roman Senator. And he alone was esteemed capable of describing the wonders of art, a sun-dial, a water-clock, or a sphere which represented the motions of the planets. From these abstruse speculations Boethius stooped, or, to speak more truly, he rose to the social duties of public and private life: the indigent were relieved by his liberality; and his eloquence, which flattery might compare to the voice of Demosthenes or Cicero, was uniformly exerted in the cause of innocence and humanity. Such conspicuous merit was felt and rewarded by a discerning prince; the dignity of Boethius was adorned with the titles of Consul and Patrician, and his talents were usefully employed in the important station of Master of the Offices."

Being suspected of some participation in a plot against Theodoric, he was confined in the tower of Pavia, where he wrote the work which has immortalized his name. Of this Gibbon speaks as follows: "While Boethius, oppressed with fetters, expected each moment the sentence or the stroke of death, he composed in the tower of Pavia the *Consolation of Philosophy;* a golden volume not unworthy of the leisure of Plato or Tully, but which claims incomparable merit from the barbarism of the times and the situation of the author. The celestial guide whom he had so long invoked at Rome and Athens now condescended to illumine his dungeon, to revive his courage, and to pour into his wounds her salutary balm. She taught him to compare his long prosperity and his recent distress, and to conceive new hopes from the inconstancy of fortune. Reason had informed him of the precarious condition of her gifts; experience had satisfied him of their real value; he had enjoyed them without guilt; he might resign them without a sigh, and calmly disdain the impotent malice of his enemies, who had left him happiness, since they had left him virtue. From the earth Boethius ascended to heaven in search of the SUPREME GOOD; explored the metaphysical labyrinth of chance and destiny, of prescience and free-will, of time and eternity; and generously attempted to reconcile the perfect attributes of the Deity with the apparent disorders of his moral and physical government. Such topics of consolation, so obvious, so vague, or so abstruse, are ineffectual to subdue the feelings of human nature. Yet the sense of misfortune may be diverted by the labour of thought; and the sage who could artfully combine, in the same work, the various riches of philosophy, poetry, and eloquence, must already have possessed the intrepid calmness which he affected to seek. Suspense, the worst of evils, was at length determined by the ministers of death, who executed, and perhaps exceeded, the inhuman mandate of Theodoric. A strong cord was fastened round the head of Boethius, and forcibly tightened, till his eyes almost started from their sockets; and some mercy may be discovered in the milder torture of beating him with clubs till he expired. But his genius survived to diffuse a ray of knowledge over the darkest ages of the Latin world; the writings of the philosopher were translated by the most glorious of the English kings, and the third Emperor of the name of Otho removed to a more honourable tomb the bones of a Catholic saint, who, from his Arian persecutors, had acquired the honours of martyrdom, and the fame of miracles."

128. Boethius was buried in the church of San Pietro di Cieldauro in Pavia.

131. St. Isidore, a learned prelate of Spain, was born in Cartagena, date unknown. In 600 he became Bishop of Seville, and died 636. He was indefatigable in converting the Visigoths from Arianism, wrote many theological and scientific works, and finished the Mosarabic missal and breviary, begun by his brother and predecessor, St. Leander.

"The Venerable Bede," or Beda, an Anglo-Saxon monk, was born at Wearmouth in 672, and in 735 died and was buried in the monastery of Yarrow, where he had been educated and had passed his life. His bones were afterward removed to the Cathedral of Durham, and placed in the same coffin with those of St. Cuthbert. He was the author of more than forty volumes; among which his *Ecclesiastical History of England* is the most known and valued, and, like the *Histories* of Orosius, had the honour of being translated by King Alfred from the Latin into Anglo-Saxon. On his death-bed he dictated the close of his translation of the Gospel of John. "Dearest master," said his scribe, "one chapter still remains, but it is difficult for thee to speak." The dying monk replied, "Take thy pen and write quickly." Later the scribe said, "Only one sentence remains;" and the monk said again, "Write quickly." And writing, the scribe said, "It is done." "Thou hast said rightly," answered Bede, "it is done;" and died, repeating the *Gloria Patri,* closing the service of his long life with the closing words of the service of the Church. The following legend of him is from Wright's *Biog. Britan. Lit.,* I. 269: "The reputation of Bede increased daily, and we find him spoken of by the title of Saint very soon after his death. Boniface in his epistles describes him as the lamp of the Church. Towards the ninth century he received the appellation of The Venerable, which has ever since been attached to his name. As a specimen of the fables by which his biography was gradually obscured, we may cite the legends invented to account for the origin of this latter title. According to one, the Anglo-Saxon scholar was on a visit to Rome, and there saw a gate of iron, on which were inscribed the letters P.P.P.S.S.S.R.R.R.F.F.F., which no one was able to interpret. Whilst Bede was attentively considering the inscription, a Roman who was passing by said to him rudely, 'What seest thou there, English ox?' to which Bede replied, 'I see your confusion;' and he immediately explained the characters thus: *Pater Patriæ Perditus, Sapientia Secum Sublata, Ruet Regnum Romæ, Ferro Flamma Fame.* The Romans were astonished at the acuteness of their English visitor, and decreed that the title of Venerable should be thenceforth given to him. According to another story, Bede, having become blind in his old age, was walking abroad with one of his disciples for a guide, when they arrived at an open place where there was a large heap of stones;

and Bede's companion persuaded his master to preach to the people who, as he pretended, were assembled there and waiting in great silence and expectation. Bede delivered a most eloquent and moving discourse, and when he had uttered the concluding phrase, *Per omnia sæcula sæculorum,* to the great admiration of his disciple, the stones, we are told, cried out aloud, 'Amen, Venerabilis Beda!' There is also a third legend on this subject which informs us that, soon after Bede's death, one of his disciples was appointed to compose an epitaph in Latin Leonines, and carve it on his monument, and he began thus,

> 'Hac sunt in fossa Bedæ   ossa,'

intending to introduce the word *sancti* or *presbyteri;* but as neither of these words would suit the metre, whilst he was puzzling himself to find one more convenient, he fell asleep. On awaking he prepared to resume his work, when to his great astonishment he found that the line had already been completed on the stone (by an angel, as he supposed), and that it stood thus:

> 'Hac sunt in fossa Bedæ Venerabilis ossa.' "

Richard of St. Victor was a monk in the monastery of that name near Paris, "and wrote a book on the Trinity," says the *Ottimo,* "and many other beautiful and sublime works"; praise which seems justified by Dante's words, if not suggested by them. Milman, *Hist. Latin Christ.,* VIII. 241, says of him and his brother Hugo: "Richard de St. Victor was at once more logical and more devout, raising higher at once the unassisted power of man, yet with even more supernatural interference,—less ecclesiastical, more religious. Thus the silent, solemn cloister was, as it were, constantly balancing the noisy and pugnacious school. The system of the St. Victors is the contemplative philosophy of deep-thinking minds in their profound seclusion, not of intellectual gladiators: it is that of men following out the train of their own thoughts, not perpetually crossed by the objections of subtle rival disputants. Its end is not victory, but the inward satisfaction of the soul. It is not so much conscious of ecclesiastical restraint, it is rather self-restrained by its inborn reverence; it has no doubt, therefore no fear; it is bold from the inward consciousness of its orthodoxy."

135. As to many other life-weary men, like those mentioned in *Purg.* XVI. 122:—

> "And late they deem it
> That God restore them to the better life."

136. "This is Master Sigier," says the *Ottimo,* "who wrote and lectured on Logic in Paris." Very little more is known of him than this, and that he was supposed to hold some odious, if not heretical opinions. Even his name

has perished out of literary history, and survives only in the verse of Dante and the notes of his commentators.

137. The Rue du Fouarre, or Street of Straw, originally called Rue de l'Ecole, is famous among the old streets of Paris, as having been the cradle of the University. It was in early times a hay and straw market, and hence derives its name. In the old poem of *Les Rues de Paris,* Barbazan, II. 247, are these lines:—

> "Enprès est rue de l'École,
> Là demeure Dame Nicole;
> En celle rue, ce me samble,
> Vent-on et fain et fuerre ensamble."

Others derive the name from the fact, that the students covered the benches of their lecture-rooms with straw, or used it instead of benches; which they would not have done if a straw-market had not been near at hand.

Dante, moved perhaps by some pleasant memory of the past, pays the old scholastic street the tribute of a verse. The elegant Petrarca mentions it frequently in his Latin writings, and always with a sneer. He remembers only "the disputatious city of Paris, and the noisy Street of Straw"; or "the plaudits of the Petit Pont and the Rue du Fouarre, the most famous places on earth."

Rabelais speaks of it as the place where Pantagruel first held disputes with the learned doctors, "having posted up his nine thousand seven hundred and sixty-four theses in all the carrefours of the city"; and Ruskin, *Mod. Painters,* III. 85, justifies the mention of it in Paradise as follows:—

"A common idealist would have been rather alarmed at the thought of introducing the name of a street in Paris—Straw Street (Rue du Fouarre)—into the midst of a description of the highest heavens. . . . . What did it matter to Dante, up in heaven there, whether the mob below thought him vulgar or not! Sigier *had* read in Straw Street; that was the fact, and he had to say so, and there an end.

"There is, indeed, perhaps, no greater sign of innate and *real* vulgarity of mind or defective education, than the want of power to understand the universality of the ideal truth; the absence of sympathy with the colossal grasp of those intellects, which have in them so much of divine, that nothing is small to them, and nothing large; but with equal and unoffended vision they take in the sum of the world, Straw Street and the seventh heavens, in the same instant. A certain portion of this divine spirit is visible even in the lower examples of all the true men; it is, indeed, perhaps the clearest test of their belonging to the true and great group, that they are continually touching what to the multitude appear vulgarities. The higher a man stands, the more the word 'vulgar' becomes unintelligible to him."

The following sketch from the notebook of a recent traveller shows the Street of Straw in its present condition: "I went yesterday in search of the

Rue du Fouarre. I had been hearing William Guizot's lecture on Montaigne, and from the Collége de France went down the Rue St. Jacques, passing at the back of the old church of St. Severin, whose gargoyles still stretch out their long necks over the street. Turning into the Rue Galande, a few steps brought me to the Fouarre. It is a short and narrow street, with a scanty footway on one side, on the other only a gutter. The opening at the farther end is filled by a picturesque vista of the transept gable and great rose-window of Notre Dame, over the river, with the slender central spire. Some of the houses on either side of the street were evidently of a comparatively modern date; but others were of the oldest, and the sculptured stone wreaths over the doorways, and the remains of artistic iron-work in the balconies, showed them to have been once of some consideration. Some dirty children were playing at the door of a shop where fagots and *charbon de terre de Paris* were sold. A coachman in glazed hat sat asleep on his box before the shop of a *blanchisseuse de fin*. A woman in a bookbinder's window was folding the sheets of a French grammar. In an angle of the houses under the high wall of the hospital garden was a cobbler's stall. A stout, red-faced woman, standing before it, seeing me gazing round, asked if Monsieur was seeking anything in special. I said I was only looking at the old street; it must be very old. 'Yes, one of the oldest in Paris.' 'And why is it called "du Fouarre"?' 'O, that is the old French for *foin;* and hay used to be sold here. Then, there were famous schools here in the old days; Abelard used to lecture here.' I was delighted to find the traditions of the place still surviving, though I cannot say whether she was right about Abelard, whose name may have become merely typical; it is not improbable, however, that he may have made and annihilated many a man of straw, after the fashion of the doctors of dialectics, in the Fouarre. His house was not far off on the Quai Napoléon in the Cité; and that of the Canon Fulbert on the corner of the Rue Basse des Ursins. Passing through to the Pont au Double, I stopped to look at the books on the parapet, and found a voluminous Dictionnaire Historique, but, oddly enough, it contained neither Sigier's name, nor Abelard's. I asked a ruddy-cheeked boy on a doorstep if he went to school. He said he worked in the day-time, and went to an evening school in the Rue du Fouarre, No. 5. That primary night school seems to be the last feeble descendant of the ancient learning. As to straw, I saw none except a kind of rude straw matting placed round the corner of a wine-shop at the entrance of the street; a sign that oysters are sold within, they being brought to Paris in this kind of matting."

138. Buti interprets thus: "Lecturing on the Elenchi of Aristotle, to prove some truths he formed certain syllogisms so well and artfully, as to excite envy." Others interpret the word *invidiosi* in the Latin sense of odious,—truths that were odious to somebody; which interpretation is supported by the fact that Sigier was summoned before the primate of the Dominicans on suspicion of heresy, but not convicted.

147. Milton, *At a Solemn Musick:*—

"Blest pair of Sirens, pledges of Heaven's joy;
Sphere-born harmonious sisters, Voice and Verse;
Wed your divine sounds, and mixed power employ
Dead things with inbreathed sense able to pierce;
And to our high-raised fantasy present
That undisturbed song of pure concent,
Aye sung before the sapphire-coloured throne
To Him that sits thereon,
With saintly shout, and solemn jubilee;
Where the bright Seraphim, in burning row,
Their loud uplifted angel trumpets blow;
And the cherubic host, in thousand quires,
Touch their immortal harps of golden wires,
With those just spirits that wear victorious palms,
Hymns devout and holy psalms
Singing everlastingly:
That we on earth, with undiscording voice,
May rightly answer that melodious noise;
As once we did, till disproportioned sin
Jarred against Nature's chime, and with harsh din
Broke the fair music that all creatures made
To their great Lord, whose love their motion swayed
In perfect diapason, whilst they stood
In first obedience, and their state of good.
O, may we soon again renew that song,
And keep in tune with Heaven, till God erelong
To his celestial concert us unite,
To live with him, and sing in endless morn of light!"

Canto XI

1. The Heaven of the Sun continued. The praise of St. Francis by Thomas Aquinas, a Dominican.

4. Lucretius, *Nature of Things,* Book II. 1, Good's Tr.:—

"How sweet to stand, when tempests tear the main,
    On the firm cliff, and mark the seaman's toil!
    Not that another's danger soothes the soul,
    But from such toil how sweet to feel secure!
    How sweet, at distance from the strife, to view
    Contending hosts, and hear the clash of war!
    But sweeter far on Wisdom's heights serene,
    Upheld by Truth, to fix our firm abode;

To watch the giddy crowd that, deep below,
For ever wander in pursuit of bliss;
To mark the strife for honours and renown,
For wit and wealth, insatiate, ceaseless urged
Day after day, with labour unrestrained."

16. Thomas Aquinas.
20. The spirits see the thoughts of men in God, as in Canto VIII. 87:—

"Because I am assured the lofty joy
    Thy speech infuses into me, my Lord,
        Where every good thing doth begin and end,
    Thou seest as I see it."

25. Canto X. 94:—

"The holy flock
Which Dominic conducteth by a road
Where well one fattens if he strayeth not."

26. Canto X. 112:—

"Where knowledge
So deep was put, that, if the true be true,
To see so much there never rose a second."

32. The Church. *Luke* xxiii. 46: "And when Jesus had cried with a loud voice, he said, Father, into thy hands I commend my spirit; and having said thus, he gave up the ghost."

34. *Romans* viii. 38: "For I am persuaded, that neither death, nor life, nor angels, nor principalities, nor powers, nor things present, nor things to come, nor height, nor depth, nor any other creature, shall be able to separate us from the love of God, which is in Christ Jesus our Lord."

35. St. Francis and St. Dominic. Mr. Perkins, *Tuscan Sculptors,* I. 7, says: "In warring against Frederic, whose courage, cunning, and ambition gave them ceaseless cause for alarm, and in strengthening and extending the influence of the Church, much shaken by the many heresies which had sprung up in Italy and France, the Popes received invaluable assistance from the Minorites and the Preaching Friars, whose orders had been established by Pope Innocent III. in the early part of the century, in consequence of a vision, in which he saw the tottering walls of the Lateran basilica supported by an Italian and a Spaniard, in whom he afterwards recognized their respective founders, SS. Francis and Dominic. Nothing could be more opposite than the means which these two celebrated men employed in the work of conversion; for while St. Francis used persuasion and tenderness

to melt the hardhearted, St. Dominic forced and crushed them into submission. St. Francis,

> 'La cui mirabil vita
> Meglio in gloria del ciel si canterebbe,'

was inspired by love for all created things, in the most insignificant of which he recognized a common origin with himself. The little lambs hung up for slaughter excited his pity, and the captive birds his tender sympathy; the swallows he called his sisters, *sororculæ meæ,* when he begged them to cease their twitterings while he preached; the worm he carefully removed from his path, lest it should be trampled on by a less careful foot; and, in love with poverty, he lived upon the simplest food, went clad in the scantiest garb, and enjoined chastity and obedience upon his followers, who within four years numbered no less than fifty thousand; but St. Dominic, though originally of a kind and compassionate nature, sacrificed whole hecatombs of victims in his zeal for the Church, showing how far fanaticism can change the kindest heart, and make it look with complacency upon deeds which would have formerly excited its abhorrence."

37. The Seraphs love most, the Cherubs know most. Thomas Aquinas, *Sum. Theol.,* I. Quæst. cviii. 5, says, in substance, that the Seraphim are so called from burning; according to the three properties of fire, namely, continual motion upward, excess of heat, and of light. And again, in the same article, that Cherubim, being interpreted, is plenitude of knowledge, which in them is fourfold; namely, perfect vision of God, full reception of divine light, contemplation of beauty in the order of things, and copious effusion of the divine cognition upon others.

40. Thomas Aquinas, a Dominican, here celebrates the life and deeds of St. Francis, leaving the praise of his own Saint to Bonaventura, a Franciscan, to show that in heaven there are no rivalries nor jealousies between the two orders, as there were on earth.

43. The town of Ascesi, or Assisi, as it is now called, where St. Francis was born, is situated between the rivers Tupino and Chiasi, on the slope of Monte Subaso, where St. Ubald had his hermitage. From this mountain the summer heats are reflected, and the cold winds of winter blow through the Porta Sole of Perugia. The towns of Nocera and Gualdo are neighbouring towns, that suffered under the oppression of the Perugians.

Ampère, *Voyage Dantesque,* p. 256, says: "Having been twice at Perugia, I have experienced the double effect of Mount Ubaldo, which the poet says makes this city feel the cold and heat.

> 'Onde Perugia sente freddo e caldo,'

that is, which by turns reflects upon it the rays of the sun, and sends it icy winds. I have but too well verified the justice of Dante's observation, particularly as regards the cold temperature, which Perugia, when it is not burning hot, owes to Mount Ubaldo. I arrived in front of this city on a brilliant autumnal night, and had time to comment at leisure upon the winds of the Ubaldo, as I slowly climbed the winding road which leads to the gates of the city fortified by a Pope."

50. *Revelation* vii. 2: "And I saw another angel ascending from the east, having the seal of the living God." These words Bonaventura applies to St. Francis, the beautiful enthusiast and *Pater Seraphicus* of the Church, to follow out whose wonderful life through the details of history and legend would be too long for these notes. A few hints must suffice.

St. Francis was the son of Peter Bernadone, a wool-merchant of Assisi, and was born in 1182. The first glimpse we catch of him is that of a joyous youth in gay apparel, given up to pleasure, and singing with his companions through the streets of his native town, like St. Augustine in the streets of Carthage. He was in the war between Assisi and Perugia, was taken prisoner, and passed a year in confinement. On his return home a severe illness fell upon him, which gave him more serious thoughts. He again appeared in the streets of Assisi in gay apparel, but meeting a beggar, a fellow-soldier, he changed clothes with him. He now began to visit hospitals and kiss the sores of lepers. He prayed in the churches, and saw visions. In the church of St. Damiano he heard a voice say three times, "Francis, repair my house, which thou seest falling." In order to do this, he sold his father's horse and some cloth at Foligno, and took the money to the priest of St. Damiano, who to his credit refused to receive it. Through fear of his father, he hid himself; and when he reappeared in the streets was so ill-clad that the boys pelted him and called him mad. His father shut him up in his house; his mother set him free. In the presence of his father and the Bishop he renounced all right to his inheritance, even giving up his clothes, and putting on those of a servant which the Bishop gave him. He wandered about the country, singing the praises of the Lord aloud on the highways. He met with a band of robbers, and said to them, "I am the herald of the Great King." They beat him and threw him into a ditch filled with snow. He only rejoiced and sang the louder. A friend in Gubbio gave him a suit of clothes, which he wore for two years, with a girdle and a staff. He washed the feet of lepers in the hospital, and kissed their sores. He begged from door to door in Assisi for the repairs of the church of St. Damiano, and carried stones for the masons. He did the same for the church of St. Peter; he did the same for the church of Our Lady of Angels at Portiuncula, in the neighbourhood of Assisi, where he remained two years. Hearing one day in church the injunction of Christ to his Apostles, "Provide neither gold nor silver, nor brass in your purse, nor scrip for your journey, neither two coats, neither shoes, nor yet staves," he left off shoes and staff and girdle, and girt himself with a cord, after the manner of the shepherds in that neighbourhood. This cord became the distinguishing mark of his future Order. He kissed the ulcer of a man from Spoleto, and healed him; and St. Bonaventura says, "I know not which I ought most to admire, such a kiss or such a cure." Bernard of Quintavalle and others associated themselves with him, and the Order of the Benedictines was founded.

As his convent increased, so did his humility and his austerities. He sewed his rough habit with pack-thread to make it rougher; he slept on the ground with a stone for his pillow; he drank water; he ate bread; he fasted eight lents in the year; he called his body "Brother Ass," and bound it with a halter, the cord of his Order; but a few days before his death he begged pardon of his body for having treated it so harshly. As a penance, he rolled himself naked in the snow and among brambles; he commanded his friars to revile him, and when he said, "O Brother Francis, for thy sins thou hast deserved to be plunged into hell;" Brother Leo was to answer, "It is true; thou hast deserved to be buried in the very bottom of hell."

In 1215 his convent was removed to Alvernia, among the solitudes of the Apennines. In 1219 he went to Egypt to convert the Sultan, and preached to him in his camp near Damietta, but without the desired effect. He returned to the duties of his convent with unabated zeal; and was sometimes seen by his followers lifted from the ground by the fervour of his prayers; and here he received in a vision of the Crucifixion the *stigmata* in his hands and feet and side. Butler, *Lives of the Saints,* X. 100, says: "The marks of nails began to appear on his hands and feet, resembling those he had seen in the vision of the man crucified. His hands and feet seemed bored through in the middle with four wounds, and these holes appeared to be pierced with nails of hard flesh; the heads were round and black, and were seen in the palms of his hands, and in his feet in the upper part of the instep. The points were long, and appeared beyond the skin on the other side, and were turned back as if they had been clenched with a hammer. There was also in his right side a red wound, as if made by the piercing of a lance; and this often threw out blood, which stained the tunic and drawers of the saint."

Two years afterwards St. Francis died, exclaiming, "Welcome, Sister Death;" and multitudes came to kiss his sacred wounds. His body was buried in the church of St. George at Assisi, but four years afterwards removed to a church outside the walls. See Note 117 of this canto.

In the life of St. Francis it is sometimes difficult to distinguish between the facts of history and the myths of tradition; but through all we see the outlines of a gentle, beautiful, and noble character. All living creatures were his brothers and sisters. To him the lark was an emblem of the Cherubim, and the lamb an image of the Lamb of God. He is said to have preached to the birds; and his sermon was, "Brother birds, greatly are ye bound to praise the Creator, who clotheth you with feathers, and giveth you wings to fly with, and a purer air to breathe, and who careth for you, who have so little care for yourselves."

Forsyth, describing his visit to La Verna, *Italy,* p. 123, says: "Francis appears to me a genuine hero, original, independent, magnanimous, incorruptible. His powers seemed designed to regenerate society; but, taking a wrong direction, they sank men into beggars."

Finally, the phrase he often uttered when others praised him may be here repeated, "What every one is in the eyes of God, that he is and no more."

51. Namely, in winter, when the sun is far south; or, as Biagioli prefers, glowing with unwonted splendour.

53. It will be noticed that there is a play of words on the name Ascesi (I ascended), which Padre Venturi irreverently calls a *concetto di tre quattrini*.

59. His vow of poverty, in opposition to the wishes of his father.

61. In the presence of his father and of the Bishop of the diocese.

65. After the death of Christ, she waited eleven hundred years and more till St. Francis came.

67. The story of Cæsar's waking the fisherman Amyclas to take him across the Adriatic is told by Lucan, *Pharsalia*, V.:—

> "There through the gloom his searching eyes explored,
> Where to the mouldering rock a bark was moored.
> The mighty master of this little boat
> Securely slept within a neighbouring cot:
> No massy beams support his humble hall,
> But reeds and marshy rushes wove the wall;
> Old, shattered planking for a roof was spread,
> And covered in from rain the needy shed.
> Thrice on the feeble door the warrior struck,
> Beneath the blow the trembling dwelling shook.
> 'What wretch forlorn,' the poor Amyclas cries,
> 'Driven by the raging seas, and stormy skies,
> To my poor lowly roof for shelter flies?'

> "O happy poverty! thou greatest good,
> Bestowed by Heaven, but seldom understood!
> Here nor the cruel spoiler seeks his prey,
> Nor ruthless armies take their dreadful way:
> Security thy narrow limits keeps,
> Safe are thy cottages, and sound thy sleeps.
> Behold! ye dangerous dwellings of the great,
> Where gods and godlike princes choose their seat;
> See in what peace the poor Amyclas lies,
> Nor starts, though Cæsar's call commands to rise."

Dante also writes, *Convito*, IV. 13: "And therefore the wise man says, that the traveller empty-handed on his way would sing in the very presence of robbers. And that is what Lucan refers to in his fifth book, when he commends the security of poverty, saying: O safe condition of poverty! O narrow habitations and hovels! O riches of the Gods not yet understood! At what times and at what walls could it happen, the not being afraid of any noise, when the hand of Cæsar was knocking? And this says Lucan, when he describes how Cæsar came by night to the hut of the fisherman Amyclas, to pass the Adrian Sea."

74. St. Francis, according to Butler, *Lives of the Saints,* X. 78, used to say that "he possessed nothing of earthly goods, being a disciple of Him who, for our sakes, was born a stranger in an open stable, lived without a place of his own wherein to lay his head, subsisting by the charity of good people, and died naked on a cross in the close embraces of holy poverty."

79. Bernard of Quintavalle, the first follower of St. Francis. Butler, *Lives of the Saints,* X. 75, says: "Many began to admire the heroic and uniform virtue of this great servant of God, and some desired to be his companions and disciples. The first of these was Bernard of Quintaval, a rich tradesman of Assisium, a person of singular prudence, and of great authority in that city, which had been long directed by his counsels. Seeing the extraordinary conduct of St. Francis, he invited him to sup at his house, and had a good bed made ready for him near his own. When Bernard seemed to be fallen asleep, the servant of God arose, and falling on his knees, with his eyes lifted up, and his arms across, repeated very slow, with abundance of tears, the whole night, *Deus meus et Omnia,* 'My God and my All.' . . . . Bernard secretly watched the saint all night, by the light of a lamp, saying to himself, 'This man is truly a servant of God;' and admiring the happiness of such a one, whose heart is entirely filled with God, and to whom the whole world is nothing. After many other proofs of the sincere and admirable sanctity of Francis, being charmed and vanquished by his example, he begged the saint to make him his companion. Francis recommended the matter to God for some time; they both heard mass together, and took advice that they might learn the will of God. The design being approved, Bernard sold all his effects, and divided the sum among the poor in one day."

83. Giles, or Egidius, the second follower of St. Francis, died at Perugia, in 1272. He was the author of a book called *Verba Aurea,* Golden Words. Butler, *Lives of the Saints,* VII. 162, note, says of him: "None among the first disciples of St. Francis seems to have been more perfectly replenished with his spirit of perfect charity, humility, meekness, and simplicity, as appears from the golden maxims and lessons of piety which he gave to others."

He gives also this anecdote of him on p. 164: "Brother Giles said, 'Can a dull idiot love God as perfectly as a great scholar?' St. Bonaventure replied, 'A poor old woman may love him more than the most learned master and doctor in theology.' At this Brother Giles, in a sudden fervour and jubilation of spirit, went into a garden, and, standing at a gate toward the city (of Rome), he looked that way, and cried out with a loud voice, 'Come, the poorest, most simple, and most illiterate old woman, love the Lord our God, and you may attain to an higher degree of eminence and happiness than Brother Bonaventure with all his learning.' After this he fell into an ecstacy, in which he continued in sweet contemplation without motion for the space of three hours."

Sylvester, the third disciple, was a priest who sold stone to St. Francis for the repairs of the church of St. Damiano. Some question arising about the payment, St. Francis thrust his hand into Bernard's bosom and drew forth a handful of gold, which he added to the previous payment. Sylvester, smitten with remorse that he, an old man, should be so greedy of gold, while a young man despised it for the love of God, soon after became a disciple of the saint.

89. Peter Bernadone, the father of St. Francis, was a wool-merchant. Of this humble origin the saint was not ashamed.

93. The permission to establish his religious Order, granted by Pope Innocent III., in 1214.

96. Better here in heaven by the Angels, than on earth by Franciscan friars in their churches, as the custom was. Or perhaps, as Buti interprets it, better above in the glory of Paradise, "where is the College of all the Saints," than here in the Sun.

98. The permission to found the Order of Minor Friars, or Franciscans, granted by Pope Innocent III., in 1214, was confirmed by Pope Honorius III., in 1223.

99. The title of Archimandrite, or Patriarch, was given in the Greek Church to one who had supervision over many convents.

101. Namely, before the Sultan of Egypt in his camp near Damietta.

104. In the words of Ben Jonson,

"Potential merit stands for actual,
Where only opportunity doth want,
Not will nor power."

106. On Mount Alvernia, St. Francis, absorbed in prayer, received in his hands and feet and breast the *stigmata* of Christ, that is, the wounds of the nails and the spear of the crucifixion, the final seal of the Order.

Forsyth, *Italy,* p. 122: "This singular convent, which stands on the cliffs of a lofty Apennine, was built by St. Francis himself, and is celebrated for the miracle which the motto records. Here reigns all the terrible of nature,—a rocky mountain, a ruin of the elements, broken, sawn, and piled in sublime confusion,—precipices crowned with old, gloomy, visionary woods,—black chasms in the rock where curiosity shudders to look down,—haunted caverns, sanctified by miraculous crosses,—long excavated stairs that restore you to daylight. . . . . On entering the Chapel of the Stigmata, we caught the religion of the place; we knelt round the rail, and gazed with a kind of local devotion at the holy spot where St. Francis received the five wounds of Christ. The whole hill is legendary ground. Here the Seraphic Father was saluted by two crows which still haunt the convent; there the Devil hurled him down a precipice, yet was not permitted to bruise a bone of him."

117. When St. Francis was dying, he desired to be buried among the malefactors at the place of execution, called the *Colle d' Inferno,* or Hill of

Hell. A church was afterwards built on this spot; its name was changed to *Colle di Paradiso,* and the body of the saint transferred thither in 1230. The popular tradition is, that it is standing upright under the principal altar of the chapel devoted to the saint.

118. If St. Francis were as here described, what must his companion, St. Dominic, have been, who was Patriarch, or founder of the Order to which Thomas Aquinas belonged. To the degeneracy of this Order the remainder of the canto is devoted.

137. The Order of the Dominicans diminished in numbers, by its members going in search of prelacies and other ecclesiastical offices, till it is like a tree hacked and hewn.

138. Buti interprets this passage differently. He says: "*Vedrai 'l corregger;* that is, thou, Dante, shalt see St. Dominic, whom he calls *corregger,* because he wore about his waist the *correggia,* or leathern thong, and made his friars wear it, as St. Francis made his wear the cord;—*che argomenta,* that is, who proves by true arguments in his constitutions, that his friars ought to study sacred theology, studying which their souls will grow fat with a good fatness; that is, with the grace of God, and the knowledge of things divine, if they do not go astray after the other sciences, which are vanity, and make the soul vain and proud."

Canto XII

1. The Heaven of the Sun continued. The praise of St. Dominic by St. Bonaventura, a Franciscan.

3. By this figure Dante indicates that the circle of spirits was revolving horizontally, and not vertically. In the *Convito,* III. 5, he makes the same comparison in speaking of the apparent motion of the sun; *non a modo di mola, ma di rota,* not in fashion of a millstone, but of a wheel.

11. Ezekiel i. 28: "As the appearance of the bow that is in the cloud in the day of rain, so was the appearance of the brightness round about."

12. Iris, Juno's messenger.

14. Echo. Ovid, *Met.,* III., Addison's Tr.:—

> "The Nymph, when nothing could Narcissus move,
> Still dashed with blushes for her slighted love,
> Lived in the shady covert of the woods,
> In solitary caves and dark abodes;
> Where pining wandered the rejected fair,
> Till harassed out, and worn away with care,
> The sounding skeleton, of blood bereft,
> Besides her bones and voice had nothing left.
> Her bones are petrified, her voice is found
> In vaults, where still it doubles every sound."

16. *Genesis* ix. 13: "I do set my bow in the cloud, and it shall be for a token of a covenant between me and the earth."

And Campbell, *To the Rainbow:*—

> "When o'er the green undeluged earth
>   Heaven's covenant thou didst shine,
> How came the grey old fathers forth
>   To watch thy sacred sign."

31. It is the spirit of St. Bonaventura, a Franciscan, that speaks.

32. St. Dominic, by whom, through the mouth of his follower, St. Francis has been eulogized.

34. As in Canto XI. 40:—

> "One will I speak of, for of both is spoken
>   In praising one, whichever may be taken,
>   Because unto one end their labours were."

38. The Church rallied and re-armed by the death of Christ against "all evil and mischief," and "the crafts and assaults of the Devil."

43. In Canto XI. 35:—

> "Two Princes did ordain in her behoof,
>   Which on this side and that might be her guide."

46. In the west of Europe, namely in Spain.

52. The town of Calahorra, the birthplace of St. Dominic, is situated in the province of Old Castile.

53. In one of the quarterings of the arms of Spain the Lion is above the Castle, in another beneath it.

55. St. Dominic.

58. Dante believed with Thomas Aquinas, that "the creation and infusion" of the soul were simultaneous.

60. Before the birth of St. Dominic, his mother dreamed that she had brought forth a dog, spotted black and white, and bearing a lighted torch in his mouth; symbols of the black and white habit of the Order, and of the fiery zeal of its founder. In art the dog has become the attribute of St. Dominic, as may be seen in many paintings, and in the statue over the portal of the convent of St. Mark at Florence.

64. The godmother of St. Dominic dreamed that he had a star on the forehead, and another on the back of his head, which illuminated the east and the west.

69. Dominicus, from Dominus, the Lord.

70. St. Dominic, Founder of the Preaching Friars, and Persecutor of Heretics, was born in the town of Calaroga, now Calahorra, in Old Castile, in the year 1170, and died in Bologna in 1221. He was of the illustrious

family of the Guzmans; in his youth he studied ten years at the University of Palencia; was devout, abstemious, charitable; sold his clothes to feed the poor, and even offered to sell himself to the Moors, to ransom the brother of a poor woman who sought his aid. In his twenty-fifth year he became a canon under the Bishop of Osma, preaching in the various churches of the province for nine years, and at times teaching theology at Palencia. In 1203 he accompanied his Bishop on a diplomatic mission to Denmark; and on his return stopped in Languedoc, to help root out the Albigensian heresy; but how far he authorized or justified the religious crusades against these persecuted people, and what part he took in them, is a contested point,—enough it would seem to obtain for him, from the Inquisition of Toulouse, the title of the Persecutor of Heretics.

In 1215, St. Dominic founded the Order of Preaching Friars, and in the year following was made Master of the Sacred Palace at Rome. In 1219 the centre of the Order was established at Bologna, and there, in 1221, St. Dominic died, and was buried in the Church of St. Nicholas.

It has been generally supposed that St. Dominic founded the Inquisition. It would appear, however, that the special guardianship of that institution was not intrusted to the Dominicans till the year 1233, or twelve years after the death of their founder.

75. Matthew xix. 21: "Jesus said unto him, If thou wilt be perfect, go and sell that thou hast, and give to the poor, and thou shalt have treasure in heaven: and come and follow me."

While still a young man and a student, in a season of great want, St. Dominic sold his books, and all that he possessed, to feed the poor.

79. Felix signifying happy, and Joanna, full of grace.

83. Henry of Susa, Cardinal, and Bishop of Ostia, and thence called Ostiense. He lived in the thirteenth century, and wrote a commentary on the Decretals or Books of Ecclesiastical Law.

Taddeo Alderotti was a distinguished physician and Professor of Bologna, who flourished in the thirteenth century, and translated the Ethics of Aristotle. Villani, VIII. 66, says of him: "At this time (1303) died in Bologna Maestro Taddeo, surnamed the Bolognese, though he was a Florentine, and our fellow-citizen; he was the greatest physicist in all Christendom."

The allusion here is to the pursuit of worldly things, instead of divine, the same as in the introduction to Canto XI.:—

"One after laws and one to aphorisms."

88. Buti says that in early times the prelates used to divide the incomes of the Church into four parts; "the first, for the prelate personally; the second, for the clergy who performed the services; the third, for the embellishment of the Church; the fourth, for Christ's poor; which division is now-a-days little observed."

90. Pope Boniface VIII., whom Dante never forgets, and to whom he never fails to deal a blow.

91. He did not ask of the Holy See the power of grasping six, and giving but two or three to pious uses; not the first vacant benefice; nor the tithes that belonged to God's poor; but the right to defend the faith, of which the four-and-twenty spirits in the two circles around them were the seed.

106. One wheel of the chariot of the Church Militant, of which St. Francis was the other.

112. The track made by this wheel of the chariot; that is, the strict rule of St. Francis, is now abandoned by his followers.

114. Good wine produces crust in the cask, bad wine mould.

117. Set the points of their feet upon the heel of the footprints, showing that they walked in a direction directly opposite to that of their founder.

120. When they find themselves in Hell, and not in Paradise. Matthew xiii. 30: "Let both grow together until the harvest: and in the time of harvest I will say to the reapers, Gather ye together first the tares, and bind them in bundles to burn them: but gather the wheat into my barn."

121. Whoever examines one by one the members of our Order, as he would turn over a book leaf by leaf, will find some as good and faithful as the first.

124. In 1287, Matteo d'Acquasparta, general of the Franciscans, relaxed the severities of the Order. Later a reaction followed; and in 1310 Frate Ubaldino of Casale became the head of a party of zealots among the Franciscans who took the name of Spiritualists, and produced a kind of schism in the Order, by narrower or stricter interpretation of the Scriptures.

127. In this line Dante uses the word *life* for *spirit*.

John of Fidanza, surnamed Bonaventura,—who "postponed considerations sinister," or made things temporal subservient to things spiritual, and of whom one of his teachers said that it seemed as if in him "Adam had not sinned,"— was born in 1221 at Bagnoregio, near Orvieto. In his childhood, being extremely ill, he was laid by his mother at the feet of St. Francis, and healed by the prayers of the Saint, who, when he beheld him, exclaimed "O *buona ventura!*" and by this name the mother dedicated her son to God. He lived to become a Franciscan, to be called the "Seraphic Doctor," and to write the Life of St. Francis; which, according to the Spanish legend, being left unfinished at his death, he was allowed to return to earth for three days to complete it. There is a strange picture in the Louvre, attributed to Murillo, representing this event. Mrs. Jameson gives an engraving of it in her *Legends of the Monastic Orders,* p. 303.

St. Bonaventura was educated in Paris under Alexander Hales, the Irrefragable Doctor, and in 1245, at the age of twenty-four, became a Professor of Theology in the University. In 1256 he was made General of his Order; in 1273, Cardinal and Bishop of Albano. The nuncios of Pope Gregory, who were sent to carry him his cardinal's hat, found him in the garden of a

convent near Florence, washing the dishes; and he requested them to hang
the hat on a tree, till he was ready to take it.

St. Bonaventura was one of the great Schoolmen, and his works are volu-
minous, consisting of seven imposing folios, two of which are devoted to
Expositions of the Scriptures, one to Sermons, two to Peter Lombard's Book
of Sentences, and two to minor works. Among these may be mentioned the
Legend of St. Francis; the Itinerary of the Mind towards God; the Ecclesiastical
Hierarchy; the Bible of the Poor, which is a volume of essays on moral and
religious subjects; and Meditations on the Life of Christ. Of others the mys-
tic titles are, The Mirror of the Soul; The Mirror of the Blessed Virgin; On
the Six Wings of the Seraphim; On the Six Wings of the Cherubim; On the
Sandals of the Apostles. One golden sentence of his cannot be too often
repeated: "The best perfection of a religious man is to do common things in
a perfect manner. A constant fidelity in small things is a great and heroic
virtue."

Milman, *Hist. Latin Christ.*, VIII. 274, 276, says of him: "In Bonaventura
the philosopher *recedes;* religious edification is his mission. A much smaller
proportion of his voluminous works is pure Scholasticism; he is teaching by
the Life of his Holy Founder, St. Francis, and by what may be called a new
Gospel, a legendary Life of the Saviour, which seems to claim, with all its
wild traditions, equal right to the belief with that of the Evangelists. Bonaventura
himself seems to deliver it as his own unquestioning faith. Bonaventura, if
not ignorant of, feared or disdained to know much of Aristotle or the Arabians:
he philosophizes only because in his age he could not avoid philosophy. . . . . .
The raptures of Bonaventura, like the raptures of all Mystics, tremble on the
borders of Pantheism: he would still keep up the distinction between the soul
and God; but the soul must aspire to absolute unity with God, in whom all
ideas are in reality one, though many according to human thought and speech.
But the soul, by contemplation, by beatific vision, is, as it were, to be lost
and merged in that Unity."

130. Of these two barefooted friars nothing remains but the name and the
good report of holy lives. The *Ottimo* says they were authors of books.

· Bonaventura says that Illuminato accompanied St. Francis to Egypt, and
was present when he preached in the camp of the Sultan. Later he overcame
the scruples of the Saint, and persuaded him to make known to the world
the miracle of the *stigmata*.

Agostino became the head of his Order in the Terra di Lavoro, and there
received a miraculous revelation of the death of St. Francis. He was lying ill
in his bed, when suddenly he cried out, "Wait for me! Wait for me! I am
coming with thee!" And when asked to whom he was speaking, he answered,
"Do ye not see our Father Francis ascending into heaven?" and immediately
expired.

133. Hugh of St. Victor was a monk in the monastery of that name near
Paris. Milman, *Hist. Latin Christ.*, VIII. 240, thus speaks of him: "The mys-
ticism of Hugo de St. Victor withdrew the contemplator altogether from the

outward to the inner world,—from God in the works of nature, to God in his workings on the soul of man. This contemplation of God, the consummate perfection of man, is immediate, not mediate. Through the Angels and the Celestial Hierarchy of the Areopagite it aspires to one God, not in his Theophany, but in his inmost essence. All ideas and forms of things are latent in the human soul, as in God, only they are manifested to the soul by its own activity, its meditative power. Yet St. Victor is not exempt from the grosser phraseology of the Mystic,—the tasting God, and other degrading images from the senses of men. The ethical system of Hugo de St. Victor is that of the Church, more free and lofty than the dry and barren discipline of Peter Lombard."

134. Peter Mangiadore, or Peter Comestor, as he is more generally called, was born at Troyes in France, and became in 1164 Chancellor of the University of Paris. He was the author of a work on Ecclesiastical History, "from the beginning of the world to the times of the Apostles;" and died in the monastery of St. Victor in 1198. He was surnamed Comestor, the Eater, because he was a great devourer of books.

Peter of Spain was the son of a physician of Lisbon, and was the author of a work on Logic. He was Bishop of Braga, afterwards Cardinal and Bishop of Tusculum, and in 1276 became Pope, under the title of John XIX. In the following year he was killed by the fall of a portion of the Papal palace at Viterbo.

136. Why Nathan the Prophet should be put here is a great puzzle to the commentators. "*Buon salto!* a good leap," says Venturi. Lombardi thinks it is no leap at all. The only reason given is, that Nathan said to David, "Thou art the man." As Buti says: "The author puts him among these Doctors, because he revealed his sin to David, as these revealed the vices and virtues in their writings."

137. John, surnamed from his eloquence Chrysostom, or Golden Mouth, was born in Antioch, about the year 344. He was first a lawyer, then a monk, next a popular preacher, and finally metropolitan Bishop of Constantinople. His whole life, from his boyhood in Antioch to his death in banishment on the borders of the Black Sea,—his austerities as a monk, his fame as a preacher, his troubles as Bishop of Constantinople, his controversy with Theophilus of Alexandria, his exile by the Emperor Arcadius and the earthquake that followed it, his triumphant return, his second banishment, and his death,—is more like a romance than a narrative of facts.

"The monuments of that eloquence," says Gibbon, *Decline and Fall,* Ch. XXXII., "which was admired near twenty years at Antioch and Constantinople, have been carefully preserved; and the possession of near one thousand sermons or homilies has authorized the critics of succeeding times to appreciate the genuine merit of Chrysostom. They unanimously attribute to the Christian orator the free command of an elegant and copious language; the judgment to conceal the advantages which he derived from the knowledge of rhetoric and philosophy; an inexhaustible fund of metaphors and similitudes, of ideas and images, to vary and illustrate the most familiar topics; the happy art of engaging the passions in the service of virtue; and of exposing the folly, as well as the turpitude, of vice, almost with the truth and spirit of a dramatic representation."

Anselm, Archbishop of Canterbury, was born at Aost in Piedmont, about the year 1033, and was educated at the abbey of Bec in Normandy, where, in the year 1060, he became a monk, and afterwards prior and abbot. In 1093 he was made Archbishop of Canterbury by King William Rufus; and after many troubles died, and was buried in his cathedral, in 1109. His life was written by the monk Eadmer of Canterbury. Wright, *Biog. Britan. Lit.,* Anglo-Norman Period, p. 59, says of him: "Anselm was equal to Lanfranc in learning, and far exceeded him in piety. In his private life he was modest, humble, and sober in the extreme. He was obstinate only in defending the interests of the Church of Rome, and, however we may judge the claims themselves, we must acknowledge that he supported them from conscientious motives. Reading and contemplation were the favourite occupations of his life, and even the time required for his meals, which were extremely frugal, he employed in discussing philosophical and theological questions."

Ælius Donatus was a Roman grammarian, who flourished about the middle of the fourth century. He had St. Jerome among his pupils, and was immortalized by his Latin Grammar, which was used in all the schools of the Middle Ages, so that the name passed into a proverb. In the *Vision of Piers Ploughman,* 2889, we find it alluded to,—

> "Then drewe I me among drapers
> My donet to lerne;"

and Chaucer, *Testament of Love,* says,

> "No passe I to vertues of this Marguerite
> But therein all my donet can I lerne."

According to the note in Warton, *Eng. Poet.,* Sect. VIII., to which I owe these quotations, Bishop Pecock wrote a work with the title of "Donat into Christian Religion," using the word in the sense of Introduction.

139. Rabanus Maurus, a learned theologian was born at Mayence in 786, and died at Winfel, in the same neighbourhood, in 856. He studied first at the abbey of Fulda, and then at St. Martin's of Tours, under the celebrated Alcuin. He became a teacher at Fulda, then Abbot, then Bishop of Mayence. He left behind him works that fill six folios. One of them is entitled "The Universe, or a Book about All Things;" but they chiefly consist of homilies, and commentaries on the Bible.

140. This distinguished mystic and enthusiast of the twelfth century was born in 1130 at the village of Celio, near Cosenza in Calabria, on the river Busento, in whose bed the remains of Attila were buried. A part of his youth

was passed at Naples, where his father held some office in the court of King Roger; but from the temptations of this gay capital he escaped, and, like St. Francis, renouncing the world, gave himself up to monastic life.

"A tender and religious soul," says Rousselot in his *Hist. de l'Évangile Éternel,* p. 15, "an imagination ardent and early turned towards asceticism, led him from his first youth to embrace the monastic life. His spirit, naturally exalted, must have received the most lively impressions from the spectacle offered him by the place of his birth: mountains arid or burdened with forests, deep valleys furrowed by the waters of torrents; a soil, rough in some places, and covered in others with a brilliant vegetation; a heaven of fire; solitude, so easily found in Calabria, and so dear to souls inclined to mysticism,—all combined to exalt in Joachim the religious sentiment. There are places where life is naturally poetical, and when the soul, thus nourished by things external, plunges into the divine world, it produces men like St. Francis of Accesi and Joachim of Flora.

"On leaving Naples he had resolved to embrace the monastic life, but he was unwilling to do it till he had visited the Holy Land. He started forthwith, followed by many pilgrims whose expenses he paid; and as to himself, clad in a white dress of some coarse stuff, he made a great part of the journey barefooted. In order to stop in the Thebaïd, the first centre of Christian asceticism, he suffered his companions to go on before; and there he was nigh perishing from thirst. Overcome by the heat in a desert place, where he could not find a drop of water, he dug a grave in the sand, and lay down in it to die, hoping that his body, soon buried by the sand heaped up by the wind, would not fall a prey to wild beasts. Barius attributes to him a dream, in which he thought he was drinking copiously; at all events, after sleeping some hours he awoke in condition to continue his journey. After visiting Jerusalem, he went to Mount Tabor, where he remained forty days. He there lived in an old cistern; and it was amid watchings and prayers on the scene of the Transfiguration that he conceived the idea of his principal writings: 'The Harmony of the Old and New Testaments'; 'The Exposition of the Apocalypse'; and 'The Psalter of Ten Strings.'"

On his return to Italy, Joachim became a Cistercian monk in the monastery of Corazzo in Calabria, of which ere long he became Abbot; but, wishing for greater seclusion, he soon withdrew to Flora, among the mountains, where he founded another monastery, and passed the remainder of his life in study and contemplation. He died in 1202, being seventy-two years of age.

"His renown was great," says Rousselot, *Hist. de l'Évang. Éternel,* p. 27, "and his duties numerous; nevertheless his functions as Abbot of the monastery which he had founded did not prevent him from giving himself up to the composition of the writings which he had for a long time meditated. This was the end he had proposed to himself; it was to attain it that he had wished to live in solitude. If his desire was not wholly realized, it was so in great part; and Joachim succeeded in laying the foundations of the Eternal

Gospel. He passsd his days and nights in writing and in dictating. 'I used
to write,' says his secretary Lucas, 'day and night in copy-books, what he
dictated and corrected on scraps of paper, with two other monks whom he
employed in the same work.' It was in the middle of these labours that
death surprised him."

In Abbot Joachim's time at least, this Eternal Gospel was not a book, but
a doctrine, pervading all his writings. Later, in the middle of the thirteenth
century, some such book existed, and was attributed to John of Parma. In
the *Romance of the Rose,* Chaucer's Tr., 1798, it is thus spoken of:—

> "A thousande and two hundred yere
> Five-and-fifte, ferther ne nere,
> Broughten a boke with sorie grace,
> To yeven ensample in common place,—
> That sayed thus, though it were fable,
> *This is the Gospell pardurable*
> *That fro the Holie Ghost is sent.*
> Well were it worthy to be ybrent.
> Entitled was in soche manere,
> This boke of whichè I tell here;
> There n'as no wight in al Paris,
> *Beforne our Ladie at Parvis*
> That thei ne might the bokè by.
>
>   . . . . .
>
> "The Universite, that was a slepe,
> Gan for to braied, and taken kepe;
> And at the noise the hedde up cast;
> Ne never, sithen, slept it [so] fast:
> But up it stert, and armes toke
> Ayenst this false horrible boke,
> All redy battaile for to make,
> And to the judge the boke thei take."

The Eternal Gospel taught that there were three epochs in the history of
the world, two of which were already passed, and the third about to begin.
The first was that of the Old Testament, or the reign of the Father; the sec-
ond, that of the New Testament, or the reign of the Son; and the third, that
of Love, or the reign of the Holy Spirit. To use his own words, as quoted
by Rousselot, *Hist. de l'Évang. Éternel,* p. 78: "As the letter of the Old
Testament seems to belong to the Father, by a certain peculiarity of resem-
blance, and the letter of the New Testament to the Son; so the spiritual
intelligence, which proceeds from both, belongs to the Holy Spirit. Accordingly,
the age when men were joined in marriage was the reign of the Father; that
of the Preachers is the reign of the Son; and the age of Monks, *ordo monacho-
rum,* the last, is to be that of the Holy Spirit. The first before the law, the
second under the law, the third with grace."

The germ of this doctrine, says the same authority, p. 59, is in Origen, who had said before the Abbot Joachim, "We must leave to believers the historic Christ and the Gospel, the Gospel of the letter; but to the Gnostics alone belongs the Divine Word, the Eternal Gospel, the Gospel of the Spirit."

Canto XIII

1. The Heaven of the Sun continued. Let the reader imagine fifteen of the largest stars, and to these add the seven of Charles's Wain, and the two last stars of the Little Bear, making in all twenty-four, and let him arrange them in two concentric circles, revolving in opposite directions, and he will have the image of what Dante now beheld.

7. *Iliad*, XVIII. 487: "The Bear, which they also call by the appellation of the Wain, which there revolves and watches Orion; but it alone is free from the baths of the ocean."

10. The constellation of the Little Bear as much resembles a horn as it does a bear. Of this horn the Pole Star forms the smaller end.

14. Ariadne, whose crown was, at her death, changed by Bacchus into a constellation.

Ovid, *Met.*, VIII., Croxall's Tr.:—

> "And bids her crown among the stars be placed,
>   With an eternal constellation graced.
>   The golden circlet mounts; and, as it flies,
>   Its diamonds twinkle in the distant skies;
>   There, in their pristine form, the gemmy rays
>   Between Alcides and the dragon blaze."

Chaucer, *Legende of Good Women:*—

> "And in the sygne of Taurus men may se
>   The stones of hire corowne shyne clere."

And Spenser, *Faerie Queene*, VI. x. 13:—

> "Looke! how the crowne which Ariadne wore
>   Upon her yvory forehead that same day
>   That Theseus her unto his bridale bore,
>   When the bold Centaures made that bloudy fray
>   With the fierce Lapithes which did them dismay,
>   Being now placed in the firmament,
>   Through the bright heaven doth her beams display,
>   And is unto the starres an ornament,
>   Which round about her move in order excellent."

23. The Chiana empties into the Arno near Arezzo. In Dante's time it was a sluggish stream, stagnating in the marshes of Valdichiana. See *Inf.* XXIX. Note 46.

24. The *Primum Mobile*.

32. St. Thomas Aquinas, who had related the life of St. Francis.

34. The first doubt in Dante's mind was in regard to the expression in Canto X. 96,

> "Where well one fattens if he strayeth not,"

which was explained by Thomas Aquinas in Canto XI. The second, which he now prepares to thresh out, is in Canto X. 114,

> "To see so much there never rose a second,"

referring to Solomon, as being peerless in knowledge.

37. Adam.

40. Christ.

48. Solomon.

52. All things are but the thought of God, and by Him created in love.

55. The living Light, the Word, proceeding from the Father, is not separated from Him nor from his Love, the Holy Spirit.

58. Its rays are centred in the nine choirs of Angels, ruling the nine heavens, here called subsistences, according to the definition of Thomas Aquinas, *Sum. Theol.,* I. Quæst. xxix. 2: "What exists by itself, and not in anything else, is called subsistence."

61. From those nine heavens it descends to the elements, the lowest potencies, till it produces only imperfect and perishable results, or mere contingencies.

64. These contingencies are animals, plants, and the like, produced by the influences of the planets from seeds, and certain insects and plants, believed of old to be born without seed.

67. Neither their matter nor the influences of the planets being immutable, the stamp of the divinity is more or less clearly seen in them, and hence the varieties in plants and animals.

73. If the matter were perfect, and the divine influence at its highest power, the result would likewise be perfect; but by transmission through the planets it becomes more and more deficient, the hand of nature trembles, and imperfection is the result.

79. But if Love (the Holy Spirit) and the Vision (the Son), proceeding from the Primal Power (the Father), act immediately, then the work is perfect, as in Adam and the human nature of Christ.

89. Then how was Solomon so peerless, that none like him ever existed?

93. 1 *Kings* iii. 5: "In Gibeon the Lord appeared to Solomon in a dream by night: and God said, Ask what I shall give thee. . . . . Give therefore thy servant an understanding heart to judge thy people, that I may discern between

good and bad: for who is able to judge this thy so great a people? And the speech pleased the Lord, that Solomon had asked this thing. And God said unto him, Because thou hast asked this thing, and hast not asked for thyself long life, neither hast asked riches for thyself, nor hast asked the life of thine enemies, but hast asked for thyself understanding to discern judgment, Behold, I have done according to thy words: lo, I have given thee a wise and an understanding heart; so that there was none like thee before thee, neither after thee shall any arise like unto thee."

98. The number of the celestial Intelligences, or Regents of the Planets.

99. Whether from two premises, one of which is necessary, and the other contingent, or only possible, the conclusion drawn will be necessary; which Buti says is a question belonging to "the garrulity of dialectics."

100. Whether the existence of a first motion is to be conceded.

102. That is, a triangle, one side of which shall be the diameter of the circle.

103. If thou notest, in a word, that Solomon did not ask for wisdom in astrology, nor in dialects, nor in metaphysics, nor in geometry.

104. The peerless seeing is a reference to Canto X. 114:—

"To see so much there never rose a second."

It will be observed that the word "rose" is the Biblical word in the phrase "neither after thee shall any rise like unto thee," as given in note 93.

125. Parmenides was an Eleatic philosopher, and pupil of Xenophanes. According to Ritter, *Hist. Anc. Phil.,* I. 450, Morrison's Tr., his theory was, that, "Being is uncreated and unchangeable,—

'Whole and self-generate, unchangeable, illimitable,
Never was nor yet shall be its birth; All is already
One from eternity.'"

And farther on: "It is but a mere human opinion that things are produced and decay, are and are not, and change place and colour. The whole has its principle in itself, and is in eternal rest; for powerful necessity holds it within the bonds of its own limits, and encloses it on all sides: being cannot be imperfect; for it is not in want of anything,—for if it were so, it would be in want of all."

Melissus of Samos was a follower of Parmenides, and maintained substantially the same doctrines.

Brissus was a philosopher of less note. Mention is hardly made of him in the histories of philosophy, except as one of those who pursued that *Fata Morgana* of mathematicians, the quadrature of the circle.

127. "Infamous heresiarchs," exclaims Venturi, "put as an example of innumerable others, who, having erred in the understanding of the Holy Scriptures, persevered in their errors."

Sabellius was by birth an African, and flourished as Presbyter of Ptolemais, in the third century. He denied the three persons in the Godhead, maintaining that the Son and Holy Ghost were only temporary manifestations of God in creation, redemption, and sanctification, and would finally return to the Father.

Arius was a Presbyter of Alexandria in the fourth century. He believed the Son to be equal in power with the Father, but of a different essence or nature, a doctrine which gave rise to the famous Heterousian and Homoiousian controversy, that distracted the Church for three hundred years.

These doctrines of Sabellius and of Arius are both heretical, when tried by the standard of the *Quicunque vult,* the authoritative formula of the Catholic faith; "which faith, except every one do keep whole and undefiled, without doubt he shall perish everlastingly," says St. Athanasius, or some one in his name.

128. These men, say some of the commentators, were as swords that mutilated and distorted the Scriptures. Others, that in them the features of the Scriptures were distorted, as the features of a man reflected in the grooved or concave surface of a sword.

139. Names used to indicate any common simpletons and gossips.

141. In writing this line Dante had evidently in mind the beautiful wise words of St. Francis: "What every one is in the eyes of God, that he is, and no more."

Mr. Wright, in the notes to his translation, here quotes the well-known lines of Burns, *Address to the Unco Guid:*—

> "Then gently scan your brother man,
>   Still gentler sister woman;
> Though they may gang a kennin' wrang,
>   To step aside is human:
> One point must still be greatly dark,
>   The moving why they do it:
> And just as lamely can ye mark
>   How far perhaps they rue it.
>
> "Who made the heart, 'tis He alone
>   Decidedly can try us;
> He knows each chord—its various tone,
>   Each spring—its various bias.
> Then at the balance let's be mute;
>   We never can adjust it;
> What's done we partly may compute,
>   But know not what's resisted."

Canto XIV

1. The ascent to the planet Mars, where are seen the spirits of Martyrs, and Crusaders who died fighting for the Faith.

2. In this similitude Dante describes the effect of the alternate voices of St. Thomas Aquinas in the circumference of the circle, and of Beatrice in the centre.

6. Life is here used, as before, in the sense of spirit.

28. Chaucer, *Troil. and Cres.,* the last stanza:—

> "Thou One, and Two, and Thre! eterne on live,
> That raignest aie in Thre, and Two, and One,
> Uncircumscript, and all maist circumscrive!"

Also Milton, *Par. Lost,* III. 372:—

> "Thee, Father, first they sung, Omnipotent,
> Immutable, Immortal, Infinite,
> Eternal King; thee, Author of all being,
> Fountain of light, thyself invisible
> Amidst the glorious brightness where thou sitt'st
> Throned inaccessible; but when thou shadest
> The full blaze of thy beams, and through a cloud
> Drawn round about thee like a radiant shrine,
> Dark with excessive bright thy skirts appear,
> Yet dazzle heaven; that brightest seraphim
> Approach not, but with both wings veil their eyes.
> Thee next they sang of all creation first,
> Begotten Son, Divine Similitude,
> In whose conspicuous countenance, without cloud
> Made visible, the Almighty Father shines,
> Whom else no creature can behold: on thee
> Impressed the effulgence of his glory abides;
> Transfused on thee his ample Spirit rests."

35. The voice of Solomon.

73. According to Buti, "Spirits newly arrived;" or Angels, such being the interpretation given by the Schoolmen to the word Subsistences. See Canto XIII. Note 58.

86. The planet Mars. Of this planet Brunetto Latini, *Tresor,* I. iii. 3, says: "Mars is hot and warlike and evil, and is called the God of Battles."

Of its symbolism Dante, *Convito,* II. 14, says: "The Heaven of Mars may be compared to Music, for two properties. The first is its very beautiful relation [to the others]; for, enumerating the moveable heavens, from whichsoever you begin, whether from the lowest or the highest, the Heaven of Mars is the fifth; it is the centre of all. . . . . The other is, that Mars dries up and burns things, because its heat is like to that of the fire; and this is the reason why it appears fiery in colour, sometimes more, and sometimes less, according to the density and rarity of the vapours which follow it, which sometimes take fire of themselves, as is declared in the first book of *Meteors*. (And therefore Albumasar says, that the ignition of these vapours signifies death of kings, and change of empires, being effects of the dominion of Mars. And accordingly Seneca says that at the death of the Emperor Augustus a ball of fire was seen in the heavens. And in Florence, at the beginning of its downfall, a great quantity of these vapours, which follow Mars, were seen in the air in the form of a cross.) And these two properties are in Music, which is wholly relative, as may be seen in harmonized words, and in songs, in which the more beautiful the relation, the sweeter the harmony, since such is chiefly its intent. Also Music attracts to itself the spirits of men, which are principally as it were vapours of the heart, so that they almost cease from any operation; so entire is the soul when it listens, and the power of all as it were runs to the sensible spirit that hears the sounds."

Of the influences of Mars, Buti, as usual following Albumasar, writes: "Its nature is hot, igneous, dry, choleric, of a bitter savour, and it signifies youth, strength, and acuteness of mind; heats, fires, and burnings, and every sudden event; powerful kings, consuls, dukes, and knights, and companies of soldiery; desire of praise and memory of one's name; strategies and instruments of battle; robberies and machinations, and scattering of relations by plunderings and highway robberies; boldness and anger; the unlawful for the lawful; torments and imprisonments; scourges and bonds; anguish, flight, thefts, pilfering of servants, fears, contentions, insults, acuteness of mind, impiety, inconstancy, want of foresight, celerity and anticipation in things, evil eloquence and ferocity of speech, foulness of words, incontinence of tongue, demonstrations of love, gay apparel, insolence and falseness of words, swiftness of reply and sudden penitence therefor, want of religion, unfaithfulness to promises, multitude of lies and whisperings, deceits and perjuries; machinations and evil deeds; want of means; waste of means; multitude of thoughts about things; instability and change of opinion in things, from one to another; haste to return; want of shame; multitude of toils and cares; peregrinations, solitary existence, bad company; . . . . breaking open of tombs, and spoliations of the dead."

87. Buti interprets this, as redder than the Sun, to whose light Dante had become accustomed, and continues: "Literally, it is true that the splendour of Mars is more fiery than that of the Sun, because it is red, and the Sun is yellow; but allegorically we are to understand, that a greater ardour of love, that is, more burning, is in those who fight and conquer the three enemies mentioned above [the world, the flesh, and the devil], than in those who exercise themselves with the Scriptures."

88. The silent language of the heart.

96. In Hebrew, *El, Eli,* God, from which the Greeks made Helios, the Sun. As in St. Hildebert's hymn *Ad Patrem:*—

> "Alpha et Omega, magne Deus,
> Heli, Heli, Deus meus."

99. Dante, *Convito,* II. 15, says: "It must be known that philosophers have different opinions concerning this Galaxy. For the Pythagoreans said that the Sun once wandered out of his way, and passing through other regions not adapted to his heat, he burned the place through which he passed, and traces of the burning remained. I think they took this from the fable of Phaeton, which Ovid narrates in the beginning of the second book of the Metamorphoses. Others, and among them Anaxagoras and Democritus, that it was the light of the Sun reflected in that part. And these opinions they prove by demonstrative reasons. What Aristotle says of this we cannot well know; for his opinion is not the same in one translation as in the other. And I think this was an error of the translators; for in the new one he appears to say, that it was a gathering of vapours under the stars of that region, for they always attract them; and this does not appear to be the true reason. In the old, it says, that the Galaxy is only a multitude of fixed stars in that region, so small that they cannot be distinguished here below; but from them is apparent that whiteness which we call the Galaxy. And it may be that the heaven in that part is more dense, and therefore retains and reflects that light; and this opinion seems to have been entertained by Aristotle, Avicenna, and Ptolemy."

Milton, *Par. Lost,* VII. 577:—

> "A broad and ample road, whose dust is gold,
> And pavement stars, as stars to thee appear,
> Seen in the Galaxy, that Milky Way,
> Which nightly, as a circling zone, thou seest
> Powdered with stars."

101. The sign of the cross, drawn upon the planet Mars, as upon the breast of a crusader. The following Legend of the Cross, and its significance, is from Didron, *Christian Iconography,* Millington's Tr., I. 367:—

"The cross is more than a mere figure of Christ; it is in Iconography either Christ himself or his symbol. A legend has, consequently, been invented, giving the history of the cross, as if it had been a living being. It has been made the theme and hero of an epic poem, the germ of which may be discovered in books of apocryphal tradition. This story is given at length in the Golden Legend, *Legenda Aurea,* and is detailed and completed in works of painting and sculpture from the fourteenth century down to the sixteenth. . . . . After the death of Adam, Seth planted on the tomb of his father a shoot from the Tree of Life, which grew in the terrestrial Paradise. From it sprang three

little trees, united by one single trunk. Moses thence gathered the rod with
which he by his miracles astonished the people of Egypt, and the inhabitants
of the desert. Solomon desired to convert that same tree, which had become
gigantic in size, into a column for his palace; being either too short or too
long, it was rejected, and served as a bridge over a torrent. The Queen of
Sheba refused to pass over on that tree, declaring that it would one day occa-
sion the destruction of the Jews. Solomon commanded that the predestined
beam should be thrown into the probationary pool (Pool of Bethesda), and
its virtues were immediately communicated to the waters. When Christ had
been condemned to suffer the death of a malefactor, his cross was made of
the wood of that very tree. It was buried on Golgotha, and afterwards dis-
covered by St. Helena. It was carried into captivity by Chosroes, king of
Persia, delivered, and brought back in triumph to Jerusalem, by the Emperor
Heraclius. Being afterwards dispersed in a multitude of fragments throughout
the Christian universe, countless miracles were performed by it; it restored
the dead to life, and gave sight to the blind, cured the paralytic, cleansed
lepers, put demons to flight, and dispelled various maladies with which whole
nations were afflicted, extinguished conflagrations, and calmned the fury of
the raging waves.

"The wood of the cross was born with the world, in the terrestial paradise;
it will reappear in heaven at the end of time, borne in the arms of Christ or
of his angels, when the Lord descends to judge the world at the last day.

"After reading this history, some conception may be formed of the impor-
tant place held by the cross in Christian Iconography. The cross, as has been
said, is not merely the instrument of the punishment of Jesus Christ, but is
also the figure and symbol of the Saviour. Jesus, to an Iconologist, is present
in the cross as well as in the lamb, or in the lion. Chosroes flattered himself
that, in possessing the cross, he possessed the Son of God, and he had it
enthroned on his right hand, just as the Son is enthroned by God the Father.
So also the earliest Christian artists, when making a representation of the
Trinity, placed a cross beside the Father and the Holy Spirit; a cross only,
without our crucified Lord. The cross did not only recall Christ to mind, but
actually showed him. In Christian Iconography, Christ is actually present
under the form and semblance of the cross.

"The cross is our crucified Lord in person. Where the cross is, there is
the martyr, says St. Paulinus. Consequently it works miracles, as does Jesus
himself: and the list of wonders operated by its power is in truth
immense. . . . .

"The world is in the form of a cross; for the east shines above our heads,
the north is on the right, the south at the left, and the west stretches out
beneath our feet. Birds, that they may rise in air, extend their wings in the
form of a cross: men, when praying, or when beating aside the water while
swimming, assume the form of a cross. Man differs from the inferior animals,
in his power of standing erect, and extending his arms.

"A vessel, to fly upon the seas, displays her yard arms in the form of a cross
and cannot cut the waves unless her mast stands cross-like, erect in air; finally,

the ground cannot be tilled without the sacred sign, and the *tau,* the cruciform letter, is the letter of salvation.

"The cross, it is thus seen, has been the object of a worship and adoration resembling, if not equal to, that offered to Christ. That sacred tree is adored almost as if it were equal with God himself; a number of churches have been dedicated to it under the name of the Holy Cross. In addition to this, most of our churches, the greatest as well as the smallest, cathedrals as well as chapels, present in their ground plan the form of a cross."

104. Chaucer, *Lament of Marie Magdaleine,* 204:—

> "I, loking up unto that rufull rode,
> Sawe first the visage pale of that figure;
> But so pitous a sight spotted with blode
> Sawe never, yet, no living creature;
> So it exceded the boundes of mesure,
> That mannes minde with al his wittes five
> Is nothing able that paine to discrive."

109. From arm to arm of the cross, and from top to bottom.
112. Mr. Cary here quotes Chaucer, *Wif of Bath's Tale,* 6540:—

> "As thikke as motes n the sonnebeme."

And Milton, *Penseroso,* 8:—

> "As thick and numberless
> As the gay motes that people the sunbeam."

To these Mr. Wright adds the following from Lucretius, II. 113, which in Good's Tr. runs as follows:—

> "Not unresembling, if aright I deem,
> Those motes minute, that, when the obtrusive sun
> Peeps through some crevice in the shuttered shade
> The day-dark hall illuming, float amain
> In his bright beam, and wage eternal war."

125. Words from a hymn in praise of Christ, say the commentators, but they do not say from what hymn.
133. The living seals are the celestial spheres, which impress themselves on all beneath them, and increase in power as they are higher.
135. That is, to the eyes of Beatrice, whose beauty he may seem to postpone, or regard as inferior to the splendours that surround him. He excuses himself by saying that he does not speak of them, well knowing that they have grown more beautiful in ascending. He describes them in line 33 of the next canto:—

"For in her eyes was burning such a smile
        That with mine own methought I touched the bottom
        Both of my grace and of my Paradise!"

139. Sincere in the sense of pure; as in Dryden's line,—

    "A joy which never was sincere till now."

Canto XV

1. The Heaven of Mars continued.

22. This star, or spirit, did not, in changing place, pass out of the cross, but along the right arm and down the trunk or body of it.

24. A light in a vase of alabaster.

25. *Æneid*, VI., Davidson's Tr.: "But father Anchises, deep in a verdant dale, was surveying with studious care the souls there enclosed, who were to revisit the light above; and happened to be reviewing the whole number of his race, his dear descendants, their fates and fortunes, their manners and achievements. As soon as he beheld Æneas advancing toward him across the meads, he joyfully stretched out both his hands, and tears poured down his cheeks, and these words dropped from his mouth: Are you come at length, and has that piety experienced by your sire surmounted the arduous journey?"

28. Biagioli and Fraticelli think that this ancestor of Dante, Cacciaguida, who is speaking, makes use of the Latin language because it was the language of his day in Italy. It certainly gives to the passage a certain gravity and tinge of antiquity, which is in keeping with this antique spirit and with what he afterwards says. His words may be thus translated:—

    "O blood of mine! O grace of God infused
        Superlative! To whom as unto thee
        Were ever twice the gates of heaven unclosed."

49. His longing to see Dante.

50. The mighty volume of the Divine Mind, in which the dark or written parts are not changed by erasures, nor the white spaces by interlineations.

56. The Pythagorean doctrine of numbers. Ritter, *Hist. Anc. Phil.*, Morrison's Tr., I. 361, says:—

"In the Pythagorean doctrine, number comprises within itself two species,—odd and even; it is therefore the unity of these two contraries; it is the odd and the even. Now the Pythagoreans said also that one, or the unit, is the odd and the even; and thus we arrive at this result, that one, or the unit, is the essence of number, or number absolutely. As such, it is also the ground of all numbers, and is therefore named the first one, of whose origin nothing further can be said. In this respect the Pythagorean theory of numbers is merely an expression for 'all is from the original one,'—from one being, to which they also gave the name of God; for in the words of Philolaus, 'God embraces and actuates all, and is but one.' . . . .

"But in the essence of number, or in the first original one, all other numbers, and consequently the elements of numbers, and the elements of the whole world, and all nature, are contained. The elements of number are the even and the odd; on this account the first one is the even-odd, which the Pythagoreans, in their occasionally strained mode of symbolizing, attempted to prove thus; that one being added to the even makes odd, and to the odd, even."

Cowley, *Rural Solitude:*—

> "Before the branchy head of Number's tree
> Sprang from the trunk of one."

61. All the spirits of Paradise look upon God, and see in him as in a mirror even the thoughts of men.

74. The first Equality is God, all whose attributes are equal and eternal; and living in Him, the love and knowledge of spirits are also equal.

79. Will and power. Dante would fain thank the spirit that has addressed him, but knows not how. He has the will, but not the power. Dante uses the word argument in this sense of power, or means, or appliance, *Purg.* II. 31:—

> "See how he scorns all human arguments,
>   So that nor oar he wants, nor other sail
>   Than his own wings, between so distant shores."

85. Dante calls the spirit of Cacciaguida a living topaz set in the celestial cross, probably from the brilliancy and golden light of this precious stone. He may also have had in his mind the many wonderful qualities, as well as the beauty, of the gem. He makes use of the same epithet in Canto XXX. 76.

The *Ottimo* says, that he who wears the topaz cannot be injured by an enemy; and Mr. King, *Antique Gems,* p. 427, says: "If thrown into boiling water, the water cools immediately; hence this gem cools lust, calms madness and attacks of frenzy." In the same work he gives a translation of the *Lapidarium* of Marbodus, or Marbœuf, Bishop of Rennes in 1081. Of the chrysolite, which is supposed to be the same as the topaz, this author says:—

> "The golden *Chrysolite* a fiery blaze
>   Mixed with the hue of ocean's green displays;
>   Enchased in gold, its strong protective might
>   Drives far away the terrors of the night;

Strung on a hair plucked from an ass's tail,
The mightiest demons 'neath its influence quail."

89. He had been waiting for the coming of Dante, with the "hunger long and grateful" spoken of in line 49.

91. The first of the family who bore the name of Alighieri, still punished in the circle of Pride in Purgatory, and needing the prayers and good offices of Dante to set him free.

97. Barlow, *Study of Div. Com.,* p. 441, says:—

"The name of Florence has been variously explained. With the old chroniclers, the prevalent opinion was, that it was derived from *Fiorino,* the Prætor of Metellus, who during the long siege of Fiesole by the Romans commanded an intrenched camp between the River and the Rock, and was here surprised and slain by the enemy. The meadows abounded in flowers, especially lilies, and the ancient ensign, a white lily on a red ground, subsequently reversed (XVI. 154), and similar to the form on the florin (*fiorino*), with the name given to the Duomo, St. Maria del Fiore, tend to show that the name was taken from the flowery mead, rather than from the name of a Roman prætor. Leonardo Aretino states that the name of the city originally was *Fluentia,* so called because situated between the Arno and the Mugnone: and that subsequently, from the flourishing state of the colony, it was called *Florentia.* Scipione Ammirato affirms that its name from the first was *Florenzia.*

"The form and dimensions of the original city have not been very accurately recorded. In shape, probably, it resembled a Roman camp. Malespini says that it was 'quasi a similitudine di bastie.' The wall was of burnt bricks, with solid round towers at intervals of twenty cubits, and it had four gates, and six posterns. The Campidoglio, where now is the Mercato Vecchio, was an imitation of that of the parent city, Rome, whose fortunes her daughter for many centuries shared. . . .

"The *cerchia antica* of Cacciaguida was the first circle of the new city, which arose from the ruins of the Roman one destroyed by Totila; it included the Badia, which the former did not; Dante, therefore, in mentioning this circumstance, shows how accurately he had informed himself of the course of the previous wall. The walls of Dante's time were begun in 1284, but not finished until nine years after his death; they are those of the present day."

98. Tierce, or *Terza,* is the first division of the canonical day, from six to nine; Nones, or *Nona,* the third, from twelve to three in the afternoon. See *Inf.* XXXIV. Note 95. The bells of the Abbey within the old walls of Florence still rang these hours in Dante's time, and measured the day of the Florentines, like the bells of morning, noon, and night in our New England towns. In the *Convito,* IV. 23, Dante says: "The service of the first part of the day, that is, of Tierce, is said at the end of it; and that of the third and fourth, at the beginning. . . . . . And therefore be it known unto all, that properly Nones should always ring at the beginning of the seventh hour of the day."

99. Napier, *Florent. Hist.*, I. 572, writes as follows: "The simplicity of Florentine manners in 1260, described by Villani and Malespini, justifies a similar picture as drawn by their great poet. 'Then,' say these writers, 'the Florentines lived soberly on the simplest food at little expense; many of their customs were rough and rude, and both men and women went coarsely clad; many even wearing plain leather garments without fur or lining: they wore boots on their feet and caps on their heads: the women used unornamented buskins, and even the most distinguished were content with a close gown of scarlet serge or camlet, confined by a leathern waist-belt of the ancient fashion, and a hooded cloak lined with miniver; and the poorer classes wore a coarse green cloth dress of the same form. A hundred lire was the common dowry of a girl, and two and three hundred were then considered splendid fortunes: most young women waited until they were twenty years old and upwards before they married. And such was the dress, and such the manners and simple habits of the Florentines of that day; but loyal in heart, faithful to each other, zealous and honest in the execution of public duties; and with their coarse and homely mode of life, they gained more virtue and honour for themselves and their country than they who now live so delicately are able to accomplish.'"

What Florence had become in Dante's time may be seen from the following extract from Frate Francesco Pippino, who wrote in 1313, and whose account is thus given by Napier, II. 542: "Now indeed, in the present luxurious age, many shameful practices are introduced instead of the former customs; many indeed to the injury of people's minds, because frugality is exchanged for magnificence; the clothing being now remarkable for its exquisite materials, workmanship, and superfluous ornaments of silver, gold, and pearls; admirable fabrics; wide-spreading embroidery; silk for vests, painted or variously coloured, and lined with divers precious furs from foreign countries. Excitement to gluttony is not wanting; foreign wines are much esteemed, and almost all the people drink in public. The viands are sumptuous; the chief cooks are held in great honour; provocatives of the palate are eagerly sought after; ostentation increases; money-makers exert themselves to supply these tastes; hence usuries, frauds, rapine, extortion, pillage, and contentions in the commonwealth: also unlawful taxes; oppression of the innocent; banishment of citizens, and the combinations of rich men. Our true god is our belly; we adhere to the pomps which were renounced at our baptism, and thus desert to the great enemy of our race. Well indeed does Seneca, the instructor of morals, in his book of orations, curse our times in the following words: 'Daily, things grow worse because the whole contest is for dishonourable matters. Behold! the indolent senses of youth are numbed, nor are they active in the pursuit of any one honest thing. Sleep, languor, and a carefulness for bad things, worse than sleep and languor, have seized upon their minds; the love of singing, dancing, and other unworthy occupations possesses them: they are effeminate: to soften the hair, to lower the tone of their voice to female compliments; to vie with women in effeminacy of person, and adorn themselves with unbecoming delicacy, is the object of our youth.'"

100. Villani, *Cronica,* VI., 69, as quoted in Note 99: "The women used unornamented buskins, and even the most distinguished were content with a close gown of scarlet serge or camlet, confined by a leathern waist-belt of the ancient fashion, and a hooded cloak lined with miniver; and the poorer classes wore a coarse green cloth dress of the same form."

102. Dante, *Convito,* I. 10: "Like the beauty of a woman, when the ornaments of her apparel cause more admiration than she herself."

108. Eastern effeminacy in general; what Boccaccio calls the *morbidezze d' Egitto.* Paul Orosius, "the advocate of the Christian centuries," as quoted by the *Ottimo,* says: "The last king of Syria was Sardanapalus, a man more corrupt than a woman, *(corrotto piu che femmina,)* who was seen by his prefect Arabetes, among a herd of courtesans, clad in female attire."

109. Montemalo, or Montemario, is the hill from which the traveller coming from Viterbo first catches sight of Rome. The Uccellatojo is the hill from which the traveller coming from Bologna first catches sight of Florence. Here the two hills are used to signify what is seen from them; namely, the two cities; and Dante means to say, that Florence had not yet surpassed Rome in the splendour of its buildings; but as Rome would one day be surpassed by Florence in its rise, so would it be in its downfall.

Speaking of the splendour of Florence in Dante's age, Napier, *Florent. Hist.,* II. 581, says:—

"Florence was at this period well studded with handsome dwellings; the citizens were continually building, repairing, altering, and embellishing their houses; adding every day to their ease and comforts, and introducing improvements from foreign nations. Sacred architecture of every kind partook of this taste; and there was no popular citizen or nobleman but either had built or was building fine country palaces and villas, far exceeding their city residence in size and magnificence; so that many were accounted crazy for their extravagance.

"'And so magnificent was the sight,' says Villani, 'that strangers unused to Florence, on coming from abroad, when they beheld the vast assemblage of rich buildings and beautiful palaces with which the country was so thickly studded for three miles round the ramparts, believed that all was city like that within the Roman walls; and this was independent of the rich palaces, towers, courts, and walled gardens at a greater distance, which in other countries would be denominated castles. In short,' he continues, 'it is estimated that within a circuit of six miles round the town there are rich and noble dwellings enough to make two cities like Florence.' And Ariosto seems to have caught the same idea when he exclaims,—

'While gazing on thy villa-studded hills
'Twould seem as though the earth grew palaces
As she is wont by nature to bring forth

Young shoots, and leafy plants, and flowery shrubs:
And if within one wall and single name
Could be collected all thy scattered halls,
Two Romes would scarcely form thy parallel.' "

110. The "which" in this line refers to Montemalo of the preceding.

112. Bellincion Berti, whom Dante selects as a type of the good citizen of Florence in the olden time, and whom Villani calls "the best and most honoured gentleman of Florence," was of the noble family of the Ravignani. He was the father of the "good Gualdrada," whose story shines out so pleasantly in Boccaccio's commentary. See *Inf.* XVI. Note 37.

115. "Two ancient houses of the city," says the *Ottimo;* "and he saw the chiefs of these houses were content with leathern jerkins without any drapery; he who should dress so now-a-days would be laughed at: and he saw their dames spinning, as who should say, 'Now-a-days not even the maid will spin, much less the lady.' " And Buti upon the same text: "They wore leathern dresses without any cloth over them; they did not make to themselves long robes, nor cloaks of scarlet lined with vaire, as they do now."

120. They were not abandoned by their husbands, who, content with little, did not go to traffic in France.

128. Monna Cianghella della Tosa was a gay widow of Florence, who led such a life of pleasure that her name has passed into a proverb, or a common name for a dissolute woman.

Lapo Salterello was a Florentine lawyer, and a man of dissipated habits; and Crescimbeni, whose mill grinds everything that comes to it, counts him among the poets, *Volgar Poesia,* III. 82, and calls him a *Rimatore di non poco grido,* a rhymer of no little renown. Unluckily he quotes one of his sonnets.

129. Quinctius, surnamed Cincinnatus from his neglected locks, taken from his plough and made Dictator by the Roman Senate, and, after he had defeated the Volscians and saved the city, returning to his plough again.

Cornelia, daughter of Scipio Africanus, and mother of the Gracchi, who preferred for her husband a Roman citizen to a king, and boasted that her children were her only jewels.

Shakespeare, *Tit. Andron.,* IV. I:—

> "Ah, boy, Cornelia never with more care
> Read to her sons, than she hath read to thee
> Sweet poetry, and Tully's Orator."

133. The Virgin Mary, invoked in the pains of childbirth, as mentioned *Purg.* XX. 19:—

> "And I by peradventure heard 'Sweet Mary!'
> Uttered in front of us amid the weeping,
> Even as a woman does who is in child-birth."

134. The baptistery of the church of St. John in Florence; *il mio bel San Giovanni,* my beautiful St. John, as Dante calls it. *Inf.* XIX. 17.

135. Of this ancestor of Dante, Cacciaguida, nothing is known but what the poet here tells us, and so clearly that it is not necessary to repeat it in prose.

137. Cacciaguida's wife came from Ferrara in the Val di Pado, or Val di Po, the Valley of the Po. She was of the Aldighieri or Alighieri family, and from her Dante derived his surname.

139. The Emperor Conrad III. of Swabia, uncle of Frederic Barbarossa. In 1143 he joined Louis VII. of France in the Second Crusade, of which St. Bernard was the great preacher. He died in 1152, after his return from this crusade.

140. Cacciaguida was knighted by the Emperor Conrad.

143. The law or religion of Mahomet.

Canto XVI

1. The Heaven of Mars continued.

Boethius, *De Cons. Phil.,* Book III. Prosa 6, Ridpath's Tr.: "But who is there that does not perceive the emptiness and futility of what men dignify with the name of high extraction, or nobility of birth? The splendour you attribute to this is quite foreign to you: for nobility of descent is nothing else but the credit derived from the merit of your ancestors. If it is the applause of mankind, and nothing besides, that illustrates and confers fame upon a person, no others can be celebrated and famous, but such as are universally applauded. If you are not therefore esteemed illustrious from your own worth, you can derive no real splendour from the merits of others: so that, in my opinion, nobility is in no other respect good, than as it imposes an obligation upon its possessors not to degenerate from the merit of their ancestors."

10. The use of You for Thou, the plural for the singular, is said to have been introduced in the time of Julius Cæsar. Lucan, V., Rowe's Tr.:—

> "Then was the time when sycophants began
> To heap all titles on one lordly man."

Dante uses it by way of compliment to his ancestor; though he says the descendants of the Romans were not so persevering in its use as other Italians.

14. Beatrice smiled to give notice to Dante that she observed his flattering style of address; as the Lady of Malehault coughed when she saw Launcelot kiss Queen Guinevere, as related in the old romance of Launcelot of the Lake.

20. Rejoiced within itself that it can endure so much joy.

25. The city of Florence, which, in Canto XXV. 5, Dante calls "the fair sheepfold, where a lamb I slumbered." It will be remembered that St. John the Baptist is the patron saint of Florence.

33. Not in Italian, but in Latin, which was the language of cultivated people in Cacciaguida's time.

34. From the Incarnation of Christ down to his own birth, the planet Mars had returned to the sign of the Lion five hundred and eighty times, or made this number of revolutions in its orbit. Brunetto Latini, Dante's schoolmaster, *Tresor,* I. Ch. cxi., says, that Mars "goes through all the signs in ii. years and i. month and xxx. days." This would make Cacciaguida born long after the crusade in which he died. But Dante, who had perhaps seen the astronomical tables of King Alfonso of Castile, knew more of the matter than his schoolmaster, and was aware that the period of a revolution of Mars is less than two years. Witte, who cites these tables in his notes to this canto, says they give "686 days 22 hours and 24 minutes"; and continues: "Five hundred and eighty such revolutions give then (due regard being had to the leap-years) 1090 years and not quite four months. Cacciaguida, therefore, at the time of the Second Crusade, was in his fifty-seventh year."

Pietro di Dante (the poet's son and commentator, and who, as Biagioli, with rather gratuitous harshness, says, was "smaller compared to his father than a point is to the universe") assumed two years as a revolution of Mars; but as this made Cacciaguida born in 1160, twelve years after his death, he suggested the reading of "three," instead of "thirty," in the text, which reading was adopted by the Cruscan Academy, and makes the year of Cacciaguida's birth 1106.

But that Dante computed the revolution of Mars at less than two years is evident from a passage in the *Convito,* II. 15, referred to by Philalethes, where he speaks of half a revolution of this planet as *un anno quasi,* almost a year. The common reading of "thirty" is undoubtedly then the true one.

In Astrology, the Lion is the House of the Sun; but Mars, as well as the Sun and Jupiter, is a Lord of the Lion; and hence Dante says "its Lion."

41. The house in which Cacciaguida was born stood in the Mercato Vecchio, or Old Market, at the beginning of the last ward or *sesto* of Florence toward the east, called the Porta San Pietro.

The city of Florence was originally divided into Quarters or Gates, which were, San Pancrazio on the east, San Pietro on the west, the Duomo on the north, and Santa Maria on the south. Afterwards, when the new walls were built and the city enlarged, these Quarters were changed to *Sesti,* or Sixths, by dividing Santa Maria into the Borgo and San Pietro Scheraggio, and adding the Oltrarno (beyond the Arno) on the southern bank.

42. The annual races of Florence on the 24th of June, the festival of St. John the Baptist. The prize was the *Pallio,* or mantle of "crimson silk velvet," as Villani says; and the race was run from San Pancrazio, the western ward of the city, through the Mercato Vecchio, to the eastern ward of San Piero. According to Benvenuto, the Florentine races were horse-races; but the Pallio of Verona, where the prize was the "Green Mantle," was manifestly a foot-race. See *Inf.* XV. 122.

47. Between the Ponte Vecchio, where once stood the statue of Mars, and the church of St. John the Baptist.

50. Campi is a village between Prato and Florence, in

"The valley whence Bisenzio descends."

Certaldo is in the Val d'Elsa, and is chiefly celebrated as being the birthplace of Boccaccio,—"true *Bocca d'Oro,* or Mouth of Gold," says Benvenuto, with enthusiasm, "my venerated master, and a most diligent and familiar student of Dante, and who wrote a certain book that greatly helps us to understand him."

Figghine, or Figline, is a town in the Val d'Arno, some twelve miles distant from Florence; and hateful to Dante as the birthplace of the "ribald lawyer, Ser Dego," as Campi was of another ribald lawyer, Ser Fozio; and Certaldo of a certain Giacomo, who thrust the Podestà of Florence from his seat, and undertook to govern the city. These men, mingling with the old Florentines, corrupted the simple manners of the town.

53. Galluzzo lies to the south of Florence on the road to Siena, and Trespiano about the same distance to the north, on the road to Bologna.

56. Aguglione and Signa are also Tuscan towns in the neighbourhood of Florence. According to Covino, *Descriz. Geog. dell' Italia,* p. 18, it was a certain Baldo d'Aguglione, who condemned Dante to be burned; and Bonifazio da Signa, according to Buti, "tyrannized over the city, and sold the favours and offices of the Commune."

58. The clergy. "Popes, cardinals, bishops, and archbishops, who govern the Holy Church," says Buti; and continues: "If the Church had been a mother, instead of a step-mother to the Emperors, and had not excommunicated, and persecuted, and published them as heretics, Italy would have been well governed, and there would have been none of those civil wars, that dismantled and devastated the smaller towns, and drove their inhabitants into Florence, to trade and discount."

Napier, *Florent. Hist.,* I. 597, says: "The *Arte del Cambio,* or money-trade, in which Florence shone pre-eminent, soon made her bankers known and almost necessary to all Europe. . . . But amongst all foreign nations they were justly considered, according to the admission of their own countrymen, as hard, griping, and exacting; they were called *Lombard dogs;* hated and insulted by nations less acquainted with trade and certainly less civilized than themselves, when they may only have demanded a fair interest for money lent at a great risk to lawless men in a foreign country. . . . All counting-houses of Florentine bankers were confined to the old and new market-places, where alone they were allowed to transact business: before the door was placed a bench, and a table covered with carpet, on which stood their money-bags and account-book for the daily transactions of trade."

62. Simifonte, a village near Certaldo. It was captured by the Florentines, and made part of their territory, in 1202.

64. In the valley of the Ombrone, east of Pistoia, are still to be seen the ruins of Montemurlo, once owned by the Counts Guidi, and by them sold

to the Florentines in 1203, because they could not defend it against the Pistoians.

65. The *Pivier d'Acone,* or parish of Acone, is in the Val di Sieve, or Valley of the Sieve, one of the affluents of the Arno. Here the powerful family of the Cerchi had their castle of Monte di Croce, which was taken and destroyed by the Florentines in 1053, and the Cerchi and others came to live in Florence, where they became the leaders of the *Parte Bianca.* See *Inf.* VI. Note 65.

66. The Buondelmonti were a wealthy and powerful family of Valdigrieve, or Valley of the Grieve, which, like the Sieve, is an affluent of the Arno. They too, like the Cerchi, came to Florence, when their lands were taken by the Florentines, and were in a certain sense the cause of Guelph and Ghibelline quarrels in the city. See *Inf.* X. Note 51.

70. The downfall of a great city is more swift and terrible than that of a smaller one; or, as Venturi interprets, "The size of the body and greater robustness of strength in a city and state are not helpful, but injurious to their preservation, unless men live in peace and without the blindness of the passions, and Florence, more poor and humble, would have flourished longer."

Perhaps the best commentary of all is that contained in the two lines of Chaucer's *Troilus and Cresseide,* II. 1385,—aptly quoted by Mr. Cary:—

> "For swifter course cometh thing that is of wight,
> Whan it descendeth, than done thinges light."

72. In this line we have in brief Dante's political faith, which is given in detail in his treatise *De Monarchia.* See the article "Dante's Creed," among the illustrations of Vol. II.

73. Luni, an old Etruscan city in the Lunigiana; and Urbisaglia, a Roman city in the Marca d'Ancona.

75. Chiusi is in the Sienese territory, and Sinigaglia on the Adriatic, east of Rome. This latter place has somewhat revived since Dante's time.

76. Boccaccio seems to have caught something of the spirit of this canto, when, lamenting the desolation of Florence by the plague in 1348, he says in the Introduction to the *Decamerone:* "How many vast palaces, how many beautiful houses, how many noble dwellings, aforetime filled with lords and ladies and trains of servants, were now untenanted even by the lowest menial! How many memorable families, how many ample heritages, how many renowned possessions, were left without an heir! How many valiant men, how many beautiful women, how many gentle youths, breakfasted in the morning with their relatives, companions, and friends, and, when the evening came, supped with their ancestors in the other world!"

78. Lowell, *To the Past:*—

> "Still as a city buried 'neath the sea,
> Thy courts and temples stand;
> Idle as forms on wind-waved tapestry

> Of saints and heroes grand,
> Thy phantasms grope and shiver,
> Or watch the loose shores crumbling silently
> Into Time's gnawing river."

"Our fathers," says Sir Thomas Browne, *Urn Burial,* V., "find their graves in our short memories, and sadly tell us how we may be buried in our survivors. Grave-stones tell truth scarce forty years. Generations pass while some trees stand, and old families last not three oaks. . . . Oblivion is not to be hired. The greater part must be content to be as though they had not been, to be found in the register of God, not in the record of man. Twenty-seven names make up the first story, and the recorded names ever since contain not one living century. The number of the dead long exceedeth all that shall live. The night of time far surpasseth the day; and who knows when was the equinox? Every hour adds unto that current arithmetic, which scarce stands one moment."

79. Shirley, *Death's Final Conquest:*—

> "The glories of our birth and state
>   Are shadows, not substantial things:
> There is no armour against Fate;
>   Death lays his icy hand on kings;
>   Sceptre and crown
>   Must tumble down,
>   And in the dust be equal made
>   With the poor crooked scythe and spade."

81. The lives of men are too short for them to measure the decay of things around them.

86. It would be an unprofitable task to repeat in notes the names of these

> "Great Florentines
> Of whom the fame is hidden in the Past,"

and who flourished in the days of Cacciaguida and the Emperor Conrad. It will be better to follow Villani, as he points out with a sigh their dwellings in the old town, and laments over their decay. In his *Cronica,* Book IV., he speaks as follows:—

"Ch. X. As already mentioned, the first rebuilding of Little Florence was divided by Quarters, that is, by four gates; and that we may the better make known the noble races and houses, which in those times, after Fiesole was destroyed, were great and powerful in Florence, we will enumerate them by the quarters where they lived.

"And first those of the Porta del Duomo, which was the first fold and habitation of the new Florence, and the place where all the noble citizens resorted and met together on Sunday, and where all marriages were made, and all reconciliations, and all pomps and solemnities of the Commune. . . . At the Porta del Duomo lived the descendants of the Giovanni and of the Guineldi, who were the first that rebuilt the city of Florence, and from whom descended many noble families in Mugello and in Valdarno, and many in the city, who now are common people, and almost come to an end. Such were the Barucci, who lived at Santa Maria Maggiore, who are now extinct; and of their race were the Scali and Palermini. In the same quarter were also the Arrigucci, the Sizii, and the sons of Della Tosa; and the Della Tosa were the same race as the Bisdomini, and custodians and defenders of the bishopric; but one of them left his family at the Porta San Piero, and took to wife a lady named Della Tosa, who had the inheritance, whence the name was derived. And there were the Della Pressa, who lived among the Chiavaiuoli, men of gentle birth.

"Ch. XI. In the quarter of Porta San Piero were the Bisdomini, who, as above mentioned, were custodians of the bishopric; and the Alberighi, to whom belonged the church of Santa Maria Alberighi, of the house of the Donati, and now they are naught. The Rovignani were very great, and lived at the Porta San Pietro; and then came the houses of the Counts Guidi, and then of the Cerchi, and from them in the female line were born all the Counts Guidi, as before mentioned, of the daughter of good Messer Bellincion Berti; in our day all this race is extinct. The Galligari and Chiarmontesi and Ardinghi, who lived in the Orto San Michele, were very ancient; and so were the Giuochi, who now are *popolani,* living at Santa Margherita; the Elisei, who likewise are now *popolani,* living near the Mercato Vecchio. And in that place lived the Caponsacchi, who were nobles of Fiesole; the Donati, or Calfucci, for they were all one race, but the Calfucci are extinct; and the Della Bella of San Martino, also become *popolani;* and the Adimari, who descended from the house of Cosi, who now live at Porta Rossa, and who built Santa Maria Nipotecosa; and although they are now the principal family of that ward of Florence, in those days they were not of the oldest.

"Ch. XII. At the Porta San Pancrazio, of great rank and power were the Lamberti, descended from the Della Magna; the Ughi were very ancient, and built Santa Maria Ughi, and all the hill of Montughi belonged to them, and now they have died out; the Catellini were very ancient, and now they are forgotten. It is said that the Tieri were illegitimate descendants of theirs. The Pigli were great and noble in those times, and the Soldanieri and Vecchietti. Very ancient were the Dell' Arca, and now they are extinct; and the Migliorelli, who now are naught; and the Trinciavelli da Mosciano were very ancient.

"Ch. XIII. In the quarter of Porta Santa Maria, which is now in the ward of San Piero Scheraggio and of Borgo, there were many powerful and ancient families. The greatest were the Uberti, whose ancestors were the Della Magna, and who lived where now stand the Piazza de' Priori and the Palazzo del Popolo; the Fifanti, called Bogolesi, lived at the corner of Porta Santa Maria; the Galli, Cappiardi, Guidi, and Filippi, who now are nothing, were then great and powerful, and lived in the Mercato Nuovo. Likewise the Greci, to whom all the Borgo de' Greci belonged, have now perished and passed away, except some of the race in Bologna; and the Ormanni, who lived where now stands the forementioned Palazzo del Popolo, and are now called Foraboschi. And behind San Piero Scheraggio, where are now the houses of the Petri, lived the Della Pera, or Peruzza, and from them the postern gate there was called Porta Peruzza. Some say that the Peruzzi of the present day are of that family, but I do not affirm it. The Sacchetti, who lived in the Garbo, were very ancient; around the Mercato Nuovo the Bostichi were great people, and the Della Sanella, and Giandonati and Infangati; great in Borgo Santi Apostoli were the Gualterotti and Importuni, who now are *popolani*. The Buondelmonti were noble and ancient citizens in the rural districts, and Montebuoni was their castle, and many others in Valdigrieve; at first they lived in Oltrarno, and then came to the Borgo. The Pulci, and the Counts of Gangalandi, Ciuffagni, and Nerli of Oltrarno were at one time great and powerful, together with the Giandonati and Della Bella, named above; and from the Marquis Hugo, who built the Abbey, or Badia, of Florence, received arms and knighthood, for they were very great around him."

To the better understanding of this extract from Villani, it must be borne in mind that, at the time when he wrote, the population of Florence was divided into three classes, the Nobles, the Popolani, or middle class, and the Plebeians.

93. Gianni del Soldanier is put among the traitors "with Ganellon and Tebaldello," *Inf.* XXXII. 121.

95. The Cerchi, who lived near the Porta San Piero, and produced dissension in the city with their White and Black factions;—such a cargo, that it must be thrown overboard to save the ship. See *Inf.* VI. Note 65.

98. The County Guido, for Count Guido, as in Shakespeare the County Paris and County Palatine, and in the old song in Scott's *Quentin Durward:*—

> "Ah, County Guy, the hour is nigh,
>   The sun has left the lea."

99. Bellincion Berti. See Canto XV. 112, and *Inf.* XVI. Note 87.

102. The insignia of knighthood.

103. The Billi, or Pigli, family; their arms being "a Column Vair in a red field." The Column Vair was the bar of the shield "variegated with argent and azure." The vair, in Italian *vajo,* is a kind of squirrel; and the heraldic mingling of colours was taken from its spotted skin.

105. The Chiaramontesi, one of whom, a certain Ser Durante, an officer in the customs, falsified the bushel, or *stajo,* of Florence, by having it made one stave less, so as to defraud in the measure. Dante alludes to this in *Purg.* XII. 105.

109. The Uberti, of whom was Farinata. See *Inf.* X. 32.

110. The Balls of Gold were the arms of the Lamberti family. Dante mentions them by their arms, says the *Ottimo*, "as who should say, as the ball is the symbol of the universe, and gold surpasses every other metal, so in goodness and valour these surpassed the other citizens." Dante puts Mosca de' Lamberti among the Schismatics in *Inf.* XXVIII. 103, with both hands cut off, and

"The stumps uplifting through the dusky air."

112. The Vidomini, Tosinghi, and Cortigiani, custodians and defenders of the Bishopric of Florence. Their fathers were honourable men, and, like the Lamberti, embellished the city with their good name and deeds; but they, when a bishop died, took possession of the episcopal palace, and, as custodians and defenders, feasted and slept there till his successor was appointed.

115. The Adimari. One of this family, Boccaccio Adimari, got possession of Dante's property in Florence when he was banished, and always bitterly opposed his return.

119. Ubertin Donato, a gentleman of Florence, had married one of the Ravignani, and was offended that her sister should be given in marriage to one of the Adimari, who were of ignoble origin.

121. The Caponsacchi lived in the Mercato Vecchio, or Old Market. One of the daughters was the wife of Folco Portinari and mother of Beatrice.

124. The thing incredible is that there should have been so little jealousy among the citizens of Florence as to suffer one of the city gates, Porta Peruzza, to be named after a particular family.

127. Five Florentine families, according to Benvenuto, bore the arms of the Marquis Hugo of Brandenburg, and received from him the titles and privileges of nobility. These were the Pulci, Nerli, Giandonati, Gangalandi, and Della Bella.

This Marquis Hugo, whom Dante here calls "the great baron," was Viceroy of the Emperor Otho III. in Tuscany. Villani, *Cronica,* IV., Ch. 2, relates the following story of him:—"It came to pass, as it pleased God, that, while hunting in the neighbourhood of Bonsollazzo, he was lost in the forest, and came, as it seemed to him, to a smithy. Finding there men swarthy and hideous, who, instead of iron, seemed to be tormenting human beings with fire and hammers, he asked the meaning of it. He was told that these were lost souls, and that to a like punishment was condemned the soul of the Marquis Hugo, on account of his worldly life, unless he repented. In great terror he commended himself to the Virgin Mary; and, when the vision vanished, remained so contrite in spirit, that, having returned to Florence, he had all his patrimony in Germany sold, and ordered seven abbeys to be built; the first of which was the Badia of Florence, in honour of Santa Maria; the second, that of Bonsollazzo, where he saw the vision."

The Marquis Hugo died on St. Thomas's day, December 31, 1006, and was buried in the Badia of Florence, where every year on that day the monks, in grateful memory of him, kept the anniversary of his death with great solemnity.

130. Giano della Bella, who disguised the arms of Hugo, quartered in his own, with a fringe of gold. A nobleman by birth and education, he was by conviction a friend of the people, and espoused their cause against the nobles. By reforming the abuses of both parties, he gained the ill-will of both; and in 1294, after some popular tumult which he in vain strove to quell, went into voluntary exile, and died in France.

Sismondi, *Ital. Rep.,* p. 113 (Lardner's Cyclopædia), gives the following succinct account of the abuses which Giano strove to reform, and of his summary manner of doing it: "The arrogance of the nobles, their quarrels, and the disturbance of the public peace by their frequent battles in the streets, had, in 1292, irritated the whole population against them. Giano della Bella, himself a noble, but sympathizing in the passions and resentment of the people, proposed to bring them to order by summary justice, and to confide the execution of it to the gonfalonier whom he caused to be elected. The Guelfs had been so long at the head of the republic, that their noble families, whose wealth had immensely increased, placed themselves above all law. Giano determined that their nobility itself should be a title of exclusion, and a commencement of punishment; a rigorous edict, bearing the title of 'ordinance of justice,' first designated thirty-seven Guelf families of Florence, whom it declared noble and great, and on this account excluded forever from the *signoria;* refusing them at the same time the privilege of renouncing their nobility, in order to place themselves on a footing with the other citizens. When these families troubled the public peace by battle or assassination, a summary information, or even common report, was sufficient to induce the gonfalonier to attack them at the head of the militia, raze their houses to the ground, and deliver their persons to the Podestà, to be punished according to their crimes. If other families committed the same disorders, if they troubled the state by their private feuds and outrages, the *signoria* was authorized to ennoble them, as a punishment of their crimes, in order to subject them to the same summary justice."

Dino Compagni, a contemporary of Giano, *Cronica Fiorentina,* Book I., says of him: "He was a manly man, of great courage, and so bold that he defended those causes which others abandoned, and said those things which others kept silent, and did all in favour of justice against the guilty, and was so much feared by the magistrates that they were afraid to screen the evildoers. The great began to speak against him, threatening him, and they did it, not for the sake of justice, but to destroy their enemies, abominating him and the laws."

Villani, *Cronica,* VIII. ch. 8, says: "Giano della Bella was condemned and banished for contumacy, ... and all his possessions confiscated, ... whence great mischief accrued to our city, and chiefly to the people, for he was the most loyal and upright *popolano* and lover of the public good of any man in Florence."

And finally Macchiavelli, *Istorie Florentine,* Book II., calls him "a lover of the liberty of his country," and says, "he was hated by the nobility for undermining their authority, and envied by the richer of the commonalty, who were jealous of his power;" and that he went into voluntary exile in order "to deprive his enemies of all opportunity of injuring him, and his friends of all opportunity of injuring the country;" and that "to free the citizens from the fear they had of him, he resolved to leave the city, which, at his own charge and danger, he had liberated from the servitude of the powerful."

134. The Borgo Santi Apostoli would be a quieter place, if the Buondelmonti had not moved into it from Oltrarno.

136. The house of Amidei, whose quarrel with the Buondelmonti was the origin of the Guelf and Ghibelline parties in Florence, and put an end to the joyous life of her citizens. See *Inf.* X. Note 51.

140. See the story of Buondelmonte, as told by Giovanni Fiorentino in his *Pecorone,* and quoted *Inf.* X. Note 51.

142. Much sorrow and suffering would have been spared, if the first Buondelmonte that came from his castle of Montebuono to Florence had been drowned in the Ema, a small stream he had to cross on the way.

145. Young Buondelmonte was murdered at the foot of the mutilated statue of Mars on the Ponte Vecchio, and after this Florence had no more peace.

153. The banner of Florence had never been reversed in sign of defeat.

154. The arms of Florence were a white lily in a field of red; after the expulsion of the Ghibellines, the Guelfs changed them to a red lily in a field of white.

Canto XVII

1. The Heaven of Mars continued. The prophecy of Dante's banishment. In *Inf.* X. 127, as Dante is meditating on the dark words of Farinata that foreshadow his exile, Virgil says to him:—

> " 'Let memory preserve what thou hast heard
>   Against thyself,' that Sage commanded me,
>   'And now attend here;' and he raised his finger.
> 'When thou shalt be before the radiance sweet
>   Of her whose beauteous eyes all things behold,
>   From her thou'lt learn the journey of thy life.' "

And afterwards, in reply to Brunetto Latini, Dante says, *Inf.* XV. 88:—

> "What you narrate of my career I write,
>   And keep it for a lady, who will know,
>   To gloss with other text, if e'er I reach her."

The time for this revelation has now come; but it is made by Cacciaguida, not by Beatrice.

3. Phaeton, having heard from Epaphus that he was not the son of Apollo, ran in great eagerness and anxiety to his mother, Clymene, to ascertain the truth. Ovid, *Met.*, I., Dryden's Tr.:—

> "Mother, said he, this infamy was thrown
>   By Epaphus on you, and me your son.
>   He spoke in public, told it to my face;
>   Nor durst I vindicate the dire disgrace:
>   Even I, the bold, the sensible of wrong.
>   Restrained by shame, was forced to hold my tongue.
>   To hear an open slander, is a curse:
>   But not to find an answer, is a worse.
>   If I am heaven-begot, assert your son
>   By some sure sign; and make my father known,
>   To right my honour, and redeem your own.
>   He said, and, saying, cast his arms about
>   Her neck, and begged her to resolve the doubt."

The disaster that befell Phaeton while driving the steeds of Apollo, makes fathers chary of granting all the wishes of children.

16. Who seest in God all possible contingencies as clearly as the human mind perceives the commonest geometrical problem.

18. God, "whose centre is everywhere, whose circumference nowhere."

20. The heavy words which Dante heard on the mount of Purgatory, foreshadowing his exile, are those of Currado Malaspina, *Purg.* VIII. 133:—

> "For the sun shall not lie
>   Seven times upon the pillow which the Ram
>   With all his four feet covers and bestrides,
> Before that such a courteous opinion
>   Shall in the middle of thy head be nailed
>   With greater nails than of another's speech,
> Unless the course of justice standeth still:"

and those of Oderisi d'Agobbio, *Purg.* XI. 139:—

> "I say no more, and know that I speak darkly;
>   Yet little time shall pass before thy neighbours
>   Will so demean themselves that thou canst gloss it."

21. The words he heard "when descending into the dead world," are those of Farinata, *Inf.* X. 79:—

> "But fifty times shall not rekindled be
>   The countenance of the Lady who reigns here,
>   Ere thou shalt know how heavy is that art;"

and those of Brunetto Latini, *Inf.* XV. 61:—

> "But that ungrateful and malignant people,
>   Which from Fiesole of old descended,
>   And smacks still of the mountain and the granite,
>   Will make itself, for thy good deeds, thy foe."

24. Aristotle, *Ethics,* I. ch. 10: "Always and everywhere the virtuous man bears prosperous and adverse fortune prudently, as a perfect tetragon."

28. To the spirit of Cacciaguida.

31. Not like the ambiguous utterance of oracles in Pagan times.

35. The word here rendered Language is in the original *Latin;* used as in Canto XII. 144.

37. Contingency, accident, or casualty, belongs only to the material world, and in the spiritual world finds no place. As Dante makes St. Bernard say, in Canto XXXII. 53.—

> "Within the amplitude of this domain
>   No casual point can possibly find place,
>   No more than sadness can, or thirst, or hunger;
>   For by eternal law has been established
>   Whatever thou beholdest."

40. Boethius, *Consol. Phil.,* V. Prosa 3, Ridpath's Tr.: "But I shall now endeavour to demonstrate, that, in whatever way the chain of causes is disposed, the event of things which are foreseen is necessary; although prescience may not appear to be the necessitating cause of their befalling. For example, if a person sits, the opinion formed of him that he is seated, is of necessity true; but by inverting the phrase, if the opinion is true that he is seated, he must necessarily sit. In both cases then there is a necessity; in the latter, that the person sits; in the former, that the opinion concerning him is true: but the person doth not sit, because the opinion of his sitting is true; but the opinion is rather true, because the action of his being seated was antecedent in time. Thus though the truth of the opinion may be the effect of the person taking a seat, there is nevertheless a necessity common to both. The same method of reasoning, I think, should be employed with regard to the prescience of God, and future contingencies; for allowing it to be true, that events are foreseen because they are to happen, and that they do not befall

because they are foreseen, it is still necessary, that what is to happen must be foreseen by God, and that what is foreseen must take place."

And again, in Prosa 4 of the same Book: "But how is it possible, said I, that those things which are foreseen should not befall?—I do not say, replied she, that we are to entertain any doubt but the events will take place, which Providence foresees are to happen; but we are rather to believe, that although they do happen, yet that there is no necessity in the events themselves, which constrains them to do so. The truth of which I shall thus endeavour to illustrate. We behold many things done under our view, such as a coachman conducting his chariot and governing his horses, and other things of a like nature. Now, do you suppose these things are done by the compulsion of a necessity?—No, answered I; for, if everything were moved by compulsion, the effects of art would be vain and fruitless.—If things then, which are doing under our eye, added she, are under no present necessity of happening, it must be admitted that these same things, before they befell, were under no necessity of taking place. It is plain, therefore, that some things befall, the event of which is altogether unconstrained by necessity. For I do not think any person will say that such things as are at present done, were not to happen before they were done. Why, therefore, may not things be foreseen, and not necessitated in their events? As the knowledge then of what is present imposes no necessity on things now done, so neither does the foreknowledge of what is to happen in future necessitate the things which are to take place."

Also Chaucer, *Troil. and Cres.*, IV., 995:—

> "Eke, this is an opinion of some
> That have hir top ful high and smoth ishore;
> Thei sain right thus; that thing is nat to come
> For-that the prescience hath sene before,
> That it shal come: but thei sain that therefore
> That it shall come, therefore the purveiaunce
> Wote it beforne withouten ignoraunce.

> "And in this maner, this necessite,
> Retourneth in his place contrary, againe;
> For nedefully, behoveth it nat be,
> That thilke thinges fallen in certaine
> That ben purveyed; but, nedefully, as thei saine,
> Behoveth it, that thinges which that fall,
> That thei in certaine ben purveyed all:

> "I mene, as though I laboured me in this,
> To enquire which thing cause of which thing be,
> As whether that the prescience of God is
> The certaine cause of the necessite
> Of thinges that to comen be, parde,

Or, if necessite of thing coming
Be the cause certaine of the purveying?

    "But, now, ne enforce I me not, in shewing
How the order of the causes stant; but wot I,
That it behoveth that the befalling
Of thinges, wistè before certainly,
Be necessarie—al seme it not therby
That prescience put falling necessayre
To thing to come, al fal it foule or faire:

    "For, if there sit a man yonde on a see,—
Than by necessite behoveth it
That, certes, thine opinion sothe be
That wenest or conjectest that he sit.
And, furtherover, now ayenwarde yet,—
Lo, right so is it on the part contrarie;
As thus; now herken, for I wol nat tarie:

    "I say, that if the opinion of the
Be sothe, for-that he sit; than say I this,
That he mote sitten, by necessite.
And thus necessite, in either, is.
For in him nede of sitting is, iwis;
And in the, nede of sothe: and thus, forsothe,
There mote necessite ben in you bothe.

    "But thou maist saine, the man sit nat therefore
That thine opinion of his sitting soth is:
But, rather, for the man sate there before,
Therefore is thine opinion sothe iwis:
And I say, Though the cause of sothe of this
Cometh of his sitting; yet necessite
Is enterchaunged bothe in him and the."

46. As Hippolytus was banished from Athens on the false and cruel accusations of Phædra, his step-mother, so Dante shall be from Florence on accusations equally false and cruel.

50. By instigation of Pope Boniface VIII. in Rome, as Dante here declares. In April, 1302, the Bianchi were banished from Florence on account or under pretext of a conspiracy against Charles of Valois, who had been called to Florence by the Guelfs as pacificator of Tuscany. In this conspiracy Dante could have had no part, as he was then absent on an embassy to Rome.

Dino Compagni, *Cron. Flor.,* II., gives a list of many of the exiles. Among them is "Dante Aldighieri, ambassador at Rome;" and at the end of the names given he adds, "and many more, as many as six hundred men, who wandered here and there about the world, suffering much want." At first, the banishment was for two years only; but a second decree made it for life, with the penalty that, if any one of the exiles returned to Florence, he should be burned to death.

On the exile of Dante, M. Ampère has written an interesting work under the title of *Voyage Dantesque,* from which frequent extracts have been made in these notes. "I have followed him, step by step," he says, "in the cities where he lived, in the mountains where he wandered, in the asylums that welcomed him, always guided by the poem, in which he has recorded, with all the sentiments of his soul and all the speculations of his intelligence, all the recollections of his life; a poem which is no less a confession than a vast encyclopædia."

See also the Letter of Frate Ilario, the passage from the *Convito,* and Dante's Letter to a Friend, among the Illustrations to *Inferno.*

52. Boethius, *Cons. Phil.,* I. Prosa 4, Ridpath's Tr.: "But my miseries are complete, when I reflect that the majority of mankind attend less to the merit of things, than to their fortuitous event; and believe that no undertakings are crowned with success, but such as are formed with a prudent foresight. Hence it is, that the unprosperous immediately lose the good opinion of mankind. It would give me pain to relate to you the rumours that are flying among the people, and the variety of discordant and inconsistent opinions entertained concerning me."

53. At the beginning of *Inf.* XXVI. Dante foreshadows the vengeance of God that is to fall on Florence, and exclaims:—

> "And if it now were, it were not too soon;
> > Would that it were, seeing it needs must be,
> > For 'twill aggrieve me more the more I age."

For an account of these disasters see *Inf.* XXVI. Note 9.

58. Upon this passage Mr. Wright, in the notes to his translation, makes the following extracts from the Bible, Shakespeare, and Spenser:—

Ecclesiasticus xxix. 24 and xl. 28, 29: "It is a miserable thing to go from house to house; for where thou art a stranger, thou darest not open thy mouth. Thou shalt entertain, and feast, and have no thanks: moreover, thou shalt hear bitter words. . . . . These things are grievous to a man of understanding,—the upbraiding of house-room, and reproaching of the lender." "My son, lead not a beggar's life, for better it is to die than to beg. The life of him that dependeth on another man's table is not to be counted for a life."

Richard II, III. 1:—

> "Myself
> > Have stooped my neck under your injuries,
> > And sighed my English breath in foreign clouds,
> > Eating the bitter bread of banishment."

Spenser, *Mother Hubberd's Tale,* 895:—

> "Full little knowest thou, that hast not tried,
> What Hell it is, in suing long to bide:
> To lose good days, that might be better spent;
> To waste long nights, in pensive discontent;
> To speed to-day, to be put back to-morrow;
> To feed on hope, to pine with fear and sorrow;
> To have thy Prince's grace, yet want her Peer's,
> To have thy asking, yet wait many years;
> To fret thy soul with crosses and with cares;
> To eat thy heart with comfortless despairs;
> To fawn, to crouch, to wait, to ride, to run,
> To spend, to give,—to want,—to be undone."

62. Among the fellow-exiles of Dante, as appears by the list of names preserved, was Lapo Salterello, the Florentine lawyer, of whom Dante speaks so contemptuously in Canto XV. 128. Benvenuto says he was "a litigious and loquacious man, and very annoying to Dante during his exile. Altogether the company of his fellow-exiles seems to have been disagreeable to him, and it better suited him to "make a party by himself."

66. Shall blush with shame.

71. Bartolommeo della Scala, Lord of Verona. The arms of the Scaligers were a golden ladder in a red field, surmounted by a black eagle. "For a tyrant," says Benvenuto, "he was reputed just and prudent."

76. Can Grande della Scala, at this time only nine years old, but showing, says Benvenuto, "that he would be a true son of Mars, bold and prompt in battle, and victorious exceedingly." He was a younger brother of Bartolommeo, and became sole Lord of Verona in 1311. He was the chief captain of the Ghibellines, and his court the refuge of some of the principal of the exiles. Dante was there in 1317 with Guido da Castello and Uguccione della Faggiuola. To Can Grande he dedicated some cantos of the Paradiso, and presented them with that long Latin letter so difficult to associate with the name of Dante.

At this time the court of Verona seems to have displayed a kind of barbaric splendour and magnificence, as if in imitation of the gay court of Frederick II. of Sicily. Arrivabene, *Comento Storico,* III. 255, says: "Can Grande gathered around him those distinguished personages whom unfortunate reverses had driven from their country; but he also kept in his pay buffoons and musicians, and other merry persons, who were more caressed by the courtiers than the men famous for their deeds and learning. One of the guests was Sagacio Muzio Gazzata, the historian of Reggio, who has left us an account of the treatment which the illustrious and unfortunate exiles received. Various apartments were assigned to them in the palace, designated by various symbols; a Triumph for the warriors; Groves of the Muses for the poets; Mercury for the artists; Paradise for the preachers; and for all, inconstant Fortune.

Can Grande likewise received at his court his illustrious prisoners of war,
Giacomo di Carrara, Vanne Scornazano, Albertino Mussato, and many oth-
ers. All had their private attendants, and a table equally well served. At times
Can Grande invited some of them to his own table, particularly Dante, and
Guido di Castel of Reggio, exiled from his country with the friends of liberty,
and who for his simplicity was called 'the simple Lombard.'"

The harmony of their intercourse seems finally to have been interrupted,
and Dante to have fallen into that disfavour, which he hints at below, hoping
that, having been driven from Florence, he may not also be driven from
Verona:—

> "That, if the dearest place be taken from me,
>   I may not lose the others by my songs."

Balbo, *Life of Dante,* Mrs. Bunbury's Tr., II. 207, says: "History, tradition,
and the after fortunes of Dante, all agree in proving that there was a rupture
between him and Cane; if it did not amount to a quarrel, there seems to have
been some misunderstanding between the magnificent protector and his
haughty client. But which of the two was in fault? I have collected all the
memorials that remain relating to this, and let every one judge for himself.
But I must warn my readers that Petrarch, the second of the three fathers of
the Italian language, showed much less veneration than our good Boccaccio
for their common predecessor Dante. Petrarch speaks as follows: 'My fellow-
citizen, Dante Alighieri, was a man highly distinguished in the vulgar tongue,
but in his style and speech a little daring and rather freer than was pleasing
to delicate and studious ears, or gratifying to the princes of our times. He
then, while banished from his country, resided at the court of Can Grande,
where the afflicted universally found consolation and an asylum. He at first
was held in much honour by Cane, but afterwards he by degrees fell out of
favour, and day by day less pleased that lord. Actors and parasites of every
description used to be collected together at the same banquet; one of these,
most impudent in his words and in his obscene gestures, obtained much
importance and favour with many. And Cane, suspecting that Dante disliked
this, called the man before him, and, having greatly praised him to our poet,
said: "I wonder how it is that this silly fellow should know how to please all,
and should be loved by all, and that thou canst not, who art said to be so
wise!" Dante answered: "Thou wouldst not wonder if thou knewest that
friendship is founded on similarity of habits and dispositions."'

"It is also related, that at his table, which was too indiscriminately hospi-
table, where buffoons sat down with Dante, and where jests passed which
must have been offensive to every person of refinement, but disgraceful when
uttered by the superior in rank to his inferior, a boy was once concealed
under the table, who, collecting the bones that were thrown there by the
guests, according to the custom of those times, heaped them up at Dante's
feet. When the tables were removed, the great heap appearing, Cane pretended

to show much astonishment, and said, 'Certainly, Dante is a great devourer of meat.' To which Dante readily replied, 'My lord, you would not have seen so many bones had I been a dog (*cane*).'"

Can Grande died in the midst of his wars, in July, 1329, from drinking at a fountain. A very lively picture of his court, and of the life that Dante led there, is given by Ferrari in his comedy of *Dante a Verona*.

82. The Gascon is Clement V., Archbishop of Bordeaux, and elected Pope in 1305. The noble Henry is the Emperor Henry of Luxemburg, who, the *Ottimo* says, "was valiant in arms, liberal and courteous, compassionate and gentle, and the friend of virtue." Pope Clement is said to have been secretly his enemy, while publicly he professed to be his friend; and finally to have instigated or connived at his death by poison. See *Purg*. VI. Note 97. Henry came to Italy in 1310, when Can Grande was about nineteen years of age.

94. The commentary on the things told to Dante in the Inferno and Purgatorio. See Note 1.

128. *Habakkuk* ii. 2: "Write the vision, and make it plain upon tables, that he may run that readeth it."

129. Shakespeare, *Hamlet*, III. 2: "Let the galled jade wince, our withers are unwrung."

Canto XVIII

1. The Heaven of Mars continued; and the ascent to the Heaven of Jupiter, where are seen the spirits of righteous kings and rulers.

2. Enjoying his own thought in silence.
Shakespeare, *Sonnet XXX*:—

> "When to the sessions of sweet silent thought
> I summon up remembrance of things past."

9. Relinquish the hope and attempt of expressing.

11. Wordsworth, *Excursion,* Book IV.:—

> "'Tis by comparison an easy task
> Earth to despise; but to converse with heaven,—
> That is not easy:—to relinquish all
> We have, or hope, of happiness and joy,
> And stand in freedom loosened from this world,
> I deem not arduous; but must needs confess
> That 'tis a thing impossible to frame
> Conceptions equal to the soul's desires;
> And the most difficult of tasks to *keep*
> Heights which the soul is competent to gain.
> —Man is of dust: ethereal hopes are his,

> Which, when they should sustain themselves aloft,
> Want due consistence; like a pillar of smoke,
> That with majestic energy from earth
> Rises; but, having reached the thinner air,
> Melts, and dissolves, and is no longer seen."

And again in *Tintern Abbey*:—

> "That blessed mood,
> In which the burden of the mystery,
> In which the heavy and the weary weight
> Of all this unintelligible world
> Is lightened."

29. Paradise, or the system of the heavens, which lives by the divine influences from above, and whose fruit and foliage are eternal. The fifth resting-place or division of this tree is the planet Mars.

38. Joshua, the leader of the Israelites after the death of Moses, to whom God said, *Joshua* i. 5: "As I was with Moses, so will I be with thee: I will not fail thee, nor forsake thee."

40. The great Maccabee was Judas Maccabæus, who, as is stated in Biblical history, I *Maccabees* iii. 3, "gat his people great honour, and put on a breast-plate as a giant, and girt his warlike harness about him, and he made battles, protecting the host with his sword. In his acts he was like a lion, and like a lion's whelp roaring for his prey."

42. *Æneid,* VII., Davidson's Tr.: "As at times a whip-top whirling under the twisted lash, which boys intent on their sport drive in a large circuit round some empty court, the engine driven about by the scourge is hurried round and round in circling courses; the unpractised throng and beardless band are lost in admiration of the voluble box-wood: they lend their souls to the stroke."

43. The form in which Charlemagne presented himself to the imagination of the Middle Ages may be seen by the following extract from Turpin's *Chronicle,* Ch. XX.: "The Emperor was of a ruddy complexion, with brown hair; of a well made, handsome form, but a stern visage. His height was about eight of his own feet, which were very long. He was of a strong, robust make; his legs and thighs very stout, and his sinews firm. His face was thirteen inches long; his beard a palm; his nose half a palm; his forehead a foot over. His lion-like eyes flashed fire like carbuncles; his eyebrows were half a palm over. When he was angry, it was a terror to look upon him. He required eight spans for his girdle, besides what hung loose. He ate sparingly of bread; but a whole quarter of lamb, two fowls, a goose, or a large portion of pork; a peacock, a crane, or a whole hare. He drank moderately of wine and water. He was so strong, that he could at a single blow cleave asunder an armed soldier on horseback, from the head to the

waist, and the horse likewise. He easily vaulted over four horses harnessed together, and could raise an armed man from the ground to his head, as he stood erect upon his hand."

Orlando, the famous paladin, who died at Roncesvalles; the hero of Pulci's *Morgante Maggiore,* Bojardo's *Orlando Innamorato,* and Ariosto's *Orlando Furioso.* His sword Durandel is renowned in fiction, and his ivory horn Olivant could be heard eight miles.

46. "This William," says Buti, being obliged to say something, "was a great prince, who fought and died for the faith of Christ; I have not been able to find out distinctly who he was." The *Ottimo* says it is William, Count of Orange in Provence; who, after fighting for the faith against the Saracens, "took the cowl, and finished his life holily in the service of God; and he is called Saint William of the Desert."

He is the same hero, then, that figures in the old romances of the Twelve Peers of France, as Guillaume au Court Nez, or William of the Short Nose, so called from having had his nose cut off by a Saracen in battle. In the monorhythmic romance which bears his name, he is thus represented:—

> "Great was the court in the hall of Loön,
> The tables were full of fowl and venison,
> On flesh and fish they feasted every one;
> But Guillaume of these viands tasted none,
> Brown crusts ate he, and water drank alone.
> When had feasted every noble baron,
> The cloths were removed by squire and scullion.
> Count Guillaume then with the king did thus reason:
> 'What thinketh now,' quoth he, 'the gallant Charlon?
> Will he aid me against the prowess of Mahon?'
> Quoth Loéis, 'We will take counsel thereon,
> To-morrow in the morning shalt thou conne,
> If aught by us in this matter can be done.'
> Guillaume heard this,—black was he as carbon,
> He louted low, and seized a baton,
> And said to the king, 'Of your fief will I none,
> I will not keep so much as a spur's iron;
> Your friend and vassal I cease to be anon;
> But come you shall, whether you will or non.'"

He is said to have been taken prisoner and carried to Africa by the Moorish King Tobaldo, whose wife Arabella he first converted to Christianity, and then eloped with.

And who was Renouard? He was a young Moor, who was taken prisoner and brought up at the court of Saint Louis with the king's daughter Alice, whom, after achieving unheard of wonders in battle and siege, he, being duly baptized, married. Later in life he also became a monk, and frightened the brotherhood by his greediness, and by going to sleep when he should have gone to mass. So say the old romances.

47. Godfrey of Bouillon, Duke of Lorraine, and leader of the First Crusade. He was born in 1061, and died, king of Jerusalem, in 1109. Gibbon thus sketches his character, *Decline and Fall, Ch.* LVIII.: "The first rank both in war and council is justly due to Godfrey of Bouillon; and happy would it have been for the Crusaders, if they had trusted themselves to the sole conduct of that accomplished hero, a worthy representative of Charlemagne, from whom he was descended in the female line. His father was of the noble race of the Counts of Boulogne; Brabant, the lower province of Lorraine, was the inheritance of his mother; and by the Emperor's bounty he was himself invested with that ducal title which has been improperly transferred to his lordship of Bouillon in the Ardennes. In the service of Henry IV. he bore the great standard of the Empire, and pierced with his lance the breast of Rodolph, the rebel king; Godfrey was the first who ascended the walls of Rome; and his sickness, his vow, perhaps his remorse for bearing arms against the Pope, confirmed an early resolution of visiting the holy sepulchre, not as a pilgrim, but a deliverer. His valour was matured by prudence and moderation; his piety, though blind, was sincere; and, in the tumult of a camp, he practised the real and fictitious virtues of a convent. Superior to the private factions of the chiefs, he reserved his enmity for the enemies of Christ; and though he gained a kingdom by the attempt, his pure and disinterested zeal was acknowledged by his rivals. Godfrey of Bouillon was accompanied by his two brothers,—by Eustace, the elder, who had succeeded to the county of Boulogne, and by the younger, Baldwin, a character of more ambiguous virtue. The Duke of Lorraine was alike celebrated on either side of the Rhine; from his birth and education he was equally conversant with the French and Teutonic languages; the barons of France, Germany, and Lorraine assembled their vassals; and the confederate force that marched under his banner was composed of four-score thousand foot and about ten thousand horse."

48. Robert Guiscard, founder of the kingdom of Naples, was the sixth of the twelve sons of the Baron Tancred de Hauteville of the diocese of Coutance in Lower Normandy, where he was born in the year 1015. In his youth he left his father's castle as a military adventurer, and crossed the Alps to join the Norman army in Apulia, whither three of his brothers had gone before him, and whither at different times six others followed him. Here he gradually won his way by his sword; and having rendered some signal service to Pope Nicholas II., he was made Duke of Apulia and Calabria, and of the lands in Italy and Sicily which he wrested from the Greeks and Saracens. Thus from a needy adventurer he rose to be the founder of a kingdom. "The Italian conquests of Robert," says Gibbon, "correspond with the limits of the present kingdom of Naples; and the countries united by his arms have not been dissevered by the revolutions of seven hundred years."

The same historian, *Rise and Fall,* Ch. LVI., gives the following character of Guiscard. "Robert was the eldest of the seven sons of the second marriage;

and even the reluctant praise of his foes has endowed him with the heroic qualities of a soldier and a statesman. His lofty stature surpassed the tallest of his army; his limbs were cast in the true proportion of strength and gracefulness; and to the decline of life, he maintained the patient vigour of health and the commanding dignity of his form. His complexion was ruddy, his shoulders were broad, his hair and beard were long and of a flaxen colour, his eyes sparkled with fire, and his voice, like that of Achilles, could impress obedience and terror amidst the tumult of battle. In the ruder ages of chivalry, such qualifications are not below the notice of the poet or historian; they may observe that Robert, at once, and with equal dexterity, could wield in the right hand his sword, his lance in the left; that in the battle of Civitella he was thrice unhorsed; and that in the close of that memorable day he was adjudged to have borne away the prize of valour from the warriors of the two armies. His boundless ambition was founded on the consciousness of superior worth; in the pursuit of greatness he was never arrested by the scruples of justice, and seldom moved by the feelings of humanity; though not insensible of fame, the choice of open or clandestine means was determined only by his present advantage. The surname of *Guiscard* was applied to this master of political wisdom, which is too often confounded with the practice of dissimulation and deceit; and Robert is praised by the Apulian poet for excelling the cunning of Ulysses and the eloquence of Cicero. Yet these arts were disguised by an appearance of military frankness; in his highest fortune he was accessible and courteous to his fellow-soldiers; and while he indulged the prejudices of his new subjects, he affected in his dress and manners to maintain the ancient fashion of his country. He grasped with a rapacious, that he might distribute with a liberal hand; his primitive indigence had taught the habits of frugality; the gain of a merchant was not below his attention; and his prisoners were tortured with slow and unfeeling cruelty to force a discovery of their secret treasure. According to the Greeks, he departed from Normandy with only five followers on horseback and thirty on foot; yet even this allowance appears too bountiful; the sixth son of Tancred of Hauteville passed the Alps as a pilgrim; and his first military band was levied among the adventurers of Italy. His brothers and countrymen had divided the fertile lands of Apulia; but they guarded their shares with the jealousy of avarice; the aspiring youth was driven forwards to the mountains of Calabria, and in his first exploits against the Greeks and the natives it is not easy to discriminate the hero from the robber. To surprise a castle or a convent, to ensnare a wealthy citizen, to plunder the adjacent villages for necessary food, were the obscure labours which formed and exercised the powers of his mind and body. The volunteers of Normandy adhered to his standard; and, under his command, the peasants of Calabria assumed the name and character of Normans."

Robert died in 1085, on an expedition against Constantinople, undertaken at the venerable age of seventy-five. Such was the career of Robert the Cunning, this being the meaning of the old Norman word *guiscard,* or *guischard*. For an instance of his cunning see *Inf.* XXVIII. Note 14.

63. The miracle is Beatrice, of whom Dante says, in the *Vita Nuova:* "Many, when she had passed, said, 'This is not a woman, rather is she one of the most beautiful angels of heaven.' Others said, 'She is a miracle. Blessed be the Lord, who can perform such a marvel!' "

67. The change from the red light of Mars to the white light of Jupiter. "This planet," says Brunetto Latini, *Tresor,* I. Ch. CXI., "is gentle and piteous, and full of all good things." Of its symbolism Dante, *Convito,* II. 14, says: "The heaven of Jupiter may be compared to Geometry on account of two properties. The first is, that it moves between two heavens repugnant to its good temperateness, as are that of Mars and that of Saturn; whence Ptolemy says, in the book cited, that Jupiter is a star of a temperate complexion, midway between the coldness of Saturn and the heat of Mars. The second is, that among all the stars it shows itself white, almost silvery. And these two things are in Geometry. Geometry moves between two opposites; as between the point and the circle (and I call in general everything round, whether a solid or a surface, a circle); for, as Euclid says, the point is the beginning of Geometry, and, as he says, the circle is its most perfect figure, and may therefore be considered its end; so that between the point and the circle, as between beginning and end, Geometry moves. And these two are opposed to its exactness; for the point, on account of its indivisibility, is immeasurable; and the circle, on account of its arc, it is impossible to square, and therefore it is impossible to measure it exactly. And moreover Geometry is very white, inasmuch as it is without spot of error, and very exact in itself and its handmaiden, which is called Perspective."

Of the influences of Jupiter, Buti, quoting as usual Albumasar, speaks thus: "The planet Jupiter is of a cold, humid, airy, temperate nature, and signifies the natural soul, and life, and animate bodies, children and grandchildren, and beauty, and wise men and doctors of laws, and just judges, and firmness, and knowledge, and intellect, and interpretation of dreams, truth and divine worship, doctrine of law and faith, religion, veneration and fear of God, unity of faith and providence thereof, and regulation of manners and behaviour, and will be laudable, and signifies patient observation, and perhaps also to it belong swiftness of mind, improvidence and boldness in dangers, and patience and delay, and it signifies beatitude, and acquisition, and victory, ... and veneration, and kingdom, and kings, and rich men, nobles and magnates, hope and joy, and cupidity in commodities, also of fortune, in new kinds of grain, and harvests, and wealth, and security in all things, and good habits of mind, and liberality, command and goodness, boasting and bravery of mind, and boldness, true love and delight of supremacy over the citizens of a city, delight of potentates and magnates, ... and beauty and ornament of dress, and joy and laughter, and affluence of speech, and glibness of tongue, ... and hate of evil, and attachments among men, and command of the known, and avoidance of the unknown. These are the significations of the planet Jupiter, and such the influences it exerts."

75. Milton, *Par. Lost,* VII. 425:—

"Part loosely wing the region, part more wise
In common, ranged in figure, wedge their way,
Intelligent of seasons, and set forth
Their aery caravan, high over seas
Flying, and over lands, with mutual wing
Easing their flight;—so steers the prudent crane
Her annual voyage, borne on winds;—the air
Floats as they pass."

78. The first letters of the word *Diligite,* completed afterward.

82. Dante gives this title to the Muse, because from the hoof-beat of Pegasus sprang the fountain of the Muses, Hippocrene. The invocation is here to Calliope, the Muse of epic verse.

91, 93. *Wisdom of Solomon* i. 1: "Love righteousness, ye that be judges of the earth."

100. Tennyson, *Morte d'Arthur:*—

"And drove his heel into the smouldered log,
    That sent a blast of sparkles up the flue."

103. Divination by fire, and other childish fancies about sparks, such as wishes for golden sequins, and nuns going into a chapel.
Cowper, *Names of Little Note in the Diogr. Dict.:*—

"So when a child, as playful children use,
    Has burnt to tinder a stale last year's news,
    The flame extinct, he views the roving fire,—
    There goes my lady, and there goes the squire,
    There goes the parson, O illustrious spark!
    And there, scarce less illustrious, goes the clerk!"

107. In this eagle, the symbol of Imperialism, Dante displays his political faith. Among just rulers, this is the shape in which the true government of the world appears to him. In the invective against Pope Boniface VIII., with which the canto closes, he gives still further expression of his intense Imperialism.

111. The simplest interpretation of this line seems to me preferable to the mystic meaning which some commentators lend it. The Architect who built the heavens teaches the bird how to build its nest after the same model;—

"The Power which built the starry dome on high,
    And poised the vaulted rafters of the sky,
    Teaches the linnet with unconscious breast
    To round the inverted heaven of her nest."

112. The other group of beatified spirits.

123. As Tertullian says: "The blood of the martyrs is the seed of the Church."

126. The bad example of the head of the Church.

128. By excommunication, which shut out its victims from the table of the Lord.

130. Pope Boniface VIII., who is here accused of dealing out ecclesiastical censures only to be paid for revoking them.

135. John the Baptist. But here is meant his image on the golden florin of Florence.

Canto XIX

1. The Heaven of Jupiter continued.

12. The eagle speaks as one person, though composed of a multitude of spirits. Here Dante's idea of unity under the Empire finds expression.

28. This Mirror of Divine Justice is the planet Saturn, to which Dante alludes in Canto IX. 61, where, speaking of the Intelligences of Saturn, he says:—

> "Above us there are mirrors, Thrones you call them,
>   From which shines out on us God Judicant."

32. Whether a good life outside the pale of the holy Catholic faith could lead to Paradise.

37. Dante here calls the blessed spirits lauds, or "praises of the grace divine," as in *Inf.* II. 103, he calls Beatrice "the true praise of God."

40. Mr. Cary quotes, *Proverbs* viii. 27: "When he prepared the heavens, I was there; when he set a compass upon the face of the depth, ... then I was by him."

And Milton, *Par. Lost,* VII. 224:—

> "And in his hand
> He took the golden compasses, prepared
> In God's eternal store, to circumscribe
> This Universe, and all created things.
> One foot he centred, and the other turned
> Round through the vast profundity obscure,
> And said: 'Thus far extend, thus far thy bounds,
> This be thy just circumference, O World!'"

44. The Word or Wisdom of the Deity far exceeds any manifestation of it in the creation.

48. Shakespeare, *Henry VIII.,* III. 2:—

> "Fling away ambition,
> By that sin fell the angels."

49. Dryden, *Religio Laici,* 39:—

> "How can the less the greater comprehend?
> Or finite reason reach infinity?
> For what could fathom God is more than He."

54. Milton, *Par. Lost,* VII. 168:—

> "Boundless the deep, because I Am, who fill
> Infinitude, nor vacuous the space."

55. The human mind can never be so powerful but that it will perceive the Divine Mind to be infinitely beyond its comprehension; or, as Buti interprets,—reading *gli è parvente,* which reading I have followed,— "much greater than what appears to the human mind, and what the human intellect sees."

65. Milton, *Par. Lost,* I. 63:—

> "No light, but rather darkness visible."

104. *Galatians* iii. 23: "But before faith came, we were kept under the law, shut up unto the faith which should afterwards be revealed."

106. *Matthew* vii. 21: "Not every one that saith unto me, Lord, Lord, shall enter into the kingdom of heaven; but he that doeth the will of my Father which is in heaven."

108. Dryden, *Religio Laici,* 208:—

> "Then those who followed Reason's dictates right,
> Lived up, and lifted high her natural light,
> With Socrates may see their Maker's face,
> While thousand rubric martyrs want a place."

109. *Matthew* xii. 41: "The men of Nineveh shall rise in judgment with this generation, and shall condemn it."

110. The righteous and the unrighteous at the day of judgment.

113. *Revelation* xx. 12: "And I saw the dead, small and great, stand before God; and the books were opened: and another book was opened, which is the book of life: and the dead were judged out of those things which were written in the books, according to their works."

115. This is the "German Albert" of *Purg.* VI. 97:—

> "O German Albert, who abandonest her
>   That has grown savage and indomitable,
>   And oughtest to bestride her saddle-bow,
> May a just judgment from the stars down fall
>   Upon thy blood, and be it new and open
>   That thy successor may have fear thereof;
> Because thy father and thyself have suffered,
>   By greed of those transalpine lands distrained,
>   The garden of the empire to be waste."

The deed which was so soon to move the pen of the Recording Angel was the invasion of Bohemia in 1303.

120. Philip the Fair of France, who, after his defeat at Courtray in 1302, falsified the coin of the realm, with which he paid his troops. He was killed in 1314 by a fall from his horse, caused by the attack of a wild boar. Dante uses the word *cotenna,* the skin of the wild boar, for the boar itself.

122. The allusion here is to the border wars between John Baliol of Scotland, and Edward I. of England.

125. Most of the commentators say that this king of Spain was one of the Alphonsos, but do not agree as to which one. Tommaseo says it was Ferdinand IV. (1295-1312), and he is probably right. It was this monarch, or rather his generals, who took Gibraltar from the Moors. In 1312 he put to death unjustly the brothers Carvajal, who on the scaffold summoned him to appear before the judgment-seat of God within thirty days; and before the time had expired he was found dead upon his sofa. From this event he received the surname of *El Emplazado,* the Summoned. It is said that his death was caused by intemperance.

The Bohemian is Winceslaus II., son of Ottocar. He is mentioned, *Purg*. VII. 101, as one "who feeds in luxury and ease."

127. Charles II., king of Apulia, whose virtues may be represented by a unit and his vices by a thousand. He was called the "Cripple of Jerusalem," on account of his lameness, and because as king of Apulia he also bore the title of King of Jerusalem. See *Purg*. XX. Note 79.

131. Frederick, son of Peter of Aragon, and king, or in some form ruler of Sicily, called from Mount Etna the "Island of the Fire." The *Ottimo* comments thus: "Peter of Aragon was liberal and magnanimous, and the author says that this man is avaricious and pusillanimous." Perhaps his greatest crime in the eyes of Dante was his abandoning the cause of the Imperialists.

132. According to Virgil, Anchises died in Sicily, "on the joyless coast of Drepanum." *Æneid,* III. 708, Davidson's Tr.: "Here, alas! after being tossed by so many storms at sea, I lose my sire Anchises, my solace in every care and suffering. Here thou, best of fathers, whom in vain, alas! I saved from so great dangers, forsakest me, spent with toils."

134. In diminutive letters, and not in Roman capitals, like the DILIGITE JUSTITIAM of Canto XVIII. 91, and the record of the virtues and vices of the "Cripple of Jerusalem."

137. The uncle of Frederick of Sicily was James, king of the Balearic Islands. He joined Philip the Bold of France in his disastrous invasion of Catalonia; and in consequence lost his own crown.

The brother of Frederick was James of Aragon, who, on becoming king of that realm, gave up Sicily, which his father had acquired.

By these acts they dishonoured their native land and the crowns they wore.

139. Dionysius, king of Portugal, who reigned from 1279 to 1325. The *Ottimo* says that, "given up wholly to the acquisition of wealth, he led the life of a merchant, and had money dealings with all the great merchants of his reign; nothing regal, nothing magnificent, can be recorded of him."

Philalethes is disposed to vindicate the character of Dionysius against these aspersions, and to think them founded only in the fact that Dionysius loved the arts of peace better than the more shining art of war, joined in no crusade against the Moors, and was a patron of manufactures and commerce.

The *Ottimo's* note on this nameless Norwegian is curious: "As his islands are situated at the uttermost extremities of the earth, so his life is on the extreme of reasonableness and civilization."

Benvenuto remarks only that "Norway is a cold northern region, where the days are very short, and whence come excellent falcons." Buti is still more brief. He says: "That is, the king of Norway." Neither of these commentators, nor any of the later ones, suggest the name of this monarch, except the Germans, Philalethes and Witte, who think it may be Eric the Priest-hater, or Hakon Longshanks.

140. Rascia or Ragusa is a city in Dalmatia, situated on the Adriatic, and capital of the kingdom of that name. The king here alluded to is Uroscius II., who married a daughter of the Emperor Michael Palæologus, and counterfeited the Venetian coin.

141. In this line I have followed the reading *male ha visto*, instead of the more common one, *male aggiustò*.

142. The *Ottimo* comments as follows: "Here he reproves the vile and unseemly lives of the kings of Hungary, down to Andrea" (Dante's contemporary), "whose life the Hungarians praised, and whose death they wept."

144. If it can make the Pyrenees a bulwark to protect it against the invasion of Philip the Fair of France. It was not till four centuries later that Louis XIV. made his famous boast, "*Il n'y a plus de Pyrénées.*"

145. In proof of this prediction the example of Cyprus is given.

146. Nicosia and Famagosta are cities of Cyprus, here taken for the whole island, in 1300 badly governed by Henry II. of the house of the Lusignani. "And well he may call him beast," says the *Ottimo,* "for he was wholly given up to lust and sensuality, which should be far removed from every king."

148. Upon this line Benvenuto comments with unusual vehemence. "This king," he says, "does not differ nor depart from the side of the other beasts; that is, of the other vicious kings. And of a truth, Cyprus with her people differeth not, nor is separated from the bestial life of the rest; rather it surpasseth and exceedeth all peoples and kings of the kingdoms of Christendom in superfluity of luxury, gluttony, effeminacy, and every kind of pleasure.

But to attempt to describe the kinds, the sumptuousness, the variety, and the frequency of their banquets, would be disgusting to narrate, and tedious and harmful to write. Therefore men who live soberly and temperately should avert their eyes from beholding, and their ears from hearing, the meretricious, lewd, and fetid manners of that island, which, with God's permission, the Genoese have now invaded, captured, and evil entreated and laid under contribution."

Canto XX

1. The Heaven of Jupiter continued.
3. Coleridge, *Ancient Mariner:*—

> "The sun's rim dips; the stars rush out;
> At one stride comes the dark."

5. Blanco White, *Night:*—

> "Mysterious Night! when our first parent knew
>   Thee, from report divine, and heard thy name,
>   Did he not tremble for this lovely frame,
>   This glorious canopy of light and blue?
> Yet 'neath a curtain of translucent dew,
>   Bathed in the rays of the great setting flame,
>   Hesperus with the host of heaven came,
>   And lo! creation widened in man's view.
> Who could have thought such darkness lay concealed
>   Within thy beams, O Sun! or who could find,
>   Whilst fly, and leaf, and insect stood revealed,
> That to such countless orbs thou mad'st us blind?
>   Why do we, then, shun death with anxious strife?
>   If Light can thus deceive, wherefore not Life?"

37. King David, who carried the Ark of the Covenant from Kirjath-jearim to the house of Obed-Edom, and thence to Jerusalem. See 2 *Samuel* vi.
41. In so far as the Psalms were the result of his own free will, and not of divine inspiration. As in Canto VI. 118:—

> "But in commensuration of our wages
>   With our desert is portion of our joy,
>   Because we see them neither less nor greater."

44. The Emperor Trajan, whose soul was saved by the prayers of St. Gregory. For the story of the poor widow, see *Purg.* X. 73, and note.
49. King IIezekiah.

51. 2 *Kings* xx. 11:—"And Isaiah the prophet cried unto the Lord; and he brought the shadow ten degrees backward, by which it had gone down in the dial of Ahaz."

55. Constantine, who transferred the seat of empire, the Roman laws, and the Roman standard to Byzantium, thus in a poetic sense becoming a Greek.

56. This refers to the supposed gift of Constantine to Pope Sylvester, known in ecclesiastical history as the patrimony of Saint Peter. *Inf.* XXI. 115:—

> "Ah, Constantine! of how much woe was mother,
>> Not thy conversion, but that marriage-dower
>> Which the first wealthy Father took from thee!"

See also the note.

62. William the Second, surnamed the Good, son of Robert Guiscard, and king of Apulia and Sicily, which kingdoms were then lamenting the living presence of such kings as Charles the Lame, "the Cripple of Jerusalem," king of Apulia, and Frederick of Aragon, king of Sicily.

"King Guilielmo," says the *Ottimo,* "was just and reasonable, loved his subjects, and kept them in such peace, that living in Sicily might then be esteemed living in a terrestrial paradise. He was liberal to all, and proportioned his bounties to the virtue [of the receiver]. And he had this rule, that if a vicious or evil-speaking courtier came to his court, he was immediately noticed by the masters of ceremony, and provided with gifts and robes, so that he might have a cause to depart. If he was wise, he departed; if not, he was politely dismissed." The Vicar of Wakefield seems to have followed the example of the good King William, for he says: "When any one of our relations was found to be a person of very bad character, a troublesome guest, or one we desired to get rid of, upon his leaving my house I ever took care to lend him a riding-coat, or a pair of boots, or sometimes a horse of small value, and I always had the satisfaction of finding he never came back to return them."

68. A Trojan hero slain at the sack of Troy. *Æneid,* II. 426: "Ripheus also falls, the most just among the Trojans, and most observant of the right."

Venturi thinks that, if Dante must needs introduce a Pagan into Paradise, he would have done better to have chosen Æneas, who was the hero of his master, Virgil, and, moreover, the founder of the Roman empire.

73. The word "expatiate" is here used in the sense given it by Milton in the following passage, *Par. Lost.* I. 768:—

> "As bees,
>> In spring-time when the sun with Taurus rides,
>> Pour forth their populous youth about the hive
>> In clusters; they, among fresh dews and flowers,
>> Fly to and fro, or on the smoothed plank,
>> The suburb of their straw-built citadel,

New rubbed with balm, expatiate and confer
Their state-affairs."

Landor, *Pentameron*, p. 92, says: "All the verses that ever were written on the nightingale are scarcely worth the beautiful triad of this divine poet on the lark. In the first of them, do not you see the twinkling of her wings against the sky? As often as I repeat them, my ear is satisfied, my heart (like hers) contented."

92. In scholastic language the quiddity of a thing is its essence, or that by which it is what it is.

94. *Matthew* xi. 12: "And from the days of John the Baptist until now the kingdom of heaven suffereth violence, and the violent take it by force."

100. Trajan and Ripheus.

105. Ripheus lived before Christ, and Trajan after.
Shakespeare, *King Henry IV.,* I. 1:—

"In those holy fields
Over whose acres walked those blessed feet,
Which fourteen hundred years ago were nailed,
For our advantage, on the bitter cross."

106. Trajan.

111. Being in hell, he could not repent; being resuscitated, his inclinations could turn towards good.

112. The legend of Trajan is, that by the prayers of St. Gregory the Great he was restored to life, after he had been dead four hundred years; that he lived long enough to be baptized, and was then received into Paradise. See *Purg.* X. Note 73.

118. Ripheus. "This is a fiction of our author," says Buti, "as the intelligent reader may imagine; for there is no proof that Ripheus the Trojan is saved."

127. Faith, Hope, and Charity. *Purg.* XXIX. 121:—

"Three ladies at the right wheel in a circle
Came onward dancing; one so very red
That in the fire she hardly had been noted.
The second was as if her flesh and bones
Had all been fashioned out of emerald;
The third appeared as snow but newly fallen."

130. *Romans* ix. 20: "Nay but, O man, who art thou that repliest against God? Shall the thing formed say to him that formed it, Why hast thou made me thus? Had not the potter power over the clay, of the same lump to make one vessel unto honour, and another unto dishonour?"

Canto XXI

1. The Heaven of Saturn, where are seen the Spirits of the Contemplative. "This planet," says Brunetto Latini, "is cruel, felonious, and of a cold nature." Dante, *Convito,* II. 14, makes it the symbol of Astrology. "The Heaven of Saturn," he says, "has two properties by which it may be compared to Astrology. The first is the slowness of its movement through the twelve signs; for, according to the writings of Astrologers, its revolution requires twenty-nine years and more. The second is, that it is the highest of all the planets. And these two properties are in Astrology; for in completing its circle, that is, in learning it, a great space of time passes; both on account of its demonstrations, which are more than in any of the above-mentioned sciences, and on account of the experience which is necessary to judge rightly in it. And, moreover, it is the highest of all; for, as Aristotle says at the beginning of his treatise on the Soul, Science is of high nobility, from the nobleness of its subject, and from its certainty; and this more than any of the above-mentioned is noble and high, from its noble and high subject, which is the movement of the heavens; and high and noble from its certainty, which is without any defect, as one that proceeds from a most perfect and regular source. And if any one thinks there is any defect in it, the defect is not on the side of the Science, but, as Ptolemy says, it comes from our negligence, and to that it should be attributed."

Of the influences of Saturn, Buti, quoting Albumasar, says: "The nature of Saturn is cold, dry, melancholy, sombre, of grave asperity, and may be cold and moist, and of ugly colour, and is of much eating and of true love. . . . And it signifies ships at sea, and journeyings long and perilous, and malice, and envy, and tricks, and seductions, and boldness in dangers, . . . and singularity, and little companionship of men, and pride and magnanimity, and simulation and boasting, and servitude of rulers, and every deed done with force and malice, and injuries, and anger, and strife, and bonds and imprisonment, truth in words, delight, and beauty, and intellect; experiments and diligence in cunning, and affluence of thought, and profoundness of counsel. . . . And it signifies old and ponderous men, and gravity and fear, lamentation and sadness, embarrassment of mind, and fraud, and affliction, and destruction, and loss, and dead men, and remains of the dead; weeping and orphanhood, and ancient things, ancestors, uncles, elder brothers, servants and muleteers, and men despised, and robbers, and those who dig graves, and those who steal the garments of the dead, and tanners, vituperators, magicians, and warriors, and vile men."

6. Semele, the daughter of Cadmus, who besought her lover, Jupiter, to come to her, as he went to Juno, "in all the pomp of his divinity." Ovid, *Met.,* III., Addison's Tr.:—

> "The mortal dame, too feeble to engage
> The lightning's flashes and the thunder's rage,

> Consumed amidst the glories she desired,
> And in the terrible embrace expired."

13. To the planet Saturn, which was now in the sign of the Lion, and sent down its influence warmed by the heat of this constellation.

27. The peaceful reign of Saturn, in the Age of Gold.

29. "As in Mars," comments the *Ottimo,* "he placed the Cross for a stairway, to denote that through martyrdom the spirits had ascended to God; and in Jupiter, the Eagle, as a sign of the Empire; so here he places a golden stairway, to denote that the ascent of these souls, which was by contemplation, is more supreme and more lofty than any other."

35. Shakespeare, *Macbeth,* III. 2:—

> "The crow
> Makes wing to the rooky wood."

Henry Vaughan, *The Bee:*—

> "And hard by shelters on some bough
> Hilarion's servant, the wise crow."

And Tennyson, *Locksley Hall:*—

> "As the many-wintered crow that leads the clanging rookery home."

43. The spirit of Peter Damiano.

46. Beatrice.

63. Because your mortal ear could not endure the sound of our singing, as your mortal eye could not the splendour of Beatrice's smile.

81. As in Canto XII. 3:—

> "Began the holy millstone to revolve."

90. As in Canto XIV. 40:—

> "Its brightness is proportioned to its ardour,
> The ardour to the vision; and the vision
> Equals what grace it has above its worth."

106. Among the Apennines, east of Arezzo, rises Mount Catria, sometimes called, from its forked or double summit, the *Forca di Fano.* On its slope stands the monastery of Santa Croce di Fonte Avellana. Troya, in his *Veltro Allegorico,* as quoted in Balbo's *Life and Times of Dante,* Mrs. Bunbury's Tr., II. 218, describes this region as follows: "The monastery is built on the steepest mountains of Umbria. Catria, the giant of the Apennines, hangs

over it, and so overshadows it that in some months of the year the light is frequently shut out. A difficult and lonely path through the forests leads to the ancient *hospitium* of these courteous hermits, who point out the apartments where their predecessors lodged Alighieri. We may read his name repeatedly on the walls; the marble effigy of him bears witness to the honourable care with which the memory of the great Italian is preserved from age to age in that silent retirement. The Prior Moricone received him there in 1318, and the annals of Avellana relate this event with pride. But if they had been silent, it would be quite sufficient to have seen Catria, and to have read Dante's description of it, to be assured that he ascended it. There, from the woody summit of the rock, he gazed upon his country, and rejoiced in the thought that he was not far from her. He struggled with his desire to return to her; and when he *was* able to return, he banished himself anew, not to submit to dishonour. Having descended the mountain, he admired the ancient manners of the inhabitants of Avellana, but he showed little indulgence to his hosts, who appeared to him to have lost their old virtues. At this time, and during his residence near Gubbio, it seems that he must have written the five cantos of the Paradiso after the twentieth; because when he mentions Florence in the twenty-first canto he speaks of Catria, and in what he says in the twenty-fifth, of wishing to receive his poetic crown at his baptismal font, we can perceive his hope to be restored to his country and his beautiful fold (*ovile*) when time should have overcome the difficulties of the manner of his return."

Ampère, *Voyage Dantesque,* p. 265, describes his visit to the monastery of Fonte Avellana, and closes thus:—

"They took particular pleasure in leading us to an echo, the wonder of Avellana, and the most powerful I ever heard. It repeats distinctly a whole line of verse, and even a line and a half. I amused myself in making the rocks address to the great poet, whom they had seen wandering among their summits, what he said of Homer,—

'Onorate l'altissimo poeta.'

The line was distinctly articulated by the voice of the mountain, which seemed to be the far-off and mysterious voice of the poet himself. . . . .

"In order to find the recollection of Dante more present than in the cells, and even in the chamber of the inscription, I went out at night, and sat upon a stone a little above the monastery. The moon was not visible, being still hidden by the immense peaks; but I could see some of the less elevated summits struck by her first glimmerings. The chants of the monks came up to me through the darkness, and mingled with the bleating of a kid lost in the mountains. I saw through the window of the choir a white monk prostrate in prayer. I thought that perhaps Dante had sat upon that stone, that he had contemplated those rocks, that moon, and heard those chants always the same, like the sky and the mountains."

110. This hermitage, according to Butler, *Lives of the Saints,* II. 212, was founded by the blessed Ludolf, about twenty years before Peter Damiano came to it.

112. Thus it began speaking for the third time.

121. St. Peter Damiano was born of a poor family at Ravenna, about 988; and, being left an orphan in his childhood, went to live with an elder brother, who set him to tending swine. Another brother, who was a priest at Ravenna, took compassion on him, and educated him. He in turn became a teacher; and, being of an ascetic turn of mind, he called himself Peter the Sinner, wore a hair shirt, and was assiduous in fasting and prayer. Two Benedictine monks of the monastery of Fonte Avellana, passing through Ravenna, stopped at the house where he lodged; and he resolved to join their brotherhood, which he did soon afterward. In 1041 he became Abbot of the monastery, and in 1057, Cardinal-Bishop of Ostia. In 1062 he returned to Fonte Avellana; and in 1072, being "fourscore and three years old," died on his way to Rome, in the convent of our Lady near Faenza.

Of his life at Fonte Avellana, Butler, *Lives of the Saints,* (Feb. 23,) II. 217, says: "Whatever austerities he prescribed to others he was the first to practise himself, remitting nothing of them even in his old age. He lived shut up in his cell as in a prison, fasted every day, except festivals, and allowed himself no other subsistence than coarse bread, bran, herbs, and water, and this he never drank fresh, but what he had kept from the day before. He tortured his body with iron girdles and frequent disciplines, to render it more obedient to the spirit. He passed the three first days of every Lent and Advent without taking any kind of nourishment whatsoever; and often for forty days together lived only on raw herbs and fruits, or on pulse steeped in cold water, without touching so much as bread, or anything which had passed the fire. A mat spread on the floor was his bed. He used to make wooden spoons and such like useful mean things to exercise himself at certain hours in manual labour."

122. It is a question whether Peter Damiano and Peter the Sinner are the same person, or whether by the latter is meant Peter Onesti of Ravenna; for both in their humility took that name. The solution of the question depends upon the reading *fui* or *fu* in this line; and of twenty-eight printed editions consulted by Barlow, fourteen were for *fui,* and fourteen for *fu.* Of the older commentators, the *Ottimo* thinks two distinct persons are meant; Benvenuto and Buti decide in favour of one.

Benvenuto interprets thus: "In Catria I was called Peter Damiano, and I was Peter the Sinner in the monastery of Santa Maria in Porto at Ravenna on the shore of the Adriatic. Some persons maintain, that this Peter the Sinner was another monk of the order, which is evidently false, because Damiano gives his real name in Catria, and here names himself [Sinner] from humility."

Buti says: "I was first a friar called Peter the Sinner, in the Order of Santa Maria. . . . . . And afterwards he went from there to the monastery at the hermitage of Catria, having become a monk."

125. In 1057, when he was made Cardinal-Bishop of Ostia.

127. Cephas is St. Peter. *John* i. 42: "Thou art Simon the son of Jona; Thou shalt be called Cephas, which is, by interpretation, a stone." The *Ottimo* seems to have forgotten this passage of Scripture when he wrote: "Cephas, that is, St. Peter, so called from the large head he had (*cephas,* that is to say, head)."

The mighty Vessel of the Holy Spirit is St. Paul. *Acts* ix. 15: "He is a chosen vessel unto me."

129. *Luke* x. 7: "And in the same house remain, eating and drinking such things as they give: for the labourer is worthy of his hire."

130. The commentary of Benvenuto da Imola upon this passage is too striking to be omitted here. The reader may imagine the impression it produced upon the audience when the Professor first read it publicly in his lectures at Bologna, in 1389, eighty-eight years after Dante's death, though this impression may have been somewhat softened by its being delivered in Latin.—

"Here Peter Damiano openly rebukes the modern shepherds as being the opposite of the Apostles before-mentioned, saying,—

> 'Now some one to support them on each side
> The modern shepherds need';

that is to say, on the right and on the left;

> 'And some to lead them,
> So heavy are they';

that is, so fat and corpulent. I have seen many such at the Court of Rome. And this is in contrast with the leanness of Peter and Paul before mentioned.

> 'And to hold their trains,'

because they have long cloaks, sweeping the ground with their trains. And this too is in contrast with the nakedness of the afore-mentioned Apostles. And therefore, stung with grief, he adds,

> 'They cover up their palfreys with their cloaks,'

fat and sleek, as they themselves are; for their mantles are so long, ample, and capacious, that they cover man and horse. Hence, he says,

> 'So that two beasts go underneath one skin';

that is the beast who carries, and he who is carried, and is more beastly than the beast himself. And, truly, had the author lived at the present day he might have changed this phrase and said,

'So that three beasts go underneath one skin';

namely, cardinal, concubine, and horse; as I have heard of one, whom I knew well, who used to carry his concubine to hunt on the crupper of his horse or mule. And truly he was like a horse or mule, in which there is no understanding; that is, without reason. On account of these things, Peter in anger cries out to God,

'O Patience, that dost tolerate so much!' "

142. A cry so loud that he could not distinguish the words these spirits uttered.

Canto XXII

1. The Heaven of Saturn continued; and the ascent to the Heaven of the Fixed Stars.

31. It is the spirit of St. Benedict that speaks.

37. Not far from Aquinum in the Terra di Lavoro, the birthplace of Juvenal and of Thomas Aquinas, rises Monte Cassino, celebrated for its Benedictine monastery. The following description of the spot is from a letter in the London *Daily News,* February 26, 1866, in which the writer pleads earnestly that this monastery may escape the doom of all the Religious Orders in Italy, lately pronounced by the Italian Parliament.

"The monastery of Monte Cassino stands exactly half-way between Rome and Naples. From the top of the Monte Cairo, which rises immediately above it, can be seen to the north the summit of Monte Cavo, so conspicuous from Rome; and to the south, the hill of the Neapolitan Camaldoli. From the terrace of the monastery the eye ranges over the richest and most beautiful valley of Italy, the

'Rura quæ Liris quietâ
Mordet aquâ taciturnus amnis.'

The river can be traced through the lands of Aquinum and Pontecorvo, till it is lost in the haze which covers the plain of Sinuessa and Minturnæ; a small strip of sea is visible just beyond the mole of Gaeta.

"In this interesting but little known and uncivilized country, the monastery has been the only centre of religion and intelligence for nearly 1350 years. It was founded by St. Benedict in 529, and is the parent of all the greatest Benedictine monasteries in the world. In 589 the monks, driven out by the Lombards, took refuge in Rome, and remained there for 130 years. In 884 the monastery was burned by the Saracens, but it was soon after restored. With these exceptions it has existed without a break from its foundation till the present day.

"There is scarcely a Pope or Emperor of importance who has not been personally connected with its history. From its mountain crag it has seen Goths, Lombards, Saracens, Normans, Frenchmen, Spaniards, Germans, scour and devastate the land which, through all modern history, has attracted every invader.

"It is hard that, after it has escaped the storms of war and rapine, it should be destroyed by peaceful and enlightened legislation.

"I do not, however, wish to plead its cause on sentimental grounds. The monastery contains a library which, in spite of the pilfering of the Popes, and the wanton burnings of Championnet, is still one of the richest in Italy; while its archives are, I believe, unequalled in the world. Letters of the Lombard kings who reigned at Pavia, of Hildebrand and the Countess Matilda, of Gregory and Charlemagne, are here no rarities. Since the days of Paulus Diaconus in the eighth century, it has contained a succession of monks devoted to literature. His mantle has descended in these later days to Abate Tosti, one of the most accomplished of contemporary Italian writers. In the Easter of last year, I found twenty monks in the monastery: they worked harder than any body of Oxford or Cambridge fellows I am acquainted with; they edu cated two hundred boys, and fifty novices; they kept up all the services of their cathedral; the care of the archives included a laborious correspondence with literary men of all nations; they entertained hospitably any visitors who came to them; besides this, they had just completed a fac-simile of their splendid manuscript of Dante, in a large folio volume, which was edited and printed by their own unassisted labour. This was intended as an offering to the kingdom of Italy in its new capital, and rumour says that they have incurred the displeasure of the Pope by their liberal opinions. On every ground of respect for prescription and civilization, it would be a gross injustice to destroy this monastery.

"'If we are saved,' one of the monks said to me, 'it will be by the public opinion of Europe.' It is the most enlightened part of that opinion which I am anxious to rouse in their behalf."

In the palmy days of the monastery the Abbot of Monte Cassino was the First Baron of the realm, and is said to have held all the rights and privileges of other barons, and even criminal jurisdiction in the land. This the inhabit ants of the town of Cassino found so intolerable, that they tried to buy the right with all the jewels of the women and all the silver of their households. When the law for the suppression of the convents passed, they are said to have celebrated the event with great enthusiasm; but the monks, as well they might, sang an *Oremus* in their chapel, instead of a *Te Deum*.

For a description of the library of Monte Cassino in Boccaccio's time, see Note 75 of this canto.

40. St. Benedict was born at Norcia, in the Duchy of Spoleto, in 480, and died at Monte Cassino in 543. In his early youth he was sent to school in Rome; but being shocked at the wild life of Roman school-boys, he fled from the city at the age of fourteen, and hid himself among the mountains of Subiaco, some forty miles away. A monk from a neighbouring convent

gave him a monastic dress, and pointed out to him a cave, in which he lived for three years, the monk supplying him with food, which he let down to him from above by a cord.

In this retreat he was finally discovered by some shepherds, and the fame of his sanctity was spread through the land. The monks of Vicovara chose him for their Abbot, and then tried to poison him in his wine. He left them and returned to Subiaco; and there built twelve monasteries, placing twelve monks with a superior in each.

Of the scenery of Subiaco, Lowell, *Fireside Travels,* p. 271, gives the following sketch: "Nothing can be more lovely than the scenery about Subiaco. The town itself is built on a kind of cone rising from the midst of a valley abounding in olives and vines, with a superb mountain horizon around it, and the green Anio cascading at its feet. As you walk to the high-perched convent of San Benedetto, you look across the river on your right just after leaving the town, to a cliff over which the ivy pours in torrents, and in which dwellings have been hollowed out. In the black doorway of every one sits a woman in scarlet bodice and white head-gear, with a distaff, spinning, while overhead countless nightingales sing at once from the fringe of shrubbery. The glorious great white clouds look over the mountain-tops into our enchanted valley, and sometimes a lock of their vapoury wool would be torn off, to lie for a while in some inaccessible ravine like a snow-drift; but it seemed as if no shadow could fly over our privacy of sunshine to-day. The approach to the monastery is delicious. You pass out of the hot sun into the green shadows of ancient ilexes, leaning and twisting every way that is graceful, their branches velvety with brilliant moss, in which grow feathery ferns, fringing them with a halo of verdure. Then comes the convent, with its pleasant old monks, who show their sacred vessels (one by Cellini) and their relics, among which is a finger-bone of one of the Innocents. Lower down is a convent of Santa Scolastica, where the first book was printed in Italy."

In the gardens of the convent of San Benedetto still bloom, in their season, the roses, which the legend says have been propagated from the briers in which the saint rolled himself as a penance. But he had outward foes, as well as inward, to contend with, and they finally drove him from Subiaco to Monte Cassino.

Montalembert, *Monks of the West,* Authorised Tr., II., 16, says:—

"However, Benedict had the ordinary fate of great men and saints. The great number of conversions worked by the example and fame of his austerity, awakened a homicidal envy against him. A wicked priest of the neighbourhood attempted first to decry and then to poison him. Being unsuccessful in both, he endeavoured, at least, to injure him in the object of his most tender solicitude—in the souls of his young disciples. For that purpose he sent, even into the garden of the monastery where Benedict dwelt and where the monks laboured, seven wretched women, whose gestures, sports, and shameful nudity were designed to tempt the young monks to certain fall. Who does not recognise in this incident the mixture of barbarian rudeness and frightful corruption which characterise ages of decay and transition? When Benedict, from the threshold of his cell, perceived these shameless creatures, he despaired of his work; he acknowledged that the interest of his beloved children constrained him to disarm so cruel an enmity by retreat. He appointed superiors to the twelve monasteries which he had founded, and, taking with him a small number of disciples, he left for ever the wild gorges of Subiaco, where he had lived for thirty-five years.

"Without withdrawing from the mountainous region which extends along the western side of the Apennines, Benedict directed his steps towards the south, along the Abruzzi, and penetrated into that Land of Labour, the name of which seems naturally suited to a soil destined to be the cradle of the most laborious men whom the world has known. He ended his journey in a scene very different from that of Subiaco, but of incomparable grandeur and majesty. There, upon the boundaries of Samnium and Campania, in the centre of a large basin, half surrounded by abrupt and picturesque heights, rises a scarped and isolated hill, the vast and rounded summit of which overlooks the course of the Liris near its fountain-head, and the undulating plain which extends south towards the shores of the Mediterranean, and the narrow valleys which, towards the north, the east, and the west, lose themselves in the lines of the mountainous horizon. This is Monte Cassino. At the foot of this rock, Benedict found an amphitheatre of the time of the Cæsars, amidst the ruins of the town of Casinum, which the most learned and pious of Romans, Varro, that pagan Benedictine, whose memory and knowledge the sons of Benedict took pleasure in honouring, had rendered illustrious. From the summit the prospect extended on one side towards Arpinum, where the prince of Roman orators was born, and on the other towards Aquinum, already celebrated as the birthplace of Juvenal, before it was known as the country of the Doctor Angelicus, which latter distinction should make the name of this little town known among all Christians.

"It was amidst these noble recollections, this solemn nature, and upon that predestinated height, that the patriarch of the monks of the West founded the capital of the monastic order. He found paganism still surviving there. Two hundred years after Constantine, in the heart of Christendom, and so near Rome, there still existed a very ancient temple of Apollo and a sacred wood, where a multitude of peasants sacrificed to the gods and demons. Benedict preached the faith of Christ to these forgotten people; he persuaded them to cut down the wood, to overthrow the temple and the idol."

On the ruins of this temple he built two chapels, and higher up the mountain, in 529, laid the foundation of his famous monastery. Fourteen years afterwards he died in the church of this monastery, standing with his arms stretched out in prayer.

"St. Bennet," says Butler, *Lives of the Saints,* III. 235, "calls his Order a school in which men learn how to serve God; and his life was to his disciples a perfect model for their imitation, and a transcript of his rule. Being chosen by God, like another Moses, to conduct faithful souls into the true promised land, the kingdom of heaven, he was enriched with eminent supernatural gifts, even those of miracles and prophecy. He seemed like another Eliseus, endued by God with an extraordinary power, commanding all nature, and, like the ancient prophets, foreseeing future events. He often raised the sinking courage of his monks, and baffled the various artifices of the Devil with the sign of the cross, rendered the heaviest stone light in building his monastery by a short prayer, and, in presence of a multitude of people, raised to life a novice who had been crushed by the fall of a wall at Mount Cassino."

A story of St. Benedict and his sister Scholastica is thus told by Mrs. Jameson, *Legends of Monastic Orders,* p. 12: "Towards the close of his long life Benedict was consoled for many troubles by the arrival of his sister Scholastica, who had already devoted herself to a religious life, and now took up her residence in a retired cell about a league and a half from his convent. Very little is known of Scholastica, except that she emulated her brother's piety and self-denial; and although it is not said that she took any vows, she is generally considered as the first Benedictine nun. When she followed her brother to Monte Cassino, she drew around her there a small community of pious women; but nothing more is recorded of her, except that he used to visit her once a year. On one occasion, when they had been conversing together on spiritual matters till rather late in the evening, Benedict rose to depart; his sister entreated him to remain a little longer, but he refused. Scholastica then, bending her head over her clasped hands, prayed that Heaven would interfere and render it impossible for her brother to leave her. Immediately there came on such a furious tempest of rain, thunder, and lightning, that Benedict was obliged to delay his departure for some hours. As soon as the storm had subsided, he took leave of his sister, and returned to the monastery: it was a last meeting; St. Scholastica died two days afterwards, and St. Benedict, as he was praying in his cell, beheld the soul of his sister ascending to heaven in the form of a dove. This incident is often found in the pictures painted for the Benedictine nuns."

For the history of the monastery of Monte Cassino see the *Chron. Monast. Casiniensis,* in Muratori, *Script. Rer. Ital.,* IV., and Dantier, *Monastères Bénedictins a' Italie.*

49. St. Macarius, who established the monastic rule of the East, as St. Benedict did that of the West, was a confectioner of Alexandria, who, carried away by religious enthusiasm, became an anchorite in the Thebaid of Upper Egypt, about 335. In 373 he came to Lower Egypt, and lived in the Desert of the Cells, so called from the great multitude of its hermit-cells. He had also hermitages in the deserts of Scetè and Nitria; and in these several places he passed upwards of sixty years in holy contemplation, saying to his soul, "Having taken up thine abode in heaven, where thou hast God and his holy angels to converse with, see that thou descend not thence; regard not earthly things."

Among other anecdotes of St. Macarius, Butler, *Lives of the Saints,* I. 50, relates the following: "Our saint happened one day inadvertently to kill a gnat that was biting him in his cell; reflecting that he had lost the opportunity of suffering that mortification, he hastened from his cell for the marshes of Scetè, which abound with great flies, whose stings pierce even wild boars. There he continued six months exposed to those ravaging insects; and to such a degree was his whole body disfigured by them with sores and swellings, that when he returned he was only to be known by his voice."

St. Romualdus, founder of the Order of Camaldoli, or Reformed Benedictines, was born of the noble family of the Onesti, in Ravenna, about 956. Brought up in luxury and ease, he still had glimpses of better things, and, while hunting the wild boar in the pine woods of Ravenna, would sometimes stop to muse, and, uttering a prayer, exclaim: "How happy were the ancient hermits who had such habitations."

At the age of twenty he saw his father kill his adversary in a duel; and, smitten with remorse, imagined that he must expiate the crime by doing penance in his own person. He accordingly retired to a Benedictine convent in the neighbourhood of Ravenna, and became a monk. At the end of seven years, scandalised with the irregular lives of the brotherhood, and their disregard of the rules of the Order, he undertook the difficult task of bringing them back to the austere life of their founder. After a conflict of many years, during which he encountered and overcame the usual perils that beset the path of a reformer, he succeeded in winning over some hundreds of his brethren, and established his new Order of Reformed Benedictines.

St. Romualdus built many monasteries; but chief among them is that of Camaldoli, thirty miles east of Florence, which was founded in 1009. It takes its name from the former owner of the land, a certain Maldoli, who gave it to St. Romualdus. Campo Maldoli, say the authorities, became Camaldoli. It is more likely to be the Tuscan Ca' Maldoli, for Casa Maldoli.

"In this place," says Butler, *Lives of the Saints*, II. 86, "St. Romuald built a monastery, and, by the several observances he added to St. Benedict's rule, gave birth to that new Order called Camaldoli, in which he united the cenobitic and eremitical life. After seeing in a vision his monks mounting up a ladder to heaven all in white, he changed their habit from black to white. The hermitage is two short miles distant from the monastery. It is a mountain quite overshadowed by a dark wood of fir-trees. In it are seven clear springs of water. The very sight of this solitude in the midst of the forest helps to fill the mind with compunction, and a love of heavenly contemplation. On entering it, we meet with a chapel of St. Antony for travellers to pray in before they advance any farther. Next are the cells and lodgings for the porters. Somewhat farther is the church, which is large, well built, and richly adorned. Over the door is a clock, which strikes so loud that it may be heard all over the desert. On the left side of the church is the cell in which St. Romuald lived, when he first established these hermits. Their cells, built of stone, have each a little garden walled round. A constant fire is allowed to be kept in every cell on account of the coldness of the air throughout the year; each cell has also a chapel in which they may say mass."

See also *Purg.* V. Note 96. The legend of St. Romualdus says that he lived to the age of one hundred and twenty. It says, also, that in 1466, nearly four hundred years after his death, his body was found still uncorrupted; but that four years later, when it was stolen from its tomb, it crumbled into dust.

65. In that sphere alone; that is, in the Empyrean, which is eternal and immutable.

Lucretius, *Nature of Things,* III. 530, Good's Tr.:—

> "But things immortal ne'er can be transposed,
> Ne'er take addition, nor encounter loss;
> For what once changes, by the change alone
> Subverts immediate its anterior life."

70. *Genesis* xxviii. 12: "And he dreamed, and, behold, a ladder set up on the earth, and the top of it reached to heaven: and, behold, the angels of God ascending and descending on it."

74. So neglected, that it is mere waste of paper to transcribe it. In commenting upon this line, Benvenuto gives an interesting description of Boccaccio's visit to the library of Monte Cassino, which he had from his own lips. "To the clearer understanding of this passage," he says, "I will repeat what my venerable preceptor, Boccaccio of Certaldo, pleasantly narrated to me. He said, that when he was in Apulia, being attracted by the fame of the place, he went to the noble monastery of Monte Cassino, of which we are speaking. And being eager to see the library, which he had heard was very noble, he humbly—gentle creature that he was!—besought a monk to do him the favour to open it. Pointing to a lofty staircase, he answered stiffly, 'Go up; it is open.' Joyfully ascending, he found the place of so great a treasure without door or fastening; and having entered, he saw the grass growing upon the windows, and all the books and shelves covered with dust. And, wondering, he began to open and turn over, now this book and now that, and found there many and various volumes of ancient and rare works. From some of them whole sheets had been torn out, in others the margins of the leaves were clipped, and thus they were greatly defaced. At length, full of pity that the labours and studies of so many illustrious minds should have fallen into the hands of such profligate men, grieving and weeping he withdrew. And coming into the cloister, he asked a monk whom he met, why those most precious books were so vilely mutilated. He replied, that some of the monks, wishing to gain a few ducats, cut out a handful of leaves, and made psalters which they sold to boys; and likewise of the margins they made breviaries which they sold to women. Now, therefore, O scholar, rack thy brains in the making of books!"

77. To dens of thieves. "And the monks' hoods and habits are full," says Buti, "of wicked and sinful souls, of evil thoughts and ill-will. And as from bad flour bad bread is made, so from ill-will, which is in the monks, come evil deeds."

79. The usurer is not so offensive to God as the monk who squanders the revenues of the Church in his own pleasures and vices.

94. *Psalm* cxiv. 5: "What ailed thee, O thou sea, that thou fleddest? thou Jordan, that thou wast driven back?"

The power that wrought these miracles can also bring help to the corruptions of the Church, great as the impossibility may seem.

107. Paradise. "Truly," says Buti, "the glory of Paradise may be called a triumph, for the blessed triumph in their victory over the world, the flesh, and the Devil."

111. The sign that follows Taurus is the sign of the Gemini, under which Dante was born.

112. Of the influences of Gemini, Buti, quoting Albumasar, says: "The sign of the Gemini signifies great devotion and genius, such as became our author speaking of such lofty theme. It signifies, also, sterility, and moderation in manners and in religion, beauty, and deportment, and cleanliness, when this sign is in the ascendant, or the lord of the descendant is present, or the Moon; and largeness of mind, and goodness, and liberality in spending."

115. Dante was born May 14th, 1265, when the Sun rose and set in Gemini; or as Barlow, *Study of Div. Com.,* p. 505, says, "the day on which in that year the Sun entered the constellation Gemini." He continues: "Giovanni Villani (Lib. VI. Ch. 92) gives an account of a remarkable comet which preceded the birth of Dante by nine months, and lasted three, from July to October. . . . . This marvellous meteor, much more worthy of notice than Donna Bella's dream related by Boccaccio, has not hitherto found its way into the biography of the poet."

119. The Heaven of the Fixed Stars. Of the symbolism of this heaven, Dante, *Convito,* II. 15, says: "The Starry Heaven may be compared to Physics on account of three properties, and to Metaphysics on account of three others; for it shows us two visible things, such as its many stars, and the Galaxy; that is, the white circle which the vulgar call the Road of St. James; and it shows us one of its poles, and the other it conceals from us; and it shows us only one motion from east to west, and another which it has from west to east it keeps almost hidden from us. Therefore we must note in order, first its comparison with Physics, and then with Metaphysics. The Starry Heaven, I say, shows us many stars; for, according as the wise men of Egypt have computed, down to the last star that appears in their meridian, there are one thousand and twenty-two clusters of the stars I speak of. And in this it bears a great resemblance to Physics, if these three members, namely, two and twenty and a thousand, are carefully considered; for by the two is understood the local movement, which of necessity is from one point to another; and by the twenty is signified the movement of modification; for, inasmuch as from the ten upwards we proceed only by modifying this ten with the other nine, and with itself, and the most beautiful modification which it receives is that with itself, and the first which it receives is twenty, consequently the movement aforesaid is signi-

fied by this number. And by the thousand is signified the movement of
increase; for in name this thousand is the greatest number, and cannot
increase except by multiplying itself. And Physics show these three move-
ments only, as is proved in the fifth chapter of its first book. And on account
of the Galaxy this heaven has great resemblance to Metaphysics. For it must
be known that of this Galaxy the philosophers have held diverse opinions.
For the Pythagoreans said that the Sun once wandered out of his path; and,
passing through other parts not adapted to his heat, he burned the place
through which he passed, and the appearance of the burning remained
there. I think they were influenced by the fable of Phaeton which Ovid
narrates at the beginning of the second book of his Metamorphoses. Others,
as Anaxagoras and Democritus, said that it was the light of the Sun reflected
in that part. And these opinions they proved by demonstrative reasons.
What Aristotle said upon this subject cannot be exactly known, because his
opinion is not the same in one translation as in the other. And I think this
was an error of the translators; for in the new he seems to say that it is a
collection of vapours beneath the stars in that part, which always attract
them; and this does not seem to be very reasonable. In the old he says, that
the Galaxy is nothing but a multitude of fixed stars in that part, so small
that we cannot distinguish them here below, but from them proceeds that
brightness which we call the Galaxy. And it may be that the heaven in that
part is more dense, and therefore retains and reflects that light; and this
seems to be the opinion of Aristotle, Avicenna, and Ptolemy. Hence, inas-
much as the Galaxy is an effect of those stars which we cannot see, but
comprehend by their effects, and Metaphysics treats of first substances,
which likewise we cannot comprehend except by their effects, it is manifest
that the starry heaven has great resemblance to Metaphysics. Still further,
by the pole which we see it signifies things obvious to sense, of which,
taking them as a whole, Physics treats; and by the pole which we do not
see it signifies the things which are immaterial, which are not obvious to
sense, of which Metaphysics treats; and therefore the aforesaid heaven bears
a great resemblance to both these sciences. Still further, by its two move-
ments it signifies these two sciences; for, by the movement in which it
revolves daily and makes a new circuit from point to point, it signifies the
corruptible things in nature, which daily complete their course, and their
matter is changed from form to form; and of this Physics treats; and by the
almost insensible movement which it makes from west to east of one degree
in a hundred years, it signifies the things incorruptible, which had from
God the beginning of existence, and shall never have an end; and of these
Metaphysics treats."

135. Cicero, *Vision of Scipio,* Edmonds's Tr., p. 294:—

"Now the place my father spoke of was a radiant circle of dazzling bright-
ness amid the flaming bodies, which you, as you have learned from the Greeks,
term the Milky Way; from which position all other objects seemed to me,

as I surveyed them, marvellous and glorious. There were stars which we never saw from this place, and their magnitudes were such as we never imagined; the smallest of which was that which, placed upon the extremity of the heavens, but nearest to the earth, shone with borrowed light. But the globular bodies of the stars greatly exceeded the magnitude of the earth, which now to me appeared so small, that I was grieved to see our empire contracted, as it were, into a very point. . . . .

"Which as I was gazing at in amazement, I said, as I recovered myself, from whence proceed these sounds so strong, and yet so sweet, that fill my ears? 'The melody,' replies he, 'which you hear, and which, though composed in unequal time, is nevertheless divided into regular harmony, is effected by the impulse and motion of the spheres themselves, which, by a happy temper of sharp and grave notes, regularly produces various harmonic effects. Now it is impossible that such prodigious movements should pass in silence; and nature teaches that the sounds which the spheres at one extremity utter must be sharp, and those on the other extremity must be grave; on which account that highest revolution of the star-studded heaven, whose motion is more rapid, is carried on with a sharp and quick sound; whereas this of the moon, which is situated the lowest, and at the other extremity, moves with the gravest sound. For the earth, the ninth sphere, remaining motionless, abides invariably in the innermost position, occupying the central spot in the universe.

"Now these eight directions, two of which have the same powers, effect seven sounds, differing in their modulations, which number is the connecting principle of almost all things. Some learned men, by imitating this harmony with strings and vocal melodies, have opened a way for their return to this place; as all others have done, who, endued with pre-eminent qualities, have cultivated in their mortal life the pursuits of heaven.

"The ears of mankind, filled with these sounds, have become deaf, for of all your senses it is the most blunted. Thus the people who live near the place where the Nile rushes down from very high mountains to the parts which are called Catadupa, are destitute of the sense of hearing, by reason of the greatness of the noise. Now this sound, which is effected by the rapid rotation of the whole system of nature, is so powerful, that human hearing cannot comprehend it, just as you cannot look directly upon the sun, because your sight and sense are overcome by his beams."

Also Milton, *Par. Lost,* II. 1051:—

> "And fast by, hanging in a golden chain,
>   This pendent world, in bigness as a star
>   Of smallest magnitude close by the moon."

139. The Moon, called in heaven Diana, on earth Luna, and in the infernal regions Proserpina; as in the curious Latin distich:—

"Terret, lustrat, agit, Proserpina, Luna, Diana,
    Ima, suprema, feras, sceptro, fulgore, sagittâ."

141. See Canto II. 59:—

"And I: 'What seems to us up here diverse,
    Is caused, I think, by bodies rare and dense.'"

142. The Sun.

144. Mercury, son of Maia, and Venus, daughter of Dione.

145. The temperate planet Jupiter, between Mars and Saturn. In Canto
XVIII. 68, Dante calls it "the temperate star;" and in the *Convito,* II. 14,
quoting the opinion of Ptolemy: "Jupiter is a star of a temperate complexion,
midway between the coldness of Saturn and the heat of Mars."

149. Bryant, *Song of the Stars:*—

"Look, look, through our glittering ranks afar,
    In the infinite azure, star after star,
    How they brighten and bloom as they swiftly pass!
    How the verdure runs o'er each rolling mass!
    And the path of the gentle winds is seen,
    Where the small waves dance, and the young woods lean.

"And see, where the brighter day-beams pour,
    How the rainbows hang in the sunny shower;
    And the morn and eve, with their pomp of hues,
    Shift o'er the bright planets and shed their dews;
    And 'twixt them both, o'er the teeming ground,
    With her shadowy cone the night goes round!"

151. The threshing-floor, or little area of our earth. The word *ajuola* would
also bear the rendering of garden-plot; but to Dante this world was rather a
threshing-floor than a flowerbed. The word occurs again in Canto XXVII.
86, and in its Latin form in the *Monarchia,* III.: *Ut scilicet in areola mortalium
libere cum pace vivatur.* Perhaps Dante uses it to signify in general any small
enclosure.

Boethius, *Cons. Phil.,* II. Prosa 7, Ridpath's Tr.: "You have learned from
astronomy that this globe of earth is but as a point in respect to the vast extent
of the heavens; that is, the immensity of the celestial sphere is such that ours,
when compared with it, is as nothing, and vanishes. You know likewise,
from the proofs that Ptolemy adduces, there is only one fourth part of this
earth, which is of itself so small a portion of the universe, inhabited by crea-
tures known to us. If from this fourth you deduct the space occupied by the
seas and lakes, and the vast sandy regions which extreme heat and want of
water render uninhabitable, there remains but a very small proportion of the

terrestrial sphere for the habitation of men. Enclosed then and locked up as you are, in an unperceivable point of a point, do you think of nothing but of blazing far and wide your name and reputation? What can there be great or pompous in a glory circumscribed in so narrow a circuit?"

Canto XXIII

1. The Heaven of the Fixed Stars continued. The Triumph of Christ.
3. Milton, *Par. Lost,* III. 38:—

> "As the wakeful bird
> Sings darkling, and in shadiest covert hid
> Tunes her nocturnal note."

12. Towards the meridian, where the sun seems to move slower than when nearer the horizon.
20. Didron, *Christ. Iconog.,* Millington's Tr., I. 308: "The triumph of Christ is, of all subjects, that which has excited the most enthusiasm amongst artists; it is seen in numerous monuments, and is represented both in painting and sculpture, but always with such remarkable modifications as impart to it the character of a new work. The eastern portion of the crypt of the cathedral of Auxerre contains, in the vaulting of that part which corresponds with the sanctuary, a fresco painting, executed about the end of the twelfth century, and representing, in the most simple form imaginable, the triumph of Christ. The background of the picture is intersected by a cross, which, if the transverse branches were a little longer, would be a perfect Greek cross. This cross is adorned with imitations of precious stones, round, oval, and lozenge-shaped, disposed in quincunxes. In the centre is a figure of Christ, on a white horse with a saddle; he holds the bridle in his left hand, and in the right, the hand of power and authority, a black staff, the rod of iron by which he governs the nations. He advances thus, having his head adorned with an azure or bluish nimbus, intersected by a cross gules; his face is turned towards the spectator. In the four compartments formed by the square in which the cross is enclosed are four angels who form the escort of Jesus; they are all on horseback, like their master, and with wings outspread; the right hand of each, which is free, is open and raised, in token of adoring admiration. 'And I saw heaven opened, and behold a white horse; and he that sat upon him was called Faithful and True, and in righteousness he doth judge and make war. His eyes were as a flame of fire, and on his head were many crowns; and he had a name written that no man knew but he himself. And he was clothed with a vesture dipped in blood; and his name is called the Word of God. And the armies which were in heaven followed him upon white horses, clothed in fine linen white and clean.' Such is the language of the Apocalypse,

and this the fresco at Auxerre interprets, although with some slight alterations, which it will be well to observe."

See also *Purg.* XXIX. Note 154.

21. By the beneficent influences of the stars.

26. The Moon. Trivia is one of the surnames of Diana, given her because she presided over all the places where three roads met.

Purg. XXXI. 106:—

"We here are Nymphs, and in the Heaven are stars."

Iliad, VIII. 550, Anon. Tr.: "As when in heaven the beauteous stars appear round the bright moon, when the air is breathless, and all the hills and lofty summits and forests are visible, and in the sky the boundless ether opens, and all the stars are seen, and the shepherd is delighted in his soul."

29. Christ.

30. The old belief that the stars were fed by the light of the sun. Milton, *Par. Lost,* VII. 364:—

"Hither as to their fountain other stars
    Repairing, in their golden urns draw light."

And Calderon, *El Principe Constante,* sonnet in Jor. II.:—

"Those glimmerings of light, those scintillations,
    That by supernal influences draw
    Their nutriment in splendours from the sun."

46. Beatrice speaks.

56. The Muse of harmony.

Skelton, *Elegy on the Earl of Northumberland,* 155:—

"If the hole quere of the musis nyne
    In me all onely wer sett and comprisyde,
Enbreathed with the blast of influence dyvyne,
    And perfightly as could be thought or devysyde;
    To me also allthouche it were promysyde
Of laureat Phebus holy the eloquence,
All were to littill for his magnyficence."

70. Beatrice speaks again.

73. The Virgin Mary, *Rosa Mundi, Rosa Mystica.*

74. The Apostles, by following whom the good way was found.

Shirley, *Death's Final Conquest:*—

"Only the actions of the just
    Smell sweet, and blossom in the dust."

78. The struggle between his eyes and the light.

85. Christ, who had re-ascended, so that Dante's eyes, too feeble to bear the light of his presence, could now behold the splendour of this "meadow of flowers."

88. The Rose, or the Virgin Mary, to whom Beatrice alludes in line 73. Afterwards he hears the hosts of heaven repeat her name, as described in line 110:—

> "And all the other lights
> Were making to resound the name of Mary."

90. This greater fire is also the Virgin, greatest of the remaining splendours.

92. *Stella Maris, Stella Matutina,* are likewise titles of the Virgin, who surpasses in brightness all other souls in heaven, as she did here on earth.

94. The Angel Gabriel.

101. The mystic virtues of the sapphire are thus enumerated by Marbodus in his *Lapidarium,* King's *Antique Gems,* p. 395:—

> "By nature with superior honours graced,
> As gem of gems above all others placed;
> Health to preserve and treachery to disarm,
> And guard the wearer from intended harm.
> No envy bends him, and no terror shakes;
> The captive's chains its mighty virtue breaks;
> The gates fly open, fetters fall away,
> And send their prisoner to the light of day.
> E'en Heaven is movèd by its force divine
> To list to vows presented at its shrine."

Sapphire is the colour in which the old painters arrayed the Virgin, "its hue," says Mr. King, "being the exact shade of the air or atmosphere in the climate of Rome." This is Dante's

> "Dolce color d'oriental zaffiro,"

in *Purg.* I. 13.

105. Haggai ii. 7: "The desire of all nations shall come."

112. The *Primum Mobile,* or Crystalline Heaven, which infolds all the other volumes or rolling orbs of the universe like a mantle.

115. Cowley, *Hymn to Light:*—

> "Thou Scythian-like dost round thy lands above
> The sun's gilt tent for ever move;
> And still as thou in pomp dost go,
> The shining pageants of the world attend thy show."

120. The Virgin ascending to her son. Fray Luis Ponce de Leon, *Assumption of the Virgin:*—

> "Lady! thine upward flight
> The opening heavens receive with joyful song;
>   Blest who thy mantle bright
>   May seize amid the throng,
> And to the sacred mount float peacefully along!

> "Bright angels are around thee,
> They that have served thee from thy birth are there;
>   Their hands with stars have crowned thee;
>   Thou, peerless Queen of air,
> As sandals to thy feet the silver moon dost wear!"

128. An Easter Hymn to the Virgin:—

> "Regina cœli, lætare! Alleluia.
>   Quia quem meruisti portare, Alleluia.
>   Resurrexit, sicut dixit. Alleluia."

This hymn, according to Collin de Plancy, *Légendes des Commandements de l'Église,* p. 14, Pope Gregory the Great heard the angels singing, in the pestilence of Rome in 890, and on hearing it added another line:—

> "Ora pro nobis Deum! Alleluia."

135. Caring not for gold and silver in the Babylonian exile of this life, they laid up treasures in the other.

139. St. Peter, keeper of the keys, with the saints of the Old and New Testament.

Milton, *Lycidas,* 108:—

> "Last came, and last did go,
>   The pilot of the Galilean lake;
>   Two massy keys he bore of metals twain,
>   (The golden opes, the iron shuts amain)."

And Fletcher, *Purple Island,* VII. 62:—

> "Not in his lips, but hands, two keys he bore,
>   Heaven's doors and Hell's to shut and open wide."

Canto XXIV

1. The Heaven of the Fixed Stars continued. St. Peter examines Dante on Faith.

Revelation xix. 9: "And he saith unto me, Write, Blessed are they which are called unto the marriage-supper of the Lamb."

16. The carol was a dance as well as a song; or, to speak more exactly, a dance accompanied by a song.

Gower, *Confes. Amant.*, VI.:—

> "And if it nedes so betide,
> That I in company abide,
> Where as I must daunce and singe
> The hove daunce and carolinge."

It is from the old French *karole*. See passage from the *Roman de la Rose,* in Note 118 of this canto. See also Roquefort, *Glossaire:* "KAROLE, dance, concert, divertissement; de *chorea, chorus;*" and "KAROLER, sauter, danser, se divertir."

> Et li borjéois y furent en present
> *Karolent* main à main, et chantent hautement.
> *Vie de Du Guesclin."*

Milton, *Par. Lost,* V. 618:—

> "That day, as other solemn days, they spent
> In song and dance about the sacred hill,
> Mystical dance, which yonder starry sphere
> Of planets and of fixed in all her wheels
> Resembles nearest, mazes intricate,
> Eccentric, intervolved, yet regular
> Then most when most irregular they seem;
> And in their motions harmony divine
> So smooths her charming tones, that God's own ear
> Listens delighted."

17. "That is," says Buti, "of the abundance of their beatitude. . . . . And this swiftness and slowness signified the fervour of love which was in them."

19. From the brightest of these carols or dances.

20. St. Peter.

22. Three times, in sign of the Trinity.

27. Tints too coarse and glaring to paint such delicate draperies of song.

28. St. Peter speaks to Beatrice.

41. Fixed upon God, in whom all things are reflected.

59. The captain of the first cohort of the Church Militant.

62. St. Paul. Mrs. Jameson, *Sacred and Legendary Art,* I. 159, says: "The early Christian Church was always considered under two great divisions: the church of the converted Jews, and the church of the Gentiles. The first was represented by St. Peter, the second by St. Paul. Standing together in this mutual relation, they represent the universal church of Christ; hence in works of art they are seldom separated, and are indispensable in all ecclesiastical decoration. Their proper place is on each side of the Saviour, or of the Virgin throned; or on each side of the altar; or on each side of the arch over the choir. In any case, where they stand together, not merely as Apostles, but Founders, their place is next after the Evangelists and the Prophets."

64. *Hebrews* xi. 1: "Now faith is the substance of things hoped for, the evidence of things not seen."

66. In Scholastic language the essence of a thing, distinguishing it from all other things, is called its *quiddity;* in answer to the question, *Quid est?*

78. Jeremy Taylor says: "Faith is a certain image of eternity; all things are present to it; things past and things to come are all so before the eyes of faith, that he in whose eye that candle is enkindled beholds heaven as present, and sees how blessed a thing it is to die in God's favour, and to be chimed to our grave with the music of a good conscience. Faith converses with the angels, and antedates the hymns of glory; every man that hath this grace is as certain that there are glories for him, if he perseveres in duty, as if he had heard and sung the thanksgiving-song for the blessed sentence of doomsday."

87. "The purified, righteous man," says Tertullian, "has become a coin of the Lord, and has the impress of his King stamped upon him."

93. The Old and New Testaments.

115. In the Middle Ages titles of nobility were given to the saints and to other renowned personages of sacred history. Thus Boccaccio, in his story of Fra Cipolla, *Decamerone,* Gior. VI. Nov. 10, speaks of the Baron Messer Santo Antonio; and in Juan Lorenzo's *Poema de Alexandro,* we have Don Job, Don Bacchus, and Don Satan.

118. The word *donnea,* which I have rendered "like a lover plays," is from the Provençal *domnear.* In its old French form, *dosnoier,* it occurs in some editions of the *Roman de la Rose,* line 1305:—

> "Les karoles jà remanoient;
> Car tuit li plusors s'en aloient
> O leurs amies umbroier
> Sous ces arbres pour dosnoier."

Chaucer translates the passage thus:—

> "The daunces then ended ywere;
> For many of hem that daunced there
> Were, with hir loves, went away
> Under the trees to have hir play."

The word expresses the gallantry of the knight towards his lady.

126. St. John was the first to reach the sepulchre, but St. Peter the first to enter it. John xx. 4: "So they ran both together; and the other disciple did outrun Peter, and came first to the sepulchre. And he, stooping down, and looking in, saw the linen clothes lying; yet went he not in. Then cometh Simon Peter following him, and went into the sepulchre, and seeth the linen clothes lie."

132. Dante, *Convito,* II. 4, speaking of the motion of the *Primum Mobile,* or Crystalline Heaven, which moves all the others, says: "From the fervent longing which each part of that ninth heaven has to be conjoined with that Divinest Heaven, the Heaven of Rest, which is next to it, it revolves therein with so great desire, that its velocity is almost incomprehensible."

137. St. Peter and the other Apostles after Pentecost.

141. Both three and one, both plural and singular.

152. Again the sign of the Trinity.

Canto XXV

1. The Heaven of the Fixed Stars continued. St. James examines Dante on Hope.

5. Florence the Fair, *Fiorenza la bella.* In one of his *Canzoni,* Dante says:—

> "O mountain song of mine, thou goest thy way;
>   Florence my town thou shalt perchance behold,
>   Which bars me from itself,
>   Devoid of love and naked of compassion."

7. In one of Dante's *Eclogues,* written at Ravenna and addressed to Giovanni del Virgilio of Bologna, who had invited him to that city to receive the poet's crown, he says: "Were it not better, on the banks of my native Arno, if ever I should return thither, to adorn and hide beneath the interwoven leaves my triumphal gray hairs, which once were golden? . . . . When the bodies that wander round the earth, and the dwellers among the stars, shall be revealed in my song, as the infernal realm has been, then it will delight me to encircle my head with ivy and with laurel."

It would seem from this extract that Dante's hair had once been light, and not black, as Boccaccio describes it.

See also the *Extract from the Convito,* and Dante's *Letter to a Friend,* among the Illustrations in Vol. I.

8. This allusion to the church of San Giovanni, where Dante was baptized, and which in *Inf.* XIX. 17 he calls "*il mio bel San Giovanni,*" is a fitting prelude to the canto in which St. John is to appear.

12. As described in Canto XXIV. 152:—

> "So, giving me its benediction, singing,
>   Three times encircled me, when I was silent,
>   The apostolic light."

14. The band or carol in which St. Peter was. James i. 18: "That we should be a kind of first-fruits of his creatures."

17. St. James, to whose tomb at Compostella, in Galicia, pilgrimages were and are still made. The legend says that the body of St. James was put on board a ship and abandoned to the sea; but the ship, being guided by an angel, landed safely in Galicia. There the body was buried; but in the course of time the place of its burial was forgotten, and not discovered again till the year 800, when it was miraculously revealed to a friar.

Mrs. Jameson, *Sacred and Legendary Art,* I. 211, says: "Then they caused the body of the saint to be transported to Compostella; and in consequence of the surprising miracles which graced his shrine, he was honoured not merely in Galicia, but throughout all Spain. He became the patron saint of the Spaniards, and Compostella, as a place of pilgrimage, was renowned throughout Europe. From all countries bands of pilgrims resorted there, so that sometimes there were no less than a hundred thousand in one year. The military order of Saint Jago, enrolled by Don Alphonso for their protection, became one of the greatest and richest in Spain.

"Now, if I should proceed to recount all the wonderful deeds enacted by Santiago in behalf of his chosen people, they would fill a volume. The Spanish historians number thirty-eight visible apparitions, in which this glorious saint descended from heaven in person, and took the command of their armies against the Moors."

26. Before me.

29. James i. 5 and 17: "If any of you lack wisdom, let him ask of God, that giveth to all men liberally, and upbraideth not; and it shall be given him. . . . . Every good gift and every perfect gift is from above, and cometh down from the Father of lights, with whom is no variableness, neither shadow of turning."

In this line, instead of *largezza,* some editions read *allegrezza;* but as James describes the bounties of heaven, and not its joys, the former reading is undoubtedly the correct one.

32. St. Peter personifies Faith; St. James, Hope; and St. John, Charity. These three were distinguished above the other Apostles by clearer manifestations of their Master's favour, as, for example, their being present at the Transfiguration.

34. These words are addressed by St. James to Dante.

36. In the radiance of the three theological virtues, Faith, Hope, and Charity.

38. To the three Apostles luminous above him and overwhelming him with their light. *Psalm* cxxi. 1: "I will lift up mine eyes unto the hills, from whence cometh my help."

42. With the most august spirits of the celestial city. See Canto XXIV. Note 115.

49. Beatrice.

54. In God, or, as Dante says in Canto XXIV. 42:—

"There where depicted everything is seen."

And again, Canto XXVI. 106:—

"For I behold it in the truthful mirror,
    That of Himself all things parhelion makes,
    And none makes Him parhelion of itself."

58. "Say what it is," and "whence it came to be."

62. The answer to these two questions involves no self-praise, as the answer to the other would have done, if it had come from Dante's lips.

67. This definition of Hope is from Peter Lombard's *Lib. Sent.*, Book III. Dist. 26: *"Est spes certa expectatio futuræ beatitudinis, veniens ex Dei gratia, et meritis præcedentibus."*

72. The Psalmist David.

73. In his divine songs, or songs of God. *Psalm* ix. 10: "And they that know thy name will put their trust in thee."

78. Your rain; that is, of David and St. James.

84. According to the legend, St. James suffered martyrdom under Herod Agrippa.

89. "The mark of the high calling and election sure," namely, Paradise, which is the aim and object of all the "friends of God;" or, as St. James expresses it in his *Epistle*, i. 12: "Blessed is the man that endureth temptation: for when he is tried, he shall receive the crown of life, which the Lord hath promised to them that love him."

90. This expression is from the *Epistle* of James, ii. 23: "And he was called the Friend of God."

91. The spiritual body and the glorified earthly body. Isaiah lxi. 7: "Therefore in their land they shall possess the double; everlasting joy shall be unto them."

95. St. John in *Revelation* vii. 9: "After this I beheld, and lo, a great multitude, which no man could number, of all nations, and kindreds, and people, and tongues, stood before the throne, and before the Lamb, clothed with white robes and palms in their hands."

100. St. John.

101. If Cancer, which in winter rises at sunset, had one star as bright as this, it would turn night into day.

105. Any failing, such as vanity, ostentation, or the like.

107. St. Peter and St. James.

113. This symbol or allegory of the Pelican, applied to Christ, was popular during the Middle Ages, and was seen not only in the songs of poets, but in sculpture on the portals of churches.

Thibaut, Roi de Navarre, Chanson LXV., says:—

> "Diex est ensi comme li Pelicans,
>   Qui fait son nit el plus haut arbre sus,
>   Et li mauvais oseau, qui vient de jus
>   Ses oisellons ocist, tant est puans;
>   Li pere vient destrois et angosseux,
>   Dou bec s'ocist, de son sanc dolereus
>   Vivre refait tantost ses oisellons;
>   Diex fist autel, quant vint sa passions,
>   De son douc sanc racheta ses enfans
>   Dou Deauble, qui tant parest poissans."

114. John xix. 27: "Then saith he to the disciple, Behold thy mother! And from that hour that disciple took her unto his own home."

121. St. John. Dante—bearing in mind the words of Christ, John xxi. 22, "If I will that he tarry till I come, what is that to thee? . . . . Then went this saying abroad among the brethren, that that disciple should not die"—looks to see if the spiritual body of the saint be in any way eclipsed by his earthly body. St. John, reading his unspoken thought, immediately undeceives him.

Mrs. Jameson, *Sacred and Legendary Art,* I. 139, remarks: "The legend which supposes St. John reserved alive has not been generally received in the Church, and as a subject of painting it is very uncommon. It occurs in the *Menologium Græcum,* where the grave into which St. John descends is, according to the legend, *fossa in crucis figuram* (in the form of a cross). In a series of the deaths of the Apostles, St. John is ascending from the grave; for, according to the Greek legend, St. John died without pain or change, and immediately rose again in bodily form, and ascended into heaven to rejoin Christ and the Virgin."

126. Till the predestined number of the elect is complete. *Revelation* vi. 11: "And white robes were given unto every one of them; and it was said unto them, that they should rest yet for a little season, until their fellow-servants also and their brethren, that should be killed as they were, should be fulfilled."

127. The spiritual body and the glorified earthly body.

128. Christ and the Virgin Mary. Butler, *Lives of the Saints,* VIII. 173, says: "It is a traditionary pious belief, that the body of the Blessed Virgin was raised by God soon after her death, and assumed to glory, by a singular privilege, before the general resurrection of the dead. This is mentioned by the learned

Andrew of Crete in the East, in the seventh, and by St. Gregory of Tours in the West, in the sixth century. . . . . So great was the respect and veneration of the fathers towards this most holy and most exalted of all pure creatures, that St. Epiphanius durst not affirm that she ever died, because he had never found any mention of her death, and because she might have been preserved immortal, and translated to glory without dying."

132. By the sacred trio of St. Peter, St. James, and St. John.

138. Because his eyes were so blinded by the splendour of the beloved disciple. Speaking of St. John, Claudius, the German poet, says: "It delights me most of all to read in John: there is in him something so entirely wonderful,—twilight and night, and through it the swiftly darting lightning,—a soft evening cloud, and behind the cloud the broad full moon bodily; something so deeply, sadly pensive, so high, so full of anticipation, that one cannot have enough of it. In reading John it is always with me as though I saw him before me, lying on the bosom of his Master at the last supper: as though his angel were holding the light for me, and in certain passages would fall upon my neck and whisper something in mine ear. I am far from understanding all I read, but it often seems to me as if what John meant were floating before in the distance; and even when I look into a passage altogether dark, I have a foretaste of some great, glorious meaning, which I shall one day understand, and for this reason I grasp so eagerly after every new interpretation of the Gospel of John. Indeed, most of them only play upon the edge of the evening cloud, and the moon behind it has quiet rest."

Canto XXVI

1. The Heaven of the Fixed Stars continued. St. John examines Dante on Charity, in the sense of Love, as in Milton, *Par. Lost,* XII. 583:—

> "Love,
> By name to come called Charity."

12. Ananias, the disciple at Damascus, whose touch restored the sight of Saul. *Acts* ix. 17: "And Ananias went his way, and entered into the house, and putting his hands on him, said, Brother Saul, the Lord, even Jesus, that appeared unto thee in the way as thou camest, hath sent me, that thou mightest receive thy sight, and be filled with the Holy Ghost. And immediately there fell from his eyes as it had been scales; and he received sight forthwith, and arose, and was baptized."

17. God is the beginning and end of all my love.

38. The commentators differ as to which of the philosophers Dante here refers; whether to Aristotle, Plato, or Pythagoras.

39. The angels.

42. *Exodus* xxxiii. 19: "And he said, I will make all my goodness pass before thee."

44. *John* i. 1: "In the beginning was the Word, and the Word was with God, and the Word was God. . . . . And the Word was made flesh, and dwelt among us, ... full of grace and truth."

46. By all the dictates of human reason and divine authority.

52. In Christian art the eagle is the symbol of St. John, indicating his more fervid imagination and deeper insight into divine mysteries. Sometimes even the saint was represented with the head and feet of an eagle, and the hands and body of a man.

64. All living creatures.

69. Isaiah vi. 3: "As one cried unto another, and said, Holy, holy, holy is the Lord of Hosts; the whole earth is full of his glory."

83. The soul of Adam.

91. "Tell me, of what age was Adam when he was created?" is one of the questions in the Anglo-Saxon *Dialogue between Saturn and Solomon;* and the answer is, "I tell thee, he was thirty winters old." And Buti says: "He was created of the age of thirty-three, or thereabout; and therefore the author says that Adam alone was created by God in perfect age and stature, and no other man." And Sir Thomas Browne, *Religio Medici,* § 39: "Some divines count Adam thirty years old at his creation, because they suppose him created in the perfect age and stature of man."

Stehelin, *Traditions of the Jews,* I. 16, quotes Rabbi Eliezer as saying "that the first man reached from the earth to the firmament of heaven; but that, after he had sinned, God laid his hands on him and reduced him to a less size." And Rabbi Salomon writes, that "when he lay down, his head was in the east and his feet in the west."

107. Parhelion is an imperfect image of the sun, formed by reflection in the clouds. All things are such faint reflections of the Creator; but he is the reflection of none of them.

Buti interprets the passage differently, giving to the word *pareglio* the meaning of *ricettacolo,* receptacle.

118. In Limbo, longing for Paradise, where the only punishment is to live in desire, but without hope. *Inf.* IV. 41:—

> "Lost are we, and are only so far punished,
>   That without hope we live on in desire."

124. Most of the Oriental languages claim the honour of being the language spoken by Adam in Paradise. Juan Bautista de Erro claims it for the Basque, or Vascongada. See *Alphabet of Prim. Lang. of Spain,* Pt. II. Ch. 2, Erving's Tr.

129. See Canto XVI. 79:—

> "All things of yours have their mortality,
>   Even as yourselves."

134. Dante, *De Volg. Eloq.*, I. Ch. 4, says, speaking of Adam: "What was the first word he spake will, I doubt not, readily suggest itself to every one of sound mind as being what God is, namely, *El,* either in the way of question or of answer."

136. The word used by Matthew, xxvii. 46, is *Eli,* and by Mark, xv. 34, *Eloi,* which Dante assumes to be of later use than *El.* There is, I believe, no authority for this. *El* is God; *Eli,* or *Eloi,* my God.

137. Horace, *Ars Poet.*, 60: "As the woods change their leaves in autumn, and the earliest fall, so the ancient words pass away, and the new flourish in the freshness of youth. . . . . Many that now have fallen shall spring up again, and others fall which now are held in honour, if usage wills, which is the judge, the law, and the rule of language."

139. The mount of Purgatory, on whose summit was the Terrestrial Paradise.

142. The sixth hour is noon in the old way of reckoning; and at noon the sun has completed one quarter or quadrant of the arc of his revolution, and changes to the next. The hour which is second to the sixth, is the hour which follows it, or one o'clock. This gives seven hours for Adam's stay in Paradise; and so says Peter Comestor (Dante's Peter Mangiador) in his ecclesiastical history.

The Talmud, as quoted by Stehelin, *Traditions of the Jews,* I. 20, gives the following account: "The day has twelve hours. In the first hour the dust of which Adam was formed was brought together. In the second, this dust was made a rude, unshapely mass. In the third, the limbs were stretched out. In the fourth, a soul was lodged in it. In the fifth, Adam stood upon his feet. In the sixth, he assigned the names of all things that were created. In the seventh, he received Eve for his consort. In the eighth, two went to bed and four rose out of it; the begetting and birth of two children in that time, namely, Cain and his sister. In the ninth, he was forbid to eat of the fruit of the tree. In the tenth, he disobeyed. In the eleventh, he was tried, convicted, and sentenced. In the twelfth, he was banished, or driven out of the garden."

Canto **XXVII**

1. The Heaven of the Fixed Stars continued. The anger of St. Peter; and the ascent to the Primum Mobile, or Cryrstalline Heaven.

Dante, *Convito* II. 15, makes this Crystalline Heaven the symbol of Moral Philosophy. He says: "The Crystalline Heaven, which has previously been called the Primum Mobile, has a very manifest resemblance to Moral Philosophy; for Moral Philosophy, as Thomas says in treating of the second book of the Ethics, directs us to the other sciences. For, as the Philosopher says in the fifth of the Ethics, legal justice directs us to learn the sciences, and orders them to be learned and mastered, so that they may not be abandoned; so this heaven directs with its movement the daily revolutions of all the others, by which daily they all receive here below the virtue of all their parts. For if its revolution did not thus direct, little of their virtues would reach here below, and little of their sight. Hence, supposing it were possible for this ninth heaven to stand still, the third part of heaven would not be seen in each part of the earth; and Saturn would be hidden from each part of the earth fourteen years and a half; and Jupiter, six years; and Mars, almost a year; and the Sun, one hundred and eighty-two days and fourteen hours (I say days, that is, so much time as so many days would measure); and Venus and Mercury would conceal and show themselves nearly as the Sun; and the Moon would be hidden from all people for the space of fourteen days and a half. Truly there would be here below no production, nor life of animals, nor plants; there would be neither night, nor day, nor week, nor month, nor year; but the whole universe would be deranged, and the movement of the stars in vain. And not otherwise, were Moral Philosophy to cease, the other sciences would be for a time concealed, and there would be no pro- duction, nor life of felicity, and in vain would be the writings or discover- ies of antiquity. Wherefore it is very manifest that this heaven bears a resem- blance to Moral Philosophy."

9. Without desire for more.

10. St. Peter, St. James, St. John, and Adam.

14. If the white planet Jupiter should become as red as Mars.

22. Pope Boniface VIII., who won his way to the Popedom by intrigue. See *Inf.* III. Note 59, and XIX. Note 53.

25. The Vatican hill, to which the body of St. Peter was transferred from the catacombs.

36. *Luke* xxiii. 44: "And there was darkness over all the earth. . . . . And the sun was darkened."

41. Linus was the immediate successor of St. Peter as Bishop of Rome, and Cletus of Linus. They were both martyrs of the first age of the Church.

44. Sixtus and Pius were Popes and martyrs of the second age of the Church; Calixtus and Urban, of the third.

47. On the right hand of the Pope the favoured Guelfs, and on the left the persecuted Ghibellines.

50. The Papal banner, on which are the keys of St. Peter.

51. The wars against the Ghibellines in general, and particularly that waged against the Colonna family, ending in the destruction of Palestrina. *Inf.* XXVII. 85:—

> "But he, the Prince of the new Pharisees,
>   Having a war near unto Lateran,
>   And not with Saracens nor with the Jews,
> For each one of his enemies was Christian,
>   And none of them had been to conquer Acre,
>   Nor merchandising in the Sultan's land."

53. The sale of indulgences, stamped with the Papal seal, bearing the head of St. Peter.

55. *Matthew* vii. 15: "Beware of false prophets, which come to you in sheep's clothing, but inwardly they are ravening wolves."

57. *Psalm* xliv. 23: "Awake, why sleepest thou, O Lord?"

58. Clement V. of Gascony, made Pope in 1305, and John XXII. of Cahors in France, in 1316. Buti makes the allusion more general: "They of Cahors and Gascony are preparing to drink the blood of the martyrs, because they were preparing to be Popes, cardinals, archbishops and bishops, and prelates in the Church of God, that is built with the blood of the martyrs."

61. Dante alludes elsewhere to this intervention of Providence to save the Roman Empire by the hand of Scipio. *Convito,* IV. 5, he says: "Is not the hand of God visible, when in the war with Hannibal, having lost so many citizens, that three bushels of rings were carried to Africa, the Romans would have abandoned the land, if that blessed youth Scipio had not undertaken the expedition to Africa, to secure its freedom?"

69. When the sun is in Capricorn; that is, from the middle of December to the middle of January.

68. Boccaccio, *Ninfale d'Ameto,* describing a battle between two flocks of swans, says the spectators "saw the air full of feathers, as when the nurse of Jove [Amalthæa, the Goat] holds Apollo, the white snow is seen to fall in flakes."

And Whittier, *Snow-Bound*:—

> "Unwarmed by any sunset light,
>   The gray day darkened into night,
>   A night made hoary with the swarm
>   And whirl-dance of the blinding storm,
>   As zigzag wavering to and fro
>   Crossed and recrossed the wingéd snow."

72. The spirits described in Canto XXII. 131, as

> "The triumphant throng
> That comes rejoicing through this rounded ether,"

and had remained behind when Christ and the Virgin Mary ascended.

74. Till his sight could follow them no more, on account of the exceeding vastness of the space between.

79. Canto XXII. 133.

81. The first climate is the torrid zone, the first from the equator. From midst to end, is from the meridian to the horizon. Dante had been, then, six hours in the Heaven of the Fixed Stars; for, as Milton says, *Par. Lost,* V. 580:—

> "Time, though in eternity, applied
>   To motion, measures all things durable,
>   By present, past, and future."

82. Being now in the meridian of the Straits of Gibraltar, Dante sees to the westward of Cadiz the sea Ulysses sailed, when he turned his stern unto the morning and made his oars wings for his mad flight, as described in *Inf.* XXVI.

83. Eastward he almost sees the Phœnician coast; almost, and not quite, because, say the commentators, it was already night there.

84. Europa, daughter of King Agenor, borne to the island of Crete on the back of Jupiter, who had taken the shape of a bull.

Ovid, *Met.,* II., Addison's Tr.:—

> "Agenor's royal daughter, as she played
> Among the fields, the milk-white bull surveyed,
> And viewed his spotless body with delight,
> And at a distance kept him in her sight.
> At length she plucked the rising flowers, and fed
> The gentle beast, and fondly stroked his head.
>
> . . . . .
>
> Till now grown wanton and devoid of fear,
> Not knowing that she pressed the Thunderer,
> She placed herself upon his back, and rode
> O'er fields and meadows, seated on the god.
>
> . . . . .
>
> "He gently marched along, and by degrees
> Left the dry meadow, and approached the seas;
> Where now he dips his hoofs and wets his thighs,
> Now plunges in, and carries off the prize."

85. See Canto XXII. Note 151.

87. The sun was in Aries, two signs in advance of Gemini, in which Dante then was.

88. *Donnea* again. See Canto XXIV. Note 118.

91. *Purg.* XXXI. 49:—

> "Never to thee presented art or nature
>   Pleasure so great as the fair limbs wherein
>   I was enclosed, which scattered are in earth."

98. The Gemini, or Twins, are Castor and Pollux, the sons of Leda. And as Jupiter, their father, came to her in the shape of a swan, this sign of the zodiac is called the nest of Leda. Dante now mounts up from the Heaven of the fixed stars to the Primum Mobile, or Crystalline Heaven.

103. Dante's desire to know in what part of this heaven he was.

109. All the other heavens have their Regents or Intelligences. See Canto II. Note 131. But the Primum Mobile has the Divine Mind alone.

113. By that precinct Dante means the Empyrean, which embraces the Primum Mobile, as that does all the other heavens below it.

117. The half of ten is five, and the fifth is two. The product of these, when multiplied together, is ten.

127. Wordsworth, *Intimations of Immortality*:—

"Our birth is but a sleep and a forgetting:
The Soul that rises with us, our life's Star,
    Hath had elsewhere its setting,
        And cometh from afar:
    Not in entire forgetfulness,
    And not in utter nakedness,
But trailing clouds of glory, do we come
    From God, who is our home:
Heaven lies about us in our infancy!
Shades of the prison-house begin to close
        Upon the growing Boy,
But he beholds the light, and whence it flows,
        He sees it in his joy;
The Youth, who daily farther from the east
        Must travel, still is Nature's Priest,
        And by the vision splendid
        Is on his way attended;
At length the Man perceives it die away,
And fade into the light of common day."

137. Aurora, daughter of Hyperion, or the Sun. *Purg.* II. 7:—

"So that the white and the vermilion cheeks
    Of beautiful Aurora, where I was,
    By too great age were changing into orange."

140. Or, perhaps, to steer, and

"Over the high seas to keep
The barque of Peter to its proper bearings."

143. This neglected centesimal was the omission of some inconsiderable fraction or centesimal part, in the computation of the year according to the Julian calendar, which was corrected in the Gregorian, some two centuries and a half after Dante's death. By this error, in a long lapse of time, the months would cease to correspond to the seasons, and January be no longer a winter, but a spring month.

Sir John Herschel, *Treatise on Astronomy*, Ch. XIII., says: "The Julian rule made every fourth year, without exception, a bissextile. This is, in fact, an over-correction; it supposes the length of the tropical year to be 365¼ d., which is too great, and thereby induces an error of 7 days in 900 years, as will easily appear on trial. Accordingly, so early as the year 1414, it began to be perceived that the equinoxes were gradually creeping away from the 21st of March and September, where they ought to have always fallen had the Julian year been exact, and happening (as it appeared) too early. The necessity of a fresh and effectual reform in the calendar was from that time continually urged, and at length admitted. The change (which took place under the Popedom of Gregory XIII.) consisted in the omission of ten nominal days after the 4th of October, 1582, (so that the next day was called the 15th and not the 5th), and the promulgation of the rule already explained for future regulation."

It will appear from the verse of Dante, that this error and its consequences had been noticed a century earlier than the year mentioned by Herschel. Dante speaks ironically; naming a very long period, and meaning a very short one.

145. Dante here refers either to the reforms he expected from the Emperor Henry VII., or to those he as confidently looked for from Can Grande della Scala, the Veltro, or greyhound, of *Inf.* I. 101, who was to slay the she-wolf, and make her "perish in her pain," and whom he so warmly eulogizes in Canto XVII. of the Paradiso. Alas for the vanity of human wishes! Patient Italy has waited more than five centuries for the fulfilment of this prophecy, but at length she has touched the bones of her prophet, and "is revived and stands upon her feet."

Canto XXVIII

1. The Primum Mobile, or Crystalline Heaven, continued.
3. Milton, *Par. Lost,* IV. 505:—

> "Thus these two,
> Imparadised in one another's arms,
> The happier Eden, shall enjoy their fill
> Of bliss on bliss."

14. That Crystalline Heaven, which Dante calls a volume, or scroll, as in Canto XXIII. 112:—

> "The regal mantle of the volumes all."

16. The light of God, represented as a single point, to indicate its unity and indivisibility.
32. Iris, or the rainbow.
34. These nine circles of fire are the nine Orders of Angels in the three Celestial Hierarchies. Dante, *Convito,* II. 16, says that the Holy Church divides the Angels into "three Hierarchies, that is to say, three holy or divine

Principalities; and each Hierarchy has three Orders; so that the Church believes and affirms nine Orders of spiritual beings. The first is that of the Angels; the second, that of the Archangels; the third, that of the Thrones. And these three Orders form the first Hierarchy; not first in reference to rank nor creation (for the others are more noble, and all were created together), but first in reference to our ascent to their height. Then follow the Dominions; next the Virtues; then the Principalities; and these form the second Hierarchy. Above these are the Powers, and the Cherubim, and above all are the Seraphim; and these form the third Hierarchy."

It will be observed that this arrangement of the several Orders does not agree with that followed in the poem.

55. Barlow, *Study of the Div. Com.,* p. 533, remarks: "Within a circle of ineffable joy, circumscribed only by light and love, a point of intense brightness so dazzled the eyes of Dante that he could not sustain the sight of it. Around this vivid centre, from which the heavens and all nature depend, nine concentric circles of the Celestial Hierarchy revolved with a velocity inversely proportioned to their distance from it, the nearer circles moving more rapidly, the remoter ones less. The poet at first is surprised at this, it being the reverse of the relative movement, from the same source of propulsion, of the heavens themselves around the earth as their centre. But the infallible Beatrice assures him that this difference arises, in fact, from the same cause, proximity to the Divine presence, which in the celestial spheres is greater the farther they are from the centre, but in the circles of angels, on the contrary, it is greater the nearer they are to it."

60. Because the subject has not been investigated and discussed.

64. The nine heavens are here called corporal circles, as we call the stars the heavenly bodies. Latimer says: "A corporal heaven, ... where the stars are."

70. The Primum Mobile, in which Dante and Beatrice now are.

77. The nearer God the circle is, so much greater virtue it possesses. Hence the outermost of the heavens, revolving round the earth, corresponds to the innermost of the Orders of Angels revolving round God, and is controlled by it as its Regent or Intelligence. To make this more intelligible I will repeat here the three Triads of Angels, and the heavens of which they are severally the intelligences, as already given in Canto II. Note 131.

The Seraphim,	Primum Mobile.
The Cherubim,	The Fixed Stars.
The Thrones,	Saturn.
The Dominions,	Jupiter.
The Virtues,	Mars.
The Powers,	The Sun.

The Principalities,	Venus.
The Archangels,	Mercury.
The Angels,	The Moon.

80. *Æneid,* XII. 365, Davidson's Tr.: "As when the blast of Thracian Boreas roars on the Ægean Sea, and to the shore pursues the waves, wherever the winds exert their incumbent force, the clouds fly through the air."

Each of the four winds blow three different blasts; either directly in front, or from the right cheek, or the left. According to Boccaccio, the north-east wind in Italy is milder than the north-west.

90. Dante uses this comparison before, Canto I. 60:—

> "But I beheld it sparkle round about
> Like iron that comes molten from the fire."

93. The inventor of the game of chess brought it to a Persian king, who was so delighted with it, that he offered him in return whatever reward he might ask. The inventor said he wished only a grain of wheat, doubled as many times as there were squares on the chess-board; that is, one grain for the first square, two for the second, four for the third, and so on to sixty-four. This the king readily granted; but when the amount was reckoned up, he had not wheat enough in his whole kingdom to pay it.

95. Their appointed place or whereabout.

99. Thomas Aquinas, the *Doctor Angelicus* of the Schools, treats the subject of Angels at great length in the first volume of his *Summa Theologica,* from Quæst. L. to LXIV., and from Quæst. CVI. to CXIV. He constantly quotes Dionysius, sometimes giving his exact words, but oftener amplifying and interpreting his meaning. In Quæst. CVIII. he discusses the names of the Angels, and of the Seraphim and Cherubim speaks as follows:—

"The name of Seraphim is not given from love alone, but from excess of love, which the name of heat or burning implies. Hence Dionysius (Cap. VII. *Cæl. Hier.,* a princ.) interprets the name Seraphim according to the properties of fire, in which is excess of heat. In fire, however, we may consider three things. First, a certain motion which is upward, and which is continuous; by which is signified, that they are unchangingly moving towards God. Secondly, its active power, which is heat; . . . . and by this is signified the influence of this kind of Angels, which they exercise powerfully on those beneath them, exciting them to a sublime fervour, and thoroughly purifying them by burning. Thirdly, in fire its brightness must be considered; and this signifies that such angels have within themselves an inextinguishable light, and that they perfectly illuminate others.

"In the same way the name of Cherubim is given from a certain excess of knowledge; hence it is interpreted *plenitudo scientiæ;* which Dionysius (Cap. VII. *Cæl. Hier.,* a princ.) explains in four ways: first, as perfect vision of God; secondly, full reception of divine light; thirdly, that in God himself they contemplate the beauty of the order of things emanating from God; fourthly, that, being themselves full of this kind of knowledge, they copiously pour it out upon others."

100. The love of God, which holds them fast to this central point as with a band. *Job* xxxviii. 31: "Canst thou bind the sweet influences of Pleiades, or loose the bands of Orion?"

104. Canto IX. 61:—

> "Above us there are mirrors, Thrones you call them,
> From which shines out on us God Judicant."

Of the Thrones, Thomas Aquinas, *Sum. Theol.,* CVIII. 5, says: "The Order of Thrones excels the inferior Orders in this, that it has the power of perceiving immediately in God the reasons of the Divine operations. . . . . Dionysius (Cap. VII. *Cæl. Hier.)* explains the name of Thrones from their resemblance to material chairs, in which four things are to be considered. First, in reference to position, because chairs are raised above the ground; and thus these Angels, which are called Thrones, are raised so far that they can perceive immediately in God the reasons of things. Secondly, in material chairs firmness must be considered, because one sits firmly in them; but this is *e converso*, for the Angels themselves are made firm by God. Thirdly, because the chair receives the sitter, and he can be carried in it; and thus the Angels receive God in themselves, and in a certain sense carry him to their inferiors. Fourthly, from their shape, because the chair is open on one side, to receive the sitter; and thus these Angels, by their promptitude, are open to receive God and to serve him."

110. Dante, *Convito,* I. 1, says: "Knowledge is the ultimate perfection of our soul, in which consists our ultimate felicity." It was one of the great questions of the Schools, whether the beatitude of the soul consisted in knowing or in loving. Thomas Aquinas maintains the former part of this proposition, and Duns Scotus the latter.

113. By the grace of God, and the cooperation of the good will of the recipient.

116. The perpetual spring of Paradise, which knows no falling autumnal leaves, no season in which Aries is a nocturnal sign.

122. Thomas Aquinas, *Sum. Theol.,* I. Quæst. CVIII. 6, says: "And thus Dionysius (Cap. VII. *Cæl. Hier.),* from the names of the Orders inferring the properties thereof, placed in the first Hierarchy those Orders whose names were given them in reference to God, namely, the *Seraphim, Cherubim,* and *Thrones;* but in the middle Hierarchy he placed those whose names designate a certain common government or disposition, that is, the *Dominions, Virtues,* and *Powers;* and in the third Order he placed those whose names designate the execution of the work, namely, the *Principalities, Angels,* and *Archangels.* . . . But to the rule of government three things belong, the first of which is the distinction of the things to be done, which is the province of the *Dominions;*

the second is to provide the faculty of fulfilling, which belongs to the *Virtues;* but the third is to arrange in what way the things prescribed, or defined, can be fulfilled, so that some one may execute them, and this belongs to the *Powers.* But the execution of the angelic ministry consists in announcing things divine. In the execution, however, of any act, there are some who begin the act, and lead the others, as in singing the precentors, and in battle those who lead and direct the rest; and this belongs to the *Principalities.* There are others who simply execute, and this is the part of the *Angels.* Others hold an intermediate position, which belongs to the *Archangels.*"

130. The Athenian convert of St. Paul. *Acts* xvii. 34: "Howbeit, certain men clave unto him, and believed; among the which was Dionysius the Areopagite." Dante places him among the theologians in the Heaven of the Sun. See Canto X. 115:—

> "Near by behold the lustre of that taper,
>> Which in the flesh below looked most within
>> The angelic nature and its ministry."

To Dionysius was attributed a work, called *The Celestial Hierarchy,* which is the great storehouse of all that relates to the nature and operations of Angels. Venturi calls him "the false Areopagite;" and Dalbæus, *De Script. Dion. Areop.,* says that this work was not known till the sixth century.

The *Legenda Aurea* confounds St. Dionysius the Areopagite with St. Denis, Bishop of Paris in the third century, and patron saint of France. It says he was called the Areopagite from the quarter where he lived; that he was surnamed Theosoph, or the Wise in God; that he was converted, not by the preaching of St. Paul, but by a miracle the saint wrought in restoring a blind man to sight; and that "the woman named Damaris," who was converted with him, was his wife. It quotes from a letter of his to Polycarp, written from Egypt, where he was with his friend and fellow-student Apollophanes, and where he witnessed the darkening of the sun at the Crucifixion: "We were both at Heliopolis, when suddenly we saw the moon conceal the surface of the sun, though this was not the time for an eclipse, and this darkness continued for three hours, and the light returned at the ninth hour and lasted till evening." And finally it narrates, that when Dionysius was beheaded, in Paris, where he had converted many souls and built many churches, "straightway the body arose, and, taking its head in its arms, led by an angel, and surrounded by a celestial light, carried it a distance of two miles, from a place called the Mount of Martyrs, to the place where it now reposes."

For an account of the *Celestial Hierarchy,* see Canto X. Note 115.

133. St. Gregory differed from St. Dionysius in the arrangement of the Orders, placing the Principalities in the second triad, and the Virtues in the third.

138. St. Paul, who, 2 *Corinthians* xii. 4, "was caught up into paradise, and heard unspeakable words, which it is not lawful for a man to utter."

Canto XXIX

1. The Primum Mobile, or Crystalline Heaven, continued.
The children of Latona are Apollo and Diana, the Sun and Moon.

2. When the Sun is in Aries and the Moon in Libra, and when the Sun is setting and the full Moon rising, so that they are both on the horizon at the same time.

3. So long as they remained thus equipoised, as if in the opposite scales of an invisible balance suspended from the zenith.

9. God, whom Dante could not look upon, even as reflected in the eyes of Beatrice.

11. What Dante wishes to know is, where, when, and how the Angels were created.

12. Every When and every Where.

14. Dante, *Convito,* III. 14, defines splendour as "reflected light." Here it means the creation; the reflected light of God.

Job xxxviii. 7: "When the morning stars sang together, and all the sons of God shouted for joy." And again, 35: "Canst thou send lightnings, that they may go, and say unto thee, Here we are?"

16. Thomas Aquinas, *Sum. Theol.,* I. Quæst. LXI. 3: "The angelic nature was made before the creation of time, and after eternity."

18. In the creation of the Angels. Some editions read *nove Amori,* the nine Loves, or nine choirs of Angels.

21. *Genesis* i. 2: "And the Spirit of God moved upon the face of the waters."

22. Pure Matter, or the elements; pure Form, or the Angels; and the two conjoined, the human race.

Form, in the language of the Schools, and as defined by Thomas Aquinas, is the principle "by which we first think, whether it be called intellect, or intellectual soul." See Canto IV. Note 54.

23. *Genesis* i. 31: "And God saw everything that he had made, and, behold, it was very good."

33. The Angels. Thomas Aquinas, *Sum. Theol.,* I. Quæst. L. 2, says: "Form is act. Therefore whatever is form alone, is pure act." For his definition of form, see Note 22.

34. Pure matter, which is passive and only possesses potentiality, or power of assuming various forms when united with mind. "It is called potentiality," comments Buti, "because it can receive many forms; and the forms are called act, because they change, and act by changing matter into various forms."

35. The union of the soul and body in man, who occupies the intermediate place between Angels and pure matter.

36. This bond, though suspended by death, will be resumed again at the resurrection, and remain for ever.

37. St. Jerome, the greatest of the Latin Fathers of the Church, and author of the translation of the Scriptures known as the *Vulgate,* was born of wealthy parents in Dalmatia, in 342. He studied at Rome under the grammarian

Donatus, and became a lawyer in that city. At the age of thirty he visited
the Holy Land, and, withdrawing from the world, became an anchorite in
the desert of Chalcida, on the borders of Arabia. Here he underwent the
bodily privations and temptations, and enjoyed the spiritual triumphs, of the
hermit's life. He was "haunted by demons, and consoled by voices and
visions from heaven." In one of his letters, cited by Butler, *Lives of the Saints,*
IX. 362, he writes: "In the remotest part of a wild and sharp desert, which,
being burnt up with the heats of the scorching sun, strikes with horror and
terror even the monks that inhabit it, I seemed to myself to be in the midst
of the delights and assemblies of Rome. I loved solitude, that in the bitter-
ness of my soul I might more freely bewail my miseries, and call upon my
Saviour. My hideous emaciated limbs were covered with sackcloth: my skin
was parched dry and black, and my flesh was almost wasted away. The days
I passed in tears and groans, and when sleep overpowered me against my
will, I cast my wearied bones, which hardly hung together, upon the bare
ground, not so properly to give them rest, as to torture myself. I say nothing
of my eating and drinking; for the monks in that desert, when they are sick,
know no other drink but cold water, and look upon it as sensuality ever to
eat anything dressed by fire. In this exile and prison, to which, for the fear
of hell, I had voluntarily condemned myself, having no other company but
scorpions and wild beasts, I many times found my imagination filled with
lively representations of dances in the company of Roman ladies, as if I had
been in the midst of them. . . . . I often joined whole nights to the days,
crying, sighing, and beating my breast till the desired calm returned. I feared
the very cell in which I lived, because it was witness to the foul suggestions
of my enemy; and being angry and armed with severity against myself, I
went alone into the most secret parts of the wilderness, and if I discovered
anywhere a deep valley, or a craggy rock, that was the place of my prayer,
there I threw this miserable sack of my body. The same Lord is my witness,
that after so many sobs and tears, after having in so much sorrow looked
long up to heaven, I felt most delightful comforts and interior sweetness;
and these so great, that, transported and absorpt, I seemed to myself to be
amidst the choirs of angels; and glad and joyful I sung to God: *After Thee,
O Lord, we will run in the fragrancy of thy celestial ointments.*"

In another letter, cited by Montalembert, *Monks of the West,* Auth. Tr., I.
404, he exclaims: "O desert, enamelled with the flowers of Christ! O solitude,
where those stones are born of which, in the Apocalypse, is built the city of
the Great King! O retreat, which rejoicest in the friendship of God! What
doest thou in the world, my brother, with thy soul greater than the world?
How long wilt thou remain in the shadow of roofs, and in the smoky dun-
geons of cities? Believe me, I see here more of the light."

At the end of five years he was driven from his solitude by the persecution
of the Eastern monks, and lived successively in Jerusalem, Antioch,
Constantinople, Rome, and Alexandria. Finally, in 385, he returned to the
Holy Land, and built a monastery at Bethlehem. Here he wrote his translation

of the Scriptures, and his Lives of the Fathers of the Desert; but in 416 this monastery, and others that had risen up in its neighbourhood, were burned by the Pelagians, and St. Jerome took refuge in a strong tower or fortified castle. Four years afterwards he died, and was buried in the ruins of his monastery.

40. This truth of the simultaneous creation of mind and matter, as stated in line 29.

41. The opinion of St. Jerome and other Fathers of the Church, that the Angels were created long ages before the rest of the universe, is refuted by Thomas Aquinas, *Sum. Theol.*, I. Quæst. LXI. 3.

45. That the Intelligences or Motors of the heavens should be so long without any heavens to move.

51. The subject of the elements is the earth, so called as being the lowest, or underlying the others, fire, air, and water.

56. The pride of Lucifer, who lies at the centre of the earth, towards which all things gravitate, and

> "Down upon which thrust all the other rocks."

Milton, *Par. Lost,* V. 856, makes the rebel angels deny that they were created by God:—

> "Who saw
> When this creation was? Rememberest thou
> Thy making, while the Maker gave thee being?
> We know no time when we were not as now;
> Know none before us; self-begot, self-raised
> By our own quickening power, when fatal course
> Had circled his full orb, the birth mature
> Of this our native heaven, ethereal sons."

65. The merit consists in being willing to receive this grace.

95. St. Chrysostom, who in his preaching so carried away his audiences that they beat the pavement with their swords and called him the "Thirteenth Apostle," in one of his *Homilies* thus upbraids the custom of applauding the preacher: "What do your praises advantage me, when I see not your progress in virtue? Or what harm shall I receive from the silence of my auditors, when I behold the increase of their piety? The praise of the speaker is not the acclamation of his hearers, but their zeal for piety and religion; not their making a great stir in the times of hearing, but their showing diligence at all other times. Applause, as soon as it is out of the mouth, is dispersed into the air, and vanishes, but when the hearers grow better, this brings an incorruptible and immortal reward both to the speaker and the hearer. The praise of your acclamation may render the orator more illustrious here, but the piety of your souls will give him greater confidence before the tribunal of Christ.

Therefore, if any one love the preacher, or if any preacher love his people, let him not be enamoured with applause, but with the benefit of the hearers."

103. Lapo is the abbreviation of Jacopo, and Bindi of Aldobrandi, both familiar names in Florence.

107. Milton, *Lycidas,* 113:—

> "How well could I have spared for thee, young swain,
>   Enow of such as for their bellies' sake
>   Creep, and intrude, and climb into the fold!
>   Of other care they little reckoning make,
>   Than how to scramble at the shearers' feast,
>   And shove away the worthy bidden guest!
>   Blind mouths! that scarce themselves know how to hold
>   A sheep-hook, or have learned aught else the least
>   That to the faithful herdman's art belongs!
>   What recks it them? What need they? They are sped;
>   And, when they list, their lean and flashy songs
>   Grate on their scrannel pipes of wretched straw:
>   The hungry sheep look up, and are not fed;
>   But swoln with wind, and the rank mist they draw,
>   Rot inwardly, and foul contagion spread:
>   Besides what the grim wolf with privy paw
>   Daily devours apace, and nothing said:
>   But that two-handed engine at the door
>   Stands ready to smite once, and smite no more."

115. Cowper, *Task,* II.:—

> "He that negotiates between God and man,
>   As God's ambassador, the grand concerns
>   Of judgment and of mercy, should beware
>   Of lightness in his speech. 'T is pitiful
>   To court a grin, when you should woo a soul;
>   To break a jest, when pity would inspire
>   Pathetic exhortation; and t' address
>   The skittish fancy with facetious tales,
>   When sent with God's commission to the heart!"

For a specimen of the style of popular preachers in the Middle Ages, see the story of Frate Cipolla, in the *Decamerone,* Gior. VI. Nov. 10. See also Scheible's *Kloster,* and Menin's *Prédicatoriana.*

118. The Devil, who is often represented in early Christian art under the shape of a coal-black bird. See Didron, *Christ. Iconog.,* I.

124. In early paintings the swine is the symbol of St. Anthony, as the cherub is of St. Matthew, the lion of St. Mark, and the eagle of St. John.

There is an old tradition that St. Anthony was once a swineherd. Brand, *Pop. Antiquities,* I., 358, says:—

"In the World of Wonders is the following translation of an epigram:—

> 'Once fed'st thou, Anthony, an heard of swine,
>> And now an heard of monkes thou feedest still:—
> For wit and gut, alike both charges bin:
>> Both loven filth alike; both like to fill
> Their greedy paunch alike. Nor was that kind
>> More beastly, sottish, swinish than this last.
> All else agrees: one fault I onely find,
>> Thou feedest not thy monkes with oken mast.'

"The author mentions before, persons 'who runne up and downe the country, crying, Have you anything to bestow upon my lord S. Anthonie's swine?'"

Mrs. Jameson, *Sacred and Legendary Art,* II., 380, remarks: "I have read somewhere that the hog is given to St. Anthony, because he had been a swineherd, and cured the diseases of swine. This is quite a mistake. The hog was the representative of the demon of sensuality and gluttony, which Anthony is supposed to have vanquished by the exercises of piety and by divine aid. The ancient custom of placing in all his effigies a black pig at his feet, or under his feet, gave rise to the superstition that this unclean animal was especially dedicated to him, and under his protection. The monks of the Order of St. Anthony kept herds of consecrated pigs, which were allowed to feed at the public charge, and which it was a profanation to steal or kill: hence the proverb about the fatness of a 'Tantony pig.'"

Halliwell, *Dict. of Arch. and Prov. Words,* has the following definition: "ANTHONY-PIG. The favourite or smallest pig of the litter. A Kentish expression, according to Grose. 'To follow like a tantony pig,' i.e. to follow close at one's heels. Some derive this saying from a privilege enjoyed by the friars of certain convents in England and France, sons of St. Anthony, whose swine were permitted to feed in the streets. These swine would follow any one having greens or other provisions, till they obtained some of them; and it was in those days considered an act of charity and religion to feed them. St. Anthony was invoked for the pig."

Mr. Howell's *Venetian Life,* p. 341, alludes to the same custom as once prevalent in Italy: "Among other privileges of the Church, abolished in Venice long ago, was that ancient right of the monks of St. Anthony Abbot, by which their herds of swine were made free of the whole city. These animals, enveloped in an odour of sanctity, wandered here and there, and were piously fed by devout people, until the year 1409, when, being found dangerous to children, and inconvenient to everybody, they were made the subject of a special decree, which deprived them of their freedom of movement. The Republic was always opposing and limiting the privileges of the Church!"

126. Giving false indulgences, without the true stamp upon them, in return for the alms received.

130. The nature of the Angels.

· 134. Daniel vii. 10: "Thousand thousands ministered unto him, and ten thousand times ten thousand stood before him."

136. That irradiates this angelic nature.

138. The splendours are the reflected lights, or the Angels.

140. The fervour of the Angels is proportioned to their capacity of receiving the divine light.

Canto XXX

1. The ascent to the Empyrean, the tenth and last Heaven. Of this Heaven, Dante, *Convito,* II. 4, says: "This is the sovereign edifice of the world, in which the whole world is included, and outside of which nothing is. And it is not in space, but was formed solely in the primal Mind, which the Greeks call Protonoe. This is that magnificence of which the Psalmist spake, when he says to God, 'Thy magnificence is exalted above the heavens.'"

Milton, *Par. Lost,* III. 56:—

> "Now had the Almighty Father from above,
> From the pure empyrean where he sits
> High throned above all highth, bent down his eye,
> His own works and their works at once to view.
> About him all the sanctities of heaven
> Stood thick as stars, and from his sight received
> Beatitude past utterance."

2. The sixth hour is noon, and when noon is some six thousand miles away from us, the dawn is approaching, the shadow of the earth lies almost on a plane with it, and gradually the stars disappear.

10. The nine circles of Angels, described in Canto XXVIII.

38. From the Crystalline Heaven to the Empyrean. Dante, *Convito,* II. 15, makes the Empyrean the symbol of Theology, the Divine Science: "The Empyrean Heaven, by its peace, resembles the Divine Science, which is full of all peace; and which suffers no strife of opinions or sophistical arguments, because of the exceeding certitude of its subject, which is God. And of this he says to his disciples, 'My peace I give unto you; my peace I leave you;' giving and leaving them his doctrine, which is this science of which I speak. Of this Solomon says: 'There are threescore queens, and fourscore concubines, and virgins without number; my dove, my undefiled, is but one.' All sciences he calls queens and paramours and virgins; and this he calls a dove, because it is without blemish of strife; and this he calls perfect, because it makes us perfectly to see the truth in which our soul has rest."

42. *Philippians* iv. 7: "The peace of God, which passeth all understanding."

43. The Angels and the souls of the saints.

45. The Angels will be seen in the same aspect after the last judgment as before; but the souls of the saints will wear "the twofold garments," spoken of in Canto XXV. 92, the spiritual body, and the glorified earthly body.

61. Daniel vii. 10: "A fiery stream issued and came forth from before him." And *Revelation* xxii. 1: "And he showed me a pure river of water of life, clear as crystal, proceeding out of the throne of God and of the Lamb."

64. The sparks are Angels, and the flowers the souls of the blessed.

66. For the mystic virtues of the ruby, see Canto IX. Note 69.

76. For the mystic virtues of the topaz, see Canto XV. Note 85.

90. "By the length," says Venturi, "was represented the outpouring of God upon his creatures; by the roundness, the return of this outpouring to God, as to its first source and ultimate end."

99. Dante repeats the word *vidi,* I saw, three times, as a rhyme, to express the intenseness of his vision.

100. Buti thinks that this light is the Holy Ghost; Philalethes, that it is the Logos, or second person of the Trinity; Tommaseo, that it is Illuminating Grace.

124. Didron, *Christ. Iconog.,* I. 234, says: "It was in the centre, at the very heart of this luminous eternity, that the Deity shone forth. Dante no doubt wished to describe one of those roses with a thousand petals, which light the porches of our noblest cathedrals,—the rose-windows, which were contemporaneous with the Florentine poet, and which he had no doubt seen in his travels in France. There, in fact, in the very depth of the chalice of that rose of coloured glass, the Divine Majesty shines out resplendently."

129. The word convent is here used in its original meaning of a coming together, or assembly.

136. The name of Augustus is equivalent to Kaiser, Cæsar, or Emperor. In Canto XXXII. 119, the Virgin Mary is called Augusta, the Queen of the Kingdom of Heaven, the Empress of "the most just and merciful of empires."

137. This is Henry of Luxemburg, to whom in 1300 Dante was looking as the regenerator of Italy. He became Emperor in 1308, and died in 1311, ten years before Dante. See *Purg.* VI. Note 97, and XXXIII. Note 43.

142. At the *Curia Romana,* or Papal court.

143. Pope Clement V. (1305–1314). See *Inf.* XIX. Note 83. The allusion here is to his double dealing with Henry of Luxemburg. See Canto XVII. Note 82.

147. Among the Simoniacs in the third round of Malebolge. Of Simon Magus, Milman, *Hist. Christ.,* II. 97, writes thus: "Unless Simon was in fact a personage of considerable importance during the early history of Christianity, it is difficult to account for his becoming, as he is called by Beausobre, the hero of the Romance of Heresy. If Simon was the same with that magician, a Cypriot by birth, who was employed by Felix as agent in his intrigue to detach Drusilla from her husband, this part of his character accords with the

charge of licentiousness advanced both against his life and his doctrines by his Christian opponents. This is by no means improbable; and, indeed, even if he was not a person thus politically prominent and influential, the early writers of Christianity would scarcely have concurred in representing him as a formidable and dangerous antagonist of the Faith, as a kind of personal rival of St. Peter, without some other groundwork for the fiction besides the collision recorded in the Acts. The doctrines which are ascribed to him and to his followers, who continued to exist for several centuries, harmonise with the glimpse of his character and tenets in the writings of St. Luke. Simon probably was one of that class of adventurers which abounded at this period, or like Apollonius of Tyana, and others at a later time, with whom the opponents of Christianity attempted to confound Jesus and his Apostles. His doctrine was Oriental in its language and in its pretensions. He was the first Æon or emanation, or rather perhaps the first manifestation of the primal Deity. He assumed not merely the title of the Great Power or Virtue of God, but all the other Appellations,—the Word, the Perfection, the Paraclete, the Almighty, the whole combined attributes of the Deity. He had a companion, Helena, according to the statement of his enemies, a beautiful prostitute, whom he found at Tyre, who became in like manner the first conception (the Ennœa) of the Deity; but who, by her conjunction with matter, had been enslaved to its malignant influence, and, having fallen under the power of evil angels, had been in a constant state of transmigration, and, among other mortal bodies, had occupied that of the famous Helen of Troy. Beausobre, who elevates Simon into a Platonic philosopher, explains the Helena as a sublime allegory. She was the Psyche of his philosophic romance. The soul, by evil influences, had become imprisoned in matter. By her the Deity had created the angels: the angels, enamoured of her, had inextricably entangled her in that polluting bondage, in order to prevent her return to heaven. To fly from their embraces she had passed from body to body. Connecting this fiction with the Grecian mythology, she was Minerva, or impersonated Wisdom; perhaps, also, Helena, or embodied Beauty."

148. Pope Boniface VIII., a native of Alagna, now Anagni. See *Inf.* XIX. Note 53, and *Purg.* XX. Note 87.

Dante has already his punishment prepared. He is to be thrust head downward into a narrow hole in the rock of Malebolge, and to be driven down still lower when Clement V. shall follow him.

Canto XXXI

1. The White Rose of Paradise.
7. *Iliad,* II. 86, Anon. Tr.: "And the troops thronged together, as swarms of crowding bees, which come ever in fresh numbers from the hollow rock, and fly in clusters over the vernal flowers, and thickly some fly in this direction, and some in that."

32. The nymph Callisto, or Helice, was changed by Jupiter into the constellation of the Great Bear, and her son into that of the Little Bear. See *Purg.* XXV., Note 131.

34. Rome and her superb edifices, before the removal of the Papal See to Avignon.

35. Speaking of Petrarch's visit to Rome, Mr. Norton, *Travel and Study in Italy,* p. 288, says: "The great church of St. John Lateran, 'the mother and head of all the churches of the city and the world,'—*mater urbis et orbis,*—had been almost destroyed by fire, with its adjoining palace, and the houses of the canons, on the Eve of St. John, in 1308. The palace and the canons' houses were rebuilt not long after; but at the time of Petrarch's latest visit to Rome, and for years afterward, the church was without a roof, and its walls were ruinous. The poet addressed three at least of the Popes at Avignon with urgent appeals that this disgrace should no longer be permitted,—but the Popes gave no heed to his words; for the ruin of Roman churches, or of Rome itself, was a matter of little concern to these Transalpine prelates."

73. From the highest regions of the air to the lowest depth of the sea.

102. St. Bernard, the great Abbot of Clairvaux, the *Doctor Mellifluus* of the Church, and preacher of the disastrous Second Crusade, was born of noble parents in the village of Fontaine, near Dijon, in Burgundy, in the year 1190. After studying at Paris, at the age of twenty he entered the Benedictine monastery of Citeaux; and when, five years later, this monastery had become overcrowded with monks, he was sent out to found a new one.

Mrs. Jameson, *Legends of the Monastic Orders,* p. 149, says: "The manner of going forth on these occasions was strikingly characteristic of the age;—the abbot chose twelve monks, representing the twelve Apostles, and placed at their head a leader, representing Jesus Christ, who, with a cross in his hand, went before them. The gates of the convent opened,—then closed behind them,—and they wandered into the wide world, trusting in God to show them their destined abode.

"Bernard led his followers to a wilderness, called the *Valley of Wormwood,* and there, at his biding, arose the since renowned abbey of Clairvaux. They felled the trees, built themselves huts, tilled and sowed the ground, and changed the whole face of the country round; till that which had been a dismal solitude, the resort of wolves and robbers, became a land of vines and corn, rich, populous, and prosperous."

This incident forms the subject of one of Murillo's most famous paintings, and is suggestive of the saint's intense devotion to the Virgin, which Dante expresses in this line.

Mr. Vaughan, *Hours with the Mystics,* I. 145, gives the following sketch of St. Bernard:—

"With Bernard the monastic life is the one thing needful. He began life by drawing after him into the convent all his kindred; sweeping them one by one from the high seas of the world with the irresistible vortex of his own religious fervour. His incessant cry for Europe is, Better monasteries, and more of them. Let these ecclesiastical castles multiply; let them cover and command the land, well garrisoned with men of God, and then, despite all heresy and schism, theocracy will flourish, the earth shall yield her increase, and all people praise the Lord. Who so wise as Bernard to win souls for Christ, that is to say, recruits for the cloister? With what eloquence he paints the raptures of contemplation, the vanity and sin of earthly ambition or of earthly love! Wherever in his travels Bernard may have preached, there, presently, exultant monks must open wide their doors to admit new converts. Wherever he goes, he bereaves mothers of their children, the aged of their last solace and last support; praising those the most who leave most misery behind them. How sternly does he rebuke those Rachels who mourn and will not be comforted for children dead to them for ever! What vitriol does he pour into the wounds when he asks if they will drag their son down to perdition with themselves by resisting the vocation of Heaven; whether it was not enough that they brought him forth sinful to a world of sin, and will they now, in their insane affection, cast him into the fires of hell? Yet Bernard is not hard-hearted by nature. He can pity this disgraceful weakness of the flesh. He makes such amends as superstition may. I will be a father to him, he says. Alas! cold comfort. You, their hearts will answer, whose flocks are countless, would nothing content you but our ewe lamb? Perhaps some cloister will be, for them too, the last resource of their desolation. They will fly for ease in their pain to the system which caused it. Bernard hopes so. So inhuman is the humanity of asceticism; cruel its tender mercies; thus does it depopulate the world of its best in order to improve it. . . . .

"Bernard had his wish. He made Clairvaux the cynosure of all contempla-tive eyes. For any one who could exist at all as a monk, with any satisfaction to himself, that was the place above all others. Brother Godfrey, sent out to be first Abbot of Fontenay,—as soon as he has set all things in order there, returns, only too gladly, from that rich and lovely region, to re-enter his old cell, to walk around, delightedly revisiting the well-remembered spots among the trees or by the water-side, marking how the fields and gardens have come on, and relating to the eager brethren (for even Bernard's monks have curi-osity) all that befell him in his work. He would sooner be third Prior at Clairvaux, than Abbot of Fontenay. So, too, with Brother Humbert, com-missioned in like manner to regulate Igny Abbey (fourth daughter of Clairvaux). He soon comes back, weary of the labour and sick for home, to look on the Aube once more, to hear the old mills go drumming and droning, with that monotony of muffled sound—the associate of his pious reveries—often heard in his dreams when far away; to set his feet on the very same flagstone in the choir where he used to stand, and to be happy. But Bernard, though away in Italy, toiling in the matter of the schism, gets to hear of his return, and finds time to send him across the Alps a letter of rebuke for this criminal self-pleasing, whose terrible sharpness must have darkened the poor man's meditations for many a day.

"Bernard had further the satisfaction of improving and extending monas-ticism to the utmost; of sewing together, with tolerable success, the rended vesture of the Papacy; of suppressing a more popular and more Scriptural Christianity, for the benefit of his despotic order; of quenching for a time, by the extinction of Abelard, the spirit of free inquiry; and of seeing his ascetic and superhuman ideal of religion everywhere accepted as the genuine type of Christian virtue."

104. The Veronica is the portrait of our Saviour impressed upon a veil or kerchief, preserved with great care in the church of the Santi Apostoli at Rome. Collin de Plancy, *Legendes des Saintes Images,* p. 11, gives the following account of it:—

"Properly speaking, the Veronica (*vera icon*) is the true likeness of Our Lord; and the same name has been given to the holy woman who obtained it, because the name of this holy woman was uncertain. According to some, she was a pious Jewess, called Seraphia; according to others, she was Berenice, niece of Herod. It is impossible to decide between the different traditions, some of which make her a virgin, and others the wife of Zaccheus.

"However this may be, the happy woman who obtained the venerable imprint of the holy face lived not far from the palace of Pilate. Her house is still shown to pilgrims at Jerusalem; and a Canon of Mayence, who went to the Holy Land in 1483, reported that he had visited the house of the Veronica.

"When she saw Our Lord pass, bearing his cross, covered with blood, spittle, sweat, and dust, she ran to meet him, and, presenting her kerchief, tried to wipe his adorable face. Our Lord, leaving for an instant the burden of the cross to Simon the Cyrenean, took the kerchief, applied it to his face, and gave it back to the pious woman, marked with the exact imprint of his august countenance."

Of the Veronica there are four copies in existence, each claiming to be the original; one at Rome, another at Paris, a third at Laon, and a fourth at Xaen in Andalusia. The traveller who has crossed the Sierra Morena cannot easily forget the stone column, surmounted by an iron cross, which marks the boundary between La Mancha and Andalusia, with the melancholy stone face upon it, and the inscription, *"El verdadero Retrato de la Santa Cara del Dios de Xaen."*

116. The Virgin Mary, *Regina Cæli.*

125. The chariot of the sun.

Canto XXXII

1. St. Bernard, absorbed in contemplation of the Virgin.

5. Eve. St. Augustine, Serm. 18 *De Sanctis,* says: *"Illa percussit, ista sanavit."*

8. Rachel is an emblem of Divine Contemplation. *Inf.* II. 101, Beatrice says:—

> "And came unto the place
> Where I was sitting with the ancient Rachel."

11. Ruth the Moabitess, ancestress of King David.

12. "Have mercy upon me," are the first words of *Psalm* li., "a Psalm of David, when Nathan the prophet came unto him."

24. The saints of the Old Testament.

27. The saints of the New Testament.

31. John the Baptist, seated at the point of the mystic Rose, opposite to the Virgin Mary. He died two years before Christ's resurrection, and during these two years was in the Limbo of the Fathers.

40. The row of seats which divides the Rose horizontally, and crosses the two vertical lines of division, made by the seat of the Virgin Mary and those of the other Hebrew women on one side, and on the other the seats of John the Baptist and of the other saints of the New Testament beneath him.

43. That is to say, by the faith of their parents, by circumcision, and by baptism, as explained line 76 *et seq.*

58. *Festinata gente,* dying in infancy, and thus hurried into the life eternal. Shakespeare, *King Lear,* III. 7: "Advise the Duke, where you are going to a most festinate preparation."

68. Jacob and Esau. *Genesis* xxv. 22: "And the children struggled together within her." And *Romans* ix. 11: "For the children being not yet born, neither having done any good or evil, that the purpose of God, according to election, might stand, not of works, but of him that calleth."

70. Buti comments thus: "As it pleased God to give black hair to one, and to the other red, so it pleased him to give more grace to one than to the other." And the *Ottimo* says: "One was red, the other black; which colours denote the temperaments of men, and accordingly the inclination of their minds."

75. The keenness of vision with which they are originally endowed.

76. From Adam to Abraham.

79. From Abraham to Christ. *Genesis* xvii. 10: "This is my covenant, which ye shall keep, between me and you, and thy seed after thee: Every man-child among you shall be circumcised."

85. The face of the Virgin Mary. Didron, in his *Christ. Iconog.,* I. 242, devotes a chapter to the "History of the Portraits of God the Son." Besides the Veronica and the Santo Volto, attributed to Nicodemus, he mentions others which tradition traces back to Pilate and St. Luke, and a statue erected to Christ by the woman who was cured of the bloody flux. In the following extract several others are referred to:—

"Abgarus, king of Edessa, having learnt, says Damascenus, the wonderful things related of our Saviour, became inflamed with Divine love; he sent ambassadors to the Son of God, inviting him to come and visit him, and should the Saviour refuse to grant his request, he charged his ambassadors to employ some artist to make a portrait of our Lord. Jesus, from whom nothing is hidden, and to whom nothing is impossible, being aware of the intention of Abgarus, took a piece of linen, applied it to his face, and depicted thereon his own image. This very portrait, continues Damascenus, is in existence at the present day, and in perfect preservation.

"At the same epoch, a minute verbal description of the appearance of Christ was in circulation. The following description, which is of great importance, was sent to the Roman Senate by Publius Lentulus, Proconsul of Judæa, before Herod. Lentulus had seen the Saviour, and had made him sit to him, as it were, that he might give a written description of his features and physiognomy. His portrait, apocryphal though it be, is at least one of the first upon record; it dates from the earliest period of the Church, and has been mentioned by the most ancient fathers. Lentulus writes to the Senate as follows: 'At this time appeared a man who is still living and endowed with mighty power; his name is Jesus Christ. His disciples call him the Son of God; others regard him as a powerful prophet. He raises the dead to life, and heals the sick of every description of infirmity and disease. This man is of lofty stature, and well-proportioned; his countenance severe and virtuous, so that he inspires beholders with feelings both of fear and love. The hair of his head is of the colour of wine, and from the top of the head to the ears straight and without radiance, but it descends from the ears to the shoulders in shining curls. From the shoulders the hair flows down the back, divided into two portions, after the manner of the Nazarenes; his forehead is clear and without wrinkle, his face free from blemish, and slightly tinged with red, his physiognomy noble and gracious. The nose and mouth faultless. His beard is abundant, the same colour as the hair, and forked. His eyes blue and very brilliant. In reproving or censuring he is awe-inspiring; in exhorting and teaching, his speech is gentle and caressing. His countenance is marvellous in seriousness and grace. He has never once been seen to laugh; but many have seen him weep. He is slender in person, his hands are straight and long, his arms beautiful. Grave and solemn in his discourse, his language is simple and quiet. He is in appearance the most beautiful of the children of men.'

"The Emperor Constantine caused pictures of the Son of God to be painted from this ancient description.

"In the eighth century, at the period in which Saint John Damascenus wrote, the lineaments of this remarkable figure continued to be the same as they are to this day.

"The hair and the beard, the colour of which is somewhat undetermined in the letter of Lentulus, for wine may be pale, golden, red, or violet colour, is distinctly noted by Damascenus, who also adds the tint of the complexion; moreover, the opinion of Damascenus, like that of Lentulus, is decidedly in favour of the beauty of Christ, and the former severely censures the Manichæans, who entertained a contrary opinion. Thus, then, Christ, in taking upon him the form of Adam, assumed features exactly resembling those of the Virgin Mary. . . . . . In the West, a century later than the time of Damascenus, Christ was always thus depicted. S. Anschaire, Archbishop of Hamburg and Bremen, who beheld Christ [in a vision], described him as 'tall, clad in the manner of the Jews, and beautiful in face, the splendour of Divinity darted like a flame from the eyes of the Redeemer, but his voice was full of sweetness."

94. The Angel Gabriel. Luke i. 28: "And the angel came in unto her, and said, Hail, thou that art highly favoured, the Lord is with thee: blessed art thou among women."

99. The countenance of each saint became brighter.

107. The word in the original is *abbelliva,* which Dante here uses in the sense of the Provençal, *abellis,* of *Purg.* XXVI. 140. He uses the word in the same sense in *Convito,* II. 7: "In all speech the speaker is chiefly bent on persuasion, that is, on pleasing the audience, *all' abbellire dell' audienza,* which is the source of all other persuasions."

108. The star of morning delighting in the sun, is from Canto VIII. 12, where Dante speaks of Venus as

> "The star
> That wooes the sun, now following, now in front."

119. The Virgin Mary, the Queen of this empire.

121. Adam.

124. St. Peter.

127. St. John, who lived till the evil days and persecutions of the Church, the bride of Christ, won by the crucifixion.

131. Moses.

132. *Exodus* xxxii. 9: "And the Lord said unto Moses, I have seen this people, and, behold, it is a stiff-necked people."

133. Anna, mother of the Virgin Mary.

137. Santa Lucìa, virgin and martyr. Dante, *Inf.* II. 100, makes her, as the emblem of illuminating grace, intercede with Beatrice for his salvation.

146. Trusting only to thine own efforts.

Canto XXXIII

1. Chaucer, *Second Nonnes Tale:*—

> "Thou maide and mother, doughter of thy son,
> Thou well of mercy, sinful soules cure,
> In whom that God of bountee chees to won;
> Thou humble and high over every creature,
> Thou nobledest so fer forth our nature,
> That no desdaine the maker had of kinde
> His son in blood and flesh to clothe and winde.

> "Within the cloystre blisful of thy sides,
> Toke mannes shape the eternal love and pees,

That of the trine compas Lord and gide is.
Whom erthe, and see, and heven out of relees
Ay herien; and thou, virgine wemmeles,
Bare of thy body (and dweltest maiden pure)
The creatour of every creature.

  "Assembled is in thee magnificence
With mercy, goodnesse, and with swiche pitee,
That thou, that art the sonne of excellence,
Not only helpest hem that praien thee,
But oftentime of thy benignitee
Ful freely, or that men thin helpe beseche,
Thou goest beforne, and art hir lives leche."

See also his *Ballade of Our Ladie,* and *La Priere de Nostre Dame.*

36. As St. Macarius said to his soul: "Having taken up thine abode in heaven, where thou hast God and his holy angels to converse with, see that thou descend not thence; regard not earthly things."

48. Finished the ardour of desire in its accomplishment.

66. *Æneid,* III. 442, Davidson's Tr.: "When, wafted thither, you reach the city Cumæ, the hallowed lakes, and Avernus resounding through the woods, you will see the raving prophetess, who, beneath a deep rock, reveals the fates, and commits to the leaves of trees her characters and words. Whatever verses the virgin has inscribed on the leaves, she ranges in harmonious order, and leaves in the cave enclosed by themselves: uncovered they remain in their position, nor recede from their order. But when, upon turning the hinge, a small breath of wind has blown upon them, and the door [by opening] hath discomposed the tender leaves, she never afterward cares to catch the verses as they are fluttering in the hollow cave, nor to recover their situation, or join them together."

78. *Luke* ix. 62: "No man having put his hand to the plough, and looking back, is fit for the kingdom of God."

86. Thomas Aquinas, *Sum. Theol.,* I. Quæst. iv. 2: "If therefore God be the first efficient cause of things, the perfections of all things must pre-exist pre-eminently in God." And Buti: "In God are all things that are made, as in the First Cause, that foresees everything."

90. Of all the commentaries which I have consulted, that of Buti alone sustains this rendering of the line. The rest interpret it, "What I say is but a simple or feeble glimmer of what I saw."

94. There are almost as many interpretations of this passage as there are commentators. The most intelligible is, that Dante forgot in a single moment more of the glory he had seen, than the world had forgotten in five-and-twenty centuries of the Argonautic expedition, when Neptune wondered at the shadow of the first ship that ever crossed the sea.

103. Aristotle, *Ethics,* I., 1, Gillies's Tr.: "Since every art and every kind of knowledge, as well as all the actions and all the deliberations of men,

constantly aim at something which they call good, good in general may be justly defined, that which all desire."

114. In the same manner the reflection of the Griffin in Beatrice's eyes, *Purg.* XXXI. 124, is described as changing, while the object itself remained unchanged:—

> "Think, Reader, if within myself I marvelled,
>   When I beheld the thing itself stand still,
>   And in its image it transformed itself."

115. Thomas Aquinas, *Sum. Theol.*, I. Quæst. xxix. 2: "What exists by itself, and not in another, is called subsistence."

116. The three Persons of the Trinity.

128. The second circle, or second Person of the Trinity.

131. The human nature of Christ; the incarnation of the Word.

141. In this new light of God's grace, the mystery of the union of the Divine and human nature in Christ is revealed to Dante.

144. Wordsworth, *Resolution and Independence*:—

> "As a cloud . . .
> That heareth not the loud winds when they call,
> And moveth all together, if it move at all."

145. 1 *John* iv. 16: "God is love; and he that dwelleth in love dwelleth in God, and God in him."

DOVER THRIFT EDITIONS

FICTION

FLATLAND: A ROMANCE OF MANY DIMENSIONS, Edwin A. Abbott. (0-486-27263-X)

PRIDE AND PREJUDICE, Jane Austen. (0-486-28473-5)

CIVIL WAR SHORT STORIES AND POEMS, Edited by Bob Blaisdell. (0-486-48226-X)

THE DECAMERON: Selected Tales, Giovanni Boccaccio. Edited by Bob Blaisdell. (0-486-41113-3)

JANE EYRE, Charlotte Brontë. (0-486-42449-9)

WUTHERING HEIGHTS, Emily Brontë. (0-486-29256-8)

THE THIRTY-NINE STEPS, John Buchan. (0-486-28201-5)

ALICE'S ADVENTURES IN WONDERLAND, Lewis Carroll. (0-486-27543-4)

MY ÁNTONIA, Willa Cather. (0-486-28240-6)

THE AWAKENING, Kate Chopin. (0-486-27786-0)

HEART OF DARKNESS, Joseph Conrad. (0-486-26464-5)

LORD JIM, Joseph Conrad. (0-486-40650-4)

THE RED BADGE OF COURAGE, Stephen Crane. (0-486-26465-3)

THE WORLD'S GREATEST SHORT STORIES, Edited by James Daley. (0-486-44716-2)

A CHRISTMAS CAROL, Charles Dickens. (0-486-26865-9)

GREAT EXPECTATIONS, Charles Dickens. (0-486-41586-4)

A TALE OF TWO CITIES, Charles Dickens. (0-486-40651-2)

CRIME AND PUNISHMENT, Fyodor Dostoyevsky. Translated by Constance Garnett. (0-486-41587-2)

THE ADVENTURES OF SHERLOCK HOLMES, Sir Arthur Conan Doyle. (0-486-47491-7)

THE HOUND OF THE BASKERVILLES, Sir Arthur Conan Doyle. (0-486-28214-7)

BLAKE: PROPHET AGAINST EMPIRE, David V. Erdman. (0-486-26719-9)

WHERE ANGELS FEAR TO TREAD, E. M. Forster. (0-486-27791-7)

BEOWULF, Translated by R. K. Gordon. (0-486-27264-8)

THE RETURN OF THE NATIVE, Thomas Hardy. (0-486-43165-7)

THE SCARLET LETTER, Nathaniel Hawthorne. (0-486-28048-9)

SIDDHARTHA, Hermann Hesse. (0-486-40653-9)

THE ODYSSEY, Homer. (0-486-40654-7)

THE TURN OF THE SCREW, Henry James. (0-486-26684-2)

DUBLINERS, James Joyce. (0-486-26870-5)

FICTION

THE METAMORPHOSIS AND OTHER STORIES, Franz Kafka. (0-486-29030-1)

SONS AND LOVERS, D. H. Lawrence. (0-486-42121-X)

THE CALL OF THE WILD, Jack London. (0-486-26472-6)

GREAT AMERICAN SHORT STORIES, Edited by Paul Negri. (0-486-42119-8)

THE GOLD-BUG AND OTHER TALES, Edgar Allan Poe. (0-486-26875-6)

ANTHEM, Ayn Rand. (0-486-49277-X)

FRANKENSTEIN, Mary Shelley. (0-486-28211-2)

THE JUNGLE, Upton Sinclair. (0-486-41923-1)

THREE LIVES, Gertrude Stein. (0-486-28059-4)

THE STRANGE CASE OF DR. JEKYLL AND MR. HYDE, Robert Louis Stevenson. (0-486-26688-5)

DRACULA, Bram Stoker. (0-486-41109-5)

UNCLE TOM'S CABIN, Harriet Beecher Stowe. (0-486-44028-1)

ADVENTURES OF HUCKLEBERRY FINN, Mark Twain. (0-486-28061-6)

THE ADVENTURES OF TOM SAWYER, Mark Twain. (0-486-40077-8)

CANDIDE, Voltaire. Edited by Francois-Marie Arouet. (0-486-26689-3)

THE COUNTRY OF THE BLIND: and Other Science-Fiction Stories, H. G. Wells. Edited by Martin Gardner. (0-486-48289-8)

THE WAR OF THE WORLDS, H. G. Wells. (0-486-29506-0)

ETHAN FROME, Edith Wharton. (0-486-26690-7)

THE PICTURE OF DORIAN GRAY, Oscar Wilde. (0-486-27807-7)

MONDAY OR TUESDAY: Eight Stories, Virginia Woolf. (0-486-29453-6)

NONFICTION

POETICS, Aristotle. (0-486-29577-X)

MEDITATIONS, Marcus Aurelius. (0-486-29823-X)

THE WAY OF PERFECTION, St. Teresa of Avila. Edited and Translated by
   E. Allison Peers. (0-486-48451-3)

THE DEVIL'S DICTIONARY, Ambrose Bierce. (0-486-27542-6)

GREAT SPEECHES OF THE 20TH CENTURY, Edited by Bob Blaisdell.
   (0-486-47467-4)

THE COMMUNIST MANIFESTO AND OTHER REVOLUTIONARY WRITINGS:
   Marx, Marat, Paine, Mao Tse-Tung, Gandhi and Others, Edited by Bob Blaisdell.
   (0-486-42465-0)

INFAMOUS SPEECHES: From Robespierre to Osama bin Laden, Edited by Bob
   Blaisdell. (0-486-47849-1)

GREAT ENGLISH ESSAYS: From Bacon to Chesterton, Edited by Bob Blaisdell.
   (0-486-44082-6)

GREEK AND ROMAN ORATORY, Edited by Bob Blaisdell. (0-486-49622-8)

THE UNITED STATES CONSTITUTION: The Full Text with Supplementary
   Materials, Edited and with supplementary materials by Bob Blaisdell.
   (0-486-47166-7)

GREAT SPEECHES BY NATIVE AMERICANS, Edited by Bob Blaisdell.
   (0-486-41122-2)

GREAT SPEECHES BY AFRICAN AMERICANS: Frederick Douglass, Sojourner
   Truth, Dr. Martin Luther King, Jr., Barack Obama, and Others, Edited by
   James Daley. (0-486-44761-8)

GREAT SPEECHES BY AMERICAN WOMEN, Edited by James Daley.
   (0-486-46141-6)

HISTORY'S GREATEST SPEECHES, Edited by James Daley. (0-486-49739-9)

GREAT INAUGURAL ADDRESSES, Edited by James Daley. (0-486-44577-1)

GREAT SPEECHES ON GAY RIGHTS, Edited by James Daley. (0-486-47512-3)

ON THE ORIGIN OF SPECIES: By Means of Natural Selection, Charles Darwin.
   (0-486-45006-6)

NARRATIVE OF THE LIFE OF FREDERICK DOUGLASS, Frederick Douglass.
   (0-486-28499-9)

THE SOULS OF BLACK FOLK, W. E. B. Du Bois. (0-486-28041-1)

NATURE AND OTHER ESSAYS, Ralph Waldo Emerson. (0-486-46947-6)

SELF-RELIANCE AND OTHER ESSAYS, Ralph Waldo Emerson. (0-486-27790-9)

THE LIFE OF OLAUDAH EQUIANO, Olaudah Equiano. (0-486-40661-X)

WIT AND WISDOM FROM POOR RICHARD'S ALMANACK, Benjamin Franklin.
   (0-486-40891-4)

THE AUTOBIOGRAPHY OF BENJAMIN FRANKLIN, Benjamin Franklin.
   (0-486-29073-5)